Praise for Anna Elliott's
TWILIGHT OF AVALON trilogy

"Fans of the TV series *Camelot* and of epic historical fiction will relish Anna Elliott's gritty, passionate evocation of Arthurian Britain. Magic, adventure, romance, and betrayal entwine in this sweeping account of the famous star-crossed lovers. Haunting and unforgettable, *Sunrise of Avalon* held me spellbound!"

> —C. W. Gortner, author of *The Confessions of Catherine de Medici*

"Enthralling! A deftly plotted, fast-paced tale of love and war, with well-drawn characters, sharp suspense, and an original portrait of Trystan and Isolde you'll never forget—I loved it!"

> —Nancy McKenzie, author of *Queen of Camelot*

"Set in a dark, richly detailed Tolkienesque world, the poignant love story of Trystan and Isolde is given shining new life in this magical retelling by Anna Elliott. *Sunrise of Avalon* kept me spellbound until the last page."

> —Sandra Worth, author of *Pale Rose of England*

"Passion, conflict, danger, and magic combine for an irresistible love story which will keep you turning the pages!"

> —Michelle Moran, author of *Madame Tussaud* and *Nefertiti*

"Elliot brings the Arthurian world to rich life, creating a Britain both familiar and distinctly alien to fans of medieval romances."

> —*Publishers Weekly* on *Dark Moon of Avalon*

"Elliott's reworking of a timeworn medieval tale reinvigorates the celebrated romance between Trystan and Isolde. . . . She paints a mystical, full-bodied portrait. . . . Fans of the many Arthurian cycles will relish this appropriately fantastical offshoot of the Arthurian legend."

> —*Booklist* on *Twilight of Avalon*

ALSO BY ANNA ELLIOTT

Twilight of Avalon
Dark Moon of Avalon

SUNRISE OF AVALON

A NOVEL OF TRYSTAN & ISOLDE

ANNA ELLIOTT

A TOUCHSTONE BOOK

PUBLISHED BY SIMON & SCHUSTER

NEW YORK   LONDON   TORONTO   SYDNEY   NEW DELHI

Touchstone
A Division of Simon & Schuster, Inc.
1230 Avenue of the Americas
New York, NY 10020

Copyright © 2011 by Anna Grube

First Touchstone trade paperback edition September 2011

TOUCHSTONE and colophon are registered trademarks of
Simon & Schuster, Inc.

For information about special discounts for bulk purchases,
please contact Simon & Schuster Special Sales at 1-866-506-1949
or business@simonandschuster.com.

The Simon & Schuster Speakers Bureau can bring authors to your live event.
For more information or to book an event contact the Simon & Schuster
Speakers Bureau at 1-866-248-3049 or visit our website at
www.simonspeakers.com.

Manufactured in the United States of America

10 9 8 7 6 5 4 3 2 1

Library of Congress Cataloging-in-Publication Data
  Elliott, Anna.
    Sunrise of Avalon : a novel of Trystan & Isolde / by Anna Elliott.—1st
  Touchstone trade paperback ed.
      p. cm.
  "A Touchstone book."
    1. Iseult (Legendary character)—Fiction. 2. Tristan (Legendary
  character)—Fiction. 3. Avalon (Legendary place)—Fiction. I. Title.
  PS3605.L443S86 2011
  813'.6—dc22
                                                    2011011984

ISBN 978-1-4165-8991-4
ISBN 978-1-4391-6457-0 (ebook)

To my mom

You may have tangible wealth untold.
Caskets of jewels and coffers of gold.
Richer than I you can never be—
I had a mother who read to me.

—Strickland Gillilan

Dramatis Personae

Dead Before the Story Begins

Arthur, High King of Britain, father of Modred, brother of Morgan; killed in the battle of Camlann

Constantine, Arthur's heir as Britain's High King, first husband to Isolde

Gwynefar, Arthur's wife; betrayed Arthur to become Modred's Queen; mother to Isolde

Modred, Arthur's traitor son and Isolde's father; killed in fighting Arthur at Camlann

Morgan, mother to Modred, believed by many to be a sorceress

Myrddin, Arthur's chief druid and bard

Rulers of Britain

Cynlas, King of Rhos

Dywel, King of Logres

Isolde, daughter of Modred and Gwynefar, Constantine's High Queen, Lady of Camelerd

Madoc, King of Gwynned and Britain's High King

Marche, King of Cornwall, now a traitor allied with the Saxon King Octa of Kent

Saxon Rulers

Cerdic, King of Wessex
Octa, King of Kent

Others

Fidach, leader of an outlaw band of mercenaries
Eurig, Piye, and Daka, three of Fidach's men, friends to Trystan
Goram, an Irish king
Hereric, a Saxon and friend to Trystan
Kian, a former outlaw and friend to Trystan, now one of King Madoc's war band
Nest, cousin and former chatelaine to King Marche
Marcia, Nest's serving maid
Mother Berthildis, abbess of the Abbey of Saint Joseph
Taliesin, brother to King Dywel of Logres, a bard
Trystan, a Saxon mercenary and outlaw, son of King Marche

Isolde's Britain

Rhegged

Ynys Mon

Gwynedd

Mercia

Anglia

Powys

Dyfed

Gwent

LONDON

Camelerd

Kent

TINTAGEL

Dumnonia

Wessex

Cornwall

Prologue

A ship sails on gentle seas
At its prow a maiden stands,
Forever young, forever fair,
Her raven locks caught on the wind.
She calls the magic from her heart
It runs through her fingers,
Like sand, like time.
The sea whitens; the moon fetches light.
All is peace at last
The King's wounds are healed.
Arthur sleeps
In Ynys Afallach, the realm of Avalon.

STRANGE HOW NOW, AT THIS twilight end of my days, the harpers' songs sung of me run again and again through my mind. An endlessly repeating curve. Like time. Like serpents of eternity, eternally swallowing their tails.

I was once that maiden of the raven hair. Morgan, half sister to Arthur the king. Morgan the enchantress, whose magic arts trapped the High King like a golden web. Morgan the sorceress, whose spite for her brother-king poisoned the land and broke Britain's hope of ever driving back the Saxon hordes.

Never do the tales mention King Marche of Cornwall, who betrayed his lord, Modred, my son. Marche, whose treason cost my son the victory at Camlann. Cost him his life.

And now Marche, ever ready to trim his sails to the way the winds of power blow, has taken my life, as well as my son's. Has walled me up in a plague-ridden garrison that I may die with all the others whose faces blacken and run with sores.

But the bards never speak of Marche. That Britain's fall was brought on by a woman's magic, a woman's spite, makes for a far better tale to sing.

Always when I hear the tales, I feel as though I have stepped into a lake, crystal clear and still. As though, with the water lapping around my waist, I draw nearer and nearer to the wavering reflection that looks back at me with my own eyes. Always and even now.

Who knows how such tales are born? To find their beginning is like unwinding the weft in a weaving on the loom. But once begun, they spread like the ripples on a pond, like dry leaves scattering before the blast of the storm.

And now new tales will be spun and told. Camlann has been fought. Arthur is dead and gone, slain by Modred, his traitor son. Our son. Arthur's and mine.

And the bards will turn all into a song of a king who was and shall be. Who sleeps in the mists of the sacred isle, and will come again in the hour of Britain's greatest need. Though whether the tales will be an eternal candle flame in the dark, or only lies to comfort children, I cannot say.

The Sight has shown me much, in my time. *May be* and *has been* and *is* and *shall be*. But now I see only dark. Perhaps the Goddess has turned her back and forgotten me. Or perhaps, with Arthur gone, there is nothing left inside me that can See.

So I lie in bed, burning with the fever of the plague that has struck the land. A punishment for my sins, I might think, did it not make me sound like some grim, black-robed and shaven follower of the Christ.

A girl sits beside me, bathes my face and brushes my hair and tries to coax me to swallow simples and drafts of herbs. I taught her the healer's craft, and she has learned it well.

She, too, might be the raven-haired maiden of the tales. Forever young, forever fair. Face a smooth, lovely oval. Skin lily pale and pure. Wide, thickly lashed gray eyes.

Isolde, daughter born to Arthur's wife, Gwynefar, by Modred, my son.

I have feared for her in the past; I fear for her still. For I have Seen love for her. Love amidst the rising dark that sweeps the land.

Perhaps one day the harpers will sing songs and tell tales of her. Isolde the fair. Isolde of the healing hands.

But how the tales will end—whether with happiness or with tears—that, too, I cannot say.

Cannot See.

BOOK 1

BOOK I

Chapter 1

ISOLDE STARED INTO HER OWN pale face: wide across the brow, small chin, thickly lashed gray eyes. Raven-dark hair. The face was hers. Unquestionably her own. Almost as though she looked in a mirror. Except that instead, she was standing apart from herself, seeing through another's eyes.

She felt . . . pity. Pity and dread, both. She was sorry for the young woman before her. Sorry that her world was about to end.

The pity curled and soured in the pit of her stomach as she opened her mouth and spoke in a voice that was at once alien and her own. "I'm sorry, Lady Isolde. He was wounded. Fatally so. He didn't—"

AND THEN THE VISION BROKE, SHATTERED, leaving her standing by an open window in the infirmary of the abbey of Saint Eucherius, her skin clammy, her breath coming quick and unsteady, the echo of the words beating in time to the drum of her own pulse. *I'm sorry, Lady Isolde. He was wounded. Fatally so.*

No name had been spoken in that brief flash of vision. But the hammering beat of her heart supplied one now. *Trystan.* Whoever it was whose eyes she'd briefly seen through had been bringing her word of Trystan. She knew it with a certainty that sank to her bones like the bite of a winter wind.

Isolde made herself draw first one breath, then another, telling herself fiercely that the Sight didn't always show true. That sometimes these flashes of the future she caught were only *may be*, and not *will be*. That the vision needn't mean that sooner or later, some man as yet unknown—the man whose pity and dread she'd just felt—was going to come and tell her that Trystan was dead.

The tight knot inside her remained, though, and the image of this vision was blotted out in her mind's eye by the memory of another, glimpsed in the scrying waters nearly three months before. Two men, locked in fierce, deadly combat, blades ringing as they slashed and struck at one another with their swords. One older, with long black hair and a coarse, heavily handsome face. The other younger, with strikingly blue eyes set under slanted brown brows. Both their faces grim and set, chests heaving, their strikes brutal as they moved in a circling dance that would plainly end only in the death of one.

Two men. Trystan and Marche of Cornwall. Marche and Trystan. Father and son.

The recollection of that vision, together with the flash that had just come, made the room seem to tilt all around her—made the queasy sickness that always assailed her at this hour of the day seem to rise up in a churning wave.

Isolde made herself turn away from the window, back to the room behind her. Daylight was breaking, making dust motes spark and dance in the air above the rush-covered floor, casting a pale, rose yellow light across the rows of wounded men who lay here in her care. She shut her eyes for just a moment, calling up a memory from two months before.

She'd been changing the bandages on a sword cut in Trystan's side. Before he'd left the abbey to get Fidach free.

Before she'd let him go.

The wound had been healing well—and she'd tended far worse hurts than Trystan's—but still she couldn't stop the sudden rush of tears to her eyes. She'd kept her face averted, not meaning for him to see, but he'd tilted her chin up.

"Isa? You're crying. What's wrong?"

Isolde shook her head. "I'm sorry. I didn't mean to. It's just . . ." She drew an unsteady breath. "I was just thinking that this wound could have killed you. It nearly did. And I—"

Trystan lifted her, bent to rest his forehead against hers. "I'm not going to die on you."

"You can't promise that. No one can." She gave him a small, crooked smile. "Especially you. Not that I'd want you to change. Even if you are too brave and reckless by half—too determined always to protect others at risk to yourself. I love you too much as you—"

She stopped as he pulled her to him, kissed the corners of her mouth, her jaw, her throat.

A long while later, he whispered against her hair, "I swear I'd come back even from the dead for you."

I'D COME BACK EVEN FROM THE dead. Now, in the dawn-lit infirmary, Isolde tried to fix that memory in place of the earlier vision in her mind.

Trystan had gone to break Fidach, friend and brother in arms, free from the prisons of Octa of Kent. Octa of the Bloody Knife, who laughed while he killed. Trystan might be in danger. But that was like saying the men who lay on straw pallets all around her in the Abbey of Saint Eucherius's infirmary *might* be in pain.

And those in pain needed her now.

Isolde started to move among the rows of soldiers, unwrapping the bandages of one to check for any sign of a poisoned wound, stooping and laying a hand on another's brow, murmuring a few words that stopped his restless turning and muttering in a dream. There were the greater hurts—the broken limbs, the sword cuts and arrow wounds—but also smaller ones, as well, to be seen to. At this season any warrior who'd been living in an army encampment was covered with the red and itching bites of insects that had to be salved with elderflower water and ivy juice if the men were to get any rest at all. Or they came to her with faces reddened, the skin hot and tight with too much time in the open sun, and needed the salve of white daisy and plantain.

This morning the sunrise was as yet only a faint thread of rose gold along the horizon, but still it was a relief to see the darkness of another night fading with the coming dawn. Death seemed, somehow, to steal into the infirmary most often in the darkest watches of the night. And as Isolde moved quietly among the men in her care, it was easier to ignore the fear that throbbed inside her like an open wound. The men in her care had lived—all of them— through one night more.

They were the High King's own men, most of them, sworn to Madoc of Gwynedd—though some wore the badges of Cynlas of Rhos and Huel of Rhegged, as well. The petty kings and lords who made up the High King's council might quarrel and jockey for power among themselves. But with a chance of halting the Saxon invasions once and for all, they were fighting united, at least for now.

As Isolde stood, looking over the rows of wounded men, she could hear two or three of the soldiers nearest her speaking in low-voiced murmurs. Their features were shadowed, little more than pale smudges in the early half-light, but the words were clear.

"Give me another day or two and then I'm up and away from here. Wounded or no, I'm not aiming to miss the fun when we drive Marche and his goat-rutting traitor army back into the sea—and their filthy Saxon allies, as well."

Isolde felt her muscles tighten, but only, or almost only, because of the recollection of her vision of Marche and Trystan. Marche had seized the High King's throne, had forced her into marriage nearly a year before—a marriage designed to stop Isolde from exposing his treason and to gain him control of her own lands.

But she'd escaped. And she'd made Marche's treason known. And now she'd stopped flinching or shrinking from the mention of King Marche of Cornwall's name. That freedom steadied her now, if only a bit.

Only a fool wouldn't have feared Marche still, if not for himself, for the ferocity with which his army fought and tore into the British forces like wolves. Half the men in her care here now had likely had Marche of Cornwall's warriors to thank for their wounds.

The nearby talk was still going on. "Not sure I'm easy about fighting alongside Cerdic's men, though." That was one of King Huel's infantrymen, a tall, thin man with a drooping mustache and a broken arm. "They're Saxons themselves, when all's said and done. What's to say they don't turn coat and stab us just when we think they're guarding our backs?"

"Cerdic make peace with Octa of Kent? Not bloody likely." The speaker, one of the men from Gwynedd, let out a derisive puff of air. "Not when Cerdic's just finished kicking Octa in the balls from here to the borders of Kent. And just lost a son and a prime fortress to Octa, to boot. Besides, I'd make alliance with the dark god himself if he offered a chance at beating Octa and Marche."

Cerdic of Wessex had dealt King Octa of Kent a smashing blow. Only to have Octa's armies rally and snatch a vital shore fortress from Cynric, King Cerdic's son and heir. Now the armies of Britain had marched south into Wessex to join with Cerdic's forces in facing Octa and Marche for what might be one final time. The war's outcome for both sides stood balanced on a knifepoint—even as the sky outside now balanced on the turning point between sunrise and dark night. But for the first time since Arthur and her father had fallen at Camlann, Isolde heard wary hope in the voices of the men around her.

Almost as though he'd heard the thought, the warrior from Gwynedd said, lowering his voice, "They say even *he's* been seen. Riding with his companions on the night before a battle."

He was Arthur, of course. The greatest king Britain had seen or would see, or so ran the harpers' tales.

Isolde wondered at times like these about the man himself—not the hero of the bards' songs, but the flesh-and-blood man who had fought a nine year's savage war with his own son, Isolde's father. And as for Morgan, her grandmother . . .

Isolde had never heard her mention her half brother's name, never heard her speak of the way Modred, her son and Arthur's, had been made.

Few were left alive, now, who'd known Arthur well; so many had died with him at Camlann. And she supposed those who had lived through Camlann might be pardoned for remembering only the Arthur of the harpers' tales. In times such as these, men needed heroes to believe in.

She moved down the line of wounded men, continuing the morning's rounds. The latest clash of fighting had sent so many wounded carried away from the fields of battle to the abbey, here, that there was scarcely room to walk between the rough pallets on which they lay. Isolde had worked over them almost without stop for the last two days, drawing arrow points from arms and shoulders, setting broken bones, salving and stitching sword wounds.

Her eyes now stung with fatigue, and the muscles of her neck and shoulders ached. But if the work couldn't keep her from thoughts of Trystan, she had forgotten to be sick quite so often as before. She was almost successfully pushing aside the knowledge, too, that Madoc of Gwynedd, Britain's High King, was expected here at the abbey tomorrow or at the latest the following day.

And that she would soon have to answer the proposal of marriage he'd made her nearly three months before.

The men were heartbreakingly grateful for whatever help she could give, for even the smallest touch of her hand. They stopped her as she moved on her rounds, begging her to touch a bandaged leg or arm for luck, rubbing their fingers against the hem of her gown as a guard against nightmares and poisoned wounds. Their unmixed adoration felt strange, still, after years of caring for injured soldiers and knowing them half grateful, half hating her as the daughter of Modred, Arthur's traitor son, who was, in a way, the cause of the wounds they bore. And more than half fearful of what powers the granddaughter of the enchantress Morgan might hold, for Morgan, it was whispered, had been able to melt a man off the earth like snow off the ditch with nothing but a look.

All that was changed by the battle of two months before. By Isolde's being at least partly to thank for the recent defeat of Octa, for the alliance with Cerdic of Wessex that had given all Britain's forces fresh hope.

Now, standing near the center of the long, timbered room, Isolde could hear soft rustlings as the wounded soldiers turned restlessly on their beds of straw, and from here and there among them came faint, raspy coughs or sometimes a low groan or sigh or a muttered prayer. She had been in too many rooms like this one to let herself hope that she could save them all. She would spoon-feed them water and broth as long as they could swallow, and wipe their faces with cool water for as long as they breathed.

But this was summer, and the fevers that always stalked infirmary halls had struck; even in the pale gray dawn light she could see the hectic flush on the cheekbones of at least half a dozen men.

One of the healthier ones, a young foot soldier with a broken collarbone, was starting to moan louder than the rest, his eyes screwed tight closed. Isolde started towards him, wishing for the countless time that she had access to her own workroom, her own medicines and stores of herbs. All that, though, was still at Dinas Emrys, in the hills of Gwynedd, a weeks-long journey across war-torn lands.

For weeks now, she had been making do with what supplies could be culled from the abbey infirmary's stores, and what roots and herbs could be dug from the surrounding woods and hills, dried, and prepared as quickly as possible for use. And at present she had far more men wounded and in pain than remained of the precious stores of poppy and the like that she had brought from Dinas Emrys nearly four months ago.

Still, she could offer the young soldier a cup of cool water, at least, and maybe an infusion of willow bark for the pain; could make sure his name was not yet to be added to those who burned with fever and so, like the war, like this new day, lay on a sword's-edge balance, this one between death and life.

Isolde threaded her way towards him between the other pallets, then checked as the door to the infirmary opened and one of the abbey sisters entered the room. Sister Olwen was perhaps forty or forty-five, and had served as infirmarer to the abbey of Saint Eucherius for some twenty years. She was a big, square-built woman, nearly as tall as a man, and her face was likewise heavy-boned and square, with piercingly clear blue eyes, a hooked nose, and an unexpectedly wide, generous mouth.

Her mouth, now, though, was set in a thin, hard line, and she pointedly refused even to glance at Isolde as she came into the room. Sister Olwen might have small experience with battle wounds, or indeed with any ailments but upset stomachs and failing eyes and the winter coughs and chilblains her fellow sisters suffered each year. But she still bitterly resented Isolde's invasion of her small domain, as hard as Isolde had tried to soften all possible offenses to her authority.

Sister Olwen, black nun's robes sweeping out behind her like raven wings, was making for one of the men who'd managed sometime during the night to fall into a deep, exhausted sleep. She carried a bowl of thin barley gruel in one arm, and as Isolde watched she bent, about to take the sleeping soldier by the shoulder and shake him awake.

Swiftly, Isolde turned aside from the groaning man and crossed to Sister Olwen, stopping her with a touch on the arm.

"That's not a good idea just now." Several of the men had turned to look as she passed, and now watched her and Sister Olwen with fever-bright eyes, but Isolde kept her voice low, mindful of any others who might be managing to catch an hour or two's rest. "He—"

Sister Olwen, though, interrupted before Isolde could finish, yanking her arm free of Isolde's touch. "He's taken no food since yesterday, he needs to eat. And I think you can trust me to feed a wounded man some gruel." She sniffed, her mouth thinning. "One hardly requires a superior healer's skill to do that much."

Isolde shook her head. "No, you don't understand. I only meant that—"

Before Isolde could move to check her again, though, Sister Olwen had bent, and seized the shoulder of the sleeping man in her firm, blunt-fingered grasp.

The soldier was barely three days out of combat, and of a certainty he'd had years of a warrior's training on other fields of battle, besides. He was a compact, barrel-chested man with a black mustache and a swordsman's powerfully muscled shoulders. He'd lost one arm to a Saxon axe blow, but he had another still whole and sound. At Sister Olwen's abrupt touch his eyes flew open and he lashed out, catching the nun a blow in the stomach that made her sit down abruptly beside him on the rush-strewn ground, the bowl of gruel upended and dripping on her lap.

For a moment, the infirmary was absolutely still. Then a man— or boy, really, for he couldn't be more than sixteen or seventeen years of age—on one of the neighboring pallets started to laugh. And as though the sound had broken a spell of silence binding the room, several more of the surrounding men started to chuckle and gasp with laughter, as well.

Isolde reached out, meaning to help Sister Olwen to her feet, but before she could so much as touch the older woman's arm, Sister Olwen had raised herself. She swayed a bit on her feet and her face

looked slightly white, but she held herself rigidly erect, even with
one hand pressed tight against her middle.

"Are you—" Isolde began.

"I am perfectly well. Thank you." Sister Olwen's voice was
slightly breathless, but she spoke with a determined, almost regal
dignity. And before Isolde could say anything more she had turned
and swept, damp black robes and all, out of the room.

Isolde saw the door shut behind her with a dull thud, then
turned back to where the man Sister Olwen had woken was still half
sitting up, blinking dazedly and looking in confusion from Isolde to
the laughing men on the pallets all around.

"Good to know we've someone to protect us if we're ever attacked
by a band of angry nuns," one of them gasped, still wheezing with mirth.

And swift as an indrawn breath, Isolde had one of those moments when she could almost see the shade of her grandmother
Morgan at her side. It usually was in the infirmary that Morgan
seemed to appear. She would glide silently up and down the rows
of wounded men, dark eyes thoughtful as she considered each case,
the hard, delicate lines of her aging but still-lovely face grave. Sometimes she would offer advice, as she might have years ago, when
Isolde was a child and still learning the healing arts from her grandmother's daily instruction.

Now Morgan's head was tipped back as she laughed along with
the other wounded men, dark eyes narrowed to amused slits.

Isolde silently shook her head at her grandmother's laughing
image. *Unkind.*

The shadow Morgan gave another chuckle. *The holy sister wasn't
harmed. Look me in the eye and say it wasn't funny seeing her sitting
there dripping porridge and looking like she'd just seen a flock of pigs flying through the air.*

The man Sister Olwen had woken was still looking dazed, and
Isolde knelt, helping him to lie back again on his pallet, touching
him gently so as not to jar the bandaged stump of his left arm.

"What just—" He swallowed, moistened his lips, and then began
again. "What happened?"

Isolde bit her lip, then gave up the struggle not to smile. The
likeness of her grandmother nodded. *No, I didn't think you could.*

"I think," Isolde said, drawing the woolen blanket back up over the black-haired soldier's chest, "that it's a good thing you're going to live, my friend. I'm not sure you'd want to take your chances on where you'd end up in the afterlife just now."

He was a young man of about Isolde's own age, twenty, or a year or two more, with a head of thickly curling black hair and dark eyes set deep under strongly marked black brows. His face was tinged with the pallor of illness, his mouth tight with pain, and he had an angry bruise across one cheekbone, but he was a handsome man, even so.

He'd been carried into the infirmary mercifully unconscious, with his left arm already gone. Isolde had cauterized, salved, and bandaged the wound, and dosed him with a measure of her remaining syrup of poppies to spare him waking to the pain as long as she could.

That had been three days ago, and she'd spoken the truth when she'd told him his life was secure. Or at least it would be, if he consented to take food and drink. But from the moment he'd woken to look blearily about him and then, in a seeming rush of remembrance, jerked upright to stare down at the bandaged stump of his arm, Isolde hadn't heard him utter a word. Not even a groan.

His fellows had told her his name was Cadell, but though Isolde had spoken to him several times, telling him where he was, what he might expect of an injury like his, he'd lain without looking at her, never once acknowledging her either by word or look. He neither looked nor spoke to any of his companions, either, simply lay day in and out, staring at the vaulted ceiling above with dull, angry eyes.

Now Cadell looked at her blankly a moment, his dark eyes still slightly dazed. But then, slowly, his mouth turned up at the edges and he started to laugh, his whole body shaking. Then abruptly, as though the laughter had cracked open a wall between him and all he was trying not to let himself feel, he stopped laughing and looked up at Isolde, eyes bleak and suddenly desperate in a rigid face.

"I've a wife waiting for me back home." His voice was barely a whisper, and Isolde saw the muscles in his throat bob up and down. He blinked angrily against the haze of moisture she could see had risen to his eyes, then jerked his head towards the missing left arm while the fingers of his good hand clutched and pulled at the loose straw on which he lay. "What's she going to say when she sees me come back to her like this?"

Isolde had guessed already that he had a wife or sweetheart waiting for him by the finely embroidered knot work woven into the hem and collar of his cloak. She saw them so often: all the charms and talismans of protection that women in every corner of the land sewed and wove into the cloaks and tunics and boots their men wore off to war. A twig of a rowan tree, tied with red ribbon. A bundle of herbs sewn into the top of a boot. An embroidered knot worked on a sword belt, the twists and turns meant to confound evil and keep the bearer from harm.

Pleas, all of them, that the man who wore it would pass through battle safely—all that the women left waiting at home could do in the way of protection.

And Isolde had been asked that same question by more men than she could even begin to count over the course of the last eight years. What would the wife or sweetheart left behind say when the man she'd sent off to war came back less than whole, after all?

Isolde gave him the same answer she always gave, the same answer her grandmother had always given. Morgan, for all her fierceness and temper, had had a streak of unexpected compassion about her that ran through her character like a wellspring of water rippling through granite.

She brushed the hair lightly back from the man Cadell's brow and, as always, concentrated every thought on the hope that her words would be true. "She's going to say that she's so happy to have you home again."

DAWN WAS BREAKING. TRYSTAN KICKED DIRT over the charred remains of last night's campfire, built in a shallow hole that when filled in would leave no trace of their presence here. Though that was essentially a waste of time. He might as well have built a bonfire, climbed one of the surrounding trees, and shouted for Octa's guard to come and pick him up. The end result was likely to be the same.

The rest of the men were grouped in a half circle around the now invisible fire pit, tearing into slabs of coarse bread and dried meat. The bedrolls were heaped in a pile to one side. Not that any of them had slept.

Eurig was the first to break the silence. His round, jowly face and bald head gleamed palely in the gray morning light, and he wiped his mouth before speaking.

"Look. I'm not for one moment suggesting we shouldn't go in after Fidach, because we all know we're going to. Live or die, I'd not leave a rabid dog in Octa of Kent's hands, much less a man who'd kept my back in battle. But what I am saying, or asking, at least, is whether we shouldn't just dig our own graves right here for Octa to throw us in before we even start on this plan."

A war band's confidence is the mirror of its leader's. Trystan remembered hearing a long dead commander utter that tidy little saying at some time or other. A long *dead* commander. Right.

They were headed to Caer Peris, Octa of Kent's newly conquered stronghold on the Saxon shore, to break out of the fortress there a man who was undoubtedly one of the Saxon king's most valued prisoners.

Octa of Kent was called Octa of the Bloody Knife for a reason, and it wasn't because of his skill at hunting rabbits. Still, Trystan resisted the urge to rub the dull throb between his eyes and instead turned to Eurig, baring his teeth in an approximation of a smile. "Not complaining, are you? Just because the holiday you've had the last three days is about to come to an end?"

In point of fact, they had all spent the last three days slogging through swamps and marshland, breathing the stench of mud and rotting leaves and waiting until nightfall to burn the day's accumulated collection of leeches off themselves.

Eurig laughed, and Trystan went on, speaking soberly, now. "I'm not saying it's going to be easy. But I'll take the most dangerous part. The rest of you just do as we agreed: take out the guards, get Fidach, and then clear the hell off."

"Oh, good." From his place nearest the fire pit, Cath shifted and addressed the surrounding trees, one hand scratching at his chin. In the thickening shadows, he looked like something between a bear and a man, broad-shouldered and heavy of build, with a head of shaggy black hair and a beard that spread over his chest. "Always know I've volunteered myself into a pig-swiving disaster when you're the one volunteering for the dangerous part."

Trystan rubbed the back of his neck, then cocked an eyebrow in the big man's direction. "You volunteering to take my place, funny man?"

Cath grinned, teeth a flash of white in his grime-smeared face. After nearly two months living rough, they were all covered in enough dirt to grow a garden. "No, no." Cath held up his hands. "I'm kicking myself in the arse enough already for once saying to call on me if there was ever anything I could do for you. Wasn't counting on your taking it quite so literal, like, you understand."

Before Trystan could answer, a sudden flurry in the underbrush made him start upright, his knife in his hand long before his mind registered *bird*. Just another bloody bird. He slid the blade back into its scabbard, his heartbeats slowing back towards normal. At least everyone else's nerves were as edgy as his own. Eurig was on his feet, and Piye and Daka had practically levitated in place.

Eurig swore under his breath. "Aye, about that"—he turned to Trystan—"your taking the part of the job with the greatest danger, I mean." He paused again, seeming to search for words, and then said, "Not sure that's right. I mean, it's one thing for me to risk my neck. Got neither kith nor kin to mourn me if the luck turns sour on me and I lose the game. But you have . . . I mean, I thought . . ."

Eurig had to be the only outlaw mercenary in six kingdoms who could actually blush. Even in the dawn light, even with the solid layer of grime on Eurig's skin, Trystan could see the color creeping up his neck.

Trystan closed his eyes and allowed himself the fervent wish that some merciful god would cleave Eurig's tongue to the roof of his mouth before he could finish. Except that Daka—it would be Daka—broke in. If Eurig and Cath were difficult to distinguish in the shadows, Daka and Piye were nearly invisible with their braided black hair and coal-black skin. "He mean you could be finding more pleasant ways to spend the nights than be sleeping alone in the mud."

Trystan opened his eyes. Perfect. He'd actually managed—what—a whole hour, now, without thinking more than a dozen times of Isolde. And now Eurig and Daka brought her up for the first time since they'd left the abbey.

A distracted soldier is a dead soldier. That was another of those tidy little sayings he'd heard somewhere or other. Memories he'd been trying to block thudded home with an actual physical jolt, and he couldn't stop the picture from appearing before him. Isolde, her wide gray eyes on a level with his as she knelt beside his bed saying, *Marry me.*

Everything—God, the only thing—he'd ever wanted in his life suddenly there before him for the taking. And just for a moment he'd believed, or at least pretended to believe, that he might even be able to keep it. Believed that the past could stay in the past, locked away.

He'd opened his idiot mouth and said, *I would love that.*

And the truly stupid thing was that if he had the same chance, the same choice to make right here and now, he knew he'd not be able to stop himself from saying the exact same thing again.

He didn't know what his expression looked like, but Daka shifted uneasily and said, "I be meaning no disrespect to your lady, you understand."

Trystan let out his breath. "Notice that I haven't ripped you into small bleeding fragments and scattered them under one of those pine trees over there." He went on before Daka could speak again, shifting his gaze to include the other three. "And as far as my taking the greatest risk goes, I'm the only one of us that can speak to Octa and his guards in their own tongue. Any of you walk into his garrison and flowers will be growing on your grave before Octa so much as spits on the earth heaped on your bones."

Cath scratched his beard again, his broad face sober now, all trace of laughter left behind. "You're sure you can get inside?"

Trystan finished filling in the fire pit, kicked some leaves over the scar of freshly turned earth, and then reached for his sword belt, lying ready to hand beside the place where he'd spent the night. "Octa has an outer ring of his men posted all around the garrison walls. We know that—we've just spent the last three weeks watching them, finding out where they patrol and who they are and when the guard changes. And the outer walls, the old Roman-built stone ones, were damaged in the siege. They've not enough men to guard all the weak points. And we know that the guards posted there are sloppy, besides. They assume no one could get through the outer ring of men. So they let their attention slip. Daka and Piye distract the outer circle of guards, and you, Eurig, and I will be able to slip inside."

Cath nodded slowly. "True enough—or could be, at least. But—"

Trystan cut him off, though, before he could finish, buckling on his sword belt and turning to Eurig, Daka, and Piye. "You're ready?"

Eurig and the other two jerked their heads in agreement. "Ready."

Trystan turned, scanning the surrounding trees, but all was still, the branches wreathed in chill ribbons of morning fog. He nodded. "Then let's be gone."

MORGAN WAS STILL BESIDE HER AS Isolde made her way down the rows of men. *So long as you're here, I don't suppose you'd like to tell me when this war will end?*

The image of Morgan smiled at that. *Out of temper today?*

Isolde had given up trying to decide whether these visions were real or only her own imagining. Either way, it was a strange comfort to be able to see her grandmother, not sick and suffering as she'd died, but regal and fierce and with the same eldritch beauty with which she'd lived. *Frightened, at least. The men may speak of Arthur—*

But the mention of Arthur was a mistake. Swift as a sword stroke, Morgan vanished. Just as in life a door had always slammed closed behind her eyes at the mention of Arthur's name.

Isolde looked down. She was standing beside another of the wounded soldiers, a man with some Pritani blood, to judge by his shock of fiery red hair. He was one of the oldest men to be brought into the infirmary, forty or forty-five, Isolde thought. His skin was fair, but weathered, with a light dusting of freckles, and he had a square-jawed, pugnacious face with heavy brows and a nose that had once been broken and inexpertly set.

He had, too, a broken leg that had not yet been set at all, since he'd shouted or growled at her wordlessly every time she'd so much as come near.

"You can open your eyes," Isolde told him now. "I know you're not actually asleep."

He lay rigid a moment longer, then his lids flickered open and he glared at her balefully from under brows as red as his hair. "Thought maybe you'd take a hint and leave me be."

Isolde made no reply, and he glowered at her again. "You see this?" He gestured to his face. "Got my nose broken and I set it myself. Didn't need an interfering female poking and prodding me then."

Isolde didn't bother to say that if she'd been the one to set the broken nose the year before, it would be straight now, and not crooked with a swelling lump at the bridge. She'd also seen more wounded men than she could count who used anger and snarling words to clamp down fear they were trying desperately to hide.

She closed her eyes, reaching towards the wounded man in her mind, casting out tiny threads of awareness that slid lightly along the muscles and sinews of his body and felt for pain. She was briefly thankful that she could now better control her sense of the wounds and injuries she saw than she'd been able to do a few months before. Busy or no, if she'd been constantly conscious of all the aches and suffering and dragging hurts in this room, she'd have been sick ten times over this morning alone.

The broken leg was agonizingly painful. And beneath the pain, she could feel a surging mass of blood-soaked memories in the man's mind. Of mud and battle and watching his closest companions cut down while he lay helpless, unable to rise to their aid.

She said, "All right. You win. Healers are useless. I'll just give up wasting my time here, shall I, and go embroider in colored wools all day?"

She could see the red-haired man fighting to keep his expression fierce, but all the same an unwilling smile twitched the corners of his tightly set mouth. He wore on his muddied tunic the badge of King Cynlas of Rhos, a bear stitched on a scarlet background. Isolde had seen many of Cynlas's men in the infirmary these last weeks, since Cynlas had responded to Madoc's call to arms.

Now Isolde gathered the skirts of her gown aside and knelt

beside the red-haired man, so that her eyes were on a level with his. "Is there a name I can call you by?" she asked him.

The soldier looked away, turning his head to stare resolutely at the opposite wall, but after a long moment he grunted, his voice grudging, "It's Cadfan."

Isolde nodded. "All right, then, Cadfan. Do you see those men over there?" She gestured to the group nearest Cadell. Three of them, at least, were among those who balanced on a sword's edge between life and death. But they were grinning, still, all the same.

Isolde turned back to the man Cadfan, and went on, keeping her voice low. "Sister Olwen—however unintentionally—has just made them all laugh one more time. But that's about as much as she or I or anyone else can do for them right now beyond waiting to see whether they live or die."

She touched Cadfan lightly on the shoulder, forcing him to turn and look at her. "So you are going to lie there quietly and let me set that broken leg of yours. Because unlike half of the other men in this infirmary, I *can* do something for you."

For a long moment, Cadfan stared at her, pugnacious jaw hard, mouth compressed in a thin, angry line, and a scowl furrowing his brow. Isolde thought, though, that the underlying fear in his eyes was perhaps a tiny bit less sharp—and yet, oddly, a shade nearer the surface, a shade less fiercely hidden, as well.

And finally, he broke away from her gaze, turned his head away, and nodded. "Not as if I'm like to go anywhere else, is it?"

As much of an agreement as Isolde was likely to get. She let out her breath and began to rise, then started at sight of the woman who, without her apparently hearing, had come to stand beside her while she spoke to Cadfan.

Mother Berthildis of the Abbey of Saint Eucherius was an almost incredibly ugly old woman. She was smaller even than Isolde, her plump body slightly stooped, and her head thrusting forward from rounded shoulders. Her face was as lined as old parchment, set with very small, sharp black eyes, and slightly toadlike, truth be told.

But that had been Isolde's first impression of her, nearly three months ago now, when she'd sat in the abbess's private parlor with the purpose of winning Mother Berthildis's permission to drug the guard of Cerdic of Wessex, the abbey's visiting patron king. Isolde had long since begun to find a kind of strange beauty in the old woman's lined and yellow face.

Now Isolde said, after answering Mother Berthildis's greeting, "Is Sister Olwen . . . ?"

"She is quite well." The abbess's face remained grave, but Isolde saw the slight crinkling of humor at the corners of her small black eyes. "She may have learned a salutary lesson in humility. We can hope so." The lines of humor deepened. "With all due humility ourselves, of course. And now," she went on briskly, "I came to see whether I might be of any assistance to you."

The abbess might be bent, old, and stoop-shouldered, her fingers gnarled and spotted with age, but Isolde had long since learned, too, that she had the strength of a woman half her years. She nodded. "Thank you. I would be glad of another pair of hands."

Mother Berthildis's small black eyes swept briskly over Cadfan, and she nodded. "Ah. A broken leg, I see. Very well. What can I do?"

Cadfan had turned away again, arms folded across his chest, his face—what Isolde could see of it—rigid as stone. She looked back at Mother Berthildis. "The break is two days old, at least. Do you see how the muscles have tightened? They're—"

Cadfan's head snapped round and he barked out, "I've got ears, haven't I? And last I checked, they still worked. No need to talk about me as though I weren't here."

The break was in his lower leg, a straight fracture of the bone just below the knee. Simple enough to set, and Isolde was almost certain he'd not even be left with a limp once the break had healed.

But she knew, too, from speaking with the other men that Cadfan had walked on the broken leg for an entire day, carrying a more badly wounded comrade on his back, after their war band had been ambushed by a patrol of Octa's men. So she said easily, ignoring his tone, "Of course. Do you see how the muscles of your leg have tightened, then?"

She gestured to the rigidly knotted muscles of his calf, visible beneath the ragged hem of the breeches she'd cut away when first he'd been carried in. Cadfan looked where she'd pointed, flinched, turned a shade paler, and then looked away. His teeth were clenched, but Isolde saw the glitter of sweat on his brow.

She touched his shoulder and said, more gently, "Your muscles are dragging the bones further out of alignment. So we'll need to relax them before I can set the break." She glanced up to include Mother Berthildis as she went on. "Usually I'd use poppy syrup, but it's in short supply just now. I'd rather save it for after I set the bone to dull the pain enough that he"—she turned back to Cadfan—"so that you can rest. But I'll let the choice be yours."

Cadfan's jaw remained tight, but his head jerked in a wordless nod, and he said, "Reckon I can stand the pain for now. You can keep your potions till later."

She couldn't help Trystan, couldn't even know for certain what dangers he faced or whether he would return, regardless of how long she waited for him here. Neither could she defeat Octa's or Marche's armies and put a halt to this endless war. She could, though, set Cadfan's leg. That had to be enough for today, for now.

Isolde nodded and then stood still, frowning at the broken leg a moment, visualizing what had to be done. Then she looked up, turning back to Mother Berthildis. "Can you have someone bring us a long wooden trough, maybe one of the ones from the stables? And enough hot water to fill it?"

OCTA OF THE BLOODY KNIFE, KING of Kent, was a big man, and powerfully built, despite his age. His matted hair and beard were streaked with silver, and his ice pale eyes were flat, almost dead-looking in a broad, battle-scarred face. And in the ordinary way, Trystan wouldn't have trusted him not to spit in a cup of ale he offered to share. Much less bargained with him for the lives of men.

He supposed he should count it a victory that he'd talked his way in past Octa's personal bodyguard, and that Octa himself hadn't— yet—gone for the heavy gold-hilted knife that lay on the table between them.

They sat at the head of Octa's great hall. The timbered walls were lined with painted shields and huge war axes and swords, and the air was thick with smoke from the central fire. The rest of Octa's warriors were sprawled in the straw that littered the floor of the lower half of the room, most too far gone in drink to pay them any mind. Two of them were fighting, chests heaving as they kicked and punched and rolled on the floor. The two combatants were surrounded by a ring of onlookers, shouting out jeers and taunts and encouragement by turns.

In many ways, a typical king's ale hall, nothing to distinguish it from a dozen others, save maybe for the richness of the gold rings on the warriors' arms and hands, showing that they had sworn oaths to an especially powerful lord. The only incongruous note was an old woman who crouched on a pile of furs and tapestried pillows in the nearest corner of the room. She was swathed in shawls and a dark head cloth so that her ancient, hook-nosed face seemed to float in the shadows.

Trystan wouldn't have marked Octa for a man to tolerate any woman's presence in his hall, except maybe that of the slave girls who served him and his men. And this old woman was no slave. Even hunched in the shadowed corner as she was, Trystan could see the heavy gold necklaces hung about her stringy neck, the gleaming glass brooch pinned to her shawls. She had looked up only once, as Trystan first came in, and for a moment had fixed him with a penetrating stare that made him feel as though she knew exactly who he was and why he had come. But she had gone back to her work of spinning a pile of wool into thread, and since then hadn't spared either him or Octa so much as a glance.

"So." Octa had a harsh, rasping voice, and he spoke almost without inflection, continuing to stare at Trystan with those pale, flat eyes. "You come here in hopes that I will release a prisoner I hold. A mercenary and leader of an outlaw band known as Fidach."

"No." Octa's brows shot up at Trystan's response, but Trystan kept his face as impassive as Octa's. He'd met with men of Octa's kind before—enough to know that the Saxon king would scent any trace of hidden fear as surely as a wolf could sniff a bloodied sheep out of a herd. Emotion in battle meant defeat. So he made himself feel nothing. No apprehension. No fear.

No past or future, either. Only this ill-lit and smoky fire hall and the man who faced him across a scarred wood table.

Octa was scrutinizing him through narrowed eyes. "No?" he repeated.

"No," Trystan agreed calmly. "Fidach is already gone."

Octa was well schooled in hiding his reactions, but Trystan saw the faint tightening at the corners of his mouth, the brief flare of shock in the pale eyes. And because he had seen the marks on Fidach's back and arms when he and Eurig had carried him out of Octa's holding cell and past the lifeless bodies of the four guards, Trystan allowed himself a moment's grim satisfaction.

In a way it was to Octa's credit—or it would have been, if Trystan had been in a mood to credit him—that he didn't argue, didn't bluster or accuse Trystan of lying or deny his claim. A white dent of anger appeared on either side of his thin mouth, but he said, only, "Then why are you here?"

Trystan lifted one shoulder. "Call it good principles. I prefer paying for what I take to theft. And I'd also prefer not to have you send men out with orders to drag Fidach back."

For a long moment, Octa stared at him. The force of his gaze was like being struck in the gut, but Trystan didn't move. One of the two men fighting in the lower hall flipped his opponent onto the floor with a resounding thud and a cheer went up from the onlookers.

Then, abruptly, Octa threw back his head and laughed harshly. "You're either very brave or very stupid, my friend. Exactly what price do you think you can offer me for your outlaw friend's life?"

Trystan let the silence rest between them a beat, then said, "Intelligence."

Octa's heavy brows shot upwards, but Trystan went on before he could speak. "I've no doubt you've informants already in—what? Madoc of Gwynedd's camp?"

Octa didn't answer, but Trystan saw the small narrowing about the corners of the other man's eyes and knew, with another quick flare of satisfaction, that he'd been right.

He knew, too, how tightly stretched Octa's resources were. Octa had months ago gained an ally in King Owain of Powys, and Owain had died. Of plague, the reports ran—which not even a newborn babe or a half-wit would have believed. Octa had installed Owain's nephew, a child of six, as king of Powys. And collected the tribute and taxes of an overlord from the land.

But maintaining that control took men—warriors stationed in Powys whom Octa could ill spare just now.

Aloud, Trystan went on, "Madoc may be High King, but his

councilmen fight among themselves like dogs over a haunch of deer. The other kings of Britain have their armies strung out all along the coast, poised to attack the string of forts your men hold. It would be to your advantage to know if one of those others planned to strike out and attack on his own." Trystan paused. Octa hadn't moved, but his flat blue gaze was fixed intently on Trystan's face.

Trystan went on. "And then there's Cerdic of Wessex. He's allied himself with Britain—for the present. But I doubt he trusts them any more than he'd trust you. His forces control the Isle of Wight." Trystan set the bronze cup of ale Octa had offered him on the table before him. "That's just opposite this fortress here—the one you've taken from Cerdic's son." He reached across the table and moved Octa's cup so that it stood opposite his own. Octa's brows lifted again, but he didn't respond, and after a moment Trystan went on. "Your forces on one side, lands Cerdic controls on the other, and only a narrow stretch of water in between that a ten-year-old child could cross in a leaky boat. You'd like to know, wouldn't you, if Cerdic is moving troops onto the island in preparation for an attack to regain this stretch of land?"

Trystan stopped. He'd laid the mission out in his mind in a series of steps. And snaring Octa was the first.

Octa's stiff features had relaxed into a look of wary speculation. He rubbed the scar that ran along his jawline, and asked, with a studied indifference that wore thin even before he'd finished speaking the words, "And you can bring me word of the plans of all these kings?"

And hooked. Trystan allowed himself a small, grim inward smile.

Those few short weeks with Isolde might have made his stomach knot with wishing he could change who he was—wishing for something he could no longer be if Arthur himself rose from the dead and touched him with his magic sword.

But if that path was forever closed off to him, he ought now at any rate to be a goddamned expert at dealing with scum like Octa of Kent.

Trystan met Octa's gaze and held it. "I can."

.   .   .

MOTHER BERTHILDIS, HER BLACK ROBES POOLING on the floor, held Cadfan's torso, but Isolde hardly had need of her. Cadfan lay absolutely still as she began to draw the broken bones gently back into alignment. He groaned occasionally, but Isolde had enough practice in blocking out men's groans while she worked that she could hold herself off from hearing Cadfan's, now.

What was harder to ignore was the fear that clung sticky as cobwebs, the echo of that earlier vision that seemed to lurk like something waiting in the shadows, ready to pounce. The recollection was making the usual gray morning nausea worse, and making Isolde's hands shake when they had to be absolutely steady.

She almost always told a story while she worked over the men in her care. She could remember her grandmother Morgan telling one of the old fire tales in a soft voice almost untouched by age as they worked together at stitching a wound or setting a broken bone. The rhythm and flow of the story was a help to both her and whichever man she cared for when they both needed something to think on besides the pain.

Usually for that reason she told one of the warrior's hero tales, a story of King Bran or Beli Mawr. Those were always the most popular among the wounded soldiers. Although sometimes, if she wanted to give a man an excuse to cry, she would tell one of the love tales—the story of Aengus Og and the swan maiden, maybe—and then keep her gaze carefully turned away when he wiped away tears.

But this time, before reaching for the mallow-root-saturated bandages that would pad the splint, Isolde drew a slow breath.

There were stories, too, of druids who could send their own souls forth from their bodies, spirits soaring like birds, high above the earth to glimpse sights unseen by human vision. And—maybe—this morning, the Sight had let Isolde's own consciousness flit, briefly, into another's body, letting her look through the eyes of a man who would one day in the future—maybe—come to tell her that Trystan had been killed.

Now Isolde tried to reach out beyond the abbey walls, to send her own thoughts, her own awareness along a gossamer, whisper-thin thread, as she did when trying to seek out the source of a wounded man's pain. Searching for—

She thought she felt something. The faintest tug, maybe, on the thread that seemed bound about her heart. A prickle, a flicker of light like the brush of wings against her mind. Trystan? She had no idea. She'd long since given up trying to question or even understand the laws that governed the Sight.

But she opened her eyes and began to speak, trying to imagine each word a link in a golden chain, a thread in a wide golden web. "In a time that once was, is now gone forever, and will be again soon, there lived a boy and a girl. Their fathers were warriors and brothers in arms, so that they knew each other almost from the time they could walk."

Isolde finished wrapping the first layer of bandages about Cadfan's leg, fastened the end in place with a bronze pin, and then reached for one of the wooden splints Mother Berthildis had brought before going on. "One day, when she was eight and the boy ten, he taught her how to track in the woods—took her out into the forest and showed her how to read the signs that meant a deer or a hare or a wild boar had passed by. The next day, he was busy training at sword play with the men. So the girl slipped off by herself into the forest. She honestly wasn't trying to be disobedient or troublesome. She was just—well, eight." Isolde finished binding the first splint in place and reached for the second. "She thought she would be back long before anyone even noticed she was gone."

Isolde glanced up to find Mother Berthildis's keen black eyes fixed on her, and smiled faintly. "She wasn't, of course. She got herself completely and utterly lost and when night started to fall she still hadn't found her way. So she sat down under a tree, shivering, because even though it was spring the nights were still cold. And she tried not to remember every story of evil spirits and night demons she'd ever heard—but of course she did.

"She was sitting there in the dark, huddled with her back against the tree trunk and more terrified than she'd ever been in her life when she looked up and saw—"

Isolde stopped, staring down unseeingly at the wooden splint in her hands. "She saw the boy standing there in front of her. She'd never in all her life been so glad to see him before. She hated to cry, and she didn't want him to think she was a coward, so she managed not to. But when her teeth stopped chattering she told him, 'I didn't think you'd find me all the way out here.'"

Isolde broke off. She hated crying. She always had. But these days she seemed to dissolve into tears for any and every and no reason at all, and before going on she had to blink away the burning in her eyes. "The boy was usually very—" She stopped, searching for a word. "Serious. He rarely ever really smiled. But he did smile then, and he tugged one of her braids and rumpled her hair and said, 'Then you're an addle-brain, aren't you?'"

She'd almost finished binding the splints in place. She tied the last knot in the wrappings as Cadfan snorted derisively through his nose. "That's the end? I've heard you tell the other men one of the war tales of Macsen Wledig. And I get a story about a couple of snotty-nosed brats? What's the point of that?"

At least she was no longer on the verge of tears. "Just to give you something else to complain of besides my treatment and your leg."

Mother Berthildis had vanished at some point while Isolde was fastening the last of the bandages, but now she reappeared, bearing a bowl of thick porridge. Isolde suppressed a sigh. She'd likely been wrong in answering Cadfan that way; she could see him now, ready to open his mouth and refuse the food out of hand, just to spite her.

Before he could speak, she cut in, reaching for the bowl herself. "Thank you, Mother. I'm sure he doesn't want it. And I'm ravenous," she added, above the lurch of her stomach. Isolde thought there was a faint twitch of amusement about the abbess's wide mouth, but she only inclined her head and then moved away to sketch light crosses in the air above the heads of some of the other men.

Isolde had managed to choke down several bites with the wooden spoon before Cadfan, fiery red brows drawn together, fairly yanked the bowl from her hands. "Give me that. There's one of us here what can walk to the kitchens for food. And I'm fair certain it's not me." He took up the spoon himself and began to devour the porridge in a series of quick, angry gulps. "Like I've not faced down trouble enough."

Isolde stood very still. Every wounded man who came into her care had his own story of the battle he'd just faced, lodged like a poison thorn in his side. Sometimes they told their stories readily, even eagerly, and the thorn was plucked out, the poison cleansed, even if the scar remained. And sometimes, like Cadfan, they held tight to their every word until the poisoned wound festered and turned bad.

Very, very slowly and carefully, Isolde sat down at Cadfan's side and asked, "What do you mean?"

Cadfan spooned up a mouthful of porridge. Isolde thought he wasn't going to answer after all. But then, finally, he lifted his head and met Isolde's gaze, a sudden blaze of anger kindling in the blue eyes. "A man expects to risk his life in battle. Be no point to it, otherwise. Kill or be killed. Stand up and take your medicine if it's your turn to die. But what he doesn't expect"—a muscle jerked in the line of Cadfan's jaw—"he doesn't expect to have his life and those of his fellows thrown away like so much rubbish for the privy pit."

Isolde thought there was a glimmer of moisture in his eyes, but he'd probably have run another entire day on the broken leg before he acknowledged the tears. Instead his voice got louder, as though anger was a cliff's edge he clung to to keep from feeling pain. "I'm oath-sworn to my lord Cynlas." He touched the badge on his tunic. "Have been these thirty years. Drank his ale, spilled my blood, and took the death oath to follow wherever he might lead. But when it comes to taking orders from a man who's either a sniveling coward or a thundering fool, for all he may be High King—"

Isolde looked over quickly. "What did you say?"

Madoc of Gwynedd had not sought the High Kingship; he'd been chosen by the king's council when Marche had betrayed Britain and the throne the previous year. He was a young man, barely a year or two past thirty, with a face that still bore the scars from an old fight with Marche. And though he'd not sought to sit on the High King's throne, he'd acquitted himself well. Few men could have held together the strained, uneasy web of alliance that united Britain's nobles and petty kings. But Madoc of Gwynedd with his warrior's blunt impatience, his warrior's drive, had done it—had led Britain's united armies in the most successful campaigns since Arthur had fallen at Camlann.

And he was loved by his men, not just obeyed. Isolde had seen it in the faces of the wounded in her care. Those oath-sworn to

Madoc—and others, besides—would have without hesitation laid down their lives for their High King.

Surprise had made Isolde interrupt Cadfan before she could stop herself. But Cadfan didn't even anger at the question. It was as though some internal dam had burst open, and he fairly spat the next words at her. "I said that High King or no, he's either a coward or a fool. And I'll say the same to his face, if he's ever man enough to come in here and risk dirtying his fine robes."

Cadfan paused, his eyes focusing on the opposite wall, his gaze turning inward and distant. "We spend nearly two weeks on the march to get down here and answer Madoc's call. Well, that's all right. We're all of us used to a life on the road. And it seems like we've got a chance of winning this once and for all—kicking Octa and his filthy Saxon dogs and traitor allies all back into the sea where they belong. So we arrive. We make camp where Madoc's got his own troops stationed. We know Octa's put out his own call for reinforcements. He's gone to ground in the fortress at Caer Peris that he won from Cerdic, and it's well enough defended that it would take more men than we've got to dig him out. So we wait to see what kind of a battle plan Madoc's come up with, because we've all heard he's got a matchless head for battle."

Cadfan broke off again to laugh shortly and harshly. "And would you like to hear the brilliant orders our High King gave us? He says to us, 'Go out and find the enemy.'" Cadfan snorted. "That's all. 'Go out and find the enemy.' Like we're going to roam about the countryside beating the shrubbery and calling 'Hallooo, Saxons, where are you?'"

Cadfan snorted again. "And then Madoc says, 'When you find the enemy, send a scout to bring word and my men and I will come.'" Cadfan paused, eyes still smoldering as he stared back across the days. Then: "Well, I'll make a long story a short one. We found the enemy, right enough. Aesc—one of Octa's lords—and his war band. Sent a scout back to bring word to Madoc. And did he come?" Cadfan gave another harsh rasp of a laugh. "Suppose he must have remembered sudden-like that he'd something else to do that day."

Cadfan stopped, and just for a moment Isolde saw the raw, aching grief in his eyes before he turned to her, jaw tight and his gaze furious once again. "It was a rutting slaughter. Fifty of us, and only a bare handful survived. And that only because my lord Cynlas called the order to retreat—which I'd never heard him do once, not in thirty years of fighting at his back."

Isolde had known of the rumors, of course, the mutters and whisperings among the wounded men, but she'd not heard the full story this way. And she was remembering how four months before, Marcia, a serving maid dying under Isolde's care, had warned her that as there had been treason on the king's council in the past, there would soon be treason again.

She asked, after a moment, "Do you know for certain that the scout sent back to Madoc got through? That Madoc actually knew you were in need and yet refused to come to your aid?"

Cadfan seemed almost to have forgotten she was there. He looked up at her as though surprised, and then grudgingly said, "Not for certain I don't. But—"

He stopped as a huge white- and brown-spotted hunting dog padded over and thrust a wet black nose interestedly in the direction of the porridge bowl.

Isolde caught hold of the big dog's collar and pulled him back. "No, Cabal." He whined and she scratched his ears and ruffled his fur. "You're going to have to start rolling instead of walking if you keep eating this way, you know."

Cabal might have been trained as a war hound, but he was proving invaluable in the sickroom, as well. From the first, he'd been a favorite among the wounded men, and even those far gone in fevers or pain would rouse to scratch his brindled coat or share with him their portions of gruel or cheese or bread.

Now Cadfan's grimly set features relaxed for what had to be the first time since Isolde had seen him carried through the abbey gates. "Oh, let the dog have it. Not much left—and anyway it's my breakfast. I say he can have it if he wants."

Cadfan set the nearly empty bowl down on the ground, and Cabal whined ecstatically and started to lap up the oats and milk, pushing the bowl across the flagged stone floor with his nose.

"Fair enough," Isolde said. In any case, well trained as Cabal was, she knew better than to try snatching food from a dog—any dog.

Instead she reached into her scrip and drew out one of her last remaining vials of poppy. "Here, take this." She poured a measure into the small horn spoon she carried for the purpose and handed it to Cadfan. "It should make you able to sleep."

Perhaps telling his story had helped in some small measure, because Cadfan accepted the dose without protest, slipping the spoon into his mouth and then handing it empty back to Isolde. And his mouth twitched into another almost smile as Cabal returned with the gleamingly polished porridge bowl clamped between his jaws and presented it to Cadfan.

"Smart dog, this."

Isolde smiled and put a hand on Cabal's head. "Yes, he is."

Cadfan took the bowl from Cabal and scratched the big dog under the chin. Then he looked up at Isolde. "Word is there's to be a meeting of the king's council in the next few days. And you're to be there?" Isolde nodded, and he went on, his voice shaking with renewed intensity, his expression again turning fierce. "Well, you ask him. Ask our High King whether the scout we sent back got through. Ask him just what he's playing at with his pussyfooting orders, because I'll make a guess that he'd like to see this war actually won, same as the rest of us here."

Isolde took the empty porridge bowl from Cadfan's hands, briefly seeing Madoc of Gwynedd's dark, bearded face, terribly scarred by fire eight months before. She could still hear his voice, as well, husky and hesitant and suddenly almost shy, as though it were as hard for him to speak the words as it would have been to step onto a field of battle without his sword. *It would be good to have someone to come home to, after the battle was done. And I would be . . . very happy, Lady Isolde, if that could be you.*

Isolde met Cadfan's gaze steadily, though, and nodded again. "Yes," she said. "If I get the chance, I will."

Cadfan looked at her intently, eyes narrowed, as though trying to judge whether she'd meant what she said. Whatever he saw seemed to satisfy him, because he gave a short, jerky nod. Isolde could see his eyelids drooping, so she laid her hand lightly on top of his.

After all these long weeks of practice, she was better able to control her sense of the wounded men's pain. And that meant that she could now send out the tiny threads of awareness again to slide through every part of Cadfan's body and then rest there, simply and silently aware of the pain.

Poppy or no, the awareness of the broken leg was still bad enough to make Isolde's own skin break out in a clammy sweat. She felt, too, the blade-sharp fragments of memory that scraped together in Cadfan's mind beneath the surface of his sullen glare: the blood and furor of battle . . . hearing his brothers in arms scream and—

God, that was Teyrn, crawling through the mud with his torn guts hanging out of his body, crying like a babe. Can't get to him . . . can't get to any of them . . . leg's not . . . bastards anyway . . . deserve to die . . . keep thinking that . . . keep pretending not to care about them getting hacked to bits while you're left alive, because . . .

As always, Isolde was filled with the ash-bitter taste of failure and frustration, because she couldn't take the pain away—she could only know it was there. And she never tried to speak to the men this way, because hearing her there, inside their own minds, would surely only frighten them more.

Cadfan, though, let out a long sigh and relaxed back onto the pallet. Oddly, it was always the same. Isolde remembered her grandmother saying that she told stories for the men in her care because the tales belonged to the Otherworld, where shades took on flesh and the past breathed and time was an endless curve.

While the story lasted, the wounded didn't have to fight the pain, didn't have to be heroic or brave. The story asked only that a sick or injured man listen, nothing more, in order to rest briefly in that Otherworld beyond the veil. Isolde sometimes thought that there must be something of the same healing in her simply listening to their stories, their pain—even if they never consciously knew she had heard.

Isolde sat with her hand on Cadfan's, watching the rise and fall of his chest as his breathing deepened and slowed. And then abruptly, his head jerked up and he looked from the empty bowl Isolde held to Isolde herself. "You did that on purpose, didn't you?" he demanded. "Said you wanted the food so that I'd take it instead?"

Isolde smiled despite herself, though the few spoonfuls she'd made herself swallow had combined with the stomach-twisting awareness of Cadfan's memories and pain, and she couldn't at that moment have spoken a word if she'd tried. So she just smiled again, rose, and—quickly—turned to go.

"YOU OFFER, THEN, INFORMATION ON THE movements and plans of the Briton forces in exchange for your friend's life." Octa was still regarding him through narrowed eyes. "Or rather, in exchange for my not seeking revenge for the loss of my property."

Trystan said nothing, and after a moment, Octa smiled, baring a row of blackening teeth. "Very well, my friend. It's a bargain." And then his smile vanished and he said, abruptly, "What do you know of the Lady Isolde of Camelerd?"

Trystan had stood with an enemy's sword at his throat and managed a convincing display of calm disinterest. A good thing, too, or Octa's words would have made him jump out of his skin. As it was, he didn't move, didn't blink, didn't startle, didn't goddamn breathe.

"Why do you ask?"

Octa picked up the jeweled knife from the table between them and turned it this way and that, caressing the edge of the blade with his thumb. "Two months ago, as I was on the verge of negotiations for peace with Cerdic of Wessex, a woman entered my camp. She claimed to be Cerdic's whore, cast off when she was far gone with child. In revenge, she had come to me, offering me the chance of defeating Cerdic and his armies once and for all."

Trystan ignored the chill that crawled unpleasantly across his neck. He had a fairly good idea where this was heading. Expect the worst, and you'll not be surprised when it jumps out and stabs you in the gut. But all the same, it would be a mistake to betray by word or glance that he'd heard this story already, and from Isolde herself. She actually had gone to Octa, deceived him into attacking Cerdic, and so dealt Octa and his army a near crippling blow.

But then she'd always been that way, ever since he could remember. He could see her at eight, already terrifyingly brave, unbelievably tough and strong.

Octa had stopped speaking, and Trystan dragged his attention back to the present. He met Octa's gaze, and saw something move behind the dead, flat eyes—something like the insane fury Trystan had seen in a wild boar or a dog gone mad. With a sudden, savage burst of movement, Octa lifted the knife and then drove it down hard into the table where it stood upright, hilt quivering, blade buried deep in the wood. "She lied. She was no more Cerdic's doxie than I am. And"—his jaw hardened as he went on, his voice harsh—"so too was the information she offered a lie. From start to finish, a lie."

Right. Plans were wonderful things, until you put them into practice.

Octa had stopped again. The wild animal look quivered briefly in his gaze and then was gone, leaving his expression flat and ice hard as his tone. "A third of my best fighting men were slaughtered in Cerdic's ambush. Men for whose lives I took payment from Cerdic when I won this fortress from his crawling coward of a son. But I have yet to take my payment from the woman whose lying tongue cost me a defeat in battle two months ago. I have learned, though, from an informant among Cerdic's men, the woman's name. Lady Isolde, daughter of the the former King Modred. Lady of Camelerd." He lingered over the final words, a small, cold smile curling the edges of his mouth.

Steady. Breathe in, breathe out. Don't think about how good it would feel to snatch up the knife on the table and erase the smile from Octa's face. Allowing yourself either anger or fear in battle got you killed.

It wasn't as though he didn't know what he'd turn into if he gave in to the simmering potential for violence that lurked under the edges of his control.

Trystan kept his voice expressionless, kept his face as devoid of emotion as Octa's, and said, "Why tell me this?"

Octa's smile broadened. "Because my informant also tells me that she was seen among Cerdic's warriors. In company with a man. A man of your description. A former companion, so the story went, of the man Fidach, who you tell me is no longer a guest of my hall."

Trystan shifted position slightly, stretching his legs out and leaning back in his chair. "And you offer me—what? A second hostage to ensure I keep my part of the bargain and bring you what you want?"

Octa moved his massive shoulders in a shrug. "You could put it that way." His eyes were like cold metal balls hanging suspended in his heavy boned face. "Bring me the intelligence we agreed on, and I may consider it adequate payment for sparing the little slut's life. Try to play me false . . ." He smiled again. "And I find her and teach her what playing whore to a king really means before I cut her throat."

Trystan sat absolutely still, pushing a spasm of fury far, far back, locking it away in that same internal holding area where he'd already been keeping all thoughts of Isolde herself.

It had better be one hell of a big space.

He made himself shift even more fully into the mind of combat, narrowed his focus to only here and now. He'd been wrong about the mission's first priority being to snare Octa. Keeping Isolde safe was—had always been—the first.

He made his voice level and very quiet as he leaned forward, bringing his face closer to Octa's. "Then let me tell you something. I've said I can get into and out of any garrison or war camp I choose to get the intelligence I've promised. If you harm the Lady Isolde— if you touch so much as a hair on her head—I swear on all the nine caverns of hell that I will prove that claim by coming into your private quarters one night, while you sleep. Maybe while you're encamped in this fortress. Maybe in your royal hall in Kent. Maybe I'll wait until you're sleeping in a war tent, out on campaign. But sooner or later, you'll wake up one night and I'll be there, standing by your bed." He allowed a small, grim smile to stretch his mouth. "There are a lot of unpleasant ways to die, King Octa of Kent. And God knows I've killed better men than you."

Octa opened his mouth, but Trystan went on, talking over him. "You may say I'd never escape after. Maybe I could kill you, but I'd never get out past your guard." He lowered his voice to an edgy near-whisper and smiled again, keeping his face expressionless, his eyes fixed on Octa's face. "But you see, I wouldn't care. Kill Lady Isolde, and I have no reason to care a single damn one way or the other whether I live or die. I could end your life and die a happy man."

Octa started to speak again, but Trystan cut him off. "I know what you're thinking. You're asking yourself why you don't simply order your guards to kill me now. And so you could. But if I don't walk out of here alive, the men who came here with me will go straight to King Cerdic's encampment and offer him all we've learned of your defenses over the last month. We got inside to take Fidach from your prison cells. I'm sure we could give Cerdic enough guidance that he could make it in. This was once his fortress, after all."

Octa's face had blanched with anger, and his nostrils flared as he spoke through clenched teeth. "You lie."

Trystan raised one eyebrow. "Do I?"

Octa's gaze narrowed. "I could hunt them down. Fidach and these men of yours."

Trystan shrugged again. "You could try. But this isn't your country. And it is theirs. And it would take more men than you can spare just now to hunt them if they're choosing not to be found."

This made his own survival even less a part of the bargain he was currently forging with both Octa and fate. But then, he hadn't much to offer Isolde in any case save his life.

Trystan let the silence rest between them a beat, and then he sat back, folding his arms as he leaned against the hard wooden chair. "But all this is unnecessary. We've come to an agreement. All you have to do is keep your hands off Fidach and Lady Isolde. And I give you what you need to win this war."

Chapter 2

"HERE. RINSE YOUR MOUTH OUT with this."

Isolde opened her eyes to find Mother Berthildis standing over her. She'd barely made it out of the infirmary and into the abbey's kitchen garden in time, and now she was sitting on the ground with her back against one of the plum trees and clammy sweat drying on her skin. The branches overhead were covered in snowy white blossoms, with a few petals drifting down onto the earth below at every faint stirring of breeze.

Isolde took the cup the abbess offered and found it filled with an herbal infusion, something with mint. Isolde took a swallow, rinsed the noxiously sour taste from her mouth, then let out her breath.

"Thank you," she said.

Mother Berthildis waved the thanks away and stood eyeing Isolde, small black eyes shrewd in her lined old face. Isolde braced herself for questions, but the abbess said, unexpectedly, "I've just come from the stables. Your Saxon companion has settled in well—and proved himself of great help, I may add. I've never seen the place in such good order."

Isolde nodded cautiously. "Yes. I'm so glad. I was afraid Hereric might not find an occupation he could still fill."

Hereric, Trystan's longtime comrade in arms, had lost an arm to a bad break turned poisonous four months before. He was Saxon by birth, and likely had been a slave at one time, but Isolde knew no more of his story than that. Strong and utterly goodhearted and kind, Hereric was yet in many ways as simple as a child. And mute, as well. He spoke in a complex system of gestures and finger signs that Isolde was slowly learning to read—but never of his past or of where he'd come from.

Hereric had been still recovering from the loss of his arm when Trystan had departed the abbey, and so had been left behind. But every time Isolde had gone to see him in the abbey stables where he'd himself chosen to work, she'd found him busy and content, nearly as well able to perform his duties with one arm as two. And seemingly able to communicate with the horses in his care in a language entirely independent of words or even sounds.

"He likes working with the horses, and he's very good with them," Isolde said. An herb-scented breeze stirred her hair. At this height of summer the thyme and rosemary were growing thickly, and the lavender was blooming, as well, the feathery purple flower stalks ready to be cut and dried. Isolde had a sudden memory of her grandmother telling her once that walking amidst a lavender bed at night, breathing in the scent, would open one's sight to visions of those who walked in the Otherworld.

She took another sip of the draft Mother Berthildis had brought, and risked swallowing it this time.

Mother Berthildis watched her and then said, "The sickness will get better. Probably somewhere around the time the child begins to show."

Of course. It was too much to hope that the abbess would have missed this. Isolde had yet to discover anything that happened under the abbey roof of which Mother Berthildis was unaware. She closed her eyes again and said, "I know. I remember."

"Ah." There was neither surprise nor condemnation in Mother Berthildis's tone. "You've borne a child before, then."

The sickness had abated enough that Isolde risked another sip of the infusion of herbs. "Yes. Once before. I was wedded before, as you know. To Constantine, the late High King. We had a child, a daughter." She looked up with a small, brief smile. "I was sick all through the whole nine months with her. Apparently she never heard the rule about an unborn babe not making its mother ill after the first three turnings of the moon."

Mother Berthildis smiled, too, wrinkles fanning out from her wide, thin-lipped mouth. "And the child? What happened to her?"

Isolde's smile faded as she stared straight ahead at the small tender green shoots sprouting from a bed of early peas. "She died. Never lived, really. She died before ever she was born."

Mother Berthildis nodded, as though she'd already guessed as much. "I'm sorry."

"Thank you." A thunderstorm two nights before had broken off a few stray branches from the plum tree overhead; one lay at Isolde's feet, the buds of blossoms still tightly furled, rose-tipped and perfect on the broken bough. She looked up at Mother Berthildis. "It hurt more than anything that's ever happened to me. But then—" Isolde stopped, searching for the words. "I started to realize that even if it did hurt, I'd never wish not to have borne her. I'd never wish not to have loved her. Even if I lost her in the end, I had her for the nine whole, precious months I carried her. Nothing can ever take that away."

Isolde picked up one of the scattered petals and held it on her palm, then tipped her hand and let it drift back to the ground. From somewhere in the branches above came the soft trill of a dove, and she was carried back to a night nearly three months ago, lying in bed with Trystan and listening to the call of a nightingale from the orchard outside their room in the guest hall.

They'd been silent a long time, and then Trystan had asked, suddenly, "Isa, are you . . ." he stopped. "Are you sure this—the two of us, like this—is what you want? Are you sure you're all right?"

Isolde had been startled by the question, but she'd answered without hesitating, reaching up to touch Trystan's face, touching her lips to his. "Of course I'm sure."

She'd held back, though, when he'd drawn her towards him. "Are you sure *you're* really all right, Trys? I don't want to hurt you, and—don't laugh. I'm a healer and it's not that long ago that you had two broken ribs and—"

Isolde broke off as Trystan drew her head down, stopping her mouth with his. He kissed her tenderly, slowly and almost reverently, in the way that never, ever failed to make her pulse skip a beat and her very bones seem to melt. For a long moment she was conscious of nothing but the movements of Trystan's lips and hands. When he finally released her, she was out of breath, but he drew back enough to say, "I wasn't laughing at you. I was laughing because you may be a healer—but right now you're a healer without any clothes on, sharing my bed. And you expect me to have wits enough to put two coherent words together and answer questions about broken ribs?"

They were both laughing as he kissed her again, but then he stopped and drew back, one hand trailing lightly from her cheek to her neck to her bare shoulder and back. "What's that line in the old stories about the Land of Youth?"

"An earthly paradise is the land, delightful beyond all dreams. Fairer than aught thine eyes have ever seen." Her voice sounded breathless in her own ears.

Trystan drew her mouth back to his, and then whispered, his own voice suddenly husky, "If this isn't paradise, I think it's the closest I'm ever likely to come."

Just for a moment, as they moved together in the dark, Isolde thought of the herbs she'd taken when she was still wedded to Con. Herbs that ensured she was safe from the pain of bearing—and losing—another child. But if they kept her safe from pain, they would cut her off from all the wonder and joy of feeling a new life inside her, as well. And right at that moment, even the thought of bearing the child who might already have been made on one of these nights—Trystan's child—brought a wave of joy so acute it stole her breath.

For a heartbeat she felt as though she held the possible future between her clasped hands. And then she spread her fingers wide, surrendering the choice to the night. She knew she'd never use the herbs again.

And then she stopped thinking anything at all.

"AND DOES YOUR YOUNG MAN, YOUR Trystan, know about the child?" Mother Berthildis asked.

They were walking across the abbey courtyard, back towards the guest hall and the small chamber where Isolde slept when she was not working among the wounded men. The room had first been

Trystan's, when he'd been carried wounded and unconscious into the abbey nearly three months before, and now everything about it, from the simple wooden furnishings to the cracks in the bare plaster walls, seemed to Isolde to speak of Trystan.

At night, when she couldn't sleep, she would lie alone on the narrow bed at night and remember every moment of every day of the three too-short weeks of marriage they'd shared. Every word they'd spoken from the moment he'd opened his eyes and returned from the brink of death. Every time he'd drawn her mouth down to his in the dark and kissed her heart-stoppingly gently, almost wonderingly, as though she'd just given him a gift both infinitely precious and sweet.

Now Isolde turned her hand over and looked down at the fine white line that ran across her palm, all the tangible signs that remained now of the handfasting she and Trystan had sworn, just the two of them, alone in a candlelit room within that hall.

She folded her fingers tight and said, "He's my husband. Though no one can know of the marriage but us two"—she smiled one-sidedly at Mother Berthildis. "And you now, I suppose. But I was born a princess, and Lady of Camelerd, as well. And princesses marry at the will of the king's council—never their own."

And Trystan was an outlaw, a mercenary who'd served as a Saxon spy. Not to mention the son of Marche, traitor High King whose armies even now fought a vicious war with the forces of Britain on the battlefields surrounding the abbey. And at least one of the kings on Madoc of Gwynedd's council—Cynlas of Rhos—had cause to wish Trystan dead. Go before the king's council and petition for Trystan to assume a place at her side as Lord of Camelerd and he'd never live long enough to take the oath of fealty to the land.

Isolde stopped. Willed a surge of helplessness away, and then at last drew breath and said, in answer to Mother Berthildis's question, "And, no. Trystan doesn't know that I'm carrying his child."

Mother Berthildis shot her a quick, shrewd glance. "But you knew—when he left the abbey in company with the other men?"

A group of black-robed sisters were filing across the court to the chapel for the morning prayers, and Isolde waited until they had passed by before she answered.

The abbey was almost a small world unto itself, Isolde had found in the months she'd been here. The main buildings were set square around a central courtyard: the long, low building where the nuns slept, the infirmary, the chapel and guest hall—all built of thatched and whitewashed wattle and daub, save for the small stone church. Then, stretching out behind, were the orchards of apple and plum trees and the small fields of oats and barley and flax. The stables and workrooms, too, stood as outlying buildings behind the main court, all likewise built of thatched wattle and daub.

And from morning to night, the whole place hummed with activity, peaceful, ordered, and comforting as the soft drone of a hive of bees. For despite the armed guards—Cerdic's men—posted at the gates, despite even the battle-wounded soldiers who lay in the infirmary, the abbey seemed almost untouched by the world outside. A tiny island of peace in a land bloodied and torn by war, where the hours of each day passed as smoothly as unrippled water flowing under a bridge, ordered by the sisters' prescribed cycle of daily work and worship and prayer.

Like the mist-shrouded Avalon of the tales might have been—although Mother Berthildis was almost as unlike one of the nine sacred faerie maids of the Glass Isle as Isolde could imagine.

Now Isolde watched the nuns' black robes flap and flutter in the soft morning breeze as they made their way, heads bowed, towards the chapel, then nodded. "Yes, I did know. Once you've known the feeling you can't mistake it. I was sure. But no, I didn't tell Trystan. I wanted to—more than I can say. And I came close. But I couldn't. He had to leave. Fidach, a man he'd fought with, had been captured by Octa's men. Even if I hadn't owed my life to Fidach, I'd have known Trystan would have to go after him—rescue him, if he could."

Isolde stopped, looking out across the flagged courtyard, bathed in the golden early morning sun, and thought of another morning sun she'd seen. A sun she'd only seen rise because Fidach, even ill with a wasting sickness as he'd been—a sickness that would sooner or later be his death—had fought his way into Octa's camp and hacked down the door of the burning building that had imprisoned her.

She could still taste the acrid smoke that had burned the back of her throat and lungs, still feel the sting of the burning embers that had showered her and Fidach both as they'd ridden across the dawn gray countryside towards safety. And she could see, still, the outlaw leader's sharp featured face, for once sober, all trace of his usual mockery or posturing gone. Fidach's strange, leaf-brown eyes had been puckered with fatigue, his hair singed.

Just because I cultivate the reputation of a man without honor—it does not follow that I have none. A man whose death hovers so clearly at his shoulder begins to be cautious what risks he takes with his soul.

Now Isolde blinked to clear the memory from her gaze, turning to Mother Berthildis again. "I do owe my life to Fidach," she said. "This child—" Almost of their own accord, her hands came up to clasp themselves over her womb. It was too soon to feel even the tiniest of fluttering movements from the baby, but if she closed her eyes she could imagine she felt a tiny, beating spark of life. "This child wouldn't never have existed if Fidach hadn't saved my life. I'd never have come back here—I'd never have married Trystan."

Isolde looked up to meet Mother Berthildis's black gaze. "I thought that I owed it to both of them—Fidach and Trystan—not to make Trystan's leaving here any harder than it already was. Not to burden Trystan with another responsibility, another worry, when all his focus had to be on getting Fidach free. So I didn't tell him. Trystan has no idea that he'll be a father before the moon has waxed and waned another seven times."

"And he's been gone . . . what . . . more than two months now?"

Again there was neither judgment nor condemnation in Mother Berthildis's tone. Isolde hadn't meant to say any more. She'd not even intended to tell the abbess about the child. But something about the older woman's steady gaze made her brush her hand across her eyes and say, "And he's neither returned nor sent word back to me. I know."

Just for a moment, she remembered the gust of sudden fear that had struck her only hours before, and felt a hard knot inside her clench and tighten. "He's not dead. I would know—I think—if he were." Since Mother Berthildis was the abbess of a house of holy women dedicated to the Christian God, Isolde didn't say how she would know. And in any case, Mother Berthildis likely knew that, as well.

She went on, "But he's—" Isolde stopped again, trying to find the right words.

The silence stretched out until at last Mother Berthildis asked, "Your story—the one you told while you were setting that man Cadfan's leg—it was about your Trystan?"

Isolde stopped, eyes on the middle distance, where the sun streamed over the abbey's outer walls. "You do see a great deal. Yes. That was a story from when the two of us were small. We grew up together. He's two years older than I am, but he was my truest friend, always, from the time I can remember. And it really did happen that way. I was eight and got myself completely lost in the woods—it was during the spring campaigns for the army, too—and Trystan came and found me and brought me home."

Isolde brushed at a shred of grass that clung to her skirt and smiled a little again. "He even helped me climb over the wall of my father's garrison so that none of the adults would realize I'd been gone. He saved me a wicked tongue lashing at the very least. My grandmother loved me, always—but even strong men knew to stay clear of her temper when she was roused."

They had reached the entrance to the guest hall, and Isolde stopped, resting a hand on the stone door frame before turning to Mother Berthildis. The abbess said nothing, but the force of her listening was an almost audible presence, and Isolde's smiled faded as she stared back across the years. "Trystan was—is," she said at last, "an exceptional swordsman. He was leading raiding parties of my father's men when he was barely fifteen. And even before then, he'd won himself the reputation of being completely fearless in battle. He'd take the most insane chances—run crazy risks—and win the day for the whole army, as like as not. And then afterwards when I or anyone else asked him why—" Isolde stopped, biting her lip, remembering, seeing again a younger Trystan's face, lean features, hard jaw, and startlingly blue eyes. "Trystan would just shrug and say, 'Someone had to do it. Why not me?'"

Isolde paused again, trying to look back across the years. To guess what had shaped Trystan into the kind of man who did shrug and say, *Why not me?* in the face of a desperate risk to be run. And she could guess, now. Some.

She looked up at Mother Berthildis again. "But no man walks away from battle unchanged. We've just come from the infirmary hall of wounded men, you'll have seen it for yourself. Their bodies may heal, but none of them will ever be the same, really the same, again. And at the battle of Camlann—when my father and King Arthur met and fought for the last time, and both lost their lives—"

Isolde stopped. "Trystan was captured in the battle," she said after a moment. "I think he must have been, because he wound up a slave in the tin mines. But he's never told me what happened. And he's told me next to nothing about what happened to him, all those years he was a slave. Though I've seen the scars."

Isolde thought of the ridged marks of lashes on Trystan's back, the missing finger joints on his left hand, marks of his time in the mines.

Mother Berthildis pursed her lips. "Many might say that you carry your own scars, as well."

"Perhaps." Isolde was quiet a moment, staring back the way they'd come across the abbey yard. "But then I had a happy childhood. Really, a very happy one. I always knew that my grandmother loved me. It's like the joy of carrying a child—nothing can ever take that away. I've always had those years with her, always known that she loved me more than anything. But Trystan—"

Isolde stopped herself, wondering how much she was willing to say of Trystan's past. "Trystan never had anything like that," she said at last. "And he's not"—she gave the abbess another small smile—"he's not like Cadfan, one who can growl and shout at any and all who come near when he's angry or afraid or both, and after he's growled and snapped a time the poison of the hurt inside him is gone so that the wound can knit clean. Trystan is—always has been—the most private person I've ever known."

The last of the abbey sisters had vanished inside the chapel, and Isolde heard the soft, rhythmic chant of the morning mass. She rubbed one hand over the other. "Trystan left to go after Fidach. But I think—if I had to guess—that he was thankful in a way to go. Because he'd let me get too close to him, too close to whatever he's still keeping locked up tight inside inside him. Though he does love me, I know."

"Child." Mother Berthildis smiled just a bit and touched her lightly on the cheek. Her fingers felt dry and cool as marble against Isolde's skin. "No one—not even a crabbed and ancient nun—who saw him look at you would ever doubt that."

Isolde pressed her eyes closed. She might hate crying, but weeks ago she'd made peace with the fact that, for her, ready tears and being sick inevitably went hand in hand with carrying a child. And in any case, she couldn't have kept the hot press of moisture from burning her eyes now. "And I love him," she said. "I do. But I'm . . . not sure he wants me to. Love is a burden to him, I think, more an added worry and care than anything else."

A knife-edged memory went through Isolde—Trystan looking down at her, his eyes the blue of the morning sky. He'd been looking at her in the way he seldom ever let himself look, with his whole heart reflected in his eyes, so that just briefly she could see the swirl of mingled longing and passion and pain. And then he'd smoothed a stray curl of hair lightly back from her brow and said, *I don't deserve you.*

Mother Berthildis's small, ugly face was still and a little remote, though not unkind. "And you think you can save him—save him from himself, if need be?"

"No." Isolde let out an unsteady breath. "I know I can't. He has to save himself. He has to choose to want to be with me. But—" She stopped and wiped her eyes. "Have you ever heard the tale of the maid whose love was stolen away by the fair folk? To win him free she had to pull him down from his faerie steed, and then hold him fast in her arms while the faerie queen's magic turned him from a roaring beast to a serpent to a red-hot burning brand."

Isolde drew a steadying breath, wiping the last of her tears away with the tips of her fingers before meeting Mother Berthildis's eyes. "So that's what I'm doing now. Holding on."

"AND YOU BELIEVED HIM?" CATH ASKED.

Fidach was asleep. Asleep, not dead—however lifeless his body

looked at present, wrapped in a thick traveling cloak and lying utterly still on the ground. His face looked almost skull-like, the skin
yellow as old tallow, and he'd not so much as twitched when Trystan
leaned over him. But Trystan had felt the light, thready pulse in his
neck.

He'd had to tell the others part, at least, of the arrangement with
Octa. Unfair not to, when he was going to have to call on them for
aid now. Six outlaws against the armies of Octa of Kent and Marche.
Though, if his plans played out as he meant them to, Octa and
Marche would do most of the work themselves.

Still, if he'd thought God owed him any favors, he would have
asked Him to at least keep any of the other five here from getting
killed.

He was still forcing his mind to focus on the task at hand. Priorities. A series of steps.

Keep Isolde safe. Neutralize Octa. Make sure that Marche
earned his own eternal reward.

Maybe in some small measure atone for past wrongs?

Beyond that Trystan wasn't letting himself think.

Now he covered Fidach more completely with the cloak, then
looked up to find that Cath was giving him a have-you-lost-your-
goat-rutting-mind look. "You think Octa's like to keep his word?"

They'd slipped past the usual reach of Octa's patrols sometime
about moonrise, but none of them had even voiced the question
of whether to risk starting a fire. They were sitting in the growing
morning light under a grove of oak trees and eating dry bread and
the chicken Daka had lifted from a nearby settlement, leaving coin
enough on the croft's doorstep to pay for the cost of the bird.

Trystan took a swallow from the skin of ale Eurig passed him
before answering Cath's question. The ale tasted faintly of the goat
the skin had been sewn from, but it was better than any of the
muddy, brackish water they'd found. "I'd not take Octa's word if he
told me the rain was wet. But he won't move until I've given him
what he wants—or until he thinks I have."

Trystan turned to Daka and Piye, their dark faces shadowed
by the branches above. "But for safety's sake, I'd like you to keep
watch. One of you on Octa, one on the abbey. Any sign that Octa is

planning a move—any at all—and you get Isolde out and get word to me. If you're willing?"

Trystan saw the brothers exchange one of their looks in which a whole conversation was captured in the curl of a lip, the lift of a brow. Then Daka turned to him. "You do not have to ask. We go."

"AND YOU STILL MEAN, THEN, TO attend the meeting of the king's council that King Madoc has called tomorrow?" Mother Berthildis asked.

Isolde could see Mother Berthildis's next words reflected in the older woman's keen black gaze, and she went on, before the abbess could speak them aloud. "I know. I know there's a risk in journeying by horseback so early on."

Involuntarily, her hands came up to clasp themselves over her still-flat stomach. "But I'll have Hereric with me, at least, to lead the horse. And I can't think I've any choice but to attend. You heard Cadfan's story."

Isolde was recalling the bleak exhaustion on Madoc's face when they'd parted three months before. Madoc might be holding the council together through sheer force of will. But he was still only one man, surrounded by allies he could never trust in full. "Whatever happened, King Madoc has need of every assenting voice just now—even that of the only woman on the council. Britain's kings are still unwilling to bury old grudges and unite, even to defeat Octa and Marche. And there's another reason." Isolde stopped, biting her lip. "I have my own lands, as you know—the kingdom of Camelerd. I've not been able to visit them myself since I was thirteen, because I was Constantine's queen, and those duties kept me for the most part in Cornwall. And now—"

She broke off. "Now the rest of the king's council may not approve of a woman holding lands in her own name, but they are mine by birthright through my mother, Gwynefar. Let any of the king's council know or even suspect that I'm with child, though, and by a husband they'd not approved . . ."

Princesses marry at the will of the council, as she had said. *Never their own.*

Madoc might have given her his word, four months ago, that

he'd not force her into any marriage not of her own choice. And Isolde knew him well enough to be certain that he would do his utmost to keep the promise he'd made. But in this case, Isolde doubted the rest of the king's council would let him.

"At best," she said, "Camelerd would be taken from me. At worst, I'd be married off to the council member who wants my lands enough that he'd suffer another man's child to be taken for his. And either way—" She stared straight ahead at the long, wattle and thatch buildings of the nuns' sleeping quarters and the guest hall. "Either way, I'd have failed utterly in my duty to all those who live on Camelerd's lands."

Though she might well have failed all the same. Four months before, Camelerd had been besieged by Octa and Marche. And with all roads controlled by Octa and Marche's forces, she'd had no word, since, of how the lands fared. It was another reason to attend the meeting of the council to be held the following day: to learn whether there was yet any news of whether Camelerd's defenses had fallen or held.

Mother Berthildis was looking at her, compassion softening the sharpness of her black gaze. She said, with a glance at Isolde's middle, "The second child is usually quicker to show than the first."

"I know." Isolde looked out over the courtyard again. The sisters had begun chanting the morning prayers, the soft Latin words drifting out through the chapel's open doors. She said, "I've likely another two months before the child starts to show, maybe three, before it shows enough that a man would notice. And after that . . ." She stopped and turned to meet Mother Berthildis's eyes. "I'd be lying if I said I could clearly see my way forward. If I said that I knew what I'm going to do when that time comes."

Especially if Trystan never did return, a voice whispered inside her. But she again pushed the thought aside. "And I know it must look as though I'd gone mad, or been completely selfish, to marry Trystan secretly this way. But I—"

She stopped, trying to put into words what she'd felt as she'd stood in almost this exact spot on a moonlit night nearly three months before. Had stood here, and listened to the chanting of the evening prayers—as she now listened to the morning ones—and thought of the choice that faced her like a bridge to be crossed into the unknown.

She said at last, "Have you ever felt so sure of a choice that it seemed as though there were no choice at all? That the path you were meant to follow was already fixed, as surely as the stars move across the heavens and the night follows the day?"

Mother Berthildis was silent, and then she nodded. "Perhaps I have."

Isolde rubbed one finger across the handfasting scar on her palm. "That was how I felt about the choice to marry Trystan. As though I could do nothing else. As though I'd been meant to wed him since the stones themselves began keeping time. Even if . . ." She folded her hand tight and began again. "Whatever happens," she said, "I'll have no regrets. Nor even doubts that marrying him was the right course to choose. Whatever the future may hold."

Mother Berthildis nodded slowly, lips pursed and gaze suddenly thoughtful, as though she were making up her mind whether to say anything more. Then she seemed to reach a decision, because she looked with sudden intensity into Isolde's face.

"You have great courage, if I may say so." She stopped. "And may I also say that with faith, the future is always perfect." She touched Isolde's cheek lightly with one hand, in a way that made Isolde think of the blessings she gave the black-robed abbey sisters as they filed out of the chapel after evening prayers. "Unexpectedly perfect, perhaps—but perfect, all the same."

THE GRAY SHADOWS OF DUSK WERE lengthening in the small, square-built room, and Isolde could hear the abbey sisters already chanting the evening prayers. After parting from Mother Berthildis, she had slept for a time, then returned to the infirmary to stitch the wounds and set the broken bones of three of Cerdic's warriors who'd just that morning been brought in.

Now she was back in her own room, her back aching with hours of bending over wounded men and her clothes saturated with the throat-catching reek of the infirmary: sweat and blood, the fug of high fevers and the cloying smell of poisoned wounds.

Isolde pulled her gown over her head with a sigh of relief and went to the washbasin to splash cool water on her sweat-sticky face, hands, and arms. Then, when she'd finished, she tipped the wash water out, filled the basin again with clean water, and set it on the floor.

That she was doing this in the midst of a house of the Christ and hadn't yet been struck by lightning she had long since decided to take as a sign that any god here didn't mind. Or at least was willing to share space with a tiny spark of the old ways and the old, small gods of the trees and streams, who had been worshipped since the rocks and earth had begun keeping time.

She wore only her thin linen shift, and the evening air felt pleasantly cool on her bare shoulders and neck as she lit the room's single wax candle and set it on the table by the bed. Then she knelt by the basin and stared at the wavering surface of the water, letting her breathing slow, letting her mind empty with each beat of her heart. She had tried this often in the long weeks since Trystan had gone. Sometimes she would see a meaningless, jumbled flash of images— a burning torch, a horse straining at the gallop, a ringing clash of swords. Sometimes she saw nothing at all but her own wavering reflection. But sometimes—just very, very rarely—she would catch a brief glimpse of Trystan's face, and the knot of fear would loosen, just a bit.

Tonight she knelt on the hard stone floor, fixing her gaze on the water in the basin, willing herself to be utterly empty of thought, utterly still. Not to think of the other vision the Sight had brought her today, without any need of scrying waters at all.

Please, she thought, in time to the beat of her pulse. *Please . . . please . . . please . . .*

And then the water seemed to flicker, to gleam with something besides the candle's reflected light. An image rippled, formed, and grew slowly clearer. A campfire. And two men sitting beside. Despite her effort at control, Isolde's breathing hitched up at the sight of them, and her heart quickened. *Pleasepleaseplease—*

One of the men was half sitting, half lying, slumped against a fallen log, as though he had scarcely the strength to hold himself upright. His face was almost painfully gaunt, bruised and streaked with dirt, but Isolde knew him at once by the swirling blue warrior's tattoos on his cheekbones. Fidach. And beside him—

Trystan looked tired, too, his blue eyes smudged with weariness, his mouth tight. He'd been in combat recently, or at least in danger. Isolde had treated too many wounded soldiers not to know the signs. He sat easily, but there was a taut, watchful control about his pose, and Isolde saw him glance up automatically, looking from side to side as he scanned their surroundings for danger.

He was alive, though. Alive, unwounded, and whole. His gold-brown hair was laced back as usual with a leather thong, and he was cleaning and polishing the blade of a sword balanced across his knees.

Isolde held very, very still. Fidach was speaking. She could see his mouth open and close. Not moving, scarcely aware, now, whether she even breathed, she concentrated every part of her attention on watching the wavering image. *Please. Please. Please.*

"—something I never thought to say. But a girl with her kind of courage could almost make me desire a woman." Fidach's voice sounded rasping and exhausted, as though the words were dragged painfully from his chest. But Isolde saw his mouth quirk and a gleam of his old mockery in his light brown eyes. "For a night or two, at least."

It was a mark of how well he knew Fidach that instead of angering, Trystan's expression lightened slightly at that, one side of his mouth twitching. He had been rubbing an oiled leather cloth along the length of the sword blade, his movements quick and controlled, but he glanced up to say, "I'll have to tell her you said so."

Fidach shifted position, and Isolde saw a spasm of pain cross his sharp-featured face, as though even that small movement had been hard to bear.

The outlaw leader had changed in the nearly three months since last she'd seen him, Isolde thought, as she stared at the wavering image of his face. She'd thought, once, that Fidach had deliberately created an identity for himself—a measure of protection, in a way, worn like a cloak. To the world at large he was a man who fed off other men's fears, and so was feared himself. A man to whom appeals of conscience were useless, because he had none. And yet all the while a man of honor lived behind his leaf-brown gaze.

And now, watching him in the waters tonight, Isolde thought that the mocking, conscienceless public persona was wearing more threadbare than before.

"You intend to be in a position to tell her, then?" Fidach's tone was still light—or as light as his rasping voice could make it—the words casual, but Isolde thought there was a curious intensity to them, as well. Fidach seemed to watch Trystan very closely as he waited for a reply.

Isolde clenched her own hands, digging her nails into her palms, to keep from reaching towards his figure, shimmeringly clear before her.

Trystan had turned back to the work of cleaning the sword, bending over the blade so that his face was turned away from both Fidach and Isolde. Isolde heard him sigh, though, and after a moment he said, "For a man supposedly at death's door, you do a hell of a lot of talking, you know that?"

Fidach sighed, and Isolde would have sworn there was a flicker of sadness or sorrow in his eyes. "And you still mean to go—"

But whatever his next words might have been were lost to Isolde. With the suddenness of a thunderclap, the vision broke, shattered, and was gone, leaving Isolde staring once more at her own reflection and the reflected image of the candlelit room.

For a long moment, she sat absolutely still. Then, moving slowly, she joined her hands over the place inside her where a tiny pulsing spark of life grew just a bit brighter each day. Too early still to feel any movement from the child. But, when she closed her eyes like this, she could feel the presence of *someone.* Someone who might have blue eyes like Trystan's or black hair like hers. A boy who would one day grow up to wield a sword—or a girl who would tell the old fire tales and sing the old songs to a babe of her own one day.

She turned her hand over, looking down at her palm, where the mark of her and Trystan's handfasting crossed another, older scar, healed now to just a barely discernible thin white line. For a moment she could see her grandmother Morgan bending over an ancient bronze scrying bowl.

Three drops of oil to sweeten the waters. Three drops of blood as payment to lift the veil.

By rowan, by ash. By maiden, mother, and crone.

She could hear her grandmother saying, too, that these old ways, the magic of the Old Ones that governed the Sight, was dying out from Britain. That first the Romans with their fish-scale armor and straight paved roads, and now the black-robed Christian priests, had broken the ties of the old gods to the land when they built their great temples of stone and declared that all gods must be shut up inside.

Isolde stopped, seeing again the brief scene she'd witnessed in the scrying waters. Brought to her by some power, for some reason—she had to believe that true.

And she ought to have been relieved. Because the vision meant that Fidach was free. Ill, maybe wounded, gaunt and weakened by what he'd endured. But alive, still, and out of Octa's grasp. And she was relieved—dizzyingly so—that she no longer had to imagine Fidach enduring whatever tortures Octa's cruelty could conceive. Fidach was safe. And Trystan—

Isolde made herself draw a breath, then another, and then she went on, speaking to the tiny someone whose presence she could sense, trying to imagine each word she spoke as a knot in a wide golden web, binding three separate points of light together. Herself, Trystan, and the part of them both she held inside her.

"I'm going to tell you about your father. Because he's—" She swallowed hard. "Because he's not here to tell you himself.

"By the time he was fifteen, he was leading raiding parties, and the men all jockeyed and fought to be put under his command. Because he'd never once let one of his warriors be taken prisoner. If they were captured, he got them back—every one. And because he never, ever allowed his men to leave a fallen comrade behind.

"And he won a reputation for himself of having nerves of iron, because through all the raids, all the battles and fighting, he never lost his temper, never showed a flicker of fear. But then, that was the way he'd always been. His father was Marche of Cornwall, his mother a Saxon princess, daughter of Cerdic of Wessex."

Isolde stopped, looking down at the reflected candle's glow, wavering beneath the surface of the water before her. Just for a moment, she wondered whether she might see another man's face, overlaying the dancing flame. A handsome, brutal, heavy-featured face, framed by black hair and with lines of weariness about small black eyes.

A year. Nearly a year since Marche had forced her into marriage—a marriage of a day and a single night of feeling his hands on her skin, his vomit-reeking mouth on hers. Since then, she'd seen Marche in other visions, where he raided settlements, cut down women and children, looked on a girl-child's splayed, bloodied body and regretted not taking her by force before she died.

But then she'd also, in glimpses of the Sight, seen Marche with his hand stuffed in his mouth, biting his knuckles to keep down sobs for all he'd lost, all he'd now become.

And now nothing appeared in the still waters. The poison of that memory, that one night, truly was gone.

If she'd not married Marche, he would have killed her. If she'd not married Marche, she'd not be here, tonight, fiercely glad with every breath she took that she was now speaking to Trystan's baby daughter or son.

She went on, her vision blurring as she stared unseeingly at the water in the basin. She would never tell all this to a child. But an unborn babe was somehow not yet a child and yet at once far more. A glowing flame of life still poised halfway between this and the Otherworld.

"Marche beat his wife—and his son. I was sorry for Trystan's mother—but I remember being angry with her, too, when I was small. Because she never stood up for Trystan, wouldn't even try to save him the beatings he got at his father's hands. I treated Trystan's hurts more times than I can count. But only because I badgered him into letting me."

But even then, even when she'd bullied him into letting her salve his bruises or strap his cracked ribs, the thirteen-year-old boy Trystan had sat as still as though he'd been carved of stone. As though he'd pushed all pain or anger or shame he might feel so far back inside him that he now felt nothing at all.

And he'd won a reputation of being fearless in battle. A name for taking insane gambles with his own life—though never the lives of his men. Because he'd halfway believed the curses and vile names his father flung at him? Because he blamed himself for not being able to protect his mother all those years from Marche's blows?

Looking back, Isolde thought it might have been that way.

Now Isolde laid a hand on her abdomen and spoke again in almost a whisper to the baby inside her. Trystan's child, as well as hers. "I think he's still that boy, in some ways. Still making sure he never loses his temper or admits he's in pain. Still blaming himself more than he ought. Still keeping everything he feels—everything that's happened to him—locked away inside."

She stopped speaking. Night had drawn in and the room was in darkness save for the single candle flame. "What I know of Trystan's story ends at Camlann. But I think that's when something happened to him—some hurt that's keeping a part of him prisoner, locked in darkness still."

The evening prayers were ended; she could hear the abbey sisters' sandaled footsteps in the courtyard outside as they crossed from the chapel to the dormitory where they would sleep until the hour for midnight prayer.

You intend to be in a position to tell her, then? Fidach had asked Trystan. Isolde could hear the echo of the words in each of the shuffling footsteps outside.

And then she thought of her final night with Trystan, their last night together before he'd gone with the other men to rescue Fidach from Octa of Kent. Trystan had been dreaming. And in the midst of the nightmare, he'd struck her, seized her and pinned her against the wall of their room—as he would have whatever enemy he fought in his dream.

Isolde could still see his face the morning after, when he'd taken a single look at the bruises on her arms and then collapsed back onto the bed beside her, one arm flung up over his eyes. *Please tell me I didn't hurt you any worse than that,* he'd said. And then, *I told you I didn't deserve you. I should never have—*

She'd argued. But Trystan had closed his eyes, as though he could no longer bear to look at her. *Please. I . . . couldn't stand it if I ever hurt you again. And it's not as though we could ever have—*

He'd never finished the words. But here, in that same small, plainly furnished room where the very walls echoed like a bard's harp with her memories of Trystan, Isolde had no trouble whatever in finishing for him.

It's not as though we could ever have stayed together. It's not as though we could ever have actually lived as man and wife.

Isolde shut her eyes. "Something happened to Trystan at Camlann," she said again. "It's tied, somehow, to his own father."

Marche, who at the battle of Camlann had betrayed his oath of allegiance to Modred and turned to King Arthur's side. That betrayal had cost Modred, Isolde's father, both the victory and his life. And then Marche had walled herself and her grandmother up in a plague-ridden garrison and left them to die.

Isolde stopped. If Mother Berthildis were here, in Isolde's chamber tonight, the abbess would doubtless say that Trystan had to forgive Marche as the Christ taught and bless him for all the blows he'd ever dealt.

The memory struck Isolde as it had that morning, with the force of a rock thrown at her stomach: Trystan and Marche, faces grim and set, their chests heaving as they they moved in the brutal, circling dance of combat. A fight whose seeds had surely been sown in every blow Marche's fists had struck when Trystan and she were young. And a fight in which, just as surely, one of them would die.

And then the image of her own face swam across the memory. Her own face, as glimpsed in this morning's flash of Sight, as she learned that someone—Trystan?—had died of a mortal wound.

Isolde made herself draw a breath, waited until her heart no longer thudded deafeningly in her ears and the fear that slid in a sickening wave through her stomach had started to recede. Then she said, speaking, still, to the child within, "But I promise you that you . . . you can always be proud that he's your father. If you know nothing else, you should know that."

THE RAIN WAS RELENTLESS, SOAKING HIM to the skin before he'd covered half the distance he had to travel tonight. But that was all to the good. The pelting hiss of raindrops on wet leaves would cover any noise he made. And no moon meant less chance of being seen.

Halfway up the hill he climbed he could see the watchfires of Arthur's camp, the guards hunched shapes about the flames as they tried to dry their sodden cloaks and warm their hands. A shadow loomed up ahead and to the right and he froze, every muscle instantly poised for either fight or retreat.

And yet a part of his mind, too, stood by and watched with detached calm. That was the part that had lived this cold, wet night over and over again. The part that knew this for a dream, knew he'd not after all been caught by the lone patrol he now watched from the deeper shadow of bush that sent an icy drip of water down his back. The part of his consciousness that knew with a mocking certainty that the worst of this memory was yet to come.

It was like being a bloody fish, gasping and jerking on a line. Mind thrashing, trying to wake before the real nightmare of blood and spilling guts and severed limbs began. He knew every minute, cursed detail of what happened from this point on. And there was no escape until he'd relived every blood-drenched moment.

He moved from his place of concealment, towards King Arthur's camp. And then—

And then the cold, the rain, the wet night vanished, and he was lying on his back in the midst of a field of sweet-smelling summer grass. The dream somehow over before he could get to the churned mud and blood and the relentless agonized screams of his men. He'd have called it a bloody miracle if he'd believed in them anymore.

And someone was bending over him.

Isolde.

Her raven-dark hair was loose about her shoulders and her gray eyes were dark with worry as she leaned towards him. He reached out a hand—and met with empty air. He couldn't touch her.

This is still a dream. He'd known it, but he felt a wave of disappointment all the same.

The dream Isolde nodded. *Yes. You're dreaming. When you wake, I'll be gone. But I always come back. All those nights in the mines when I came and sat with you in the dark and the cold—remember them? All those nights after battle? I always came to hold your hand and tell you to stay strong. To just keep breathing, keep your heart beating. To just stay alive, and you'd get through one more day.*

I'd have gone completely out of my mind if it hadn't been for you. Trystan laughed and flung an arm up over his eyes. *Maybe it's a good thing you're only a dream. Otherwise I'd never be able to say that out loud.*

I know. He thought there was a note of sadness in the softly spoken words. But then she settled lightly on the grass beside him, tucking her feet under her. *You were dreaming something else tonight, before I came—what did you dream of?*

He looked up to find her watching him, gray eyes soft. *What did you dream of, Trys? Tell me.* Even in a dream, her voice made him think of sweet, cool water.

I can't.

Yes, you can. Her fingers moved as though to touch his hair, though he felt nothing at all. *You can tell me anything and it will be all right.*

You don't want to hear.

Yes, I do. Tell me, Trys. Tell me the story. Look, I'll begin it for you: In a time that once was, is now gone forever, and will be again soon . . . Now you go on.

Ah, gods. You're going to make me say it, aren't you? There was . . . there was a boy, once. Grown too close to being a man for his father to beat him as he once had. But he was afraid of the bastard all the same. Because there was a space inside him where he'd locked away all the fear and pain and rage he'd ever felt. And every time his father looked at him, the walls of the space started to shift and shake and he was afraid he would . . . afraid of becoming—

I can't do this.

Yes, you can. He was afraid of becoming like his father, is that what you were going to say? That if he ever unlocked the fetters on all he held prisoned inside, he was afraid he'd turn into the man his father was? She stopped. *What did your father used to say to you, Trys? What did he call you?*

Cur. Bastard Brat. Midden scum. Instantly, the words pounded behind his eyes. Trystan looked up at her. *You were the only thing that kept me from completely believing it.*

You did believe it, though. You still do, don't you? That's really why you left me, isn't it? Why you haven't come back?

God. Maybe. But I can't—

You can. I know you can. Just tell the story. First one word, then another and another after until you reach the end. It's not so hard.

There was a boy who should no longer have feared his father—but he did. And so when he had a choice to make, he chose . . . he chose wrong . . . and it meant . . . it meant that—

If there was a God, he'd be able to wake up now. Trystan's skin was clammy and his heart was trying to pound its way out of his chest. *I really can't do this.*

Hush, it's all right. Again he felt nothing, but he saw her hand move and knew that she'd laid the tips of her fingers lightly against his cheek. *It's all right, Trys. If you can't tell the story, then I'll tell one for you. Close your eyes. This one is a tale you already know.*

HE WAS LYING ON THE NARROW bed of the abbey's guest hall, with Isolde's body warm and soft against his. Her hand rested on his chest, and she didn't move, but he knew by her breathing she wasn't asleep.

"Isa?"

He felt her shift, as though to look up at him, though it was too dark in the room to see. "Yes?"

"Do you remember telling me once that you could read my thoughts?"

He felt her nod.

"So can you tell what I'm thinking now?"

"Perhaps." She propped herself up on one elbow, and he imagined the smile curving the edges of her mouth. "At least I think I can."

"And?"

"And I thought you said you usually knew what I was thinking, as well."

He threw the pillow at her, and she caught it, rolling onto her back and laughing. "And I love you, too."

And then she stopped laughing and settled close back against him. "I mean it, Trys." Her voice was a soft breath of warmth as she rested her head on his shoulder. "I love you. For always—as long as I breathe."

Chapter 3

"Υου can tell 'King Cerdic that I'll beat his cock-breathed toady of a champion into the ground and cut off his ballth." Dywel of Logres's face was suffused, twisted with anger. "And any other Thaxon scum's, too, if Cerdic himself is too much a withered old man to raise his own prick, much leth fight his battles like a man."

He fairly spat the final words, dividing a furious glance between Cerdic of Wessex and Isolde. King Dywel was a big, darkly handsome man, with tightly curling black hair beneath the gold torque of kingship he wore about his brow. And off the field of battle, he was straightforward, good-natured and slightly simple, speaking with a slight lisping awkwardness because his front teeth had been lost to battle or age.

Dywel was also, though, a king without a land; Logres had been lost to Cerdic and his thanes in the years after Camlann. Now Dywel depended on the hospitality of his fellow kings, lived at their halls, and commanded a band of warriors he could not afford to pay—save with whatever they might loot from either the field of battle or raids of enemy settlements. Isolde had heard stories of the rage that seized Dywel in battle, of how Dywel had even been known to attack his own men, because in the heat of the fighting he stopped recognizing friend from foe.

She and all the rest of the king's council were catching more than a glimpse of that side of Dywel now.

Isolde turned to where King Cerdic himself sat at the head of the room. The walls and timbered roof of the hall were new, hastily constructed when Madoc and his army had turned this ancient hill fortress into their garrison nearly two months before. These lands had long been in Saxon hands, and yet the ancient Briton hill fortress of the Old Ones had remained, almost untouched by centuries of war and change. Like a giant asleep underground, waiting and ready to be refurbished and refortified by Madoc's men.

Or at least it would have been good tonight to think so.

Cerdic was an old man, scarred with the marks of countless past battles, but his frame was still upright and tall, with the remnants of a warrior's strength. His white beard was plaited into a single long braid, and he wore his snow-white hair long, as well, with several strands here and there capped with gold. His features were lean, hawklike, with startlingly blue eyes set deep under slightly tilted brows. And at the moment they were utterly, coldly expressionless, betraying no hint of his private thoughts.

As Isolde's eye met his, one slanted brow lifted in faint inquiry, inviting a translation of what Dywel had said.

"The king of Logres accepts your challenge," she said.

The other of Cerdic's brows rose, as well, and he said, in a cultured, if faintly gutteral tone, "A long answer, surely, for such a brief translation into the Saxon tongue."

Cerdic knew exactly what Dywel had said. He both spoke and understood far more of the British tongue than she herself did of the Saxon. Though after two months of nursing his men, she'd had practice in stringing words together and understanding what Cerdic's warriors said. And then, too, growing up with Trystan she'd learned a bit of the language, as well. His mother had spoken Saxon with him, and he'd—

Isolde caught herself, forced her mind back to the council and the men all around her. And tried to block out the awareness of how much Cerdic of Wessex's lean features mirrored those of Trystan, his grandson.

Cerdic's request that she serve as his translator tonight was intended merely to gain Cerdic an advantage in the bargaining that went on tonight, buying him twice the time as any of the other men to take the measure of the faces around him and consider his answers. Not that Isolde could blame him for that, after what Dywel and his men had done.

"The king of Logres seems to further hope you'll get up from your chair and tear him limb from limb."

Cerdic's expression didn't alter, but she thought a glint of amusement showed in his eyes at that, and Isolde steadied herself on the back of her own chair. The air of the hall was hazy with smoke and thick with the smells of dirt and stale sweat and the mutton-fat lamps that hung on the walls—and she'd managed to eat some of the roasted meats and coarse bread that had been served, because, as she'd told Mother Berthildis, none of the men around her could guess or even suspect she was two months gone with child.

But right now it was guilt that churned in her stomach. Not that she was herself responsible for what had occurred. And her winning Cerdic over into an alliance against Octa and Marche had been Britain's final—only—hope; if she'd failed, the men around her, and countless others besides, would be lying dead in the trampled mud of a battlefield. But even so, she knew she ought to have foreseen this moment, this confrontation, from the first moment she'd entered Cerdic's private apartments at the abbey three months before.

She was tired, too, after the long day's ride. She'd slept only fitfully the night before, and had woken this morning to a jumbled recollection of dreams: cold rain and soldiers hunched in their cloaks against the night's chill. Danger and dread—and Trystan. Trystan had been there. She thought she could dimly remember a memory of reaching towards him, wishing she could take away the grim shadow in his eyes.

She'd woken with a tugging ache in her chest and something of the same ashy bitter taste that filled her when she sensed a wounded man's pain but was powerless to take it away.

Now Cerdic inclined his snowy white head in answer to her translation, only a faint shadow of irony marring his cool blue gaze. "King Dywel outdoes himself in courtesy." He turned with a questioning look to the High King's place beside him, where Madoc of Gwynedd sat.

Following Cerdic's gaze, Isolde thought that Madoc, too, looked tired, his black eyes lined and drawn-looking above the scarring burns that covered his face, though his dark beard covered the worst of the damage to his neck and chin.

Save for a brief exchange of greetings when she'd first arrived, Isolde had yet to speak with Madoc alone—for which she was conscious of a cowardly relief. Now Madoc made a quick, impatient gesture with one hand that was instantly checked, and instead raised the hand slowly and let it fall. "So be it. Begin."

At the signal, two men stepped forward into the circular space that had been cleared at the head of the room, swords drawn. Dywel of Logres and Cerdic of Wessex's champion.

Cerdic's warrior was a tall, burly Saxon with braided blond hair, a crooked nose, and a scar running the length of his face on the right side. He and Dywel faced each other, raised their swords, and saluted, their eyes glinting bright and hard in the torchlight that illumined the hall. A tense, expectant hush fell over the room. And then the two were locked in combat, circling the cleared space in a savage dance of slashing attack and counterattack, grunts and ringing clashes of swords.

They'd kicked off their boots and fought barefoot, poised on the balls of their feet, weaving this way and that, advancing, retreating, probing for an opening, coming together then drawing apart to begin the circling dance all over again. Dywel drove forward, hacking the air between him and his opponent with quick, brutal chops of his sword. His face was mottled and so distorted as to be almost unrecognizable, his beard flecked with spittle and sweat, and Isolde held her breath, wishing she could look away as he slashed furiously at the other man. But Cerdic's champion rallied and recovered, wielding his own blade in a series of two-handed, overhead blows that blunted the power of Dywel's attack and drove him backwards, towards the ring of the circle in which they fought.

The Saxon champion was the heavier of the two, and taller than Dywel by half a head and more. But even so, Isolde thought the king of Logres might have recovered. He was the more skilled swordsman of the two, his thrusts more than matching the sheer brute strength of the Saxon man's, and far exceeding his opponent's speed.

But as Dywel fell back, he stepped on a patch where ale had been spilled, turning the rush-strewn earthen floor to mud. And all at once, in barely more than the space of an indrawn breath, the fight was over. King Dywel slipped, twisted trying to recover, and then fell, sprawling back on the churned ground. And Cerdic's warrior was on him in a flash, raising his own sword, preparing to strike the blow that would end his opponent's life.

Isolde sat very still, her teeth clenched. It was at moments like these that she utterly, absolutely hated such meetings as this one—hated everything about the quarreling and jockeying for power and the endless battles of the world of men. Every single man in the hall tonight from Cerdic himself to the lowest petty king's bodyguard knew what Dywel and his warriors had done.

During the most recent clash of fighting, while Cerdic's army had been pinned down to the north by a fresh offensive on the part of Octa's men, a band of Dywel's warriors had sacked one of the small villages near the Wessex border, thieving the grain and livestock and what meager wealth could be pillaged and killing every man, woman, and child.

Everyone knew it. Dywel's men had been openly boasting these last three weeks and more of the successful raid. And yet when Cerdic had charged Dywel with the act tonight, Dywel had given a blustering affirmation of innocence that Isolde could, she thought grimly, have scripted for him before ever he opened his mouth, down to his use of the word *honor* four times, and *vile lie* twice. He'd denied all knowledge of the attack, though. Hence the trial by combat that Cerdic had proposed.

Now the very air seemed to have been sucked out of the hall as for an instant time itself hung still. Then the silence shattered and broke, a ripple of shock running the length of the room, Dywel's leather-clad warriors erupting into bellows of "unfair" and "foul," Cerdic's blond and bearded men howling victory and drumming on their shields with the butts of swords and spears.

Cerdic's champion had stopped, the blade of his sword just touching Dywel's neck, and Isolde dug her nails hard into the palms of her hands as the Saxon warrior's shoulders bunched and tightened. Then, with slow deliberation, he turned to his king.

Cerdic's glance moved from the Saxon man to King Dywel, whose face was still twisted with rage, though the flush of color was draining gradually away as he lay prostrate with his opponent's sword blade at his throat. Not to save her life—or, for that matter, Dywel's—could Isolde have guessed what order Cerdic was about to give.

And then Cerdic raised his hand and made a sign—one that meant nothing to Isolde, but that his guardsman must have understood, for the man lifted his blade away from the fallen man's throat. And then, with deliberation, the Saxon man raised his sword and with a quick, contemptuous flick opened up a cut across King Dywel's left cheekbone.

As though the sting of the blade had loosed a spring, Dywel was all at once on his feet, rounding on Cerdic, blood dripping from his chin.

"And how many of my thettlements were razed by your armies theven years ago?" he demanded, taking a step towards the Saxon king's chair. The slight lisp from his missing teeth was more readily apparent as his anger grew. "How many of my freemen now therve as your thlaves? How many of their wives were dragged off to pleasure your filthy warriors?"

Cerdic didn't move, nor did his expression alter by so much as a twitch of muscle in the face of Dywel's anger. And to Isolde's surprise, Madoc made no move to check Dywel's outburst.

Madoc of Gwynedd was a man of contradictions. Isolde had always known that. He heard Mass every morning, even had his own priest ride out with his army on campaign. And he was, despite the taunts of his fellows, faithful to the memory of the wife he'd lost in childbed years before. Yet his reputation for quick temper was nearly the match of Dywel's own, and he usually governed such meetings as this with an iron hand. It was the reason he'd held the council together this long.

But now it was Cynlas of Rhos who rose to take Dywel's arm.

The king of Rhos was a broadly built, hatchet-faced man of fifty, or thereabouts, who until four months ago had looked younger than his years by far. Now, though, Isolde could still in his gaze the shadowed reflection of a day months before when they'd watched his only living son die in an ambush attack. There were deep lines etched about the corners of Cynlas's mouth and eyes and his once fiery red hair had turned nearly white.

And the confrontation—the confrontation Isolde actually had been expecting tonight—never occurred. After what the wounded in the abbey infirmary had told her, she had been waiting for Cynlas to call Madoc to account for the defeat he and his army had suffered weeks before. No matter why that defeat had occurred, no matter whether the plea for aide Cynlas had sent Madoc had arrived or no.

Cynlas had spoken no word of it, though. Indeed, as he spoke to Dywel in a voice slightly hoarse as though with long disuse, it came to Isolde that these were the first words she'd heard from Cynlas tonight.

"What's done is done. Lose a battle, bury your dead, and move on."

Dywel's face was still dark with anger, his jaw tight, and Cynlas leaned close, speaking in an undertone. Isolde didn't hear what he said, but it was enough to make Dywel allow himself to be pushed back onto his bench, mopping blood from his cut cheek.

The man seated to Cynlas's right, though, looked up. King Meurig of Gwent was a small, meager-chested man, and bald, save for a fringe of wiry black hair above his ears. He wore a glove of heavy leather, padded thickly at the wrist, and on it perched a sleek falcon with a speckled breast and cruelly hooked beak. From time to time, Meurig stroked the bird, making it ruffle its plumage, or fed it scraps of meat from the platter before him.

The king of Gwent's thin mouth relaxed a bit whenever his gaze fell on the falcon, but save for those rare times he sat sullen and scowling throughout. His skin had a yellowish cast, and his face bore the perpetual lines of ill temper and impatience. His eyes were dark, set close together under black brows, and he now shot Cynlas a look in which cold dislike mingled with resentment.

"Hardly surprising that you would say so, my lord Cynlas. Considering how Caer Peris fell."

Cynlas of Rhos turned sharply to face Meurig, some of his old fire flashing in his steel blue gaze. "Speak plain, my lord Meurig. Are you saying I bear the blame for the loss of the fort?"

The smaller man seemed to shrink, slightly, under Cynlas's steady stare, but shrugged, ran a finger across the falcon's neck, and said, an odd mixture of nerves and belligerence in his tone, "I'm saying, at any rate, that there seems small chance it was a bird flew over the walls and chittered in Octa's ear to tell him how to fight past our defenses."

Isolde, watching, was all at once back four months ago, keeping watch at Marcia's bedside as the other girl died her protracted death from bleeding out an unborn child. *There was a traitor on the king's council once before. And now there's a traitor amidst them again.*

Now, her glance moving from Meurig and Cynlas to Dywel and back, Isolde thought the only wonder was that Marcia had spoken of only one traitor and not a half dozen or more.

If Cerdic, the Saxon, the outsider and sometime enemy, had demanded a trial by blades to prove the crimes committed by Dywel's men, he had still provoked the fewest quarrels here today. And if any had the right to question the loss of the fortress at Caer Peris it would have been he, who had lost not only his fortress but his eldest son, Cynric, as well.

Glancing towards him, Isolde thought that Cerdic might have spoken. But Meurig had gone too far, and from his place at the head of the assembly Madoc broke in sharply. "Enough. We meet here today to plan for the future, not to sling muck in each other's faces as we wallow in the past like a bevy of hogs."

Isolde could almost see the concentrated effort Madoc made to set his own weariness aside, summon the energy to settle one snarling quarrel more, and she felt another quick pang.

I've few friends, Lady Isolde, Madoc had said when he'd asked for her hand in marriage. *Fewer, since I took the throne as king.*

If not for Trystan, she might have married him. Might even have grown to love him, in time. And now, watching Madoc's exhausted face she wished for a moment not that she might have accepted Madoc's proposal—no, not that. But she wished just for an instant that she could have wanted to, for Madoc's sake.

Madoc regarded Meurig steadily until the king of Gwent lapsed into sullen silence. Then Madoc turned to fix a steady dark gaze on Dywel. "You, Dywel of Logres, will pay King Cerdic whatever he deems fair for the destruction of his settlement." Dywel opened his mouth, but Madoc spoke over him, his voice hard and biting as his dark gaze. "And unless you wish to be granted a very small new kingdom—one consisting of the patch of earth over your grave—you will in the future keep better control over your men."

ISOLDE WAS HERE. AT THE COUNCIL meeting.

He might have known. He might have goddamn known that whatever god with a sense of humor ruled the fates wouldn't be able to resist this.

Trystan focused on keeping his heart beating steadily. On *not* crossing the length of the council hall that stood between them and snatching her up into his arms.

He couldn't stop watching her, though. Even though standing at the back of the smoke-filled hall, watching her translate King Dywel's insults, eat and drink and smile just a bit at something Hereric signed, was torture, he couldn't seem to turn his gaze away. Like the irresistible urge to test an injured muscle to see if it still hurt.

Trystan saw her turn pale and tense during the fight between Dywel and Cerdic's champion, but apart from that she looked well enough. And Hereric was with her, which meant that the looks the fighting men around him were casting at her only set his teeth on edge and didn't make him wish overwhelmingly that he could drag her out of here.

He'd come here, because giving Octa of Kent enough rope to hang himself was going to require some firsthand knowledge of the council's plans. Octa would be expecting results, and soon. And he'd wits enough to see through intelligence that was entirely false.

He'd come alone because he'd enough on his conscience without getting Cath or Eurig or any of the others captured or killed along with himself. Though as it happened it had been almost childishly easy to get inside the hill fort. Madoc's men were still working at restoring the concentric rings of earthworks that formed the fort's defenses. And the network of guards they'd posted were meant to defend against an army, not a single man.

With his sword belt and leather tunic, he passed easily for just another fighting man. And with so many kings and their war bands grouped here, no one thought twice about seeing a strange face. He'd slipped into the council meeting unnoticed and unchallenged.

And now stood in the shadows at the far end of the room, unable to keep from staring at Isolde, who sat amidst the swirling smoke like some faerie from the Otherworld, dark hair held back from her brow by a thin circlet of gold, skin seeming to shimmer with the pale glow of starlight.

He watched her one moment more, and then deliberately turned his gaze away. That was a lesson he'd learned long ago. Whether in life or in battle, when you had a job to be done, you took all the memories that tried to haunt you, all the unwanted emotions that clogged up your thoughts, shut them in a box, and then took a step forward, leaving them behind.

And if you got lucky, if you waited long enough, you never had to open the box and deal with what was inside at all.

He did that now, pushing the ache in his chest, the thought of Isolde, far, far back, until it was distant enough that he could bring his focus back to the discussion going on at the front of the room. Because it might have been easy getting in here, but it was still wasted effort if all he learned was that Isolde was as heart-stoppingly beautiful as ever before.

The talk had moved on from the recriminations and name-calling surrounding the loss of Caer Peris, and now the council was discussing future plans. Another council meeting was planned for a month hence. And in the meantime, Meurig, the small, rat-faced king of Gwent, was fondling the bird on his arm and making a whining petition for support in defending his borders against Marche's armies, camped directly to the south of his lands.

Marche. Trystan had long since trained himself not to flash on a memory of his father's face at the mention of that name, to step away from the whole churning, seething mass of memories hearing it called up. But tonight his gaze went inevitably to Cerdic of Wessex, sitting beside Madoc at the front of the room.

What would the old man do if he knew he, Trystan, was here tonight?

Order his champion to cut his throat, probably, kin or no. Trystan's fingers felt briefly slippery with the remembered wetness of blood and he couldn't stop a memory of his mother's battered face from appearing before him.

Seeing Cerdic, his mother's father—and with Isolde sitting within sight, under the same roof for the first time in more than two months—was bringing it back, making him wish a lot of utterly goddamn impossible things.

Like that he could go back seven years and ask his fifteen-year-old self what the hell he was thinking of taking the word of a man he knew firsthand to be about as trustworthy as a rabid dog.

Or—here was another impossible one—that he could somehow now make himself the kind of man who deserved to be up there at Isolde's side.

Trystan ground his teeth and forced his attention back to the talk at the front of the room. After some debate, Meurig's request had been granted, on the grounds that the council couldn't afford to have Marche's forces free to join with Octa's, here in the south. In a show of good faith and renewed alliance, Cerdic volunteered fifty of his own spearmen to join with Meurig's men and reinforce the borders of Gwent.

And from there the talk turned to Cerdic's son, Cynric, who'd been taken by Octa of Kent together with the whole of his army when the fortress at Caer Peris had fallen and was now the gods only knew where. Cynric, who was, he supposed, his mother's brother—not that he'd ever so much as exchanged a greeting with the man.

Trystan made himself to take note of the particulars: rumors that had been followed, informants who had come back empty-handed.

Snaring Octa. That was the first part of the job. And to do it he needed what information could be gathered here.

None could find the smallest evidence of where Cynric and his warriors were being held. If they were still aboveground and not tossed into some shallow grave. Trystan wouldn't have wagered a hell of a lot on the expected life span for any prisoner of Octa of Kent.

At one point, though, Cerdic rose and made one interesting contribution. "My informants may not have been able to discover the fate of my son or his men. They do, however, report that rumor holds the relation between Octa of Kent and his own son to be fracturing. They say that Octa drove his son Eormenric away from Caer Peris in a rage."

In his dark, smoky corner, Trystan frowned. If it were true, he'd seen no sign of it himself at Octa's court. But the rumor was something to be remembered, all the same.

The talk went on. Reports of Octa's numbers, the strength of his armies, his warlords and spearmen. Underestimated report, though Trystan wasn't exactly in a position to put the men right. One fact was plain, though. Cynric and his army were key. With the field of battle divided between facing Marche in the north and Octa in the south—with the loss of nearly half of Cerdic's troops—Octa of Kent would triumph if it came to a pitched final battle.

No one actually said as much—the talk was all of strategies, of routes to be traveled, and divisions of troops and supplies. But the councilmen knew it, all the same, from Madoc of Gwynedd to the whining Meurig of Gwent.

Trystan listened to the talk. Forced himself not to look at either Cerdic or Isolde again. Or to notice that Madoc, in the High King's place at the head of the room, was also keeping his gaze carefully turned away from Isolde, save for the occasional quick, betraying glance.

If he loved her, he had to keep his distance. He owed her that. He couldn't stand the thought of hurting her again.

ISOLDE STEPPED OUT FROM THE HALL'S main entrance and into the night. Behind her, the council meeting had ended and turned to a feast, and at least some of the taut, strained atmosphere had begun to lift. She could hear the sounds of laughter and the shouts of men as they vied for the hero's cut of the ox that Madoc had ordered roasted and brought in.

She had left just as Taliesin, both brother and bard to Dywel of Logres, had begun to play his harp. His voice drifted out to her, still, clear, and sweet above the raucous noise of the other men, like a lark's call amidst a summer storm.

Where his brother Dywel was big, darkly handsome, and square-jawed, Taliesin was sleekly plump, with an oiled dark beard and a face that ought to have been good-humored but was instead marred by a look of sullen, smoldering bitterness about his dark eyes. His voice, though, was piercingly, almost painfully beautiful, with a chiming cadence that made Isolde think of a clear stream flowing from deep underground, and the song he played floated out to Isolde as she paused just outside the entrance to the great hall.

Men went to Camlann with the dawn.
Their bravery cut short their lives.
They stained their spears, splashed with blood.
Men went to Camlann with the dawn.
Quicker to a field of blood
Than to a wedding.

A slight stirring of breeze lifted Isolde's hair, and she drew a breath and started towards the women's quarters, where she'd been assigned a bed for the night. She'd taken only a step or two, though, when a voice behind her made her start.

"Lady Isolde."

She turned to find that Cerdic, too, had come out of the hall. He was accompanied by two bodyguards—the man who had won the trial by combat and one other—though they stayed a few paces behind. Cerdic's hair and beard gleamed white in the moonlight, though until he moved closer, his face was little more than a shadowed blur. He made her a grave, formal bow.

"You do not care to stay for the feasting?"

Isolde glanced back at the pool of torchlight that spilled out of the hall's open door along with the laughter and shouts and bursts of song. "I don't think there's a place for a woman in there."

"Nor, it would seem a place for old men." Cerdic's voice was dry. "I confess that the lure of a comfortable bed is stronger these days than any other pleasures of the flesh. Though"—Cerdic inclined his head slightly towards Isolde—"for tonight I'm glad of an old man's aching bones, since it gives me the chance of speaking with you alone."

Isolde looked up into the Saxon king's weathered, hawk-featured face. Four months ago, she had deceived and drugged his private guard to gain the chance of a private audience with Cerdic of Wessex. And somehow the events of that night had forged between them— not friendship, exactly, but a link that made Isolde speak now more frankly than she might otherwise have done.

"I wasn't sure you'd want to speak with me alone." She paused, then added, "I am truly sorry for what Dywel's men have done."

Cerdic, though, lifted one shoulder in a shrug, all trace of his earlier anger done. "King Dywel is quite right," he said calmly. "I and my men have burned dozens of his settlements, pillaged and claimed his lands and the people on them for our own these last twenty years and more. Warmed our beds with countless numbers of his women, too. Honor demanded I demand redress for the attack tonight. But if I am honest, Lady Isolde, in King Dywel's place, I might have acted the same." Cerdic paused, then added with equal calm, "And so long as I am being honest, were I regretting the alliance, I would spare little thought to breaking it. Never trust the aged, Lady Isolde. We grow vain and capricious enough to believe that any means are justified in achieving our own desired ends."

Cerdic rubbed his fingers lightly together and said, with a glance back towards the hall, "Oaths of allegiance sworn between countrymen are fragile enough. Those between Briton and Saxon would need to be written in a river of blood to hold, unless both parties find it convenient to honor the treaty's terms."

Isolde thought of King Dywel, of the tense, snarling exchange tonight between Cynlas of Rhos and Meurig of Gwent, and couldn't argue or even keep the bitterness from her tone. "It's a great shame."

A little distance away, a serving maid hurried towards the hall bearing a tray of food and a fresh pitcher of ale. Save for her and the guards, though, Cerdic and Isolde were alone. The rows of leather war tents where Madoc's men slept were dark and still, the torchlit wooden ramparts manned by sentries too far away to hear any of what they said.

And to her surprise, Cerdic inclined his head, letting out his breath in a rasp of a sigh. "Yes, it is. A great waste and a shame. But perhaps an inevitable one, as well. Our longboats bring to these shores men who are hungry for lands. We plow the soil, till it, water it with the blood of our finest warriors. We will not be driven out. Until Britain accepts this, there will be war." He paused and looked up, away from her, towards the vault of stars above their heads. "I think I told you once, Lady Isolde, that we Saxons have a saying: *Gæð a wyrd swa hio scel.* Fate moves ever as she shall. But there is another saying about fate. *Wyrd bið ful aræd.* Fate remains wholly inexorable."

Taliesin still played; the words drifted out and seemed to Isolde to wind around them in the silence that followed.

> *The young, the old, the lowly, the strong,*
> *True is the tale, death o'ertook them at Camlann.*
> *Since the brave one, the wall of battle, was slain,*
> *Since the earth covered Arthur,*
> *Poetry is now gone from Britain.*

"*Since the earth covered Arthur.*" Cerdic's voice was dry. "Since he and I fought as enemies through twenty years and more of war, I can scarcely agree that his death banished all poetry from the land. Though I remember the battle at Camlann well." Cerdic looked round them at the ancient hill fort, the guards pacing atop the ramparts, torches whipped into tatters of flame by the breeze, and then he said, "It seems to me that the ghosts of the past draw very near on such nights as this—and in such places as these."

Isolde thought of Morgan, alive in the Otherworld of the old magic, the old tales. "In many ways, I would be glad to believe that true."

Cerdic exhaled through his nose. "Or it may be only that I've grown old enough to be nearer their world than this one." He gestured with one hand towards the hall, where Taliesin still played. "Since my own life, my own battles, are now a matter for bards' tales."

His voice sounded suddenly weary, and he looked for that moment less like a king and more like what he had claimed to be—a world-weary, old man, face and body scarred by a lifetime's worth of battles and war. He was still for a moment, then said, in a slightly altered tone, "I did have another reason for seeking a private interview with you, Lady Isolde." He gave her a sharp glance from beneath his brows. "I hear stories that you have, in the past, been able to . . ." Cerdic frowned, as though choosing his words. "That you have the power to see the future as it may unfold. Or to see events far removed from where you are. Or to sense the location of certain men."

Only Marche. And she'd paid a high enough cost for that.

Cerdic was still speaking, still looking steadily out into the night, without meeting Isolde's gaze. "I had thought to ask you, Lady Isolde, whether you might use that power to see Cynric. My son."

"I could try," Isolde said. But she knew, even without trying, that the effort would be useless. Since those visions of Marche had finally gone, she'd been able to See nothing but those occasional glimpses of Trystan. And even those . . . those seemed to come with no particular pattern, no hint of what power chose to grant them, much less why or when.

And maybe that was the true difference between the Old One's magic and whatever small sparks or remnants of their power lingered now. Maybe once, in the great stone circles, or within the walls of hill forts like this one, Seers had commanded visions. Paid the price of the triple death, that their spirits might hover a moment between this world and the Other and tell, in their death throes, what they had Seen. And now such visions came only in snatches, in whatever fragments the lingering gods of Britain—or the Christian God, if He'd truly banished all others—chose to bestow.

"I could try," she said again. "But . . . I would not give you false hope. I doubt I would succeed." She added, "I'm truly sorry. If I had such power, I would use it to help you."

But she had gone too far. Cerdic was not the man to accept a woman's sympathy or admit to the weakness of human feeling before her. He was still a warrior, who had carved out and held a kingdom through a lifetime of battles and war. He straightened, giving Isolde another wintry smile. "I have many sons, Lady Isolde. Too many, it sometime seems to me."

He stopped, and Isolde thought he was about to make his farewells and leave. But instead he said, still not meeting her gaze, "I have many sons. But only one daughter. And the last time we met, Lady Isolde, you were in the company of a young man you told me was her son."

Taliesin was still playing; Isolde could hear the harp's lilting tune drifting out of the hall, though the words were drowned, now, by a burst of raucous song. One of the warriors must have started a drinking game. She said, "Trystan."

Cerdic inclined his head again. "Did the young man recover from his wounds?"

Cerdic knew nothing of her marriage to Trystan. Nor could he. At least, not for now. "Yes. He did recover. He's left the abbey now. Gone to . . . to the aid of a friend."

"I see." Cerdic paused, then said, with a look Isolde couldn't quite read, "I would have liked to know him better."

Isolde thought again of the song Taliesin had sung. The story of the battle at Camlann, in which Marche, Trystan's father, had betrayed both Cerdic and Modred and cost them a brutal, killing defeat.

She said, "Even knowing that Trystan is Marche of Cornwall's son? The son of the man who took your daughter's life? You wish to meet him, still?"

There was time for Isolde to count several beats before Cerdic answered. Then: "A man does not choose his father. And if this young man, this Trystan, bears Marche of Cornwall's blood, he also bears in equal measure my daughter's blood—and mine. So, yes, I would like to meet with him. My only daughter's only son."

There was a brief silence where the last, lingering notes of the harp hung in the still night air. Isolde bowed her head. "Then I promise you that I will tell him so. If I . . . if I see him again."

ISOLDE WATCHED CERDIC WALK AWAY, FLANKED by his two bodyguards, towards the thatched dwelling he had been allotted for the night. Save for the assembly hall and the armorer's forge, few of the hill fort's original tumbled buildings had as yet been remade. But a row of small wattle and thatch roundhouses against the northern ramparts had been restored, and it was there, away from the noise and smoke and mud of the rows of army tents, that Cerdic and the other kings on the council had been housed.

Isolde's own bed was in one of those buildings: a long, low-built structure built for the wives and serving maids and children who followed Madoc's men on the march. She had been intending to make her way there after leaving the council hall, but now she found herself all at once too restless to think of sleep. She turned instead towards the fenced corral on the opposite side of the encampment where the horses were kept. Hereric would have gone to feed and water and settle their mounts for the night. Likely he would be there still.

She found him sitting on an upturned empty barrel outside the paddock's gate. The flaming torches set at intervals around the fort's timbered outer walls showed her Hereric's straw-fair hair and big, square-built form—and showed her the man who sat beside him, as well. A barrel-chested older man, with powerful shoulders and a head of grizzled hair, whose craggy face was marked by a long scar down one cheek and a leather patch over one eye.

"Kian!" Isolde crossed the remaining distance between them, all worry forgotten, for the moment, at least. She would have embraced the older man had she not been certain that Kian would utterly hate any display of that kind.

Kian had looked up at her approach and at once risen to greet her, and she settled for squeezing his hand. "I hadn't realized you'd be here. Are you well? We'd heard you'd been wounded in the fighting last month."

Kian's face was never expressive—Isolde had sometimes thought that his features might as well have been carved in wood or stone. But he must have been glad to see her, as well, because he gave her hand a clumsy pat with one of his horned and callused ones and the grim line of his mouth twitched upwards into what might almost have been a smile.

"Wounded? Nay, 'tweren't nothing but a scratch." He stretched out an arm, showing a scar cleanly healed to a thin pink line, and he patted her hand again. "Thought I told you once before I'm not that easy to kill."

"Tough as old boot leather—I know."

Kian gave a brief chuckle at that. "Oh, aye. That's me." He dropped back down to sit beside Hereric on another upturned barrel. There was a bale of hay for the horses beside them, and Isolde perched on top, breathing in the sweet, grassy scent that rose up all around her. Cabal had been lying at Hereric's feet, but his head lifted as Isolde sat down and he snuffled into her hand.

Isolde rubbed the big dog's ears, and thought that she didn't have to ask Kian whether he was really all right—she could see for herself that he was.

Kian had once fought as a mercenary soldier alongside Trystan; now he was oath-sworn to king Madoc's war band. He'd been Isolde's only trusted companion during the five months she'd spent in Gwynedd at Dinas Emrys—the months before Trystan's return four months ago.

The last time she'd seen Kian had been only days after the loss of his eye, after he'd been tortured, though not quite to breaking, by Marche's men. Then his whole body had been rigid, and he'd held himself as though he were afraid he might shatter apart. As though his every thought, his every bit of focus were turned inward, towards containing the sharp fragments of memory that grated together inside.

Now he sat easily on the barrel beside Hereric, and he drew from his belt a knife and one of the little wooden animal carvings he worked on in moments of ease. A squirrel, this one, tiny front paws clasped around an acorn, small carved eyes seeming somehow almost bright with life. Kian turned the piece over, propping it on his knee, and started to work on the details of the bushy tail. Parchment-fine shavings of wood started to drift down, forming a little pile on the ground at his feet.

No, she didn't have to ask. Kian truly was well.

"Hereric was just telling me about Trystan," Kian said after a moment's silence. He tipped his head in the Saxon man's direction, and Hereric nodded. "Says he's gone to get Fidach out of Octa of Kent's hands."

Isolde nodded. "Do you know Fidach, then?"

Kian shook his head. "That was before I knew him that Trystan was one of Fidach's band. Heard of him, though. Got a name for himself in fighting circles, Fidach has." His mouth thinned. "Don't envy him Octa of Kent's hospitality none."

Isolde hesitated. But this was Kian and Hereric, who, all else aside, deserved any reassurance she could give. She said, after a moment, "I'm . . . nearly certain that Trystan and the others have already gotten Fidach free."

"Oh aye?" Kian's head lifted at that, and he gave her a sharp look from under his bushy brows. He asked nothing more, though, only turned back to his carving. "Well, glad to hear it, if it's true. You think Trystan will soon be back, then?"

Isolde bit her lip and looked past Hereric and Kian to where the tethered horses made sleek, graceful shadows in the night. This was harder, because not even Hereric knew that she and Trystan had exchanged handfasting vows before he'd gone—much less that she now carried Trystan's child.

"I don't know."

It wasn't that she didn't trust the two men—she did, absolutely. And she knew that if she swore them to silence about what lay between her and Trystan, they would never speak of it to a living soul. But still, something made the words stick in her throat. So long as she held the secret hugged tight within herself, she could keep it safe, secure.

Hard enough, just now, to believe that the tale might end happily for her and Trystan. But telling anyone else, even Kian and Hereric, made it harder still.

Kian gave her another sharp glance, but then to her relief only nodded and went back to shaving off tiny, precise curls from the squirrel's tail. "Well, I hope he does come back. I'm not sure how long we'll be posted here and I'd like to see him again."

Isolde looked up quickly. She'd been startled when Cerdic had said much the same, and she was surprised now, though in a different way. "Would you?" she said.

Kian shrugged slightly. He let the knife rest idle against his leg a moment, letting out a long breath, and moved his shoulders again, as though easing a heavy load. "I know . . . I know I went out of my way not to see him before, when he turned up at Dinas Emrys. It was—well, it was on account of this." He touched the leather patch over his eye, and seemed to search for words. "Because I knew if I saw him, he'd be thinking about it and minding it the whole time. And I'd know it, and not be able to help thinking of it, as well." Kian shifted position, the corners of his mouth turning downwards. "Sounds a bit cowardlylike, put like that. But it was Trystan I was thinking of, too."

Isolde thought of all the wounded men she'd known—men with

injuries that would never heal, who couldn't even look their former companions in the eye—and thought that only Kian would read cowardice into his feelings. But she said, only, "Because you knew Trystan would blame himself for it, do you mean?"

Kian glanced up at her, one eyebrow cocked. "Well, didn't he? I'm guessing you told him, sooner or later."

Isolde thought of Trystan's look when she'd had to tell him that Kian had been captured and tortured by Marche's men. Tortured because Marche was bent on likewise capturing his son—and Kian was the first link to Trystan to fall into his hands.

She didn't even have to speak. Kian read the answer on her face, nodded, and let out a breath that was half grunt, half exasperated sigh. "Aye, I know. One fine day the gods are going to wake up and find they've nothing left to do, because Trystan will have taken over thinking he's responsible for the whole bloody world."

Isolde watched one of the horses out in the paddock stamp and switch its tail to dislodge a bothersome fly. "You know him very well," she said softly.

Kian shrugged. "Well enough. He's been a good friend to me, these last years. And I would like to see him again. Tell him I don't hold him to blame for what no one but he would think was his fault."

"I hope you get the chance," Isolde said softly. She hesitated, looking from Kian to Hereric, then asked, "Did Trystan ever . . . ever talk to you about himself? About his past?"

"Not to me, he didn't." Kian shot a questioning look at Hereric, but the Saxon man shook his head. He could sign almost as fluently with one hand now as he had once done with two; he made a rapid series of gestures. *Trystan . . . not like . . . talking of the past.*

"He never spoke to you of"—Isolde hesitated briefly— "Camlann?"

"Camlann?" Kian's brows shot up. "No. But then he wouldn't have, would he?" As though by reflex, Kian's hand came up to touch the scar that ran down his face from temple to jaw. The scar he'd won on the fields of Camlann, where, in another life from the one he lived now, he'd been oath-sworn to a king who was Modred's man.

Kian had fought on the side of Isolde's father—and like most on that losing side of the war, had lost all save his life. *Poetry is now gone from Britain.* Isolde seemed to hear the mournful echo of the ending to Taliesin's song in the silence that followed Kian's words. Then Kian moved his shoulders, as though breaking free of a memory. "Anyway, you'd know more about his past than either of us, I reckon. You grew up with him, after all."

Isolde nodded, a vivid memory rising before her of herself at ten, and Trystan twelve or a few months more, holding himself stiffly, his face so absolutely expressionless she knew he was in pain. Though he never once admitted it, even when she bullied and nagged him into letting her rub sorrel ointment into the angry purpling bruises across his back.

He's still that boy, she'd told the baby she carried.

Kian was watching her, and said, with an unaccustomed frown of worry between his brows, "You'd best be finding your bed if you're meaning to leave tomorrow with Madoc and the rest. Want one of us to walk you to the women's hall?"

She was tired, Isolde realized all at once. Tired and achy from the long days' ride and the still longer meeting in the council hall. She shook her head, though, and got to her feet. "No, that's all right. I'll take Cabal—he'll not let me come to any harm."

She clicked two fingers, and instantly the big dog was on his feet, butting his head against her hand. "Good night." She looked from Hereric to Kian. And then impulsively she leaned down and kissed Kian's bristly cheek. "If I don't see you tomorrow, take care of yourself. Keep safe."

ISOLDE WALKED PAST THE ROWS OF war tents, where a few torches burned now, and voices could be heard as the men made their way from the feasting to their beds. She kept her hand on Cabal's leather collar, and had few thoughts but of finding her own rest. As she neared the women's quarters, though, a figure stepped out of the shadows and into her path.

"Lady Isolde."

Even had he not spoken, Isolde would have recognized him by the spotless cream-colored wool of his tunic and cloak, and by the glitter of gold on his neck, brow, and hands. Taliesin. And as she drew up sharply, one hand burying itself in Cabal's thick fur, Isolde felt a cold tightening about her heart.

Once before, Taliesin had gifted her with a tale that had sketched out the future like a map scratched in the sand. And cowardly though it might be, Isolde absolutely didn't want to hear another tale foretelling what was to come for her and Trystan. Not tonight.

Taliesin took a step towards her, the left leg dragging slightly behind, and Isolde remembered his crippled left foot, clubbed and turned in. He made her a slight bow from the waist.

"Did you enjoy the playing tonight?" Taliesin's speaking voice was quite unlike his singing one, acerbic and tinged with a slight, caustic mockery. His eyes, too, held a glint of bitter malice—and yet, beneath that, Isolde felt as though the cool dark gaze were reading, weighing, and judging her on some private balance.

She looked out into the surrounding darkness, half wondering whether the likeness of her grandmother would appear. *Poetry is now gone from Britain.*

Morgan had never told her the story of how Arthur had forced himself on her in the drunken flush following battle and left her to bear his son alone. But Isolde had known it all the same; she'd read it in Morgan's every silence, her every look at Modred, her and Arthur's son.

"It was beautiful," Isolde said at last. "Though it's a tale with a sorrowful ending."

One of Taliesin's plump white hands moved in a brief, dismissive flutter. "Many of them are."

The feasting in the hall was breaking up; from across the shadowed encampment, Isolde could hear the last, faint bursts of drunken song, ragged laughter and shouts. And from the women's dwelling before her came a baby's sleepy wail and the low murmur of its mother's voice, soothing the child back to sleep.

Isolde hadn't meant to say any more; the words seemed to speak themselves of their own accord. "And do you think the ending of a tale can ever be changed?"

In the flickering torchlight, Taliesin's black eyes looked bottomless, fathomlessly deep. He was still a long moment, and then a faintly mocking smile touched his mouth. "Perhaps they can. But then, what is an ending? Maybe all tales would finish differently if we could only follow them past the endings we bards impose."

Isolde opened her mouth to answer, then stopped, looking past Taliesin. They stood in a pool of light cast by the torches on either side of the door to the women's quarters. And beyond that circle of light, near the looming shadow of the ramparts, Isolde seemed to see not the image of Morgan she might have expected, but instead the deeper shadow of a man's form, broad-shouldered, lean and tall.

Isolde shivered, remembering another story she'd heard many times before. Of a maiden who saw the fetch, the spirit sending, of her love, and knew by the omen that he was soon to die.

Heart beating hard, she strained her eyes to see into the dark. But there was nothing. Only the darkened encampment, surrounded by great earthen ramparts that seemed to speak in a slow, deep voice of the protection of all who had gone before. Finally, Isolde made herself turn away, back to Taliesin, meaning to bid the bard good night.

But when she looked round, Taliesin, too, was gone.

Chapter 4

IF THE SAXONS WEREN'T MAKING quite as much noise as a herd of angry bulls while they crashed through the underbrush, they were at least running the bulls a close second. Trystan had stopped moving to listen to the Saxon men's approach. He knew they were Saxon born; he'd caught a word or two as they hit a patch of brambles and stuck, cursing the thorns and one another.

Trystan stepped noiselessly into the shadow of a spreading oak tree, turning back to silently signal Cath and Daka. *Men. At least five. Get under cover and wait.* Cath and Daka signaled understanding, then melted back into the shadows, soundlessly drawing the knives from their belts as they moved. Piye had been lagging behind, helping Fidach along, but he must also have seen Trystan's signal, because Trystan caught a flash of Piye's black hand and a glimpse of Fidach's gaunt face before they, too, vanished behind a screen of bushes that ran along one side of the old hunting trail they'd been following.

Trystan held still, listening again, keeping his breathing to a shallow, even rhythm that made next to no noise. The Saxons were coming closer; the crunch of their footsteps and the sounds of their clumsy attempts to move quietly were louder. Closer . . . Closer . . .

They passed within a spear's cast of where he stood. Five of them, dressed in leather and skins, dirty blond hair tangled around sunburned, weathered faces. All armed with two-headed axes and swords.

And they never so much as glanced Trystan's way.

Trystan watched them tramp off through the underbrush, hacking at overhanging branches with their weapons, twigs snapping beneath their booted feet. He almost jumped when Cath appeared noiselessly at his side. Cath's large white teeth were bared in a grin. "Company, eh?" His voice was a nearly silent breath. "You want to invite them to join us in a friendly cup of ale?"

Trystan looked towards the Saxon men's retreating backs. "I want to see where they're headed, at any rate." He kept his voice to the same soundless murmur—though with the noise the five of them were making, he could probably have recited an entire bard's song in normal speaking tones before any of them thought to turn around. "I'd have said Octa had sent them after us. But even men who make that much noise hacking their way through the woods would know enough to look around once in a while if they're tracking fugitives."

Trystan glanced around to see Piye and Daka's heads emerging from the thick green leaves on either side of the trail, dark faces nearly invisible in the shadows save for a gleam of eyes. Trystan raised a hand, signaling them as before. *Keep quiet. Follow.*

It was a distraction, at any rate, from tramping along and trying with every step to block out the memory of Isolde. Pale and still as she watched the fight in the council hall. Smiling as she spoke with Hereric and Kian outside.

Hereric and Kian.

Even now, with most of his attention fixed on moving soundlessly after the five men, Trystan flinched inwardly at thought of them. Hereric now without one arm, Kian with a leather patch over his missing eye.

Two more who deserved to have him stay far, far away from them.

A shout from up ahead made Trystan break off and freeze again, his head snapping up to listen. And then all question of how much noise they were making became irrelevant, as, from somewhere over the next rise of land, came the unmistakable sounds of battle. Angry shouts, the screams of frightened horses, the ringing clash of swords on swords.

Trystan stood stock-still. Two choices: turn back or go on. The fight was nothing to him; neither, it seemed, were the men they'd followed.

Nothing save that he'd seen Isolde ride out with the rest of Madoc's party at dawn. And this was unquestionably the route they would take.

He turned to Cath. "Get Daka and Piye. Tell them to follow my lead."

HERERIC STOPPED SHORT, TIGHTENING HIS GRIP on the mare's reins so that Isolde had to hold tight to the saddle to keep from losing her balance. The mare nickered and flicked her ears at the abrupt halt, blowing irritably through her nose, but Hereric quieted her at once with a gentle press on her neck and a soft click of his teeth. Hereric was so tall that his head nearly topped the mare's, and at his touch the horse whickered again and affectionately lipped his shoulder-length flaxen hair.

They had ridden out from the hill fort just after dawn, part of the company made up of Madoc, Cynlas of Rhos, and a chosen number of each king's war band. As had been decided at the meeting of the council, the men were to escort Isolde and Hereric back to the abbey and then continue south, organizing the strengthening of the fortifications their troops held along the coast. Just as Huel's and Cerdic's men were now riding east and north.

They had left behind the old Roman road that ran to the north of the hill fort and onto a winding track that led through a forest of oak and holly trees. Occasionally the trill of bird song broke the hushed stillness all around, or the rat-a-tat drilling of a woodpecker, and once Isolde caught a glimpse of the russet brown coat of a red deer. The soil here was peaty, poor for farming, but even still they'd passed by a few settlements, and several small fields thick with ripening grain. The settlements were deserted, though—doors leaning ajar on broken hinges, hearth fires cold—and in several fields cut hay lay rotting on the ground without anyone to gather it into bales. Save for the birds and deer, the occasional stray sheep or goat—and once a mangy-looking dog that snarled at Cabal, then turned tail and fled—they met with no one at all.

Nearly all who lived and farmed on these lands had fled during the recent fighting with what possessions could be gathered, taking refuge in one or another of Cerdic's forts. And not without reason. Two of the settlements they passed by had been burned, the huts kicked apart and trampled into mud, the air thick with the greasy stench of ashes and death.

Now their party was crossing a stretch of open meadow that Isolde thought must be halfway back to the abbey. Hereric was standing very still, head slowly turning as he scanned the green landscape around them, and without knowing why, cold prickles danced across Isolde's skin as she followed his gaze.

To the right, the ground sloped upwards towards a patch of thick forest, and as his eyes fell on the screen of trees, Hereric stopped. Isolde saw his hand move automatically to the amulet strung on a leather thong about his neck, his thumb rubbing the smooth surface of the wolf's tooth that rested against his collarbone. Without looking at her, he made a rapid series of gestures. *Someone there. In woods.*

It was past midday, the summer sun hot overhead, but even still the forest looked shadowed and dark behind the thick curtain of green. Isolde stared at the closely twined branches, the thick tangled underbrush. She could see no sign that Hereric was right, but all the same she felt cold skitter along her spine.

"How can you tell?"

For answer, Hereric gestured to Cabal, now standing at his side. *Dog knows. Can smell.*

Isolde looked down at Cabal and saw that the big dog was indeed staring fixedly in the direction of the trees on the crest of the hill. His paws were planted wide, the fur on the back of his neck bristling, and Isolde heard him give a low, rumbling growl.

They had been riding somewhere near the middle of the train of mounted warriors who made up the party; now, before Isolde could answer, her attention was caught by a sharp cry of alarm from up ahead, where the leaders of the party were just rounding a curve in the path. Her first, heart-stopping thought was that Hereric and Cabal were right; they were surrounded and about to come under attack. But then the wavering line of horses and armed and helmeted men in front of her shifted and moved forward enough that she, too, could see beyond the path's curve to where four or five men lay prone and in pools of blood on the ground.

In an instant, Isolde had slipped off the brown mare's back and turned to Hereric. "Someone's been hurt up there—I'm going to see."

As she moved closer, she saw that the wounded men wore Madoc of Gwynedd's badge stitched to their leather tunics. Scouts, maybe, sent on ahead to be sure the way the larger party passed was secure. There were four of them, all lying facedown on a patch of ground that had been churned and muddied, the grass uprooted and torn. Even apart from the bodies, it would have been plain a brutal fight had occurred.

Madoc himself and several of his men were standing in a loose half ring around the space where the bodies lay. But the scouts—if scouts they had been—must have been mounted, for one horse now remained—a big black stallion with a blaze of white on his wide brow, standing close by the nearest man's motionless form.

The animal was plainly terrified; he was tossing his head, dancing in place and snorting, his tail switching quickly from side to side. And any attempt on the men's part to move closer frightened and angered the stallion further. Each time one of Madoc's warriors took a step forward, the horse plunged forward, teeth snapping and eyes rolling as he snorted angrily through his nose.

"No," Madoc said before any of the other men could try approaching again. "Frighten him any more and the men on the ground will be crushed—if any of them is still alive."

Hereric had come up behind Isolde and now touched her arm, making a rapid series of signs. *Hereric will try . . . can calm . . . get horse away.*

There wasn't time to ask whether he was sure; already the black stallion's plunging hooves were coming perilously close to the body of the man who must have been his rider. Isolde moved quickly to Madoc's side.

"Let Hereric try. He says he can calm the horse enough that you'll be able to lead him away."

Madoc's gaze moved from Isolde to Hereric, and Isolde could almost see the rapid debate going on behind his dark gaze. Madoc was a war leader, though, accustomed to making even the gravest decisions on the turning of a breath. He seemed to weigh Hereric's appearance against his claim, and then abruptly he nodded. "Right, then. Go ahead."

Hereric at once turned to the stallion, brow furrowing as he watched the stallion shift his weight uneasily from side to side. The horse's muscles were trembling hard, its eyes frightened and ears flat back. Hereric frowned a moment, then drew out from his belt a small horn container. He flicked the cork open with his thumb, tipped out a small measure of the contents—what looked to be a grayish, gritty powder—and smeared it over his palms. And then, with infinitesimal slowness he started to move forward, holding a hand out towards the terrified war mount.

Isolde saw that he kept his body turned sideways and that he was careful never to make eye contact with the big animal as he edged slowly forward. One step . . . two . . . three . . .

Isolde held her breath, expecting at every moment to see the stallion rear up, lethal front hooves flashing towards Hereric's head. But instead the stallion stood, powerful muscles still tense and trembling, but with all four hooves planted firmly on the ground.

Four steps . . . five . . . and then Hereric was close enough for his outstretched hand to touch the stallion's black muzzle. The horse shied back and whinnied—but then seemed to catch the scent of whatever Hereric had rubbed onto his palm. The big nostrils dilated, blew out a gusty breath, and then the horse lowered its head, nuzzling Hereric's fingers.

Hereric's other hand came up, rubbing the stallion's neck in light circles. Isolde saw the stallion's sides ripple as he drew and then blew out another great gust of air. One last tremor shook him, and then his muscles relaxed. He stood quiet, neck bent, head down, nose resting on Hereric's shoulder.

A collective sigh of relief seemed to go up from all who had been watching, and Isolde relaxed muscles she hadn't realized had been clenched. Still rubbing the horse's neck, Hereric led the great animal away, and Isolde was able to step forward, along with several of Madoc's other men, towards the wounded who lay on the ground.

The two men Isolde checked were both past help; in neither

one's throat or wrist could she find even the smallest flutter of a pulse. A shout from Madoc, though, made her start up and cross quickly to the man the black stallion had guarded. Madoc was kneeling beside the man, his scarred face as tight with anger and grim as ever Isolde had seen it, though his expression relaxed, slightly, at sight of her.

"This man's still alive—just."

Isolde nodded and moved quickly to kneel in the grass beside the wounded man, forcing herself to narrow her focus, to block out the rest of the bodies that lay sprawled on the ground. Before she started to take stock of the man's injuries, though, Isolde looked up at Madoc, squinting against the dazzle of the sun's midday glare. "Cabal scented men in the trees there." She gestured towards the woods at the crest of the hill.

Madoc had fought battles with Cabal at his side; he trusted the big dog's instincts as completely as Isolde did. He didn't argue, didn't hesitate, only nodded and turned to scan the trees himself. "Another ambush?" He frowned, speaking more to himself than to Isolde. "If that were it, we'd be dead—or at least fighting for our lives— by now." He narrowed his eyes at the stretch of woods again, then abruptly turned away and started to speak in an undertone to the men at his side.

Isolde was vaguely aware of Cynlas coming up from the rear of the train to join in the men's talk. Of Madoc and Cynlas speaking briefly together, and then Madoc ordering a party of eight warriors to ride ahead and circle round, entering the woods from behind. She was conscious, too, of the warriors taking their mounts and departing to do as Madoc said—but only peripherally so.

Her hands were moving lightly over the injured man's body, finding the pulse in his neck, thready and light, seeking the source of the blood that had puddled beside him in a patch of sticky crimson on the ground.

Isolde drew in a breath, steadying herself, keeping the door open in her mind. Beneath the pain she could feel a confused swirl of memories, buzzing like a cloud of stinging insects. *Riding . . . scanning the path ahead, the trees . . . Christ, what was that? Someone's ragged shout of alarm . . . and then from nowhere, men, shouting, cursing*

men on all sides. Flashing swords, screaming horses, his mount bucking
under him—

Isolde was concentrating so hard that she had no warning at
all. The first she heard was a pounding of horse's hooves. And then
rough hands seized her from behind, a length of course fabric was
thrown over her face, and she felt herself dragged forcibly upwards,
onto a horse's back.

Blinded, choking on the reek of horse from the blanket over her
face and head, Isolde heard Madoc, or it might have been one of his
men, give a shout of alarm. But it was too late. They'd been standing
at a distance, discussing plans. And the man—it had to be a man—
who had seized her had turned his mount and was pounding away
at a gallop.

AFTER THE FIRST MOMENT'S STUNNED SHOCK, Isolde kicked out, twisting, trying to fight her way free. The blanket had been wrapped
tightly around her whole body, though, effectively pinning her arms
to her sides. She heard her captor grunt as she kicked out, but his
grip on her only tightened, powerful hands biting painfully into her
skin.

She was half sitting, half lying across the front of the saddle, the
horse's jarring gate and the hot airlessness of the blanket making her
head swim. She'd lost all sense of direction, had no idea even how far
they'd ridden. But from beneath the blanket, she felt a shadow fall
across them, felt the horse's pace slacken, if only slightly, and heard
the sound of its hooves change from a pounding on earth and grass
to a crunch on dry bracken and leaves. They must have entered the
forest.

Panic flooded every part of her, making it harder still to breathe.
Because as realization of her situation struck her, her thoughts flew
instantly to the small, beating spark of life growing each day inside
her.

She didn't know—couldn't guess—who the man who held her
was, or where he was taking her. But she'd been captured for a reason. She must have been. And unless she could escape, her baby
would be born in captivity.

Or, if she were killed, her baby would die as well.

Isolde had to fight against the hot tide of stomach-churning anger and self-reproach that threatened to overwhelm her. Stupid . . . stupid . . . stupid. The word seemed to beat in her mind in time to the drum of the horse's hooves. How could she have been so careless? By the crone, how could she?

She'd known there was danger, despite what Madoc had said. If she'd been more on her guard, if she'd taken better care, she'd not be here, at the mercy of an unknown, faceless captor, dragging her the gods only knew where. She'd not be here, helpless as a swaddled babe herself, with the tiny, fragile life of her own child every moment in greater peril.

Like a swimmer kicking free of dragging water weeds, Isolde made herself push that thought aside.

Think. She had to stay calm and think, or she'd be no good to her baby or to herself. That Madoc and Cynlas would send men after her, she didn't doubt. Almost certainly, men were already riding in pursuit of her and her captor. So she had to—

And then, all at once, she felt the mount beneath her startle, rear and shy back, so that she was thrown hard against her captor's chest. She heard the man who held her shout something, felt him dragging on the reins, trying to bring the horse back under control. The animal reared again, though—and this time Isolde felt both herself and the faceless attacker tip and slide, and then she was falling, tumbling to the ground with a jolt that seemed to run through every nerve in her body and drove the air from her lungs.

For a moment she lay still, unable to move, everything forgotten in the desperate, pulse-pounding struggle to draw in a breath of air. And then realization tore through her, and she sat up, frantically clawing her way free of the blanket's scratchy folds. Stupid—stupid—stupid! This could be your only chance.

The fabric covering her face fell away, and Isolde took in a great gulp of cool, sweet, leaf-scented air. And then she froze, a jolt like lightning seeming to run through her as she wondered whether she could have struck her head harder than she'd realized in her fall. Or whether shock or fear were making her conjure visions from the air.

They were in a small clearing. And the horse—she now saw it

was a big, dappled gray stallion—hadn't bolted, but stood perhaps ten paces away, muscles quivering. And just before her, not within her reach, but nearly so, two men faced each other beneath the spreading canopy of oak trees. One man she didn't know—a big, raw-boned man with a head of greasy blond hair and a face she knew she'd never seen before. Though by the burly strength in his shoulders and arms, she knew in an instant he had to be her captor.

But she spared him barely a glance. All her attention was transfixed, locked on the man who stood at most five paces away, his sword at the ready and drawn. A young man, with a warrior's spare, broad-shouldered build, dressed in tunic and breeches of an indeterminate shade between green and gray. He had gold-brown hair laced back in a leather thong, a lean face with a thin, flexible mouth and startlingly blue eyes set under slanted brows.

Trystan.

Isolde blinked, but Trystan's image didn't waver, didn't flicker or disappear. His face was set and hard, his blue eyes unwavering in their fix on the other man, his every muscle tight as a coiled spring. She'd seen him in combat before, and knew that right now he was completely a soldier, his every other thought, every purpose pushed aside to focus on the enemy who faced him. She knew he was waiting for her captor to make a move. And she knew—absolutely—that if the other man took a single step in her direction, Trystan would be on him in a flash.

Evidently her would-be captor knew it, too. She saw the blond man's fingers twitch and his glance flick, just briefly, to the knife he wore at his belt. Saw him weigh it against the sword Trystan held, and conclude, as she had, that even if he drew the weapon he wouldn't stand a chance. And then, so quickly Isolde barely had time to register the movement, he had bolted sideways, seized the horse's dangling reins, and vaulted into the saddle in a single smooth leap. He dug his heels into the horse's side hard and was gone, vanishing into the trees in a spatter of churned leaf mold and flying hooves.

And in an instant, Trystan had sheathed his weapon and dropped to kneel beside her, pulling her close, smoothing her hair, running his hands lightly down her arms as though to check for broken bones. "Holy mother of God, Isa, are you all right?"

For once, he sounded nearly as shaken as Isolde felt. She could feel the rapid drumming of his heart in his chest, feel the tension in the muscles that held her. She tried to answer, but she couldn't make her voice work, so she nodded against his shoulder. Reaction was setting in, and she couldn't stop herself from starting to shiver. She had to clamp her teeth together to keep them from chattering.

Trystan pulled her closer, wrapping his arms around her. "God, I'm sorry. I shouldn't have let him get away. But I didn't want a fight if I could help it. Not with you right in the middle—and without knowing how badly you were hurt."

Isolde closed her eyes, resting her head against the solid strength of his chest, and felt the shivering ease a bit.

"I'm really all right," she managed to say. "I wasn't hurt at all." And then she lifted her head, looking up at him, reaching to touch his face, trace the line of his brow and cheekbone, still unable to quite believe that this wasn't some delusion or dream. His jaw was stubbled by several days growth of beard that pricked under her fingers, and his skin felt warm. "You're here," she whispered. "You're alive."

She thought she saw something, swift as a shadow, cross his blue gaze. But then he pulled her close again and said, his voice muffled by her hair, "I'm here."

His arms about her were solid and strong, and he was holding her so tightly, as though he were never, ever going to let go. It felt, Isolde thought, like coming home. Like seeing the sun rise after the darkest night. Her every muscle ached from the ride and the fall from the horse, but even still she didn't want this moment ever to end. She could have sat here forever, listening to the gradually slowing beat of Trystan's heart under her cheek, just knowing that he was here with her, was alive and safe.

And then a thought struck her like a gust of icy rain and she jerked back. "Trys, you can't be found here. You can't be seen. Madoc and his men will be combing these woods searching for me. And Cynlas of Rhos was riding with us, as well. He'll recognize you—he's bound to."

Cynlas held Trystan to blame for the death of his eldest son four years before. Blamed him unjustly—but there was almost no chance of proving that, after all this time.

"At the least, they'll think you might have had something to do with the attack down there on Madoc's men."

Trystan was silent. "And you don't?" he said at last.

"Of course not!" Isolde drew back. But then she touched his cheek and said again, softly, "Of course not. Of course I don't think that."

Again Trystan just looked at her, his whole body very still. She was getting better at reading the looks in his eyes. Now she thought they held a cloud of sadness, and something like astonished wonder, as well—as though he couldn't, or didn't dare let himself believe whatever it was he saw in her face. And then, too, she read in his blue gaze a longing that twisted her heart.

"Isa," he said. "You shouldn't—"

But from somewhere close by came the sound of men, shouting her name, and a bark Isolde recognized as Cabal's. She put a hand across Trystan's mouth, stopping him before he could say more. "Please," she said. "I couldn't bear to have anything happen to you—especially if it were my fault for keeping you here."

Trystan made no move, though, only looked at her a long moment more. Finally, he said, "You deserve—" he stopped.

With every part of her, Isolde wished he would offer to take her with him—even though she knew he'd be able to move far faster, and in far greater safety, alone. Or, failing that, she willed him to say that he'd come for her at the abbey as soon as he could—that he'd see her again soon.

Instead, very slowly and carefully he reached out and brushed her cheek with the backs of his fingers, traced the line of her mouth with his thumb. His blue eyes were on hers, looking at her as though he were trying to memorize every line of her face, to fix this moment forever in his mind.

He said, "I'll be watching until Madoc's men find you. Until I know you're safe."

Isolde could hear the men's shouts coming nearer, hear Cabal's excited barks and the sound of the search parties crashing through dry brush and leaves. Another moment and they'd burst on the scene.

Trystan had started to rise, but she tightened her grip on his hand. "Wait—where will you go? What have you—"

But there was no time. No time to ask him how he came to be here at all, appearing as if by some magic or charm, as though her needing him had conjured him from the air. She heard a shout—one of Madoc's men, she supposed. "I see her. Up ahead. This way."

Involuntarily, she turned, catching a flash of a drawn sword, a glimpse of an approaching blue tunic through a gap in the trees. And when she turned back, Trystan was gone, vanished as though he'd never been there at all.

ISOLDE, ALL RIGHT?

Hereric's brow was creased with worry as he sat beside Isolde on the ground. He and Cabal had been amongst the first of the searchers to reach her in the woods, and the Saxon man's broad face had lit in a sunrise blaze of relief at finding her safe and unharmed. Together they'd made their way back to the horses and the rest of the party. And now Isolde was back exactly where she'd been when she'd been seized by her still unknown captor: kneeling beside the earlier attack's single survivor, bandaging his wounds and readying him to ride.

Hereric's anxious question made her thoughts fly instantly to the baby inside her. She was still aching and stiff from the fall, and aware at every twinge or throb of a bruise of the harm such accidents could do an unborn child. She was trying as hard as she could to block out the fear, though, at least for now. If there had been damage, it was already done. She could do nothing just now for herself or the child. And she had work to do in trying to keep the unconscious man at her feet alive.

Madoc had identified the man as Cei, sent out early that morning, as Isolde had guessed, to make sure the route they were to travel was secure. And the black stallion that Hereric had calmed must belong to the wounded man. The animal stood quiet, now, but all the same put its ears back and tossed its head when anyone tried to lead it far from Cei's side. And as Isolde nodded in response to Hereric's question and tried to reassure him that she truly was fine, she happened to glance up at the horse and was struck by remembrance.

"What was that powder you put on your hands before?" she asked.

Hereric's face cleared a bit. *Made from . . .* Hereric made a sign Isolde didn't recognize, and seeing her blank look he gestured to the stallion's inner forelegs, where the dark calluses common to all horse's grew. *Smell calms when horse is frightened. Don't know why.*

"I'd never heard that before." Isolde bent to secure a thick pad of bandage over the wound in Cei's side. The cut was still oozing blood, and it would be a miracle if the jolts of the ride back to the abbey didn't make it break open again. But there was nothing more she could do. Clearly, they couldn't remain here, where afternoon shadows were already lengthening, foretelling the coming dusk, and a second attack could happen at any time.

Madoc had come at once, as soon as Hereric had found her, to be sure she was truly unharmed, and to assure her that he would send riders after the man who had tried to drag her away. His intent dark gaze had held a naked relief that had made Isolde feel another sharp pang of guilt. But there'd been no time for any further speech with him. Both Madoc and Cynlas had agreed that they must press on to the nearest place of safety. Even now, the riders were moving into formation, readying the horses and preparing to move out. They would be leaving in only a short while more.

Isolde hesitated, as she always did when touching the subject of Hereric's past. But then she asked, "Where did you learn to care for horses so well?"

Hereric's pale blue eyes went faintly distant, his heavy-boned brow furrowing—though whether because he couldn't recall or because the question troubled him, Isolde couldn't tell. He rubbed at his beard, then finally gestured, *Know some already . . . Trystan teach more. Good with horses. You know?*

Isolde did know—though she'd almost forgotten, it had been so many years. But she remembered, now, how many hours Trystan had spent in her father's stables when they were growing up. Partly, Isolde had guessed, because it saved him having to go back to the men's hall, where his father Marche would be. Though of course Trystan would never, ever have admitted as much, even to her.

But the crabbed and bent old man who had been the official horse trainer had gladly welcomed any aid as it came. And Trystan had been good with the horses—very good. Patient and skilled at training the war mounts to respond to the commands necessary in battle. In equal parts patient and entirely without nerves when it came to breaking the wildest horses to tolerate the restraint of a saddle and rider.

For just an instant, Isolde felt again the brush of Trystan's fingers on her cheek. *I'll be watching until Madoc's men find you,* he had said. *Until I know you're safe.*

She looked up towards the woods at the top of the hill, darker and more shadowy, now, as the sun sank further in the west. She could see nothing. No sign that Trystan or anyone else might now be watching; Cabal lay quiet at her side, head on his paws, body relaxed. And the riders Madoc had sent out hadn't returned—as they would, if they'd found anyone. Trystan or the man who'd dragged her off.

Isolde turned back to Hereric, wondering whether she should tell him that she'd seen Trystan. What could she say, though? *Trystan was here, but now he's gone again? And I've no idea when or even whether he'll return.*

And before she could make up her mind whether to speak or keep silent, Cei's eyelids fluttered and opened, and he fixed a bleared, pain-glazed gaze on her face. His throat worked as he tried to swallow and his lips moved. "What—"

Instantly, Isolde bent over him and slipped her hand into his. "You were attacked, but you're safe, now. I'm a healer. I'm going to help you."

The panicked confusion in Cei's gaze cleared a bit, and his head moved in a feeble nod. "We were . . . set on." The words came in whispered bursts. "Too many to fight off. Thought I was . . . done for. But then . . . more men . . . strangers . . . came out of nowhere. Drove the men who'd hit us off."

A half dozen questions at least sprang to Isolde's mind, but she forced herself not to ask. Cei was panting, sweat beading his brow, his lips drawn back in a grimace of pain.

So instead she said, "Shhh. It's all right. Don't try to talk."

Cei's mouth twisted in a fresh spasm of pain, but he gave another weak nod.

His face was chalky white, tinged with gray about the edges

of his mouth. And thinking of the oozing gash, now covered by bandages, Isolde felt dread that bordered on certainty curl inside her. Still, she squeezed Cei's hand, opened the door inside her, and sent out her threads of awareness to slide through him, from the swelling lump she could now feel on the back of his head, to the ache of several cracked ribs, to the wrenching, searing agony of the sword gash.

She let the awareness rest there inside him until she felt, too, all the desperate horror of the ambush, still raw in Cei's mind, still like a nightmare tale he was telling himself over and over again. She saw through Cei's eyes the men erupt from the trees, felt his heart start to pound as—

Get your sword, up, fool. Ah, God's rotting bones, that was Essa who just fell and was coughing and screaming and thrashing in agony on the ground. Essa, and—

After the terror of her own abduction, the shock of seeing—and losing—Trystan, sharing this with Cei was almost sickening; Isolde had to force herself not to jerk her mind back from the contact, snap the fragile threads that bound her awareness to his. She felt the ashy bitterness of failure, too, at not being able to take either pain or memory away.

But Cei was breathing more easily, and his face, if still the color of clay, was less agonized. Isolde took his hand. "You're safe now. We'll be back at the abbey soon." She squeezed his fingers in hers and added, softly, "You fought bravely. No man can do more."

"I WANT YOU AND PIYE TO watch the abbey again. Isolde sets foot outside the walls, you follow. Anyone unexpected tries to gain access— you come and find me."

Daka's brows drew together.

They had come far enough north and east of Caer Peris that Octa's patrols were unlikely to venture upon them, especially with Madoc's hill fort encampment less than a half day's ride away. Trystan had risked a small fire tonight, kindled in a shallow hole. The light wouldn't be seen from a distance, but sitting next to it as he was, the flames cast a flickering orange glow across Daka's dark face. "You think we be needing to guard her? I see the way King Madoc looked at her. He guard her close himself, I'd say."

Trystan gritted his teeth. The knowledge that Madoc—damn his eyes to hell—was undoubtedly the better man for her was no help whatever in isolating the urge to knock Daka's head against the rock he was sitting on. "Just do it, right?"

He was spared hearing Daka's reply by a violent fit of coughing from Fidach. The injured man was half sitting, half lying on the ground beside the fire, propped up by one of their traveling packs and covered by the heap of all their traveling cloaks. But he was still shivering, and the spasm of coughing that seized him bent him nearly double.

Trystan steadied him with one hand, mindful of the healing wounds on Fidach's back. But even still, one of the deepest cuts must have opened up, because a scarlet stain had appeared on the back of Fidach's tunic.

Trystan said nothing. He didn't doubt that Fidach considered blood a small price to pay for the satisfaction of having fought and won against men who almost certainly came from Octa.

When the worst of the fit passed, Fidach looked up at him with streaming eyes. He was wiping blood away from his mouth, but he said, "I half kill myself to do your job for you and I don't even get a cup of ale in thanks?"

Cath put a cup into Trystan's outstretched hand, and Trystan guided it to Fidach's mouth, clapping him lightly on the shoulder. "All right, then, you've earned your ale. But Christ, man, the next time you want an extra cup, just ask."

Daka and Piye had been carrying on a low-voiced conversation in their own tongue, and now Daka came to lay an extra branch on the fire and squat down next to Trystan. He spoke as though they'd never been interrupted before. "Look, you be wanting Piye and me to guard Lady Isolde, we do it. You know that. But I not understand. Why you don't do this yourself?"

Trystan's mind slid to the memory of Isolde, caught roughly up by the man on horseback and dragged off at a gallop. Gods, even thinking of it set his pulse pounding blackly against his eyes.

He'd told Isolde he'd not fought the man because he'd not

wanted to risk putting her in the middle of a fight. Which was true enough, in a way. But the real reason was that he absolutely hadn't trusted himself to be able to stamp down his rage if the encounter had come to an actual meeting of swords.

He was gutter scum himself enough not to want Isolde to see that. Not to want her there if the simmering potential for violence for once slipped beyond his control.

And still the most he could say about the men they'd fought was that they had moved and operated like an organized band of fighting men, not just stray bandits or masterless men.

But nothing to show he or any of the rest had been Octa's men, sent with the express purpose of snatching Isolde. And though he'd have thought this early for even Octa to break the bargain they'd made, it was yet another reason he couldn't stay here. She was safer inside the abbey walls than he could keep her. And ensuring she stayed that way meant keeping to his side of the bargain with Octa. Concentrate on the pragmatics, on getting the job done.

And yet—serpents of hell—if he had to stay here another day, even, he knew he was going to get up from here and head for the abbey at a run.

Trystan drew in his breath. "I think Octa of Kent is not a patient man. If I want to have any leverage at all with him, I'm going to have to give him what he wants—and soon."

What he'd learned at the King's Council meeting was a start— but only a start. He doubted he now knew more than the rest of Octa's informants and spies. No, for that he needed an informant of his own.

Not that Garbhán, the informant he'd contacted, had any particular loyalty to him. Or compunction about selling his knowledge to the highest bidder. But whatever else he was, Garbhán was at least no friend of Octa of Kent.

Now Trystan answered Daka, "You heard the message Garbhán's emissary brought. He's agreed to a meeting in two days' time. Which means I have to leave tonight."

Silently and for the hundredth time, Trystan swore at the ill chance that two months before had reduced his ship to a pile of rubble and ash. A boat now would have meant covering the same distances in less than half the time. Not to mention providing a means of escape if things went wrong.

Across the fire, Cath threw another log on the blaze and spoke for the first time. "Reckon Eurig and Fidach will do well enough on their own here. I'll go along."

Trystan looked at him sharply through the rising smoke. "You're sure?"

"Oh, aye." Cath stretched his booted feet out in front of him, black beard splitting in a grin. "Unless Garbhán's been hatched over and hatched different, as my mam used to say, you'll need someone to guard your back."

ISOLDE PICKED UP THE HEATED CHAMOMILE and garlic poultice. It was nearly hot enough to burn the tips of her fingers, but Cei didn't even stir when she pressed it tight against the sword cut in his side.

Now, still holding the poultice in place, Isolde glanced up at Madoc, who stood at the foot of the narrow bed. "Thank you for bringing the fresh stores of medicines from Dinas Emrys. I've been desperately short of supplies here."

Madoc had been staring down at Cei's face and seemed at first scarcely to have heard Isolde. Then he jerked his shoulders, dismissing the thanks. "Much good may it do this poor devil." He raised his head, meeting Isolde's gaze. "He is dying, is he not?"

Isolde looked down at Cei, wishing she could deny Madoc's words. She couldn't, though. Cei's skin was the color of wood burned to pale ash, his breathing rasping and shallow. For a time, Isolde had been able to rouse him enough that he could swallow scant mouthfuls of water. But he'd lapsed into unconciousness hours ago, and now not even shaking him drew any response.

"I'm sorry."

They had reached the abbey near nightfall of the previous day, and Cei had been carried at once to a pallet in the infirmary. Isolde had done for him what she could, and then had consented to go to her own bed and sleep for a time, leaving Cei and the other wounded in Sister Olwen's care.

Sister Olwen had been, if not exactly friendly, at least a shade less prickly and hostile. And though Isolde wasn't sure rest would counter any damage that had been done by the day's ride and the fall, it was as much as she could do. She'd been tense with waiting for any sign that she might be about to lose the child. But there'd been nothing at all—no pain, no blood. And—for once reassuringly—she'd been as sick as ever when she'd tried to eat the bread and broth one of the abbey sisters had brought.

Now it was evening again, and she was once more kneeling beside Cei's pallet in the infirmary. The room was dimly lit by a fire in the hearth at the far end of the hall, and by a guttering lantern that Isolde had asked to be hung just above Cei's bed. All about them the abbey was quiet, the time for evening prayers not yet come, the infirmary filled with the soft rustles and sighs of the men who slept on the pallets all around.

Even as she tended to Cei's wound, Isolde was struggling against a feeling of complete disconnection from her surroundings. The past two days felt fragmented, and try as she would she couldn't seem to fit the pieces together into any kind of coherent whole.

The council meeting at the ancient hill fort . . . her moonlit encounter with Taliesin . . . the ride back . . . the attack . . . her capture . . . and then, the most disconnected fragment of all, that fleeting, almost completely unbelievable meeting with Trystan.

If not for the story Cei had told, she might have thought the whole encounter just her own imagination. Or some cruel trick of the forest folk, like the tales of travelers lured into faerie mounds and lost for a hundred years and more. But Cei had recounted at least fragments of what had happened to her, and then later to Madoc during a brief lucid spell here at the abbey.

He and the rest of the scouting party had been set upon by a band of men who'd come screaming out of the forest and attacked with axes and swords. They'd been caught off guard, and quickly overpowered. And then, as he'd lain bleeding on the ground and thought himself a dead man, a second band of men had appeared from nowhere and driven the first attackers off.

Cei had been too weak to describe the men who'd saved him. But when Isolde had reached again towards his mind she caught more quick, splintered glimpses of the memories that swirled beneath the wounded man's fear and pain.

Four men . . . or five . . . couldn't tell. Two like some demons of the night, with braided black hair and skin black as coal. One with the swirling tattoos of the Pritani tribes on his high cheekbones, who wielded his sword with a speed like lightning.

Isolde supposed the images she caught from Cei's mind should have been a comfort. And in a way, they were. Because wherever Trystan now was, he was with Daka and Piye, the Nubian twins whom Isolde would have trusted as she did Hereric and Kian. And Fidach. If he'd been among those to come to Cei's aid, driving off the attackers, ill as he was, Isolde had been right that the decent man who lived behind his public face was now nearer the surface than before.

Isolde couldn't stop herself, though, from seeing again and again the look in Trystan's eyes just before they'd parted—the look of a man leaving for a battle he didn't expect to survive.

She spread a layer of cloth over the poultice to hold it in place, then felt Cei's brow, his neck, the joining of his chest and arm. All frighteningly hot and dry, without any trace of cooling sweat. Despite her efforts with the wound, he'd fallen into a fever sometime during the night before, and it had only continued to rise.

Isolde bit her lip, then happened to glance up and catch sight of Madoc's face. His expression was set, unflinching and hard, but something about the look in his eyes made Isolde say, "You know, you needn't stay here. I doubt he'll wake."

Madoc's head lifted and he looked at her almost as though he'd forgotten her presence. But he shook his head and said, "Cei was my man. He was wounded in a battle fought on my orders. So I'll stay. I owe him that much." Madoc's mouth twisted as though at a bitter taste. "No king should be allowed to order his men into battle without seeing firsthand the consequences that can befall."

Isolde was quiet a moment, watching his scarred, weary face, then said, "You're a good king, my lord Madoc. But you ought to rest. I'm sure the abbey sisters would grant you a bed in the guest hall."

Madoc's expression went so blank with surprise that Isolde wondered with another pang how long it had been since anyone had expressed concern for his welfare. Then he smiled, though it seemed to Isolde slightly forced. "I must look worse even than I thought. I'll do well enough. I need little sleep, as a rule."

Both Madoc's and Cynlas's forces were camped on the hills surrounding the abbey, their journey south for the moment halted so that riders could be sent to ascertain what yesterday's attack might mean. The slaughter of Madoc's scouts might have been only chance—a stray raiding party of Octa's or Marche's men. But it might mean, too, that Octa and Marche had a large force massed somewhere nearby.

Isolde dampened a clean cloth in a basin of water and started to wipe Cei's fever-flushed neck and face. "Have you learned anything yet of the men who did this?"

Madoc rubbed his eyes and said, wearily, "Nothing. I begin to believe it must indeed have been a stray raiding party, or even a band of masterless men. The scouts I've sent back have seen no sign that anything of substance has changed. Octa and his forces still hold the shore forts. Marche's men are still massed to the northwest, near the borders of Gwent."

"And Cerdic is still to join with King Meurig and move north?" Isolde asked. "To ensure that Marche's armies cannot join forces with Octa's?"

"So we agreed. So Meurig of Gwent believes."

Something in Madoc's tone struck Isolde and she said, "You don't trust him?"

Madoc's shoulders moved in a weary shrug. "After the raid by Dywel's men?" He grimaced. "I'd be the son of a flaming goat if I trusted even my own countrymen."

Isolde's eyes strayed to where the red-haired man, Cadfan, slept on the opposite side of the infirmary, his splinted leg propped straight out under the blankets that covered him, and she recalled the story he'd told, of a plea for help that had seemingly never arrived. She thought, too, of the council meeting, of the snarling tension between Meurig of Gwent and Cynlas, between Dywel and the other men. Of the loss of Caer Peris and the capture of Cerdic's son.

She dampened the cloth again, then asked, "And there is still no word of Cerdic's son Cynric or the other captive men?"

Madoc shook his head. "They might as well have stepped through one of the portals of the Fair Folk and into the hollow hills for all we can learn of where Octa has taken them."

Madoc stopped, his thoughts plainly following some winding track of their own. Then he seemed to recall himself and turned again to Isolde. "But I've not yet had time to give you what news I do have, Lady Isolde. News I hope will be welcome, even here." He glanced about them, his face hardened again as his gaze fell on Cei's unconscious face.

"Yes?"

"I can at last give you word of Camelerd. As you know, for some time we had been unable to get past Marche's forces to reach the borders. And I know that you—and I—feared the worst. But now I can tell you that matters are not as dire as we had thought. Your man, Drustan, who has ruled the land in your absence has acquitted himself well. Remarkably so, I may say. He has been hard pressed by Marche's army, but he has held the borders of Camelerd strong."

"You were there?" Isolde asked quickly. "You saw Drustan yourself?"

Madoc nodded. "Saw him and fought with him, besides. Two weeks ago my men and I at last fought our way through Marche's forces, joined with Drustan and the warriors of Camelerd, and drove Marche and his army back."

Isolde had gone still at the first mention of Camelerd, her every muscle tensing. But now she let out her breath, briefly closing her eyes as relief washed through her in a wave. "That is good news." She looked up. "Thank you, my lord Madoc. I am . . . more grateful to you than I can say."

Madoc waved the thanks away. He seemed to search for a way to begin, looking across the infirmary as though suddenly unwilling to meet Isolde's eyes.

"My lord Madoc?" she said, a cold hand tightening about her heart once again. "Is something wrong? Is Camelerd—"

Madoc looked round at that. "No. You may be easy on that score. I've left fifty of my own spearmen to guard the borders. But now that Marche's forces have drawn off, I believe the country out of danger." Madoc's mouth lifted wryly. "Or as much out of danger as any land can be in these times."

He stopped. Plainly, he hadn't finished, though, and so Isolde was silent, waiting. After a long moment, Madoc let out a breath and said, "It's just that I'm not sure you should be thanking me, Lady Isolde. I fear"—his mouth twisted—"I must give you other news. Of a far less welcome kind."

Isolde set down the basin and rag and looked up at him. "Tell me. Please."

Madoc met her gaze, mouth lifting in another small, wry smile. "I beg pardon, Lady Isolde. I know you are not one to flinch from facing the unpleasant or the hateful. The news is simply this: King Marche has offered a price in gold for your capture. And I believe our driving him off from Camelerd was what prompted him to do so. You are Camelerd's lady. Capture or kill you, and Marche would hope that the army's will to fight would be gone—that the country's defenses would fall."

Isolde made herself hold very still. She might not hate Marche; She might be—was—fiercely glad that she'd chosen brief marriage to Marche, and life, over certain death. And she might, in a way, feeling unwilling pity for the man who filled himself with rage to drive away a constant, cold, deadly fear and revulsion for what he now was. But Madoc's words sent a sliding sickness through her all the same.

She said, without letting herself flinch away from the idea, "Then the men who attacked your scouts . . . the man who tried to abduct me . . ."

Marche met her gaze and gave an unwilling nod. "I would be shocked to learn that all were not Marche's men." He paused, then added, "And I do apologize, Lady Isolde, for not telling you of this latest threat from Marche earlier, as soon as I myself heard."

Isolde couldn't find it in herself to be angry—not when, if she were honest, a cowardly part of her would far rather have remained unknowing, still. There was a brief moment's silence and then Madoc said, in a different tone, "I do have one final piece of news for you."

Isolde had been focused on holding her hands steady as she started to wipe Cei's face again, but something in Madoc's words made her look up sharply. "Oh?"

Madoc nodded. "I have had word that King Goram of Ireland is wedded. He has taken to wife one of the Ui Neil clan—a powerful connection, as I'm sure you know." Madoc paused and said, turning again to look at the opposite wall, not meeting her gaze, "But I think this news means that you may consider his offer for your hand in marriage withdrawn."

And with it, the most pressing reason for Madoc's own marriage proposal was likewise withdrawn. Madoc didn't speak the words aloud, but Isolde could feel them, hanging in the space between them, palpable as the fraying coils of smoke that drifted up from the lantern's flame.

She had been dreading—and still dreaded—having this conversation. But she couldn't in conscience put it off any longer. She drew in her breath and made herself say, "I never gave you an answer, Lord Madoc. To what you asked of me at Dinas Emrys four months ago."

Madoc was still for a long moment, face averted, shoulders tight beneath the linen of his tunic, then, slowly, he turned back to meet her gaze and said, quietly, "And you needn't now. I already know."

It was a side of Madoc few saw, beneath the authority and determination of the warrior and king. "I'm truly sorry," Isolde said softly.

Madoc's eyes met hers a moment longer, and Isolde couldn't stop herself from flinching at the look in their depths. But then he forced another smile. "Don't be, Lady Isolde. If anyone should be sorry, it's I. For . . . for hoping for more than you could ever be willing to give."

Chapter 5

ISOLDE MADE HER WAY SLOWLY back to the abbey's guest wing. She was utterly exhausted—her very bones seemed to ache with weariness—and very, very sad. Cei had died in the hour just before dawn. And if she'd sat beside many wounded men and held their hands while they drew their last gasps of air, she felt the same, afterwards, every time.

Now the morning sun was bathing the abbey in a soft, golden glow, and the air felt fresh and cool. It seemed almost an insult to Cei. That, too, was the same every time: the small tragedy that countless men might breathe their last in the night, and the sun would shine in the morning unchanged.

She came around a corner of the guest hall and then stopped short. A stone bench stood at the joining of two walls, and huddled on the bench was a black-robed figure Isolde recognized as Sister Olwen, head buried in her hands, crying with the complete abandonment of a child.

Madoc had stayed with Isolde in the sickroom until the hour for the midnight prayers, when he'd had to return to the army encampment. When Madoc had gone, Sister Olwen had come to take his place, and Isolde had been unreservedly glad to have her. Especially when, towards the end, Cei had cried out and tried to rise from the sleeping bench. It had taken all Isolde and the sister's combined strength to hold him down. And then, at the last, Sister Olwen had wiped Cei's face with unbelievable gentleness, her lips all the while mouthing the words of soundless prayers.

But never, ever would Isolde have expected to find her here, weeping as though Cei had been her own son. Sister Olwen hadn't seen her, and for a moment Isolde hesitated, wondering if the older woman would only be humiliated or angry at having her privacy violated this way. But she looked so pitiful, curled in on herself, her shoulders hunched and shaking as she sobbed, that Isolde found she couldn't just turn away and leave.

Instead she approached quietly and sat down on the bench beside the nun. Sister Olwen jerked upright, gasped, and then turned her face quickly away to hide her tears.

Isolde, too, turned away, likewise pretending not to notice Sister Olwen's blotched face and red, swollen eyes. "Do you mind if I join you?" she asked.

She heard Sister Olwen draw in a ragged breath. "If you like." Her voice was unsteady, thick, and clogged with crying.

They must, Isolde thought, have made a comical picture, sharing a bench but sitting so far turned away from each other that they were almost back to back, each addressing the empty air. She kept silent, though, letting Sister Olwen decide whether she wanted to speak or only sit and be still.

In the abbey's work sheds, some of the sisters were beating retted flax fibers to be spun into the linen that was traded with local settlements for cheese and vegetables and ale. The dull, rhythmic thumping made a counterpoint to Sister Olwen's hiccuping breaths.

Finally, Isolde said, "Thank you for your help last night. I couldn't have done without you."

Sister Olwen made a soft, indeterminate noise, and Isolde heard her black robes rustle as she shifted position on the bench. Then she said, still in a low, choked tone, "I owe you an apology, Lady Isolde. There is a good deal I don't know about caring for wounded men. I see that now."

Isolde turned to find that Sister Olwen was facing her, her body drawn up stiffly, her expression a faint, sorry echo of her usual dignified stare. Isolde smiled a bit. "If you mean knowing not to wake a warrior when he's just out of battle, I only learned that lesson through painful experience. The first year I was nursing wounded men I got a split lip and two black eyes."

Surprisingly, Sister Olwen's mouth curved, too, in a faint, watery smile. Then she bit her lip, dragging one of her sleeves wearily across her face. "How do you keep doing it?"

Isolde knew the sister wasn't speaking of waking combat-trained men. She looked away, tilting her head up a bit so that the warmth of the sun played on her face, listening to the soft sounds of foot-steps and voices as the whole small, peaceful island that was the abbey went about its day.

Isolde said slowly, after a moment, "Because when I'm working with the wounded, I feel as though nothing exists but each moment I'm living right there and then. As though I'm exactly where I'm supposed to be, doing what I'm meant to be doing."

Sister Olwen watched her a moment. Her gray hair was falling in wisps about her face, and she made a futile effort to push a stray lock back into place. Then: "I envy you, Lady Isolde—sin though that may be. I've found that feeling in prayer. But only very, very rarely."

"Thank you." Isolde smiled a bit again. "But I'm not sure you need feel envy. You've just told me that what you find in prayer, I find in lancing boils and salving suppurating wounds."

Sister Olwen stared at her a moment. And then, amazingly, she gave a small hiccup of a laugh and scrubbed at her reddened eyes again. "I suppose that's true."

They sat quiet a long moment, and then Sister Olwen said, suddenly and unexpectedly, "I knew your mother, you know."

Isolde turned and looked at the older woman in blank astonishment. "My mother?" she repeated.

Sister Olwen leaned back a little on the stone bench. She had recovered some of her usual composure, but her face looked gentler, the harsh lines softened by weariness and the tracks of her recent tears. She nodded. "Gwynefar. Yes. She took the veil at the convent where I was first a sister. Not here. This was an abbey in the Summer Country. It must now have been"—she glanced up at Isolde—"well, I suppose it must have been twenty years ago now."

Isolde nodded. "Twenty years." She stopped. "She betrayed her marriage vows to Arthur to wed my father while Arthur was on campaign with his armies, fighting in Gaul. And then when Arthur returned, she was too afraid of what he might do to her. With good reason. The punishment for an adulterous queen is death by burning. And from what I've heard I can't imagine Arthur would have spared her. So she fled the world and took the veil. Just after I was born."

And she might never have hated or even blamed Gwynefar for fleeing the world and leaving her behind. But now she felt a faint qualm, wondering whether she wanted her mother to be more to her than simply a name, a remote figure in the bards' tales. Gwynefar of the white hands and golden hair.

Especially at this time, when her every thought, her every movement was centered around awareness of her own unborn babe.

Sister Olwen had settled back in her place, her gaze turning distant as she looked back across twenty years. "She was very beautiful, of course. And very sweet and kind. And I'll have to say—" Sister Olwen hesitated, a line appearing between her scanty brows as she searched for words. "There are some people who face life as though they were great, centuries-old oaks. Storms and wind scarcely touch them; they just stand solid through it all. And then there are others like spring saplings. They may be slight, but they're strong and they're supple. They can bend and sway whichever way the wind may blow, and then spring back afterwards unharmed. And then . . ."

Sister Olwen paused. In the sky above them a swallow was sketching great, circling loops, the elegant outspread wings a dark shadow against the bright morning blue. Sister Olwen's piercingly blue eyes seemed to track its swoops and dips for a time, and then at last she went on. "And then there are some who can't stand up to life any more than a spring blossom can keep from getting crushed in a hailstorm. And I'll have to say that lady Gwynefar was one of those." Sister Olwen paused, then glanced at Isolde. "I think, really, that she willed herself into the illness that killed her. She'd no wish to keep living anymore. So she died."

Isolde's vision blurred, and she blinked hard. But she was in some way relieved, too, that she still felt only simple pity for the woman who'd been her mother—nothing more. There was a moment's silence, and then Sister Olwen said abruptly, "She'd meant it for the best, though. Weak she may have been, but she didn't betray Arthur because she was wicked or a wanton—or a fool."

Isolde looked up. "How do you mean?"

Sister Olwen sighed again. Her big, callused hands flexed, then rested still in her lap. "I was infirmarer, then as now, and I nursed her when she took ill that last time. She talked to me, some."

Sister Olwen paused, eyes turning unfocused, as though she could hear a ghost's echo of long-ago spoken words in the quiet bustling sounds of the abbey and the drunken buzzing of bees in the gardens. "Arthur thought he'd brought peace to the land. At best he'd only beaten the Saxons into temporary retreat. We all knew they'd be back. But Arthur left Britain to fight in Gaul. And Gwynefar was lady of Camelerd." Sister Olwen cast a sidelong look at Isolde, and said, "As you are, now, I understand."

Isolde thought of her talk with Madoc the night before. "Yes, I am."

"Then you'll know it's a heavy burden for a woman to carry alone." Sister Olwen pursed her lips, and added, with a gleam of her usual tone, "Not that I don't believe a woman could uphold the duties of ruler every bit as well as a man. Only that you'd look long and hard before you'd find an assembly of men ready to let her."

Isolde felt her mouth curve in a small smile. "Very true."

Sister Olwen shifted on the bench. "Your mother said once that Arthur had spent half a lifetime battling the Saxons back with every force Britain's armies could muster, and won nothing but at best an uneasy peace, and at God alone knows what cost. And Modred"— Sister Olwen glanced at Isolde as though in faintly surprised realization—"your father, I suppose, said that instead of battering our armies bloody against an immovable stone wall, we make allies of those who had been foes. And it worked—or at least it was beginning to. You'll know, of course, of Modred's alliance with King Cerdic."

Isolde did know; she'd counted on that same old alliance when she'd entered Cerdic's private chamber three months ago and persuaded him to take a chance on an alliance with Britain's forces again. She nodded, and Sister Olwen went on. "Gwynefar chose the man—the king—she believed could best defend Britain and, too, the lands she held in her own right. And she might have been proved right. But it was no use, of course. Arthur wasn't the man to sit by and let his own heir seize both his wife and throne."

Sister Olwen's voice held a bitter edge and she added, mouth twisting, "At least Gwynefar died long before Camlann. I've always been glad of that."

Isolde rubbed a faint, darkening bruise on her arm, remnant of her near capture the day before. "I know," she said. "I'm glad, as well."

They sat quiet for a moment. Isolde thought again of what Madoc had told her the night before—that between them, he and Drustan, her mother's man, had successfully defended her lands.

She thought, too, of all she'd told Mother Berthildis. She would stake her own baby's life on the councilmen between them being able to outfit a small army with their own bastard sons. Save Madoc, perhaps. Rumor held him to be unfailingly faithful even to the memory of the wife who had died in childbed five years before.

But snow would fall on the fires of Beltain before the rest of the council would consider her anything but dangerously uncontrollable and unchaste for bearing the child of a husband they'd not hand-chosen for her themselves.

For a moment, she tried to conjure a likeness of Gwynefar as she sometimes conjured Morgan, tried to imagine what her mother would wish now for the lands that she had in a way given her life for.

After a long moment, Isolde turned back to Sister Olwen and said, "You said that my mother took the veil at the first abbey you entered. How did you come to leave there?"

Sister Olwen had been staring into the middle distance, her gaze lost in the past, and she looked up, surprised at the question. She didn't answer at once, and then her mouth thinned again. "The abbey was sacked—raided. By Arthur's men." She stopped, her blue eyes turning steel-hard. "Arthur is said, now, to be a great war hero. Perhaps he was. But he needed what small wealth and stores of grain we had for his armies. He asked. Our abbess refused. He gave his war band leave to attack us and pillage at will."

She drew breath, then went on in a voice flat with remembered fury, the words coming in short bursts. "Myself and the other sisters of our house fled across country. It was the dead of winter. And we had nothing save the clothes on our backs and what little we'd managed to catch up as we fled. A few of us, not nearly all, survived to reach this place here."

She paused, turning to meet Isolde's gaze. And then the corners of her mouth turned up just a bit. It was just a small smile, and a grim one. But it was also an offering, if not quite of friendship, at least of alliance, something Isolde wouldn't have thought possible before today.

YEARS HADN'T CHANGED GARBHÁN. HE HAD the same greasy brown hair, the same bulging greenish eyes and wide, thin-lipped mouth, the same paunch hanging over his leather belt. Irish by birth and blood, he now earned a sizable if unsavory living thieving from wrecked ships that foundered on the coast, and—the reason Trystan had arranged this meeting—selling the information his network of informants gathered to the highest bidder.

Garbhán shifted from one foot to the other, weighing the bag of coin he held in one hand.

"You've come here unarmed, as we agreed. So what's to stop me, friend, from just taking this and slitting your throat here and now?"

Right. Same old Garbhán.

Trystan said, pleasantly, "The same spirit of goodwill that's stopping Cath there from putting an arrow through your heart." He gestured upwards into the tree above their heads.

Garbhán's pale gooseberry eyes swiveled upwards. Dusk was falling, but Cath was still plainly visible, sitting astride one of the thicker branches, an arrow nocked back in his bow and trained on Garbhán's beefy chest. As the Irishman looked up, Cath gave him a wolfish grin and a tip of his shaggy head, his aim never faltering, his body remaining unmoving by so much as a hair.

If Garbhán was shaken he didn't show it. He laughed appreciatively. "Ah, well. Worth asking the question, you understand." He stowed the coins in some inner fold of his tunic and said, "Very well. To business, then." Garbhán pursed his lips and seemed to marshal his thoughts, then said, "The word I hear is that though a certain Saxon king has allied himself with Britain, the truce is at best an uneasy one."

Trystan's brows lifted again. "Cerdic of Wessex, you mean. And if that's the information you're giving in exchange for payment, I may have Cath put an arrow through you after all."

"Patience, my friend. Patience." Garbhán lifted his hands in a pacifying gesture, but Trystan saw him turn slightly pale and cast an uneasy glance upwards into the trees. "That was only the beginning. This Saxon king—Cerdic of Wessex, as you say—has agreed to send troops towards Gwent, to reinforce the borders against attack by king Marche. However . . ." Garbhán paused, glanced round, and lowered his voice. "Certain sources tell me that Cerdic has not been entirely forthright with his British allies about the number of troops under his command. He has more than suspected. And plans to use those added troops in a surprise attack on Octa at Caer Peris. Already he begins to amass food and other supplies in that area to maintain a siege."

Trystan considered the Irishman closely, but could detect no sign that Garbhán was lying. He asked a few more questions and got in response a rough map, sketched by Garbhán in the dirt at their feet. Trystan studied it, committing its lines to memory, then wiped it out with the toe of his boot.

"And you'll keep me informed if you happen to hear anything more?"

"Of course." Garbhán patted the coins in his pocket. "We've a bargain, haven't we?"

Trystan raised an eyebrow, and Garbhán said with a fine show of righteous indignation, "What's that for? I'm a man of my word."

"When it suits you to keep it."

Garbhán's anger collapsed in another wheezy chuckle. "You wound me to the quick, my friend. Unkind . . . but true enough." He started to turn away, then looked back over his shoulder, a kind of sly curiosity in the prominent green eyes. "Why come to me?" he asked. "Not that I don't appreciate the business, but there are others you could have gone to for information."

Trystan shrugged. "Call it care for your immortal soul—giving you a chance to atone for past sins."

"Care for my—" Garbhán broke off and laughed until his eyes watered and his breath came in gasps. "That's good. That's very good." And then he sobered, and said, with another curious glance at Trystan, "And why are you doing this, then?"

Trystan thought of Isolde, sitting amidst the smoky heat of the king's council hall. He shook his head, and a too-familiar memory of a woman's crumpled body replaced the vision of Isolde in his mind's eye, followed almost instantly by a second too-familiar picture, a field of battle. Men screaming and dragging their guts behind them in the mud. Corpses stacked like so much corded wood.

Trystan wrenched his focus back to the present. Garbhán was watching him. But his green eyes were mildly curious, nothing more. Trystan clapped Garbhán on the shoulder and said, easily, "It's a rare man who's nothing to atone for."

THE SMALL, STONE-BUILT CHAPEL WAS DIM and cool, the air faintly musty, scented with wax candles and incense. Golden rays of afternoon sunlight slanted in through the door. Isolde paused a moment in the doorway, momentarily blinded after the bright sun in the courtyard outside, before her eyes adjusted and she saw Madoc, seated on one of the wooden benches at the front of the room.

She'd been in the infirmary when the sister whose duty was to keep the abbey gatehouse had come to say that Madoc was arrived and would wait for her in the chapel until she was finished making her rounds of the wounded men.

She would have expected to find Madoc kneeling, head bowed and arms outstretched in prayer; even before being crowned High King, Madoc had been a devoted believer in the God of the Christ. But instead he was merely sitting motionless on the hard, backless bench, head lifted as he stared unblinkingly at the thick white candles that burned day and night on the raised altar at the chapel's apse. He seemed lost in thought, though, for he didn't even glance round at Isolde's approach, and it was only when she took the place on the bench beside him that he looked up with a start. He blinked, his gaze seeming to return from a long way away.

"Your pardon, Lady Isolde. I didn't hear you come in."

Isolde smoothed the blue linen veil with which she'd covered her hair, in deference to the abbey's rule. "Thank you for coming so quickly, Lord Madoc. I know you and King Cerdic must be occupied with making plans."

Madoc waved away the acknowledgment, and Isolde drew in her breath. "I wanted to speak to you of Camelerd."

Madoc looked surprised. His dark brows drew together. "Of Camelerd? But I told you, Lady Isolde, that the danger to your lands is—"

"I know." Isolde stopped him before he could finish. "The worst of the danger to Camelerd is passed. I believe you—and I truly thank you for all you've done to defend the land." She paused, then drew breath and looked up to meet Madoc's gaze. "That's what I wished to speak with you about. Even if I cannot marry you, I could sign a charter, granting you, as High King, control of my lands."

For a long moment, Madoc sat without speaking, looking at her with intent dark eyes, and an expression Isolde couldn't quite read on his scarred face. Then, at last, he said, "Do you mean that is your wish?"

"It is." Isolde folded her hands tight in her lap, then looked up at Madoc again. "You've defended Camelerd these last months—you've surely won the right to hold them in name as well as deed. A better right than I, at any rate. I've not set foot inside Camelerd's borders in years."

"Hardly by choice. You had your duties as Constantine's High Queen to keep you away."

Isolde lifted one shoulder in a half shrug. "Even so." She thought of what Sister Olwen had said. *Not that I don't believe a woman could uphold the duties of ruler every bit as well as a man. Only that you'd look long and hard before you'd find an assembly of men ready to let her.* "But the council will never willingly accept a woman who rules a land without a husband by her side." She raised her gaze briefly to Madoc's. "We both know that. I can fight it, or . . ." She stopped, lifted one hand and let it fall. "Or I can grant control of the lands to a man of my choice, who can both rule and guard them better than I."

Madoc didn't speak. Then, after the quiet stretched out between them, he said, "You are sure?"

"I am." At least this way she herself chose the man who gained control of Camelerd. And she had a chance, at least, of her marriage to Trystan's one day being more than a secret vow between them.

If Trystan lived.

If he came back to her.

Holy Goddess, great mother of all. Isolde closed her eyes. One impossibility at a time.

She shifted on the bench to look up at Madoc again. "I'm sure," she said. She held out the roll of parchment written and witnessed for her by Mother Berthildis and Sister Olwen in the abbess's rooms that morning. "This is a charter granting you full control of Camelerd."

Madoc seemed to hesitate. Then he reached to take the parchment from her, bowed his head and said, eyes dark and very grave, "I will present this at next month's council meeting. And I thank you, Lady Isolde, for the trust you have placed in me."

"And I thank you. For being worthy of the trust."

They sat quietly a moment, and then Madoc asked, in a different, easier tone, "And for the rest—you are well here at the abbey? You have all you need for your work with the wounded?"

Isolde nodded. "For the present, yes."

"And your guardsman—the man who guided you here from Dinas Emrys—he is no longer with you?"

Isolde stiffened. Madoc was speaking of Trystan. She'd told Madoc that Trystan was her messenger, a guardsman from her own estates in Camelerd. Though she doubted Madoc believed it, then or now. She said, carefully, "No. He was called away. And I gave him leave to go."

Madoc's brows drew together. "He went overland, then? I understood that his boat had been—" He stopped.

If Isolde had stiffened before, she now utterly froze, every muscle in her body locking, the blood in her veins running snow-melt cold. Trystan's boat had been burned when a party of raiders had attacked them on the journey that had ended here. But she'd never told Madoc that. She'd told no one at all. There was no way—none—that Madoc could know of that attack. Unless . . .

Isolde's gaze fixed on the parchment Madoc still held in one hand. *Breath of all the gods.* What had she just done?

Feeling as though her head were being drawn by a wire, she looked up, meeting Madoc's eyes, and saw in their depths awareness of what he had just revealed. She couldn't have spoken. She felt almost exactly as she had in the moment after the jarring fall from her would-be captor's horse in the forest; the stunning force of realization had driven all the air from her lungs, making it impossible even to breathe. She only sat, staring at Madoc.

It was he who faltered first, looking away, towards the burning candles on the altar. "I'm sorry."

"You're sorry?" Isolde had caught her breath, at least. "You're sorry?" She would have liked to shout, to catch hold of Madoc and shake him. But something in Madoc's face stopped her and made her speak in barely more than a whisper instead. "There are men in my infirmary crippled and dying because of you."

Even now, she was half hoping he would deny it, but his scarred face worked, as though the words were torn from his chest. "I know. God, do you think I don't know?" He dropped his head into his hands.

Isolde felt as though a new, incomprehensible reality were taking shape before her, like a likeness in the scrying waters. She said, her voice sounding far-off and strange, "You're the traitor. The traitor Marcia spoke of."

Madoc flinched at the name, and she said, the words coming more easily, now, as she started to become accustomed to the truth that had struck her like a slap in the face, "Marcia's child. It was—"

"Mine." The word was half whisper, half groan. Madoc had been staring at the altar, but now dragged his gaze to meet Isolde's. He inhaled and then exhaled slowly, as though the effort of breathing was painful. "Spit on me. Strike my face. Tell me I disgust you. Believe me when I say that you can call me nothing that I've not called myself."

He stopped, closing his eyes. "She came to me. Just after . . ." He gestured to the scars on his face. "I'd not been with a woman since my wife had died. I'd sworn I never would. But she—Marcia—threw herself at me . . . flattered me." Madoc made a disgusted sound in the back of his throat. "Made me think she'd long loved me from afar. She all but climbed naked into my bed, and I—" Madoc's jaw tightened, as though he had to force the words out. "I should have been strong enough to refuse her, turn her away. But it had been so long. And after this"—he touched the scars on his face again—"after this happened, I wanted—"

He broke off with another noise of disgust. "It doesn't matter. She was Marche's spy. That was why she took up with me. She was acting for Marche. I found that out soon enough. But I swear to you"—Madoc stopped and turned to look at Isolde, his voice shaking with sudden intensity—"I swear on my life, Lady Isolde, that I didn't know about the child."

Isolde's lips felt stiff, and she was still finding it difficult to think clearly. But she said, "I believe you." And she did. She had no doubt whatever that Madoc spoke the truth. That he would have dealt honorably with Marcia, Marche's spy or no, if he'd known she was to bear his daughter or son.

And then she thought of something else. She said, "There's a man in the infirmary, Cadfan. One of Cynlas's army. I set his broken leg. And he said that he and his raiding party had sent word to you, asking for reinforcements. But that you'd never come. And I—" the words almost choked her. "I told him that the messenger couldn't have made it back to you in time. But—"

Slowly, Madoc bowed his head. Then he looked up at her and said, very quietly, "I told you, Lady Isolde, that there was nothing— no vile name—you could possibly call me that I had not already called myself." He let out an explosive breath that was half mirthless, bitter laugh. "Did this Cadfan also tell you about the orders I'd given him and his men? God, I heard myself telling them, *Go out and find the enemy.*" Madoc gave another harsh laugh. "Like some kind of goat-rutting idiot. I kept expecting someone to say, *Why, have you lost them?*"

The first shock was wearing off. Isolde said, slowly, "And you have made secret alliance with whom? Octa? Marche?" The effort of thinking clearly was like trying to see through fog. "But I don't understand—you defended Camelerd. Unless . . ." She went suddenly icy cold as a thought struck her. "Was that also a lie?"

Madoc flinched slightly, mouth tightening, but he said, "No. It was the truth. The . . . agreement I made was with Octa alone. Not with Marche. Octa finds himself—disappointed in his sometime ally. Allegiance with Marche has not won him the strategic advantage he'd hoped for. Octa would be quite pleased if Marche were to fall in combat. Marche has no heir. Cornwall would be vulnerable to anyone who could conquer and hold it."

"I see. And so, having succeeded in turning one High King of Britain traitor, Octa of Kent decided to try his luck with a second?"

This time Madoc didn't flinch at the hardness of Isolde's tone. His shoulders slumped, and he stared at the opposite wall, as though unable to meet her gaze. The only sounds came from the bustle in the courtyard outside. Then he said, at last, "Do you know, I had a bargain with myself, back at Dinas Emrys. That if you consented to marry me, I'd be the kind of man you could be proud to stand beside. That if you'd be my wife, I'd tell Octa of Kent to go to the devil."

Isolde wanted—desperately, at that moment—to be angry with him. She would have welcomed a jolt of clean, hot fury just now, even if it meant losing her temper and saying something that might make matters worse yet. Above all else, she didn't want to feel pity for Madoc of Gwynedd. But she did.

Isolde felt a flicker of self-disgust. Maybe it was true what they said about pregnancy softening a woman's brain. But still her next words came out sounding more flat than angry.

"Are you saying that your turning traitor was my fault?"

Madoc's mouth twisted again in a small, mirthless smile, though his eyes remained achingly sad. "No. I didn't mean that. I only meant—" He broke off, shaking his head. "No. I'll not try to excuse myself. It hardly matters now."

Isolde felt as though she'd seen the tide come in with a rush on the beach, then just as quickly ebb, leaving an entirely new landscape in its wake. She said, slowly, "That means . . . you must have been approached by Octa long since—more than four months ago. Before ever you agreed to my journeying to seek Cerdic's aid."

Madoc said nothing, but his dark head tipped in slight agreement.

"And you listened to Octa. Considered his offer. Why?"

Marche, Octa's ally, had been solely responsible for the disfiguring burns on Madoc's face, for the long weeks Madoc had spent in nerve-wrenching pain. And no man—no sane man—would trust Octa of Kent to keep a treaty unless it were written in Octa's own life-blood.

Madoc let out a slow breath and said, in a quiet voice, "Because he has my son."

After the the shocks of the last few moments, Isolde should have been impervious to any further surprise. But at that she caught her breath. "What?"

Madoc rubbed his eyes, then turned to face her. "I said, he has my son. I'd kept him away from me—not told anyone where he was being raised—for just this reason. But Octa's spies discovered his location. Maybe they bribed Marcia for the knowledge; I don't know. But my son, Rhun, is now hostage to Octa of the Bloody Knife." Madoc paused, staring straight ahead, and then said, in a voice tight with control, "He turned five years old in the spring."

"I'm sorry," Isolde said quietly. And she meant it. Even in the midst of shock, even wishing she could feel anger, it made her heart twist to think of a five-year-old boy imprisoned by Octa, alone and afraid and ripped from everything and everyone he'd ever known.

Madoc was silent, then gathered himself again. "Thank you." He stopped, drawing a heavy breath. "But I'd be lying, Lady Isolde, if I told you that was the only reason I considered Octa's offer of allegiance. I said I'd not try to make excuses for what I've done, but—"

He broke off, swearing under his breath. "You've sat through nearly as many meetings of the council as I have. You've seen and heard what goes on. Britain's kings may unwillingly unite to face a common threat, but they hate each other as much as they do any Saxon. They'd be as happy to plunder each other's lands and slaughter each other's warriors and rob each other's wealth as they would Octa's or Marche's. And that's not even taking into account acts like Dywel's—stabbing our supposed allies as soon as their backs are turned."

Madoc's voice had roughened, but then he stopped and passed a hand across his face again. When he went on, the words were flat with fatigue. "How many atrocities can we commit—how many lives can we take in the name of protecting Britain and still remain a Britain worth protecting?"

Isolde could think of no possible answer she could make to that. She felt as though a yawning chasm had appeared at her feet, with Madoc on one side and her on the other. And yet she could agree with him, in a way. Madoc's hands clenched on his knees. "I was king of Gwynedd, Lady Isolde, before the council made me king of all Britain. I swore a blood oath when I was nineteen to defend Gwynedd to my last breath. Five months ago, when Octa's emissary approached me, Britain's forces had been driven back to our last strongholds in the Welsh hills, and we were a hair's breadth from utter defeat. I had Gwynedd to consider. Lands where women and children had been left to do the planting and harvesting for more seasons than could be counted, because the men were at war—where the people were starving, because as hard as they worked, they couldn't accomplish what their menfolk should have been home to do themselves."

Madoc's hands tightened again. "Five months ago, it seemed to me that Britain lay in its death throes. That all question of my son's life aside, Gwynedd's best hope of survival lay in alliance with Octa and Marche." He stopped, looking up to meet Isolde's gaze. "You know already the choice I made."

Isolde wished again that she could hate the man who sat beside her on the hard, backless bench, his face somber, the burden of his own treachery in his dark eyes.

If Madoc hadn't actually ordered the attack on Trystan's boat, he had at least turned a blind eye, set Marche's guardsmen on their track, and given them what they needed to find her and Trystan. Trystan or Hereric or she herself, or all three, might easily have died.

And yet she'd seen enough men suffering dire agony to know that Madoc was in such pain now.

He was still speaking, still staring at the altar with its cross and surrounding glow of candle flame. "In wars of this kind there are no victors, only a side that suffers fewer crushing defeats. And Britain may have a chance of survival now—but it is only a chance, and growing ever slighter with each fresh quarrel amongst the council. Each insult to Cerdic drives him ever further towards regretting that he ever allied his forces to ours. Go back on my agreement with Octa and Marche, and Gwynedd will be utterly destroyed, even if by chance Britain as a whole manages to weather the war battered but unbroken as a whole. And then . . . and then, there is my son."

Madoc stopped and Isolde saw the muscles of his throat bunch, his voice altering, growing suddenly husky in tone. "Rhun is my only son—my only child. And Gwynedd's only heir to the throne. Even if I felt nothing for him at all, Gwynedd would need an heir, a man to rule when I am gone, if the land is not to plunge into the blood feuds and chaos that befall any kingdom without a king. No—"

Madoc's voice shook slightly, and Isolde saw a spasm cross his scarred face as he looked up at the altar one final time. "I may no longer sleep at night. I may no longer be able to pray, when the oaths to Britain I have broken rise up and choke off the words before they can leave my throat. But I may at least know this: that I have become what I most abhor and broken my own soul in order that my son's reign of Gwynedd may be one of peace instead of war."

"Peace? Owain of Powys allied with Octa and died for it. Hasn't it occurred to you that you may very well do the same?"

Madoc only shook his head, though, and after a moment Isolde said, "What are you planning to do with me, then? Kill me to ensure my silence? Force me to marry you after all?"

Her voice was hard, though she was abruptly aware of how alone they were, here in the chapel, and of the strength of Madoc's powerfully muscled arms and hands.

But Madoc actually flinched at the suggestion and closed his eyes. "I deserved that, I suppose." He sat still, let out a breath, then at last looked up at her with exhausted, red-rimmed eyes. "No, Lady Isolde. I may be a traitor, but I've not fallen quite that far." He glanced down at the roll of parchment he still held in one hand, and his mouth tightened in another of those small, humorless smiles. "This makes matters easier, I must say."

Isolde made herself draw another slow breath. Time enough, later, to call herself every kind of name she could think of for having willingly signed Camelerd over to this man, effectively delivering her lands as a gift to Octa and Marche.

She made her voice sound calm. "What do you mean?"

Madoc rubbed his forehead. "I see no reason that you cannot remain here, where you are. I will post added guards, with orders to be sure you do not leave the abbey walls. And I will take your groom—Hereric, his name is?—with me, when I go."

Isolde couldn't stop the stomach-wrenching rush of fear that tightened her every nerve. "No! You can't take Hereric. He's a mute, simple-minded and crippled, besides. He can be no danger to—"

Madoc stopped her before she could finish. "He will be safe. I'll offer him work with my own horses. I could see he has a way with them."

Isolde clenched her hands to stop them shaking. Now, when

it could do no good whatever, she felt hot fury flooding her veins. "Give me your word," she said fiercely. She was hardly in a position to make demands, but she was too angry to care. "Your sworn oath, that if you take Hereric away from here you'll not hurt him."

Madoc looked at her in silence a long moment, a strange look in his dark eyes. "Would you believe my sworn oath?" he asked.

Isolde met his gaze steadily, searching his scarred face. And then finally, she nodded. "Yes," she said. "I would."

Something crossed Madoc's expression, stirred behind his eyes, and then was gone. He looked at her in silence a long moment, then in a swift movement drew the knife from his belt, kissed first the jeweled hilt and then the blade. "I swear to you, Lady Isolde, that so long as you stay within these walls I will do neither you nor your man Hereric any harm."

Isolde looked up at him. "You could still turn back. You could. It's not too late."

She thought something flickered just briefly at the back of Madoc's eyes, but he gave her a brief, bitter smile and said, "You're a healer, Lady Isolde. And a fine one. But has it not occurred to you that there is that in this world which cannot be healed?"

SHE CAME WALKING TOWARDS HIM ACROSS the grassy meadow. The breeze lifted the night-dark hair from her face, and she settled beside him as lightly as before.

He reached out a hand to her. He hadn't really expected to be able to touch her, but the same hollow disappointment filled his chest all the same when his fingers met with only empty air. She was looking at him the same way she'd looked in the forest, when she'd touched his face and said, *You're here. You're alive.* With a shining gladness in her gray eyes that felt like a punch in the gut.

He knew this time it was only a dream. And yet Trystan still threw an arm up over his eyes to keep from having to meet her gaze.

I should have made you hate me.

She was quiet a moment, and then he heard her soft voice say, *Why, Trys?*

He couldn't stop himself. He looked up at her, his gaze dragged towards her face by some will far stronger than his own. She looked as she always did. Beautiful and delicate, like the princess in some harper's tale. Black hair. Milk-pale skin. Thick-lashed, widely spaced gray eyes.

Because I swore I'd keep you safe.

She sat still, watching him, and then she said, *You were going to tell me a story. About a boy who feared becoming the man his father was—wasn't that it? About what happened to you at the battle of Camlann.*

Her gray eyes held the look that said, You can tell me anything and it will be all right. Filled with such complete, utter understanding that dream or no, he felt his chest ache.

It was the kind of look she gave him in every impossible fantasy he'd ever had—the ones where he told her the truth, the whole story, and she didn't pull back in horror, didn't turn her back on him, fold her arms, or avoid meeting his gaze.

Even in a dream, though, he couldn't believe those fantasies more likely than the rain suddenly starting to fall upwards.

You asked me that question once before, remember? He laughed humorlessly. *I mean, the real you asked me. Not just like this, in a dream. And I said if you trusted me, not to ask me to give you an answer.*

She was still gazing at him with that look of utter understanding in her eyes. Gods, he wished he weren't always so aware that this was just a dream. He'd have given almost anything for just a few brief moments of believing this actually was real.

Why do you keep coming this way? He felt as though the words were torn from his throat. *I don't deserve to see you even like this.*

She lifted one slim hand to touch his brow, though still he felt nothing at all. Her voice was soft. *Why, Trys?*

Because protecting you doesn't mean just protecting you from Octa. It means protecting you from myself, as well. I know it. And yet I'd sell whatever's left of my soul to have you actually here tonight.

Her face was starting to shift and shimmer, a thickly blanketing darkness closing in that meant he would soon wake. But he heard her whisper amidst the swirling black, *Maybe I always am.*

BOOK II

Chapter 6

ISOLDE WOKE WITH A START and a gasp. She was in Mother
Berthildis's bedchamber, sitting by the abbess's bed. And though
she'd tried again and again over the last weeks to see something of
Trystan in the scrying waters, she'd been granted not even a flash
of a vision, not a hint of where he might be now. Only when she'd
dozed off by a sick woman's bedside had she dreamed of him.

At least, she thought the dream had been of Trystan. Her rec-
ollections were still clouded, hazy with sleep, but she remembered
battle images flashing before her like glass-edged shards. Screaming
horses and screaming men, mud and gore and flashing swords. And
amidst it all, a gnawing, stomach-churning sense of guilt. A feeling
that this slaughter, this bloodshed was her fault somehow.

And then the dream had shifted, changed to an almost equally
frightening one of trying again and again to reach Trystan. Of
knowing he was somewhere near, but on the other side of a high
wall, with a door whose key she couldn't find. Only at the very, very
end, just before waking, had she caught a glimpse of Trystan's face.

I'd sell whatever's left of my soul to have you actually here tonight,
he'd said. And his look had been unguarded, for once everything he
felt for her visible in his eyes.

Which was purely the wishful thinking of the dream. He almost
never let himself look at her that way in real life.

Isolde rubbed her eyes and shifted, trying to loosen the stiffness
in her neck. Three weeks. Three interminable, endless weeks had

dragged passed since Madoc had ridden out from the abbey and left her here, a prisoner in fact, if not precisely in name. He'd taken Hereric, as well.

Isolde had told Hereric nothing of the truth. Instead, summoning up every bit of self-control she could muster, she had smiled and told him not to worry over leaving her, she would be perfectly safe at the abbey; that going with Madoc was what Trystan would want him to do. And the Saxon man had been half anxious, half pleased that the High King needed and asked his assistance with the king's war mounts.

Which was all to the good. If she could do nothing to stop Madoc's imprisoning them both, she could at any rate spare Hereric the fear that was a constant fist about her heart.

The days since had been an excruciating mixture of tension and boredom, until two days ago, when Mother Berthildis had been found lying crumpled and insensible amidst the rushes on her floor. She had eventually regained consciousness and opened her eyes. But the left side of her wide, yellowed face was drooping and slack, her left eye wandered listlessly, and she could neither sit up nor even move the fingers on her left hand.

It was utterly unexpected, completely, cruelly unfair—and though she'd sat by the abbess's bedside almost continually since then, there was absolutely nothing Isolde could do that would mend whatever inner damage had been done.

Mother Berthildis had woken now, as well. Glancing over, Isolde found the older woman's one good eye fixed on her with a faint shadow of its usual sharpness. "Not going to get any better than this, am I?"

Her voice was a little slurred, and she looked far older than she had done only days before. Without her veil to cover her head, her scalp looked pink, wrinkled, and somehow pathetic, covered in scanty wisps of snow-white hair. Her squat, square-built body, too, seemed suddenly smaller, almost fragile.

Still, Isolde made herself hold the abbess's gaze without looking away. She never, ever stopped hating the feeling of being helpless in the face of illness or hurt, yet it still happened, and far more often than she liked. "I honestly don't know," she said. "I've not seen sickness like yours many times before. There's a chance, I think, that you may recover. Not fully—but enough that you'll be able to sit up and maybe even stand and walk with a crutch or cane. Or—"

Isolde stopped, hesitating. The hour was near midnight, the room in darkness save for a pair of candles on the small wooden side table. All about them the abbey was silent, utterly still, though before too long, Isolde knew, they would hear the chanting from the chapel of the night prayers.

The darkest watch of the night had always seemed to her the most honest, the time when all pretense, all artifice was stripped away and questions could be answered only with truth. And besides, Mother Berthildis was regarding her steadily, and Isolde knew the abbess wouldn't thank her for a half-truth or a comforting lie.

"Or you may get very much worse," she finished, still meeting Mother Berthildis's black gaze. "Though whether sooner or later, I'm afraid I can't say."

Mother Berthildis searched Isolde's face, then nodded, her breath escaping in little puffs through her drooping lips. "I see." One side of her mouth tightened, and she said in the same hoarse, slightly blurred tone, "So I may improve or I may spend the rest of my days lying here helpless and having to be tended like a newborn babe."

"I'm—"

The abbess cut Isolde off before she could finish, with a gesture of her good hand that, feeble as the motion was, managed to be imperious all the same. "No. Don't say you're sorry. It's no fault of yours, and pity's a thing I never could abide." Her voice was more vigorous than before, but the effort tired her. She exhaled heavily and her eyes drifted shut. "Though I confess this is not the way I'd have chosen to meet my Lord God and Christ. A drooling infant without even the use of her arms and legs."

Isolde had no answer to that, so she said, instead, "You have many here who will gladly be your legs and arms for you as long as you need."

Mother Berthildis's face relaxed and she gave a small smile. "Thank you, child. And such things are sent to try us and keep us humble. There is wisdom in this, as in all."

The abbess spoke the words with a small, distant sadness in her eyes—but with such utter, absolute assurance that Isolde felt a pang of something that was almost envy.

Mother Berthildis's eyes had drifted closed once again, and for a moment Isolde thought she'd fallen asleep. But then the abbess's shriveled lids flickered and opened, her one good eye suddenly sharp and concerned. "And you—are you well? You look pale. There's nothing amiss with the babe, is there?"

Isolde shook her head. "No, nothing like that."

It made it easier, when she was lying on her narrow bed at night, trying to block out the memory of that last look Trystan had given her, to be able to lay her hand over her now slightly rounded abdomen and say to that small companion, *You must be very strong. Very determined to be born.*

It was a help, as well, during the countless hours she had spent over the last weeks staring at the blank walls of her own room and wondering what, if anything, she was to do now.

Madoc had betrayed Britain. Unless the rest of the council could be warned, Britain's forces would be crushed. And yet . . .

There was Marche, who had offered a price in gold for her capture. Whose men had tried at least once to drag her off. Tried and nearly succeeded, but for Trystan.

And always, at this point in her inner debate, Isolde's thoughts would turn to the helpless life she carried, the life she would risk if she left the abbey and laid herself open to another attack.

Though if Britain lost this war, if her defenses fell, the chaos and destruction would be no place into which she'd wish to bring a child.

She smoothed the coverlet over Mother Berthildis's wasted frame. "Don't trouble yourself. I promise you, I'm quite well."

She thought there was a look of disbelief in Mother Berthildis's keen black eyes. Hardly surprising. Sick or well, the abbess still could penetrate a lie with a single glance. But before the older woman could argue, the door of the chamber opened quickly, hitting the wall behind them with a bang.

Isolde looked round to see Sister Magdalen—Isolde thought that was her name—standing at the threshold, her features tight, and her hands clasped and twisting together at her waist.

"I'm sorry," she said. "I know Mother Berthildis is in no way to be disturbed." Sister Magdalen's gaze fell on the bed, and Isolde saw her flinch, even in the midst of whatever was troubling her, at sight of Mother Berthildis's half-slack face.

Isolde knew that Mother Berthildis, too, had seen, but she said only, "And I know that you would not have come here without good cause. What has happened?"

Sister Magdalen's glance flicked from Mother Berthildis to Isolde and back again, and then she swallowed, visibly. "Men—two men have arrived at the main gate, demanding that Lady Isolde come with them."

Isolde felt her heart seize hard, jerking against her ribs even as her every muscle froze. She'd succeeded—almost—in suppressing the recollection of the vision she'd seen weeks before. But now it flashed instantly across her mind: a man, as yet unknown, coming to tell her that Trystan had been wounded—fatally so.

Isolde willed the darkening at the edges of her vision to clear. Trystan couldn't be dead. She would have known. She would have felt it, felt something, if he were.

Still, she had to swallow twice before she could make her voice work. "Who are these men?" she asked. "Did they say what their business is with me?"

"They claim to be king Dywel of Logres's men." Sister Magdalen was a small, plump woman with pale hazel eyes, and she now turned a wide, frightened gaze to Isolde's face. "And they carry the seal of the High King Madoc. They say that King Madoc has determined you are no longer safe here, and has ordered you removed to a place of greater security."

Isolde saw Mother Berthildis turn her head on the pillow. She was plainly hoarding her strength, for she didn't speak, but the question in the abbess's black gaze was plain: *Do you believe it?*

Slowly, willing herself to think clearly and be calm, Isolde said, "I think they're lying. They must be. Madoc would have sent his own men."

He'd never have risked trusting Dywel's men to act as her escort, not when it would give her the chance of revealing his alliance with Octa of Kent.

"And I doubt that these men are from King Dywel, either—what reason has he to wish me taken from here? But it's a safe pretense, probably the safest they could make. Because the abbey is guarded by Madoc's soldiers and Cerdic's men. None of them would know all Dywel's warriors by sight. None of them would know or even suspect that these men are not what they claim to be."

And she could appeal to none of them, either. Count on none of them for aid. Maybe if she could have spoken to Cerdic's guardsmen alone. But she knew the five men Madoc had posted here as her guards would never allow that. She didn't know what orders Madoc had given his men—whether they even knew the reason for their sudden change of duty. None of the five had ever spoken to her. But wherever she went about the abbey, one or more of them was there, watching, following a few paces behind. She knew absolutely that when she stepped outside Mother Berthildis's room, she would find at least one of Madoc's warriors waiting for her in the courtyard outside.

Mother Berthildis had been watching her keenly, and now gave a feeble nod of her head. "Very well." She spoke as though a decision had been reached, and she turned to Sister Magdalen. "Go now, and fetch a novice's robe for Lady Isolde. Quickly. And then show these men asking for her in to me here." The right side of her mouth tightened in a small, grim smile. "If they're like most of their sex, setting foot in an old woman's sickroom will make them unable to think of anything but getting far, far away as quickly as may be."

Sister Magdalen hesitated and seemed about to speak, but at Mother Berthildis's unwavering look from her pillows, she bowed her head instead and turned for the door. It fell closed behind her, and Isolde and Mother Berthildis were once more alone.

Isolde looked at the fragile old woman's body lying motionless beneath the blankets, at the yellow, crumpled face and drooping left eye. "I can't let you—" she began.

But the abbess cut her short with a flutter of her good hand. Her hands, too, seemed suddenly more fragile, but the authority with which she spoke was unchanged. "I can't see that you've any choice in the matter," she said. "You may not have wished to involve the abbey in whatever coil you are caught up in, but it appears we are about to become involved all the same. Wait here until Sister Magdalen returns, then dress in the robe she brings. If we're to hide you, it had best be in plain sight. Few men have the wit, either, to look beyond the nun's robe and veil to the woman who wears them. You will be dressed as a novice. And these men will be told that the Lady Isolde was called out yesterday evening to attend a difficult birth of one of the women in the crofters' cottages nearby."

"The guards posted at the gate will know that's not true."

Mother Berthildis shrugged with one shoulder. "Perhaps. But guards have been known to be mistaken—or fall asleep at the watch. And it will be my word against theirs."

Isolde watched the abbess a moment in silence, then said, "They may find me, even so."

"I know." Mother Berthildis's voice sounded tired, but the steadiness of her black gaze didn't falter or even change. "You said a few moments ago, Lady Isolde, that you were willing to serve as my arms and legs while the strength of my own had failed." She paused for another breath, smiled a bit grimly again, then said, eyes still black on Isolde's, "If I were not trapped helpless in bed here, I would be in the chapel, praying as I had never prayed before."

"AND YOU'RE SURE IT WAS HERERIC?" Trystan asked.

Daka just looked at him for answer. Right. Stupid question. Trystan rubbed the space between his eyes. Huge, one-armed Saxon man built like an oak tree. Not easy to mistake.

"Hereric ride away five mornings ago," Daka said. "Then tonight two men ride up to the abbey gates. We come find you. Lucky you already heading back this way."

They were camped in a thick grove of pine trees near the place where they'd parted seven days before. When Trystan and Cath had gone to keep the meeting with Garbhán, Piye and Daka to keep watch on the abbey, Eurig and Fidach had stayed here. They hadn't risked even a fire in a pit tonight, and with the shadows cast by the thickly needled branches above, Daka was little more than a disembodied voice.

The back of Trystan's neck pricked disagreeably at Daka's words. "The two men who arrived tonight—what direction did they come from?"

He felt rather than saw Daka's shrug. "Look like north. Mean little, though."

"Armed?"

He sensed Daka's nod. "Spears. Shields. Probably axes, too, but we not able to tell. We have to be staying far enough away that they won't see."

Trystan nodded. He was supposed to be on his way back to Octa.

And this could well have nothing to do with Isolde. But that didn't stop an unpleasant, prickling sense of danger.

He hadn't lived this long without learning to trust that instinct.

Trystan said, "We go in."

ISOLDE SAT IN THE COOL, MUSKY scented chapel where she had sat with Madoc five days before. The thick white candles on the altar were lighted at even this hour of the night; their flames cast a flickering yellow glow that didn't quite reach to the shadowed corner where she sat on one of the hard wooden benches.

She wore the robe and veil that Sister Magdalen had brought her, and with luck, anyone looking into the chapel would see only one of the nuns keeping midnight vigil at her prayers. But Isolde had chosen a place in the darkest part of the vaulted chamber, all the same.

She had caught just a glimpse of the men who'd come for her as she and Sister Magdalen crossed the courtyard to come here. Big men, both, one with a head of thickly curling black hair and a beard, one with lighter coloring and a drooping mustache. Isolde hadn't recognized either, but it made little difference. They might well be Marche's men all the same.

She'd seen one of them, the black-haired man, roughly kick over a basket of plums from the orchards that had been stacked and ready to be carried to the abbey kitchens, and say something angry to the sister who was escorting him. And she'd had to clench her hands and force herself to hurry after Sister Magdalen, towards the safety of the chapel, without looking back.

The men, whoever they were, would surely begin their search in the infirmary. And even the thought of the harm and the hurt they could do the wounded men there was making Isolde's stomach churn and her fingers clench. Her nerves felt stretched tight and quivering with the urge to run there herself. But that would be to stupidly throw away whatever small chance of escape Mother Berthildis and the other abbey sisters were granting her.

Isolde closed her eyes briefly, trying to let something of the chapel's living stillness soak into her. She'd never sat like this, alone with the candles and cross on the high altar. But she could feel . . . something. If not quite a presence, at least a sense of peace. As though the prayers and chanted worship of the abbey sisters had soaked into the walls so that they now hummed like a harp's plucked string.

Isolde drew a steadying breath, then looked into the shallow basin she'd asked Sister Magdalen to bring. The sister had given her a quick, curious look at the request, but had brought both basin and water without question or argument.

Months before, whatever caprices governed the Sight had granted her visions of Marche; had let her slip the bounds of her own senses, hear Marche's thoughts, see through Marche's eyes.

For three months, now, the visions hadn't come. But now, in the flickering half-light and musky, incense-rich stillness, Isolde stared at the water's surface, let her breathing steady and slow. Let her mind float upwards, into the raftered shadows of the chapel's roof beams above. She could feel the pulse of the Sight like a second pulse of blood through her veins, surrounding her, then reaching out like tendrils of mist into the night beyond the chapel walls.

Nothing appeared on the water's surface, though. Even when Isolde deliberately conjured a memory of Marche's heavy, brutal features, black hair, and pouchy black eyes.

Finally, she let out her breath and sat back, staring up at the altar with its soft halo of candle flame. Maybe the visions wouldn't come in a chapel of the Christ. Or maybe the scrying waters refused to grant her a glimpse of Marche because she was, in her heart, so thankful to have those flashes gone, that particular window of the Sight closed.

Mother Berthildis had said to her three months ago that the visions of Marche were a gift from God, sent that she might forgive herself for that one night's marriage to him. And she had—at least, the poison of the memory was now gone.

But then the abbess had also said that she would have to forgive King Marche.

Isolde leaned back against the hard wooden bench and thought of Mother Berthildis lying in bed with half her body made useless and her strength all but gone, and saying *There is a wisdom in this, as in all things.* Telling her that the future was always perfect, with faith.

For a moment, Isolde wondered whether the abbess's faith would be as perfect, as solid and secure, if she'd lived her life in the world, instead of shut away in a small island of peace devoted to her God.

And yet she did envy that faith, in a way, because she could see that it made Mother Berthildis face even her own illness and possible death without fear, and Isolde would have been desperately glad of some of that fearlessness just now.

Her eyes were starting to ache with weariness, and she raised a hand and rubbed her lids. Then froze as an image of her grandmother's face appeared against the black. Almost as unlikely an answer to prayer in a Christian church as an image of Marche would have been. But just then Isolde was thankful for any answer at all.

And stone-walled domain of the Christ or no, there was something about the fragrant, vaulted peace of the chapel that did make it easier to believe in an Otherworld beyond the veil. Where Morgan might now walk on an endless curve of time, and so—perhaps— it didn't matter that the Romans and Christians had driven the Old magic of Britain from the land.

Her grandmother looked as she always did when Isolde saw her this way: black hair streaked with gray, pale, delicately sculptured face lined with age but beautiful still. Fiercely proud. A woman who throughout her life did her weeping in private and carried her burdens alone.

She stood very still and looked back at Isolde with exactly the same clear-sighted, penetratingly direct gaze she'd always possessed in life. *Well? Are you going to stay cowering here, living your mother's story all over again?*

Isolde sat up. She supposed it was true, in a way. She'd been left without a husband, with a duty to protect the land that was hers by right of birth, and carrying a child that, in the eyes of the king's council, should never have been made. Like Gwynefar.

Part of her wanted to simply sit here in the chapel's cool stillness as long as she could. Until the men searching for her either gave up and left or discovered her and dragged her out of this small place of sanctuary like a rabbit from its den. In a way, she would be glad to have the choice taken out of her hands.

But she shook her head. *No. I'd have to be dead before I stop fighting to protect my baby. Or the land. Even if I don't blame my mother for her choice.*

The likeness of Morgan nodded and said, with an odd gentleness in her voice, *I was wrong to blame her myself. Gwynefar did the best she could with the lot fate dealt her in life. So must we all.*

Isolde rubbed her aching eyes again. The Morgan she'd known had loved her, she knew, and had been capable of her own kind of fierce tenderness. But certainly she'd never heard her admit to being mistaken. The imagined Morgan's lips curved in a small, wry smile. *Eventually, even I can learn something new.*

Isolde's own brief smile faded. *What am I going to do?*

Real or no, Isolde felt a cold hand touch her heart at the wordless, unflinching answer she could read in her grandmother's eyes.

I'm still afraid I'm going to fail.

Isolde could almost imagine she heard the word *Courage* breathed into the incense-scented air. And then, more sharply, *Afraid or not, I didn't raise you to be a coward.*

Isolde half smiled despite herself. *All right, maybe it is actually you after all.*

Even before the words had formed in her mind, though, her grandmother was gone, vanished in a flash of vision that fell like a sword stroke and blotted out the chapel, the altar and candles, the rows of wooden benches and all.

In their place, Isolde saw a boy's face. A handsome boy, with gold-brown hair and startlingly blue eyes. She thought for an instant it was Trystan, as he'd been at eight or nine. But then she saw that this boy's brows were rounded, not slightly tilted as Trystan's were, and that he was grinning, a joyful, unguarded grin, as Trystan surely never had.

Then the vision was gone, and Isolde struggled to draw breath, tried to slow the hard drumming of her heart. She closed her eyes. *Was that vision true? The baby's a boy? A son?*

But seemingly she'd been granted all the answers she was going to get tonight. Nothing stirred in the chapel save the soft sighing of the night breeze in the eaves. Morgan seemed well and truly gone.

Still, she sat without moving, without even breathing, and tried to fix every detail of the vision in her mind. Let herself imagine, for one heart-stopping, achingly sweet moment, a day when she'd hold her baby in her arms, see him look up at her with his father's blue eyes.

Then, finally, she let out her breath and looked up at the altar again. She was supposed to be praying. That was what Mother Berthildis had all but commanded her to do. But as she gazed towards the flickering candles, she seemed instead to see Trystan, looking at her a long moment and then vanishing amidst the trees. Hear a voice that was both a stranger's and her own saying that Trystan had died of a fatal wound.

She wondered whether Mother Berthildis would call that vision, too, a gift from God. Whether if she had some of the abbess's perfect faith, she could make sense of a Power that bestowed both that cruel flash and a vision of the child in her womb. That granted her glimpses of Trystan in the scrying waters, but denied her the power to find King Cerdic's son.

Isolde shut her eyes. Tried again to imagine herself slipping free of the abbey walls, flying eagle-swift towards wherever Trystan was tonight. And the words that formed of their own accord in her mind were less a prayer than a reaching out into the night darkness all around.

I need you. Where are you?

TRYSTAN STUDIED THE ABBEY GATES, PUSHING back the anticipation of seeing Isolde again. Not that it helped much; it was drumming in his head like the ache of a bruise.

There were lights dancing inside the abbey walls where no lights should be at this hour of the night. Piye and Dake were right. Something— And then he swore violently under his breath and looked up as realization struck. "We're known there." He turned to where Daka and Piye stood behind him, hands on the hilts of their swords. "The three of us, and Eurig, as well."

Set foot inside the abbey walls and unless they were lucky to the point of a miracle, someone would recognize them. And he'd learned a long time ago that the one certain thing about luck was that it would run against you if you were fool enough to base a plan around its being on your side.

"So what are we going to do?"

That was Cath's voice. Cath, the only one of them who had never been near the abbey, who could be recognized by no one there.

Trystan turned to where Cath's bulk was a looming shape in the dark. "How convincing a beggar in search of alms do you think you can make?"

ISOLDE SAT WATCHING THE ENORMOUS STRANGER opposite her. He was a giant of a man, with legs like tree trunks and a chest like an ox; the callused hands resting on his knees were double and more the size of Isolde's. He had long black hair that he wore loose, falling straight to his shoulders, and a black beard that gave him the look of a forest wildman. Above the beard, his face was weathered, though Isolde judged his age at not more than thirty or thirty-five, and set with small and very bright blue eyes under bushy black brows.

Cath, he'd said his name was. And that he came from Trystan.

According to Sister Olwen, he'd come to the infirmary begging treatment for a pain in his gut. How he'd talked his way from there into Mother Berthildis's sickroom, and from the abbess to this meeting, Isolde had no idea. But apparently he had managed to persuade both Sister Olwen and the abbess of his good intent. Because Isolde was sitting with him in Sister Olwen's sleeping cell, herself on the hard wooden sleeping bench, the man called Cath dwarfing the room's single wooden chair.

It was early morning; all about them the abbey was stirring to life, the sisters passing to and fro in the courtyard on their way to the day's work in the gardens and workrooms. Sitting in the darkest corner of the chapel the night before, Isolde hadn't meant to sleep. But she'd been too exhausted to keep her eyes open. She'd woken at dawn, her every muscle stiff from a night on the bare wooden bench, to find Sister Olwen standing beside her.

Sister Olwen had had a bruise on her cheekbone that had made Isolde feel dizzy and sick all over again. But when Isolde had asked her about it, the older woman had said only, her mouth hardening into a grim line, "The men wished to search the infirmary and disturb the wounded men. They did not, however, succeed in what they'd planned."

If Sister Olwen's resentment of Isolde had gone, she was still a force to be reckoned with, and Isolde had been grateful beyond words that the wounded men were now in her care. Sister Olwen had gone on to say that the two strangers had been given the story that Lady Isolde was outside the abbey walls, attending a difficult birth, and apparently they had accepted it, if grudgingly.

Though even now they were waiting in the abbey courtyard for Isolde's return.

Isolde dragged her attention back to the man before her. Cath was speaking, finishing telling Isolde of his predawn encounter with Mother Berthildis. He had a deep, gravelly voice that, quietly as he was speaking, still echoed in the tiny room.

"So the holy mother looked up at me and said I just might be an answer to prayer. And I said I was much obliged, though I'd tell her straight out, that was something I'd never been called before." His eyes crinkled and, teeth flashed white in the black beard. "And here I am."

Isolde studied his broad-featured, weathered face. Something about the big man made her instinctively trust him—and like him, as well. But she couldn't stop herself from asking, "You've just come from seeing Trystan? He's safe?"

"Oh, aye. Parted from him—him and Piye and Daka, as well—not two hours ago. He's safe." Cath's grinned again, this time slightly wryly. "Or as safe as he ever is, considering he's reckless as the devil himself when it comes to risking his own neck in a fight."

Isolde smiled just a bit. "You really do know Trystan."

"That's convinced you, has it?" Cath gave her an answering smile. "Ah, well. Least he's a bit choosier about risks to his friends' necks, eh?"

"But you're here."

Cath waved one meaty hand. "No danger about that. Or next to none. If I can't keep myself out of trouble here, I deserve what's coming to me." He paused, planting his hands once more squarely on his knees. "Now, what I need from you, Lady Isolde, is just to tell me everything that's been going on. Quickly as you can."

Isolde made up her mind. She drew in her breath, and, as quickly and clearly as she could, told Cath everything. She began with the king's council meeting, and Cerdic's revealing that Marche had offered a reward for her capture. And then she told him of Madoc's betrayal of Britain and the High Kingship, of his making her captive here, and then at last of the arrival of the armed men the night before.

When she'd finished, Cath sat in silence, rubbing his nose with the back of his thumb, brows drawn. "The High King's turned traitor? That's bad, that is."

Watching him, Isolde wondered what possible connection this huge, genial stranger had to Trystan. "You could say so."

Cath looked up at that, beard splitting in another quick show of teeth. "Aye, bit of an understatement, like. I know. But what I meant to say was that there's not much you or me can do about the High King's choices just now. What we've got to do now is to figure a way of getting you out of here safe. Because I'd say you're dead right. If those men out there"—he nodded towards the door—"are actually who they claim, I'm a Gaulish dancing girl."

Cath rubbed his nose again. "Trouble is, we can't exactly just walk out through the gates, not with all those guards posted." He touched the carved bone hilt of a knife in his boot top. "Got this, but no other weapons on me. Wouldn't exactly have done for a poor beggar like myself to come strolling in with a sword what costs enough to feed a family for a year, you understand. Not but what I couldn't do a fair bit of damage with the knife and my bare hands—but I'd as soon avoid trouble till we don't have a choice." He paused, frowning slightly. "There may be only two of these men asking for you inside the abbey, but that's not to say they don't have a dozen and more of their nearest and dearest friends camped in the trees and watching all that goes on, if you see what I mean. And we could try sneaking out, the two of us. But I'd as soon not bring a pack of trouble down on the good sisters here, either. Which we would, if you suddenly disappear."

Isolde made herself sit quietly, without shivering. She was still stiff from sleeping in the chapel, and the crumpled novice's robe she wore was rough and itchy against her skin. She said, "You're right. I agree. Just tell me what you need me to do."

Cath frowned a moment. Then: "Look, if I ask you to wait an hour after I leave here, then go to these men and agree to go with them, do you think you can do it? And make them believe you've no suspicions at all that they're not just what they want you to think?"

Isolde didn't let herself hesitate. "Yes."

Cath's frown relaxed slightly. "Good. That's what I want you to do, then. Wait an hour, get whatever you want to take with you packed and ready to go. Then tell these men you're ready for them to take you wherever it is the High King Madoc has in mind."

"And you—"

"We'll get you away from them. As soon as you're well outside the abbey gates." Cath's bright blue gaze was abruptly serious as he looked into her face, all teasing and laughter gone. "You can trust us, lady."

Isolde nodded. "I do."

Cath let out a gusty breath and braced his hands on his knees, preparing to rise, and as quickly as it had come, the grave, serious look was gone. "Well, that's all right then." He flashed her another grin. "Or right as anything that's not me sitting with my boots off and a full cup of ale in my hand can be."

He got to his feet and gave a light rap on the door, which opened to reveal Sister Olwen's broad, black-robed form in the passage outside. Even Sister Olwen looked slight and small compared to Cath. Cath made her a bow that brought his shaggy head nearly on a level with hers. "Be taking my leave, now, Sister. Many thanks for the draft you fixed me to settle my stomach." He clapped a hand to his belly and gave Sister Olwen a broad wink. "Made a new man of me, it has."

If Sister Olwen had softened towards Isolde, she was usually no less acerbic with everyone else. Now, though, to Isolde's amazement, the grim line of the nun's mouth relaxed in a small, wry smile. "I'm delighted I could be of help."

Cath paused in the doorway and scratched his beard. "Ah, well, now. There's another way you could help me if you would, come to think of it. These men—the ones asking for Lady Isolde. Happen they should come back here tomorrow, maybe, or the next day, asking questions, like, about any other strangers you might have seen about . . ." Cath cocked one bushy dark brow. "I understand the church takes lying for a sin, Sister, but . . ."

Sister Olwen watched him intently a moment, glanced at Isolde, then nodded her head. "Lying is a sin, that's true. But then, I've been having more and more trouble lately remembering faces." Sister Olwen pursed her mouth regretfully. "Old age, you know." She paused, meeting Cath's eyes directly. "I've no doubt I'll have forgotten yours the moment you walk out of here."

Chapter 7

"Satan's hairy black arse." Cath coughed. "You smell like a brew house." They were alone; Eurig had remained behind at their camp to guard Fidach, and Piye and Daka were already in position.

"I know. I haven't actually drunk a single swallow and I still may never be able to look at ale again." Trystan finished soaking his leather jerkin, then tossed the empty aleskin into the bushes.

"So the Lady Isolde's already threatened by Madoc and Marche. You going to tell her Octa wants her dead, as well?"

Trystan's head snapped round. "No. And I want your word that you'll not tell her anything, either."

Cath looked surprised by the sudden vehemence in his tone. "But if—"

"No buts." He knew Isolde. There wasn't a chance in hell she'd stand by and let him risk himself for her this way if she knew the whole. "I'll talk to the others later, but I want your sworn blood oath that you'll not breath a word of what passed between me and Octa. Not to Isolde—not to anyone."

Cath was frowning, but he nodded slowly, drew the knife from his belt, and pressed his first two fingers firmly over the blade. A bright bead of blood sprang up and he made the mark of binding over his heart and mouth. "If that's what you want."

Trystan let out a breath and nodded brief acknowledgment before turning to scan the trees for any sign that the men they were watching for approached. When he turned back, Cath's eyes were still on him, and Trystan cocked an eyebrow at the other man in silent question.

Cath held up both hands, eyes flaring in exaggerated innocence. "What? Did I so much as breathe the word *pig-swiving disaster* aloud?"

"That's three words." Trystan's brief smile faded and he let out his breath. "Look—"

But Cath stopped him, abruptly sober, as well. "You don't have to say anything more. Something goes wrong, something happens to you, and we get the Lady Isolde out of there. You don't care if we're crawling on our bellies with both arms hacked off, we see she's safe before we roll over and die. I know."

Trystan had already locked away all thoughts of what could go wrong. Of what would happen if Isolde was trapped in the midst of a fight. Or if—Christ's blood—they were too late. If the goat bastards had already hurt her.

He couldn't afford to so much as think of that now, so he only nodded.

Cath wasn't finished, though. He was frowning, eyes were still grave, and he shifted his grip on his own sword, running a finger lightly down the polished blade. "See, now," he said. "A band of men like us, we fight for pay, not for the honor of any lord. But we both know that once that battle starts it's not about the reward. Battle starts and you're fighting for the man on your right and the man on your left and the one guarding your back. And you've been all three to me often enough that you know you can count on me not to fail you now."

"I do know." Trystan tipped his head in brief acknowledgment, then met Cath's eyes. "And thanks."

Cath nodded again, then blew out a gusty breath, the moment of seriousness gone. "What I was going to say was, just don't take any bigger risks than you can help, right?" He bared his teeth in a ferocious grin. "You get us all killed today and I swear to God I'll follow you to hell and drag you back so I can kill you again."

.   .   .   .

ISOLDE KEPT HER EYES FIXED STRAIGHT ahead, at the screen of trees ahead. They were passing through a thickly wooded area. The ground was patched with dappled pools of golden afternoon sunlight and the air held the sweet, slightly musty smell of the carpet of decaying leaves underfoot.

She was riding the small gray donkey that her two escorts had brought for her, a hideously uncomfortable, swaybacked animal that plodded dispiritedly along and kept trying to bite the hands of the man who had hold of the rope bridle. Isolde's escorts were on foot, one man leading the donkey, the other following a few paces behind.

And both of them looking at her in a way that made Isolde wish she had a traveling cloak to pull close about her, despite the heat of the morning sun on her head and neck. Though she supposed she should be thankful that they'd neither touched her nor even spoken to her since they'd left the abbey, save to tell her that their names were Derog and Glaw, and to grunt, when she'd asked where they were taking her, "To King Madoc's camp. Not far."

At least she had Cabal with her. Isolde glanced down at the big dog, padding along beside the donkey. She'd flatly refused to leave without him, and had collected him from the stables before she agreed to accompany the two men.

Now Cabal was shooting her quick, anxious glances and whining from time to time. He trusted their two escorts no more than did Isolde.

The donkey's saddlebags held her two changes of clothing and her medicine scrip. Sister Olwen had helped her pack up as many of the salves and prepared herbs as could be spared from the abbey stores, and promised Isolde that she would care for Mother Berthildis and the other wounded men. Then the older woman had hugged Isolde tightly, which Isolde thought had likely surprised Sister Olwen even more than it had surprised her.

"My prayers go with you," Sister Olwen had said. "And take care."

The man in the lead—Derog, the big one with the head of curling dark hair—was watching her again. His face was scarred by the marks of a lifetime of battles, and he had a thin mouth, with something cold and flat about the stare of his dark eyes.

Isolde suppressed a shiver. The forest seemed unnaturally quiet, without even a trill of birdsong to break the stillness. The only sounds were the rustle of leaves beneath their feet and the drum of blood in Isolde's own ears.

Isolde's skin felt clammy, and her heart was racing, every nerve was stretched taut with waiting for Cath and the others to make their move. *You can trust us, lady,* Cath had said. And she did. They would intercept Derog and Glaw. It was only a matter of waiting, of time.

But even still, when Trystan stepped abruptly out from behind a clump of oak trees on the path ahead, her heart stumbled and her chest squeezed as though a giant hand had wrapped around her, driving the air from her lungs.

"Stop!" Trystan had drawn a knife from his belt, and he held it aimed at Derog, in the lead. "Don't anyone move!"

Derog and Glaw were no less taken aback. Derog pulled up abruptly, hauling on the donkey's lead rope. "Who in hell are you?"

Isolde was struck by a dizzying sense of unreality. Hours ago, she'd been sitting at Mother Berthildis's bedside, feeding the stricken woman broth with a spoon. Now she was in the midst of a forest, watching Trystan confront the two men who'd come to abduct her for a reason she still didn't know.

And she felt, just for a moment, as though it couldn't be real—as though she were again watching a far-off scene played out in the waters of a scrying bowl.

Trystan wore a leather jerkin over breeches, and his arms were bare, the muscles of his shoulders and swordsman's wrists and hands plain in the slanting afternoon sun. "Doesn't matter who I am. All you need to know is that I'm taking the girl."

Trystan's voice sounded deeper and strange, but it was a moment before Isolde realized he was speaking with a thick Saxon accent, as though British were clearly not his native tongue.

Glaw had come up from behind to stand at Derog's shoulder, and Isolde saw the two men exchange an incredulous look. "You and what army?" Derog drew his own blade. "The girl's ours."

Trystan laughed. "What, do you have some kind of written charter saying you're the only ones with the right to abduct her? I don't think so."

Trystan took a step forward, and Isolde's heart stumbled again, because he was weaving slightly, lurching and unsteady on his feet as though he were ill or injured. Then she caught, even from a distance, the reek of ale.

Trystan took another lurching step forward, blinking as though he were trying to focus his vision on Derog and Glaw. "Just two of you, am I right? Or is it four?" He shook his head. "Well, doesn't matter. Just hand her over and no one gets hurt."

As Derog and Glaw exchanged another bemused glance, Trystan's eyes flashed just for an instant to Isolde's, their intensely blue gaze keen and utterly focused, so that Isolde knew—not that she'd ever truly doubted it before—that the drunkenness was just an act.

"Not likely." That was Derog, sounding less angry than contemptuously amused. Derisive laughter edged in his tone, his mouth—what Isolde could see of it—curving in a tight, scornful smile. "Look, friend, if anyone gets hurt here, it will be you. Just clear out and go sleep it off under a bush, all right?"

Isolde's heart was pounding hard enough to make her vision blur. But, mindful of the two men standing within arm's reach of her, on either side of the donkey's head, she started to ease her way back along the blankets that formed the makeshift saddle. Slowly . . . slowly . . . bit by bit, readying herself to jump backwards off the animal's back.

She kept her eyes locked on Trystan's lean face. He had a smear of ash across one cheek and his jaw was stubbled by several days' growth of beard.

"Clear out?" Trystan took another staggering step towards Derog and Glaw.

It was a good act, too; his eyes blazed with the sudden, instantly kindled outrage of the profoundly drunk. But for that quick, clear-eyed look Isolde would almost have believed it herself. "Clear out? You know what my job's been this last year? Digging privy pits for Octa's guards and then shoveling the dirt over them when they're full. Ever since I burned down his private storehouse of beer and ale. Was it my fault I tripped and dropped the torch just as I was getting another barrel for the evening's meal in the fire hall?" he demanded in an aggrieved tone. "You'd think Octa would see that I was lucky to get out alive before the whole roof fell in. But no."

He blinked again and wavered unsteadily on his feet. "Any rate, if you think I'm going to go back without the Lady Isolde—give Octa reason to set me digging latrine pits for another ten years more—I'll tell you right now you're wrong."

As Trystan spoke, he'd been moving forward, closing the distance between him and the other two men. Still completely unsure what to make of him, Derog and Glaw had seemed hardly to notice. Until . . .

Isolde saw the moment when Derog, at least, realized that Trystan was now barely an arm's length away. His muscles jerked to attention and he gave a startled shout, raising the fist that held his knife. But the realization of danger had come too late.

In a movement so swift Isolde scarcely saw it, Trystan's hand shot out; the blade of his own knife flashed and landed with a dull, meaty thud in Derog's chest. Derog jerked, staggered, then dropped to the ground, and in the same moment Glaw charged at Trystan with a bellow of rage, spear upraised.

Trystan was without a weapon. But he raised his shield, blocking Glaw's blow with the spear and thrusting so hard that Glaw staggered back, momentarily off balance. And then, in one fluid, lightning-quick movement, Trystan bent his head and spun to the side, ducking under Glaw's guard and seizing back his knife.

Glaw should have charged, but instead he cast a glance back over his shoulder at her. Isolde could almost see the quick debate take place behind his eyes. Grab her, hold a knife at her throat, and he stood a chance of ending this fight. Trystan moved forward with another quick, slashing blow that Glaw only just blocked in time, and it dragged his attention away from Isolde.

For now.

Glaw shouted again and charged at Trystan, and it took every last vestige of Isolde's will to pull her eyes away, to turn so that she could jump from the donkey's back to the ground. She had to trust Trystan to win in a fight with Glaw.

He'd just given up the advantage the act of drunkenness had gained. It had gotten him close enough to attack, had made his opponents dismiss him as a threat. But Glaw was a fool if he didn't realize by now that Trystan was as sober as he himself was.

And Trystan had done it because he'd wanted her out of danger. She had to move, or he'd be distracted by waiting to be sure she was safe.

As soon as her feet touched the ground, Cabal was beside her, butting his head against her side, whining high in his throat. Isolde pulled him close, holding the leather thong of his collar, keeping him from charging towards Trystan and Glaw. Cabal might be trained as a war hound, but she absolutely couldn't risk anything that would divert Trystan's attention from the fight.

The two men were locked in a savage struggle, circling each other as they wove back and forth, each seeking an opening in the other's defenses. Trystan must have deflected Glaw's second strike with the spear, because the weapon now lay useless on the ground. He held the bloodied knife poised before him, ready to parry the strikes of the knife Glaw had now drawn.

The breath scraped in Isolde's throat and every beat of her heart seemed to last an eternity, but it couldn't have been more than a few moments before strong hands seized her from behind. Isolde's heart lurched sickeningly again before she recognized Cath, lifting her up and moving her aside.

He gave her a grin and a quick nod. "Told you to trust us, didn't I?" And then he stepped past her on the narrow wooded path, towards the fight, sword already drawn. At the same moment, Isolde saw two men with coal-black skin and braided hair close in on Trystan and Glaw from either side. Daka and Piye.

Cath's bulk blocked her view of the fight, so that she heard only one of the men cry out. A harsh, pained cry as though at a mortal wound. The breath froze in Isolde's throat before her mind registered the certainty that the voice hadn't been Trystan's. Not Trystan's.

Cath moved forward and she saw that it was over. Trystan was standing, breathing hard. The man Glaw lay facedown on the ground in a pool of crimson. And one of the Nubian twins, she thought Piye, was wiping blood from the blade of his sword.

Cath had bent over Derog, still prone on the ground where he'd fallen under Trystan's strike with the knife.

"This one's still alive," Cath said.

Though not for long. Isolde saw the bubble of blood on Derog's lips, heard the sudden, almost deafening silence that had fallen on the forest, the harsh rattling gasp of Derog's breath. Trystan glanced from the dying man up to Cath, and he gave a short, wordless nod. And Cath seemed to understand, for he crouched beside Derog, turning the prostrate man's face to his.

Isolde heard Cath say, his gruff voice blunt, "You've not many breaths left to take. I can make them come easier and hurt less. And I will, if you tell me what I want to know."

All at once she couldn't listen to any more. Cath was right— Derog was dying, and there was nothing she or anyone else could do to help him. Her hand still clenched tight on Cabal's collar, she stepped back, back, until she almost tripped over a fallen log.

Derog must have agreed to talk, because Cath was putting pressure on the wound in his chest with one hand, while Piye and Daka between them lifted Derog's legs, propping his feet up on what looked like a couple of leather traveling packs. The three of them— Cath, Daka, and Piye—moved in swift concert, without needing to speak about what they did, as though they'd done this already many times before.

Which probably they had.

Isolde sank down on the dead log and hugged her knees, trying to stop shivering.

"Are you all right?" Trystan had been standing watching the other three men, but when Isolde opened her eyes she saw that he'd come to crouch down near her.

Isolde had another dizzying moment of unreality, of feeling as though she'd been plunged from sunlight into thick, swirling mist. All through the last long weeks since Trystan had left her, she'd been picturing this moment, the moment when she saw him again. Living it over and over again in her mind, as though the imagining were a talisman, a charm against fear and dark.

And now Trystan was here, before her, blue eyes concerned as he searched her face.

He hadn't touched her, though. This time he had himself under control. He stayed back, a careful three paces away from where she sat.

Isolde nodded, trying to keep her teeth from chattering. And then she caught sight of the sticky smear of scarlet on Trystan's upper arm. "You're bleeding."

Trystan glanced down as though surprised to see the blood. "This? It's nothing much. I'm fine."

Isolde had always believed that caring for the sick and the wounded taught patience like nothing else. She had nursed Cadfan through his broken leg back at the abbey—and cared for dozens more men like him, besides. Had nursed them for weeks and not lost her temper even once.

And all that hard-won experience was doing her absolutely no good whatsoever facing Trystan now as he stood, his face shuttered and controlled, bleeding from a wound in his arm that he'd never in a hundred years admit hurt or needed care.

"Fine meaning you don't have a gaping knife cut in your arm, or fine meaning you're not yet dead?" She blinked, but she couldn't stop angry tears from rising to her eyes.

Trystan's slanted brows drew together at her tone, but his gaze softened again as he looked at her. "Isa, I'm fine. It's going to hurt like a ring-tailed devil for a few days and then eventually it will stop. I'll live to tell the tale."

The concern in his blue eyes was harder to bear, in a way, than anger or indifference would have been. Isolde's heart twisted tight inside her and she said, unable to stop her voice from shaking, "You nearly didn't, though. You could have died today. Because of me."

Trystan's eyes were steady on hers. His gold-brown hair had come loose from the leather thong in the fight and he pushed a few strands back from his face, then reached out, as though about to touch her face. For a brief moment a tiny spark of hope flickered to life in Isolde's chest. But then Trystan checked the movement, clenching his hand into a fist as his arm fell back to his side. He said, quietly, "You know I would always die to protect you."

Isolde waited until her vision cleared—*Do* not *cry*—then said what she'd been thinking a few moments before; what she'd known from the moment she set eyes on Trystan's face. "But if it hadn't been a question of risking your life to protect me, you wouldn't be here, would you?" She had to swallow before going on. "If these men hadn't tried to abduct me, would I ever even have seen you again?"

Trystan had gone utterly motionless, his face so expressionless it was as though a curtain had been wrung down behind his eyes. Isolde felt as though they stood on opposite sides of a rocky, yawning chasm. Or, again, as though she were still watching him in the scrying waters, and any attempt to reach out and touch him would shatter the image, driving him even further away than before.

She didn't know whether he intended any answer, but in any case, there was no chance for either of them to say any more. The low murmur of Cath's voice as he spoke to Derog had stopped, and now Cath let Derog's head fall back onto the carpet of dead leaves and rose to his feet, crossing to where Trystan sat in a few brief strides. "He's dead. He says they were sent by Marche of Cornwall."

If Isolde had thought Trystan motionless a moment ago, it was nothing to the complete, utter stillness that came over him now. His muscles might have been turned to stone, and his face and eyes were absolutely, utterly blank. It was as though he'd taken an internal step backwards, somehow leaving his body behind.

And then, in barely more than a heartbeat, the moment passed and he was present again, focused and with his self-control still absolutely intact and whole. He turned to Cath. "And you think he told the truth?"

Cath's right hand was still stained with Derog's blood, and there was a smear of crimson on the knees of his breeches, too, where he'd knelt at Derog's side. But if anything of what just happened had shocked or troubled him, it didn't show in his face or his deeply set eyes. "I'd say so." He shrugged, hawked, and spat on the ground. "Vicious bastard, and not a thought in his head but for his not getting the reward he was promised after all, and for cursing us all for getting in his way. But I don't think he lied. Said orders were to bring the Lady Isolde in alive. Kill her only if she gave any trouble."

For a moment, Trystan's glance strayed to the two men who now lay dead on the ground a few paces away, Daka and Piye still standing like ebony sentinels on either side. Something hard crossed Trystan's lean face, but then he turned back to Cath. "Were they alone?"

Cath shrugged again. "Don't know. Died before I could get the chance to ask."

Trystan nodded. "Right. We'd better get away from here." He shaded his eyes with one hand and squinted up at the afternoon sun, setting the leaves above them ablaze as it sank lower in the western sky. "I don't think we'll make it back to Eurig and Fidach before nightfall. But we can make a start."

TRYSTAN STARED UP AT THE BRANCHES overhead, rustling slightly in the night breeze. He'd volunteered to take first watch, and by rights he should have woken Cath an hour ago. But he'd decided he might as well finish out the night. The chances of him actually sleeping, with Isolde lying not ten paces away, were almost nonexistent.

The moon was nearly at the full, and if he turned his head he could see Piye, Daka, and Cath, stretched out on their bedrolls asleep. And Isolde, sleeping curled on her side under their only spare woolen blanket, with the dog Cabal lying close by.

At least, he'd thought her asleep. A soft step behind him made him look round to see that she'd slipped out from under the blanket and was making her way across the small camp towards him. Her dark hair was loose on her shoulders and her feet were bare.

Gods be merciful.

She stopped when she reached the tree stump he was sitting on and sank down beside him, tucking her feet under her. "Is everything all right?"

The moonlight silvered her face and reflected in her eyes. It might have been his dream come to life. Trystan nodded and made himself tear his own gaze away. "No sign of trouble."

She looked down at her own hands, clasped lightly together in her lap, then back up at him. "I never said thank you, Trys. For being there today. For getting me away from those men. And for rescuing me before." She touched his hand. "I'm incredibly grateful, though. Truly. I don't know how you managed both times to be there just when I needed you. You must be my own guardian spirit in disguise."

Not bloody likely. Especially not when she was sitting as close to him as this and he had to ignore her touch vibrating through his every nerve.

She smiled just a bit. "That was quite a performance. You

sounded as though you'd just crawled your way out of the nearest ale hall."

Trystan made himself lean back, away from her, and shrug. "It wouldn't have worked at all if you hadn't known to get out of their reach as quickly as you did."

There was a moment's quiet. And then Isolde said, "Please let me see to the cut on your arm."

The cut was aching dully, but Trystan said, automatically, "It's fine."

Isolde didn't say anything, just raised her brows and looked at him, and Trystan said, "Would a disguised guardian spirit lie?"

She laughed at that, but then said, "Please, Trys. I don't think it needs stitching—it looks like the kind of cut that's best left open to bleed clean. But let me put a salve on it at least and a bandage to keep the dirt out. Even a small wound can be dangerous if it turns bad."

"And I'm not going to win this argument, so I may as well give up now?"

She smiled again. "Something like that."

She'd brought her bag of medicines with her, and she sorted through it quickly, taking out a pot of ointment and a vial of cleansing oil. She poured a measure of the oil onto a clean linen pad and touched it gently to the cut in his arm, wiping the dried blood away.

"You know, I should probably give you an award," she said after a moment. "For being the man I've bandaged and salved and stitched together the most number of times."

Trystan had been desperately trying to ignore the awareness of her cool fingers on his skin, but at that he raised an eyebrow. "You keep count?"

She gave him another brief, crooked smile. "No. I stopped a long time ago. After you'd won by enough of a margin that no one was ever likely to catch up."

Trystan laughed. "God, I—" *missed you.* Trystan clenched his jaw before he could open his idiot mouth and say the words aloud.

After a moment she turned her attention back to the cut in his upper arm, dipping one finger into the pot of salve and spreading it lightly over his skin.

As long as she wasn't watching him, Trystan let himself gaze at her, momentarily losing himself in the play of moonlight and shadow across her face.

And then she looked up, meeting his eyes. All about them, the forest was quiet save for the whisper of wind in the trees above. Her gaze searched his for a long moment, and then she said, softly, "You really wouldn't have come back, would you?"

Right. It had never been anything but completely futile to think he could escape this. He'd never known her to flinch away from something in her entire life.

Trystan made himself hold her gaze, forced himself not to look away. "Isa, the two of us, together, was always impossible. We both know that. Someone like you and someone like me. It was . . . It was very nice for that short while, but—"

"Very nice?" Isolde interrupted him before he could finish. Her hands clenched the roll of bandage she was holding, and her voice rose. But then she cast a glance back at the three sleeping men behind her and lowered it again, speaking through gritted teeth. "Very *nice*? So, if I'd not been in danger—if Cath had come to the abbey and found everything as it should be, he would have told me . . . what? 'Trystan says he's glad you're all right but he didn't actually mean that marriage vow he swore with you three months ago? Oh, but he did think sharing a bed with you for a few weeks was *very nice*'?"

Trystan made another of those laughable futile efforts to slam the door on the flood of memories her words brought. He held still, waiting for her to . . . right, no, she probably wouldn't cry. Hit him, maybe, but not cry.

Instead, though, she came to an abrupt and total stop and sat staring at him. From somewhere far off in the trees came the trill of a night bird. Then Isolde closed her eyes. "Goddess mother. I wasn't going to let this happen. I promised myself I wasn't going to let you do this."

"Do what?"

She gave him a look that said he already knew, but said, "Let you make me lose my temper and give you an excuse to walk away and never come back."

She gave a small, humorless laugh and looked up at him again. "Do you want to give it another try? You could tell me that you're already married to someone else—a beautiful foreign princess, maybe?"

And then she stopped, still looking up at him, her wide, moonlit gray eyes suddenly flooding with tears. She blinked, then whispered, "I must really scare you to death."

She was looking at him as she always had, ever since he'd known her. As though she could see straight through him, read his every thought. But there was a sadness in her eyes, too, that made something in his chest clench.

For an instant, Trystan saw everything in unnaturally clear fragments. A scrap of dry leaf caught in her tumbled hair. The sparkle of tears trapped on her lashes.

Trystan tried to draw a breath. He didn't want this for her. This was exactly why he'd sworn he was going to keep his distance, stay away. And yet . . . he'd already been exercising every last scrap of self-control he had not to reach for her. And, looking into her swimming gray eyes, Trystan knew it was all over. He was lost. He was going to reach out and pull her into his arms.

But then she wiped her eyes with the back of her hand—which shouldn't have surprised him, she's always been tough—and said, "Those men today, they said they were from Marche."

Trystan nodded, and Isolde said, "You should know that Madoc told me Marche has offered a reward for my capture."

At any rate, he was able to stop himself from reaching for her. Trystan felt an explosion of red behind his eyes, and drew a breath, forcing himself to step back from a thick wave of anger that threatened to sweep him away. "Why?"

"Because he's been driven back from taking Camelerd." Her mouth twisted. "And because he doesn't like to lose. Capture me and he'd think there's a greater chance Camelerd would fall."

Trystan focused on keeping the door to that inner holding area firmly shut. But something must have shown on his face, because Isolde watched him, her eyes steady, her head a little on one side, and after a moment asked suddenly, "Did you ever love him? Your father, I mean?"

"Not as much as I hated him."

God damn it. Her question had caught him so completely off guard that the words were out before Trystan could stop them. He'd flashed instantly to a memory of his mother's bruised face—the one he saw in nightmares, lips split and bleeding, one eye swollen shut. He supposed he owed Marche a debt, in a way. He remembered practicing swordfighting for endless hours, day after day.

As if Marche would somehow magically stop beating the hell out of his mother if only he, Trystan, got good enough at swordplay.

Isolde was watching him, her gaze still soft and luminous in the pale moonlight. The way she looked when he conjured her from memory so that he could silently tell her things he'd never admit to aloud. Or when she walked lightly in and out of his dreams. Trystan could feel words trying to jostle their way out of his chest. He clenched his teeth.

"Why are you asking this? You were there—you already know everything that happened back then."

Isolde watched him a moment, then she said, softly, "I don't know that. Whether you ever loved him. Even when we were younger, you barely ever mentioned his name. Much less how you felt about him."

Trystan didn't trust himself to speak. He kept silent, and after a moment Isolde let out a small, resigned sigh and sat back. He'd hurt her. Again.

She watched him without speaking for a moment, then shifted position, tucking her feet under her again, and said, "I can tell you that Marche at least in some measure regrets the oath of allegiance he swore with Octa of Kent. Octa makes for a poor ally; those closest to him tend to end up dead, their lands absorbed into Octa's own. Marche fears him—and hates him because of that fear. I don't think it would take much to destabilize the alliance between them. Already it's balanced on a knife edge. Neither one trusts the other."

She stopped, pushing a stray lock of hair back behind her ear, then went on, in a different, quieter tone, "I can tell you, too, that he's not entirely a monster. Or maybe he is, but there's a part of him, still, that hates himself for it. I'm not sure that part of him is strong enough to be his salvation. But it might be his weakness."

Control. Steady. When Trystan could manage a reasonably convincing degree of calm, he said, "Why are you telling me this?"

Isolde turned her head to look up at him again, that same warmly penetrating look in her eyes—the one that said she could see through to his very soul. "Because I know you, Trys," she said quietly. "Because if I had to guess, I'd say you intend to go after Marche and keep him from doing any more harm than he already has. Both to me and to Britain. That it's insanely dangerous and you want to keep me out of it, which is why you're not telling me the truth and why you're pushing me away." And then she reached out and touched his face, just lightly, with one hand. "And I was hoping that the more you know about Marche, as the man he is now, the safer you'll be."

Her gray eyes were the color of the ocean at dawn, and for a moment Trystan felt as though he could fall into their gaze and drown. And this time he couldn't stop himself. He reached for her, touched her, fingers tracing the delicate curve of her cheek, feeling the soft warmth of her skin. "Isa, please." He had to clear his throat before he could go on. "Please, promise me you won't try to come after me. Promise me you're not going to put yourself in danger on my account."

Isolde didn't answer at once. She was still holding the length of bandage, and she looked down at it, then slowly leaned forward, slipping it around his upper arm and drawing it over the salved knife cut. Only when she'd knotted the strip of linen securely in place did she pull back enough to look up. Her eyes were still bright with unshed tears, but she blinked. And then she said, with a very small twist of a smile, "No."

ISOLDE WOKE TO THE MURMUR OF voices from somewhere nearby. She'd slept fitfully, waking often to look over at where Trystan still sat on guard. And each time she'd turned her head in his direction, he'd been sitting absolutely motionless, looking at once utterly vigilant and inhumanely remote. But for the steady rise and fall of his breathing, she wouldn't have been entirely convinced he was even still alive.

Now she was instantly awake and she sat up, pushing tangles

of hair from her eyes. Dawn was breaking; the forest all around them was hushed and ghostly in the pale light, the grass and leaves that carpeted the ground silvered with the morning dew. Cath and Trystan were standing several paces away and carrying on a low-voiced conversation, the words too quiet and indistinct for her to hear. Seeing her sit up, though, Trystan said something final to Cath and came to crouch beside her.

Cabal had started awake with Isolde and now, recognizing a friend, whined and licked Trystan's hand. Trystan ruffled the big dog's ears, but the gesture was quick and barely more than perfunctory. He looked tired this morning, Isolde thought, his mouth tight and his eyes slightly red-rimmed. But his face was still shuttered, unapproachable and remote, and as his gaze met Isolde's, she couldn't see even a glimmer of remembrance of last night's conversation.

He wore his sword belt, and his knife was sheathed in its leather scabbard, as well. "Piye and Daka were out scouting just before dawn and spotted a patrol of Octa's soldiers heading this way," Trystan said. "You go with Cath. He'll take you back to where Eurig and Fidach are camped."

Isolde might have sworn to herself that she wouldn't let Trystan make her lose her temper. But her head was aching after her nearly sleepless night on the ground, and at Trystan's calm, even-voiced dismissal, she felt a hot flash of anger surge through her veins.

Looking at Trystan, though, she was achingly reminded of the boy she'd grown up with years ago, who'd borne his father's beatings in stony silence, without any outward show of anger—without even tears. He looked so much the same now, so grim and controlled and utterly shut off and alone that Isolde reached out and touched his face.

"Is there any point in my asking you to come back safely to me?"

Trystan closed his eyes as though he could no longer stand to look at her. "Isa, please. Everything else aside, I can't give you the kind of life you deserve. You know that."

Cath had moved off to the opposite side of the clearing and was readying the donkey to ride, giving the beast water from a half-empty skin, buckling on the saddlebags. He was out of earshot of anything they might say.

Isolde said, "I know you won't even try."

"You want to be an outlaw's wife?" Trystan's voice roughened just slightly, and he gestured to the clearing all around them. "Spend the rest of your life living outcast, sleeping on the ground without even a roof over your head? Constantly traveling, and never openly, always by stealth? Never knowing from which direction the next threat will come?"

Isolde's temper slipped. "So I should have married Madoc when I had the chance? I could be a traitor's wife now, instead of an outlaw's."

For a moment, Isolde thought she'd at last succeeded in breaking Trystan's self-control. He went very still and then said, in the dangerously quiet voice she knew meant he was really, truly angry, "Madoc had the nerve to tell you he'd turned traitor and then afterwards ask you to marry him?"

Isolde shook her head. "No. He asked me to marry him before we left Dinas Emrys, four months ago."

"And you didn't—" Trystan stopped. *Tell me,* Isolde knew he'd been about to say, but instead he drew in a breath and let it out again, a muscle tensing in the line of his jaw. "It doesn't matter. You're safe from him. And from Marche, as well." His blue eyes met hers, and then, just lightly, he reached to smooth a stray curl of hair back from her brow, as he had the night before. "I swear to you, Isa, I'll keep you safe. But to do it, I have to go now."

His touch was gentle, but his face was shuttered, detached and remote once more, and Isolde blinked back angry tears. "You—" she began.

You can walk away from me without looking back, but can you walk away from your son or daughter, as well? That was what she'd been about to say. Tell Trystan she was carrying his child, and even if she didn't persuade him to come back to her, she would, at the very least, shake him out of his detachment, the control that shut him off so completely he might as well have been a walking dead man.

But she caught herself before she could say aloud the words she'd intended. Not for Trystan's sake, this time, or for her own, but because she absolutely refused to tell Trystan about the tiny life growing inside her in anger. Her baby—their baby—deserved better than that.

So she drew in her breath and said, instead, "Go where?"

"With Daka and Piye. They've already started." He nodded towards the tree line. "We'll see if we can draw the attention of the patrol off, away from you. Keep them from following you and Cath or finding the camp."

"The camp?"

"Not far from here. You'll be safe there."

"And I'm to stay there? With Cath and the others? Until you—" Isolde stopped.

Soon she was going to have to face the question of where she herself went from here. With Trystan or without him. She'd escaped Marche's men. Escaped Madoc's guard. Madoc, whose treason might any day cost Britain the war.

But now, here before her, was Trystan. *I love him,* she'd told Mother Berthildis, *but I'm not sure he wants me to.* How much could she ask of him now, or persuade him to give her?

Something of what she felt must have showed in her face, because Trystan's own expression softened and he said, "I'll be careful. It will be all right."

"You'll be careful," Isolde repeated. "And that's meant to make me feel better? Coming from you?"

One side of Trystan's mouth tipped up at that, if only briefly. But then his gaze darkened. "You've been the best—almost the only good thing that's ever happened to me. But that doesn't mean I don't know—God, don't I know—that I'm about the worst thing that could ever happen to you."

He stopped. "Please, Isa." His voice was suddenly low and husky with the effort he was making to keep it steady. "Please don't make me add one more wrong to my conscience, and a wrong against you, besides. Let me at least walk away from here knowing that for once I acted with honor—did what I should have done three months ago."

Isolde felt hot tears sting at the back of her eyes. "The worst thing that could ever happen to me?" Her voice was a whisper. "Why?" She touched his cheek. "And how could you ever, ever think that?"

He looked at her, and just for a moment, Isolde saw in his blue gaze an echo of all the love and pain and longing he was trying not to let himself feel. But then it was gone. He shook his head, and his muscles bunched, preparing to rise.

Isolde had a memory, sharp and sudden as a sprung arrow shaft, of sitting beside Trystan's sickbed two months ago while he lay unconscious with a deep sword wound in his side. Knowing that unless she could find a way to reach him, draw him back to her, he would die. And impossible as that task had seemed at the time, it felt childishly simple compared to what she faced now.

Even still, the anger was still hissing through her veins, and she had to clench her jaw shut to keep from flinging the words at him like knives: *You're going to be a father.*

Knowing about the child would be only another burden for him to carry now, another care. Might even drive him further from her. If he thought himself unworthy of her, how much faster and farther would he run from a baby, an innocent child?

But it was only the awareness that they were nearly out of time, and the lead-heavy knowledge that this might be the last time she ever saw Trystan, that let her say, steadily, "I knew what choice I made when I married you, Trys," she said. "But even if you want to forget we ever pledged handfasting vows, even if you won't come back to me, you're still my best friend. Please, promise me you really will take care of yourself."

For a long moment, Trystan's eyes met hers and she saw his hand move jerkily, as though about to touch her hair. Instead, though, he took her hand, lowered his head, and pressed his mouth to the inside of her wrist.

And then he rose and stepped back, as though he didn't trust himself to be so close to her a moment more. "You take care, as well," he said. He wore what Isolde always thought of as his combat face, steady and hard-eyed, all emotion shut down, and she knew he was already gone. Gone far away from her to a place where she couldn't follow.

Cabal whined again, and Isolde looped an arm around the big dog's neck, pulling him close as she watched Trystan cross to where Cath was still busy packing up the camp. She realized after a moment that she was cradling her wrist with one hand, as though she could hold in the warmth of Trystan's lips, the feel of his breath on her skin.

She watched as the two men spoke briefly, the words too low for her to make out until at last Cath nodded. "Right, then. Watch your back."

"Always." Trystan held out a hand, and they clasped wrists briefly.

And then Trystan was gone, swinging the round Saxon shield over his shoulder and striding towards the trees. Isolde watched him until he disappeared. He didn't look back.

Chapter 8

THE RISING SUN WAS TWINING rose fingers above the trees to the east. It was the dawn of a new morning. Isolde and Cath had found Eurig and Fidach's camp the night before, after a day spent tramping through thick forest, avoiding anything like a road or even a trail, leading the donkey she'd ridden from the abbey—because, as Cath had pointed out, you could never tell when the beast might come in useful.

Now the donkey was browsing in a patch of thick grass that grew on the far side of the clearing, and Isolde was sitting with Eurig and Cath beside the small rippling stream that ran through the forest glade. Cabal was lying at her feet, snapping up stray crumbs of the hard, dry bread she was trying to choke down.

At the head of the stream, where the clear water bubbled up out of the rocks, a rough-hewn archway had been fashioned out of three great slabs of gray stone, and rounded hollows had been carved from the rock up and across and then down the face of the arch. All but one of the hollows was empty now, but Isolde thought they must once all have been filled, as the one at the very top of the arch was, with an age-yellowed, grinning skull.

A holy place, once. An entrance to the Otherworld, where worshippers gathered to pay homage to the white or green lady of the spring. They would have dropped bracelets or swords or other precious things into the waters as payment, then drunk from one of the skulls lining the arch, hoping for healing or wisdom or both.

Cath followed Isolde's glance towards the head of the stream, and nodded, tearing off another mouthful of his own share of the bread. "Ought to be a bit creepy, like," he said, with a gesture at the skull. "But it's not somehow."

He was right about that, as well, Isolde thought. The bone-white grin that might have been menacing was somehow mellowed by age, benign and strangely protective. Whatever earth gods had once been worshipped here had faded graciously away without anger. Or maybe they simply continued on, as before, unaffected and ungrudging of their shrine's having been abandoned and left to fall into disrepair.

Despite the call of birdsong and the bubbling voice of the stream, there was a hushed stillness about the place that made Isolde think of the chapel in the abbey, where she'd sat only three nights before.

Isolde crumbled some of her own bread and tossed it out across the stream. Dozens of small fish, lithe, slippery bodies flashing under the water's surface, darted towards the crumbs, hungry mouths agape. She watched the water boil with their thrashing struggle for the food, then made herself look up at Eurig and Cath. She said, "Trystan's not coming back, is he?"

Cath and Eurig exchanged an uneasy glance. Then Eurig cleared his throat. "How's Fidach, then?"

"Apart from the fact that he's dying, do you mean?"

Isolde's glance went automatically back towards the camp, where Fidach still slept beneath a pile of heavy traveling cloaks. She'd seen him the night before, and had almost embarrassed them both by crying over the outlaw leader's condition—the marks of Octa's torture on his shoulders and back and his painfully emaciated frame. And then, when she'd let herself open her senses to Fidach's pain, she'd felt, too, the searing ache in Fidach's chest, like red-hot iron bars about his lungs.

Now Isolde made her clenched fingers relax, one by one. Unfair to blame Eurig and Cath for the choices Trystan made. "I'm sorry," she said, more quietly. "Only, please just tell me the truth. I promise you I won't weep or scream or make you try to tell me anything you've sworn not to."

Cath and Eurig exchanged another glance, and then Eurig said, a flush of embarrassment creeping up his neck, "Sorry. We can't tell you what we don't know, and neither of us know where Trystan is now. Just said he had a job to do and that we were to keep you safe."

Watching the color rise in Eurig's face, seeing the way his brown eyes shifted away from hers, Isolde knew that he, at least, knew more than he'd just said—though how much more, she couldn't be sure. But she also knew that he wasn't going to tell her anything else.

She glanced at Cath, whom she didn't know as well as Eurig. But if his loyalty was even half what Eurig's was, he'd keep silent, as well. So instead she hesitated a moment, then said, "You know, both of you, that Trystan was a prisoner, once, a slave in the tin mines. Eurig, you were actually a prisoner with him."

She saw Eurig wince slightly, as though at the dark rush of memories her words recalled, and felt a stab of compunction. But she'd come too far not to go on. "Does either of you know how Trystan was captured—how he came to be in the prison camp?"

Oddly, both men relaxed at the question, and Cath snorted around a swallow of mead from the jar by his side. "Not goat-rutting likely. Begging your pardon, Lady," he added with a glance at Isolde. "I've known Trystan these four years and I could use my thumbs to count the number of times he's said anything of himself. And I'm talking does he like mead or ale, or fighting with a knife or a sword. Never said a word about his past history that I can recall."

Cath glanced questioningly at Eurig, who shook his head. "Nor to me." He gave a quick, rueful smile, rubbing a hand over his bald pate. "Not exactly a believer in that old saying about a trouble shared is a trouble halved, Trystan isn't. Keeps his past in his past and doesn't talk of it—not to anyone that I've ever heard."

Isolde hadn't really let herself hope for anything else, but she felt a sharp twist of disappointment all the same. "And yet you like him, both of you," she said. "You'd count him a friend."

Both men looked surprised at the question, though it was Cath who answered. "Oh, aye. Don't have to know where a man comes from to know what he's made of."

WHEN CATH HAD GONE TO MAKE another patrol of their camp, Isolde turned to Eurig. "Was Cath one of Fidach's band?"

Again Eurig looked surprised by the question she'd asked. "You didn't know? Aye, Cath was one of us. For a time, anyway. Left the band . . . let's see, now . . . woulda been three years ago, maybe a bit more."

"It's an unusual name—Cath."

Eurig nodded agreement. "Aye, it is. Not his proper, name, though. Just a nickname, like. Short for *cath fach*."

Isolde almost choked on a bite of the hard bread. "*Cath fach*? Kitten?"

Eurig chuckled at the expression on her face. "Aye, that's right." Eurig leaned back against the slender trunk of a birch tree behind him, clasping his hands over his middle. "Cath joined up with the Fidach's band just after Trystan and I did. He was some different, then, though. Would fight a man just for looking at him funny. Never laughed. Never even smiled. Wouldn't tell us his proper name, either—said he'd answer to 'Wolf' and that was all."

Eurig's brown eyes turned distant at the memory, a smile twitching the edges of his mouth. "So Trystan's sitting there, as he tells us this, looking kind of thoughtful. And then Trystan says as how he's been thinking lately that we're scaring the enemy a bit too much. That what we ought to do is try and come across as a friendlier, gentler kind of outlaw. So he starts calling this Wolf fellow *Kitten*. And the name just stuck. *Cath Fach*—Cath for short."

"And Cath hasn't murdered Trystan yet?"

Once more Eurig's look was surprised, but he said, "Nah, not likely. Cath'd step in front of an arrow aimed at Trystan any day."

And then he stopped short, as Cath himself reappeared, breathing heavily, gasping between words. "Band of armed men, heading this way."

"Men?" Eurig was instantly on the alert. "Whose men, could you see?"

Cath sucked in another breath, then nodded, mouth flattening into a grim line. "Carried shields painted with the four gold lions of Gwynedd."

TRYSTAN PAUSED, SCANNING THE FOREST PATH ahead of him. Nothing. No sign of anything out of the way. Just trees and branches and a carpet of decaying leaves. No reason the back of his neck should have been prickling with an awareness of danger, but it was. And no reason he should automatically have drawn the knife from his belt, but when he looked down, there the blade was, ready in his hand.

"Something wrong?" Daka asked behind him.

Trystan held up one hand for quiet. They'd led Octa's patrol in a wide, arcing loop the day before, leaving them hopelessly lost in a patch of foggy swamp at least a full day's journey from the glade where they'd left Eurig and Fidach camped. Where Isolde must be now.

Trystan dragged his attention back to the present. Make sure that Marche earned himself his own just reward. That was the next part of the job.

They were in the no-man's-land of forested region surrounding Caer Peris. Following up on what Garbhán had told him: that Cerdic planned a secret, surprise attack on the fortress he'd lost to Madoc a month before. That he'd already begun massing the supplies his army would need to sustain a seige.

They'd been combing the thick woodlands for hours when Trystan's eye had been caught by a flash of white. Just a scrap of linen caught on a branch at about shoulder height. It could easily have been torn off some traveler's shirt. But on inspection, it had proved to mark the entrance to a narrow track through the trees, and it had set the back of Trystan's neck prickling.

They'd been following the path for some time—an hour or more. And now his skin was itching with awareness of a different kind.

Somewhere up ahead was a threat. Nothing to show it—but he was certain of it, just the same.

Trystan held very still, scanning the stretch of path ahead again. Left to right, right to left. He could hear the call of birds in the trees—which he wouldn't, if they were about to walk into an ambush. So, no one hiding in the trees. Probably.

Now he let his eyes travel once more across the stretch of ground in front of them. Left to right. Right to left. Keeping his breathing steady and slow. Left to—

And then he stopped. There. On the ground not three paces away. One single green leaf lying amidst the sea of brown.

Trystan shook his head. Satan's breath, his nerves were in bad shape if a single leaf had his inner alarms jangling.

"What—" Daka began again, and took a step forward, past Trystan. Instantly, and more by reflex than anything else, Trystan's hand shot out, catching hold of his arm and dragging him back. Just as the ground collapsed beneath Daka's feet.

When the dust settled, Daka lay panting on the ground, a mere handspan from the pit that had a moment before been disguised by a matting of crossed leaves and branches. Daka said something vehement and undoubtedly profane in his own tongue, and Trystan, letting out his breath, moved to the edge of the hole and looked down. Piye moved past his brother to stand beside him and commented, shortly, and likewise in his native language, "Nasty."

The pit had been dug nearly to the depth of a man's height, the bottom lined with sharpened wooden stakes. And the points of the stakes were smeared in filth, so that any wound they made would turn poisonous fast enough to kill.

Daka was on his feet, though still breathing hard. He and Piye exchanged a look and then Daka said, "You sure this trail be worth following?"

Trystan slipped his knife back into his belt and nodded, eyes still on the trap. "No one goes to this much trouble to protect a place unless there's something worth protecting. We go on." He looked up from the pit of stakes, turning back to the other two. "I'll stay in the lead. Just keep behind me, this time."

ISOLDE SAT WITH HER HEAD BOWED, willing herself not to look up or protest as Madoc's men kicked their way through the camp. Silently, she willed Cabal to keep silent as well.

She'd sent the big dog with Cath and Eurig to the place of concealment they'd decided on amongst the trees. But still, her fingers were clenched with the fear that he'd bark or come running back to her and give the other two men's hiding place away. Cabal was well trained, but he was always uneasy at being separated from her, and she couldn't be sure he'd obey orders if he sensed she was in danger.

The leader of the group, a heavy-set older man with a red

face and a drooping mustache, strode across her line of sight, and Isolde risked a quick look up at him from under the hood of the cloak. He was standing staring at the stone altar at the head of the stream, and the one grinning, age-yellowed skull that remained in the hollowed-out recesses. Isolde saw him shift his weight uneasily before he turned away to paw roughly through a basket of dried meat and parchment-wrapped cheese.

Beside her, she could almost feel the tension radiating from Fidach in waves—but he sat as still and as silent as she did, only following the movement of the guardsmen with his eyes.

Fidach had woken at Cath's return. He'd listened, eyes flat as brown pain, to Cath's report, then drawn himself upright and said, "Leave me. It's the only way you're likely to outrun them."

Cath and Eurig had exchanged a glance, and then Cath said, "Went to a deal of trouble to get you out of Octa's clutches. Not so sure I'm anxious to go through the whole load of bother all over again if you're captured by Madoc's men today."

Fidach's face had been gaunt and ashy pale, save for bright spots of fever over his high cheekbones. He'd sat staring at Cath a long moment, an unreadable expression in his leaf-brown gaze. And then at last he'd coughed again.

"Very well, then." His voice was slightly raspy, but it still cracked with the authority of a man who'd for ten years and more commanded the obedience of an outlaw band. "Eurig . . . Cath. Get into the trees and stay there unless there's trouble. And you"— he turned to Isolde—"you're my wife. Understand?"

They'd been able to hear already the snap of twigs and leaves under approaching booted feet by then, but even so, Fidach had given her a brief flash of his old sharp-toothed grin. "And that's something I never thought to say to a woman."

Now the mustached guardsman pushed the basket of foodstuffs aside and rose, turning to Fidach. "And you say you're bound for Dumnonia?"

There was a note in the man's voice that sent unease crawling down Isolde's spine . . . and as he spoke he bent, peering into Fidach's face. Isolde's heart tightened. She had no reason to think that Madoc's men would recognize or even know of Fidach's existence—in that they were lucky, that these were not Octa's men who'd found them here. And moreover, Madoc's men should believe her abducted from the abbey by Marche's men—as she very nearly had been. Not traveling in company with a single man, pretending to be his wife.

But all the same, she didn't want the guardsman studying either of their faces too closely. Or questioning the tale they'd told. Evidently Fidach had sensed something in the guardsman's tone, as well; Isolde saw his hand shift almost imperceptibly nearer the knife at his belt.

Before he could speak, though, and before the red-faced leader could ask any more, she said, quickly, "My lord, your pardon, but could I get a bit o' bread from the basket over there?" She doubted the guardsman merited the title of lord, but he looked the kind of man who would be glad to have her think he did. She went on swiftly before he could give her an answer, clasping her hands over her stomach, slurring her words a little, trying to make her voice sound soft and uneducated. "I'm feeling most dreadfully ill, like." She turned to Fidach and added in an aggrieved voice, "It's your fault. I told you I couldn't travel. Not fair to expect me to—not with a child on the way, and me being sick every other moment."

She felt Fidach stiffen with surprise. But ill or no, half dead from a month of starvation and torture or no, he had lived a lifetime by his quickness of wit, his ability to react instantly in the face of threat. He recovered almost at once and said, "And you're the one that wouldn't trust me to keep my bed free of other company while I was gone." With a derisive snort, he spread out a hand towards the surrounding forest. "As if there's just bevies of doxies lurking behind every tree."

Fidach's eye caught Isolde's and she thought she caught a gleam of amusement—almost enjoyment—in his. A kind of joy of combat that made her inwardly shake her head—and yet at the same time feel both glad and a bit amazed that it hadn't been crushed out of him by all he'd endured. Fidach's face was sober, though, as he turned to the leader of the guardsmen and said in a resigned tone, "Best let her have the bread, my lord. Or take a good step back if you value the leather on your boots."

The mustached man's face creased with distaste and he did take a hasty step back, but he gave a curt nod. Isolde rose. Her stomach was churning enough that she felt as though Fidach's warning might well be proved true.

From behind her, though, she heard the lead guardsman's tone as he asked Fidach, "And you've seen no one else in these parts? Met with no one on the road?"

Isolde heard a note of boredom creeping into the guardsman's tone, as though the questions were perfunctory and he were already impatient to be gone. She let herself draw a cautious breath as Fidach said, without hesitation, "No, my lord. No one at all."

Chapter 9

I T WAS A STOREHOUSE.

They'd come to the end of the trail, having discovered three more concealed pits in the ground. The heat of the late-summers afternoon seemed to press in close around them, and Trystan's nerves were on edge, his eyes aching and his neck muscles wire-tight with the effort of constant vigilance needed to spot the damned things. But they'd avoided all the traps they found, and hadn't even had any calls as close as Daka had had with the first one.

And now they came on this, here.

The structure was concealed by a pile of brush and a network of cross-woven green branches and leaves, so that its outlines were scarcely visible unless you knew what to look for. From a distance, it looked to be just a ruined goat herder's hut, overgrown by vines and young saplings. But an abandoned hut didn't merit two armed guards posted outside.

Trystan studied them from his place of concealment behind a thick oak tree. Only two, but armed with bows and arrows, as well as swords, their shields painted with the colors of Cerdic of Wessex.

Not that that was a surprise, after what Garbhán had told him. Still, it was a welcome discovery. Carefully, and shutting down all thoughts of anything else, he let himself recall one single fragment of his talk with Isolde. *I don't think it would take much to destabilize the alliance between Octa and Marche*, she had said.

Now, if they played this correctly, Cerdic's storehouse could be used not only to win an added measure of Octa's trust, but to drive an effective wedge into that already shaky arrangement of allies.

Soundlessly, careful to avoid stepping on any dry twigs or branches, Trystan stepped backwards until he reached the spot where he'd left Daka and Piye.

"Only two guards," he reported, when they'd fallen back to a point out of earshot, behind a clump of some flowering shrubbery.

Daka frowned. "You're sure?"

Trystan didn't answer at once. He'd seen no sign of anyone else. But on the other hand, he didn't want to die thinking, *Well, you asked for that one, didn't you, fool?*

"Almost sure. I'd say that's the point of the staked pits we found. To catch any who comes near this place and make added guards unneeded. But to be absolutely sure, we should circle around behind and make sure there aren't any more posted on the other side."

"And assuming you be right?" Daka asked. "What we do then?"

Trystan glanced back in the direction of the hut—fully hidden now by the thick screen of leaves and trees. His mind flipped through the various possibilities. Assuming there were no other guards, the odds were in their favor. Two against three. But attack openly, and the two existing guards would be on them in a heartbeat. And above all else he didn't want to get them into a position where it was kill or be killed.

Trystan made up his mind. "Here. Put these on." He slipped his traveling pack from his shoulder and drew out armbands marked with the blue boar of Cornwall—also bartered from Garbhán, who augmented his living by trading in looted battlefield goods, as well as information. They weren't much of a disguise, but they did clearly bear the mark of Marche's army. With any luck, they'd serve.

Trystan handed an armband to each of the other men, then said, "Right. Now listen carefully. This is what we're going to do."

TRYSTAN LEANED AGAINST THE SOLID TRUNK of another tree, catching his breath, wiping sweat from his eyes with the back of his wrist. They'd attacked in a screaming rush at the guards posted outside the hidden storehouse. And, as expected, the two guards had driven them back, shooting a hailstorm of arrows after the first moment of stunned disbelief.

They'd retreated under a rain of arrow fire, turning and running for cover in the trees. They hadn't gone far before Trystan had heard Piye, running between him and Daka, give a harsh cry of pain and shout, "I'm hit!"

Now Daka knelt on the ground beside a prostrate form, hands shaking as he used his knife to slice a strip of bandage from the hem of his shirt. "You be all right. Just stay with me, brother. We tie the wound up, and you be fine."

Trystan concentrated on steadying his breathing, then froze. From somewhere close by, came the sharp snap of a dry branch. Someone was coming.

Daka was still bending over the fallen body on the ground. "No. I not let you die, Piye," he was saying. "You hear me? You going to be fine."

He didn't even look round as the two guardsmen stepped past Trystan's place of concealment and moved forward, swords drawn.

"You hear me, Piye? You going to be—"

Trystan stepped out from behind his tree and hit the nearer of the two guards a sharp blow across the back of the neck, sending him crumpling to the ground, just as Piye stepped out from behind a screen of bushes and dealt similarly with the second man.

"Thank the gods!" Daka rose to his feet and stepped back from Trystan's spare shirt and traveling cloak that they'd arranged over a mound of dry leaves on the ground. He grimaced. "Even I be sick of listening to myself."

Trystan moved to gather up the shirt and cloak, and Piye said something in their own language that made a dusky flush of color rise in Daka's face. Daka hunched his shoulders and gestured to the unconscious guards. "Come on. Better be getting these two tied up before they come around."

Working quickly, they used the guards' own belts and the leather straps on their quivers of arrows to bind their hands and legs. When they had finished, Daka stood up. "What now?"

Trystan glanced from the trussed-up guardsmen back towards the hut, and from there up at the sky. Shadows were lengthening; it would be dark in another hour. "Anything of value and easy to carry we take. The rest we burn. We'll travel as far as possible tonight, then find somewhere to hole up and rest as soon as it's light."

"HOW'S HE FARING?"

Isolde looked at Fidach, sleeping half sitting up beside her because he couldn't get his breath lying down. The skin was tightly stretched over the bones of his face, the swirling tattoos standing out in sharp relief on his cheekbones. She turned back to Cath, who had the first watch of the night, but after making a slow circuit of the camp had come to crouch beside her by the small fire they were keeping alight.

Isolde felt tears prick behind her eyes and swallowed. "I honestly can't think he's more than a few days left."

Cath nodded, face sober but unsurprised. "Aye, thought as much." His glance traveled to Fidach's sleeping form and rested there a moment. "There's others—others of the band—that would have come in a heartbeat and fought to get him out of Octa's prison. But Trystan said no—that it was the kind of job where a small band of men had a better chance of getting the job done than a larger group."

Cath's gaze rested again on Fidach's face. "Well, just let me know if there's aught I can do."

Isolde nodded. "Thank you."

They were quiet a moment, and then Cath asked her, "Can't sleep?"

She hadn't even bothered to try. Not when every word she'd spoken to Trystan and he to her kept echoing in her mind like an endlessly repeating tale. Or when every time she closed her eyes she saw Trystan turning and walking away.

She said, "Maybe in a bit. I'm hoping Fidach wakes soon. I want to give him another dose of horehound and fennel. It should make it a bit easier for him to breathe."

Cath nodded again. The moon was waning, but still bright overhead, and all about them the forest was hushed, the only sounds the chirp of crickets from the trees and the bubbling voice of the stream.

Eurig was asleep, rolled in a blanket on the far side of the clearing, guarding the place where the remaining stores of food were hid. Isolde had expected Cath to move off, back to his patrol of the camp, but instead he settled on a rock beside her, stretching his legs towards the flickering fire.

He didn't speak, though, and after a moment's hesitation Isolde said, "Eurig told me the story behind your name."

Cath looked round, teeth flashing instantly in one of his ready grins. The firelight deepened the shadows about his eyes and twined fiery fingers in his shaggy black hair and beard. "And you're wondering why it is that I'm still on speaking terms with Trystan?" Cath gave a rumbling chuckle. "Well, it's a bit of a story, that. You're sure you want to hear the whole?"

She wanted—desperately, just now—to hear anything at all connected to Trystan, if only because it seemed to bring him one step nearer to where she sat by a campfire and watched through the long, chilly night. "If you don't mind telling it."

Cath settled back on his elbows. "I don't mind." His voice was still easy and genial, but his expression changed in some indefinable way, becoming suddenly graver, more sober. He was quiet a moment, eyes on the dancing flames.

At last he blew out a breath and said, "Sorry—bit hard to know how to start. Suppose I'd better just say plain that it starts with me getting myself roaring drunk in a tavern and buying the favor of . . . well, of the kind of girl that'll treat a man nicely for a bit of ready coin."

He stopped and glanced up. "I was some different then. Maybe Eurig's told you a bit. I can't even remember what this girl said to make me angry, but all of a sudden I was hauling off and belting her across the face."

He looked towards the fire. "Not something I'm proud of, but that's what happened. And the next thing I know, Trystan's got me by the shoulder and spinning me around and beating the—uh, the daylights out of me." Cath glanced up at Isolde. "You ever see Trystan lose his temper?"

Isolde looked out towards the rippling stream and the crudely carved altar, with its single skull mute testament to the worship of a god whose name had been lost to the swirling mists of time. But whose presence perhaps could still be felt here in this small glade. "Not often."

Cath nodded. "Aye, well, neither had I till that night. He ended by dumping me in a watering trough in the stable yard. Well, that sobered me up. Nothing like almost drowning to clear a man's head. My ears were still ringing, like. But I'd just about wits enough left to be able to take in what he said."

Cath paused, frowning as if in an effort to recall the exact words. "He says to me, 'You can be a crawling coward and tell yourself it was all the girl's fault—that she shouldn't have made you angry if she didn't want a beating. Or you can be a man about it and decide that you're not going to be the kind of sack of dirt who'd lay violent hands on a woman again. Your choice.'"

Cath stopped again and was silent so long that Isolde asked, "And you changed—just like that?"

"Ah, well." Cath rubbed his jaw. "Well, I'll admit Trystan might have added something about taking his knife and, uh, making sure I never fathered children did he ever catch me beating a woman again." He grinned, then sobered. "But no, it was like he said—I'd a choice about the man I was going to be, and I made it. And that's the debt I owe Trystan."

"And what happened to the girl?" Isolde asked.

"The one in the tavern?" Cath gave another rumbling chuckle. "Well, that'll be the other part of what I owe Trystan. Got her and a boy and girl waiting for me to come home to 'em after this is done."

Isolde looked at him in surprise. "You married her?"

Cath had been watching the fire, but he glanced up and nodded. "Oh, aye. I went to her the next day, though I still had the two black eyes Trystan had given me and a nose swollen up like a ripe plum and hurting like nothing on earth." Cath touched his nose gingerly, as though recalling the pain. "It's a wonder she didn't run screaming. But I took her a bag of coin—all the money I had in the world—and said she could take it and order me from her sight and I'd swear never to trouble her again."

Cath paused. "Or she could marry me, and we'd use the coin to buy a house and maybe a patch of land." He stopped, gaze turning distant again, and rubbed his beard. "I told her I knew marriage had to be a gamble for a woman. Don't know if you're going to get a man who treats you right or one who'll do . . . well, what I'd done to her. But I told her she was one up on that with me, because she could be certain I was never, ever going to lay hand on her again so long as we both lived."

He stopped, still watching the fire's crackling flames, and for a moment the sound of the crickets in the surrounding trees filled the night quiet. He was still smiling, but his expression altered, somehow, as he said, softly, "And I've thanked God every day since that she decided to take a chance on trusting what I said and agreed to be my wife."

Cath looked up, his gaze focusing once more on Isolde. "Got the girl and boy now, like I say. Girl's just turned one, and the boy's nearly three. Boy's named for Trystan." Cath flashed another grin. "Thought I owed him a thanks for not making good on what he'd threatened with the knife."

Isolde laughed at that and he joined her, then looked at her in concern. "You all right, Lady? Didn't mean to make you cry."

Isolde wished for what must have been the seven hundredth time that carrying a child didn't mean that every other time she turned around she found herself crying like a baby herself. Cath might be happily wedded, but he still looked at a weeping female with the usual man's expression on his face that said he'd far rather be facing a wall of enemy swords.

She wiped her eyes with the back of her hand. "And yet you still came to help Trystan get Fidach free?"

Cath looked at her in mild surprise, the orange glow of the fire flickering in his deep-set gaze. "Oh, aye," he said again. "Even if I wanted to refuse, Glenda—that's my wife—would have my liver did I ever try it." Cath grinned. "She's a redhead, you understand." Then he spread his hands, showing callused palms. "I'm a smith now, with my own forge and all and a fair business in trade. Not much call to raise one of these anymore"—he touched the sword at his belt—"unless it's to beat out a new blade for someone else. But aye, I'd come any time Trystan called."

. . .

"YOU KNOW, YOU'RE ONLY WASTING YOUR time here." Fidach's voice was raspy. He had woken in a fit of coughing a short while ago, and now lay back exhausted on his bedroll, face as gaunt and hollow eyed as the ancient skull in the glade's stone shrine. "It's not as though you've any hope of curing me. And it could be dangerous for you to stay here too long."

Isolde had been pouring a measure of horehound mixed with fennel and honey into a cup, but she glanced up at that. "It could be dangerous? Oh, well, in that case, I'll just forget you ever saved my life and leave you here to die alone. Here, take this," she added. She put the draft into Fidach's hand. "And don't waste your breath. I feel the same as Cath and Eurig. I'm here for as long . . . for as long as you need me."

Fidach laughed, though he winced as though the laughter tore at his lungs. "I begin to think that Trystan was right about you."

Isolde's hands stilled on the blankets she'd been straightening, but she didn't trust herself to ask what Trystan had been right about. So she kept silent, waiting until Fidach had downed the remainder of the dose, and then took the empty cup back.

She and the outlaw leader were alone. Cath had gone to trade places with Eurig and sleep out the rest of the night, and Eurig was now patrolling the camp. From time to time, Isolde saw just a glimpse of him as he made his way on a slow circuit of the glade, a shadowed deeper blackness against the looming darkness of the surrounding trees. The fire was dying down, but the moon was still bright overhead, a polished globe of palest gold, hanging amidst the branches above.

Fidach drew several harsh, labored breaths, then asked, "And where will you go, after you leave here?"

He said the words as though he were speaking of a change in the weather and not his own death. But then, by now, Isolde would have expected nothing else.

Isolde stared into the fire. If she were honest, she'd known from the time she'd left the abbey what she had to do. She was only putting it off, moment to moment, in hopes that Trystan would come back and find her here. She couldn't wait forever, though. Nor even much longer than another few days.

"I'm the only one who knows Madoc has turned traitor. I have to try to warn the rest of the council of what he plans."

She paused, eyes on the fire's orange and yellow flames. "I've thought that maybe if a campaign could be launched to rescue Madoc's son, he might reconsider the alliance with Octa and Marche. But I don't even know where the boy is being held."

Beside her, Fidach gave the ghost of another laugh, mirthless this time. "Well, I can tell you that, at any rate. He's at Caer Peris."

Isolde's hands jerked so that she almost spilled the remains of the draft. "He is? You're sure?"

"Oh, yes." Fidach smiled, but again without humor. Something hard crossed his thin features as he said, "That happens to be where I . . . enjoyed Octa's hospitality, as well. But news and gossip reach even into the filthy depths of a prison cell. I'm sure. The boy is there— or was two weeks ago. I've no reason to think he's not there still."

Isolde's gaze went to Fidach's emaciated shoulders, the angry scars and healing marks of flogging, hidden now by his thick tunic and cloak. She said, quietly, "Thank you. That may do some good."

Fidach's smile was easier, this time, if still wry. "Consider it partial payment for your care here." He was quiet a moment, tipping his head back, eyes drifting from the fire up to the vaulted night sky above. And then he said, "You know, I was going to congratulate you on your performance this afternoon with the patrol. Of a woman sick and with child. But it wasn't an act, was it?"

Isolde went still. They were alone, the other men posted out of earshot, on guard around the clearing. And it was the darkest watch of the night, the hour of change, when the veil between this world and the Otherworld shifted and thinned.

She turned to Fidach. "How did you know?"

"Ah, well." Fidach coughed, covering his mouth with one thin hand. "I'd a sister, once. Long ago."

It was more than Isolde had ever heard the outlaw leader say of himself. But then he shook his head. "It hardly matters now. Did you tell Trystan before he left?" The corners of Fidach's mouth lifted once again. "You'll notice I don't even bother asking whether the child is his."

"Thank you—I suppose. And, no." Isolde bit her lip. "I didn't tell him." She looked unseeingly out at the darkness beyond their fire's circle of light, hugging her knees. "He still doesn't know."

Fidach shifted under the blankets and he grimaced again, head turning as he sought a position of ease. Then he said, his voice neutral, "A man might want to know that. He might think he deserved to be told."

Isolde turned to him and asked, "Would you?"

The firelight picked out with merciless clarity the hollows in Fidach's face, the sharp angles of temple and jaw and the hectic flush of fever on his high cheekbones. He gave another short rasp of a laugh. "It's not exactly a question that's ever come up in the course of my life."

"Well, then." Isolde turned her gaze to the dying embers of the fire, willing her voice not to shake. "What I think is that right now Trystan deserves *not* to be told."

It had been hard, waiting at the abbey, knowing Trystan was either dead or had chosen not to send any kind of message back to her. It was harder still, now, to tell herself that his spirit was marked by a lifetime's worth of scars. That she couldn't simply shake him and demand he tell her of hurts he'd buried too deeply to share.

She fixed on the memory forcing herself to turn away when he'd battled Glaw. She'd trusted him then to save both his life and hers. She had to trust him again now.

"He's caught in something. Some mission. I know him. I know the signs. And I have to trust that if he thinks the mission vital enough to make him risk his life, it is. And I can't distract him from the job he's on—or make him worry for me and the child. Any distractions, any more worries, and he's only more likely to die."

Fidach's light brown eyes were on her, thoughtful and for once without mockery. Isolde thought there might even have been sympathy in their depths.

"Hard on you, though."

"Perhaps." Isolde blinked the sting of wood smoke from her eyes. "But I chose this—chose him—knowing it was going to be a difficult road to walk. I can hardly complain when it is."

Fidach watched her a moment and then he said, "Trystan's a lucky man."

Isolde called up again the image of her two points of light. One far distant, one glowing just inside her. Thought of the rare moments when Trystan let himself look at her, his whole heart reflected in his eyes, with such love and longing in their depths that it stopped her breath.

"No. I'm the lucky one." And then she turned to Fidach. "Please, promise me you won't tell any of the other men. Or Trystan, if he comes back."

Fidach started to nod, but a harsh, tearing fit of coughing interrupted him, bending him double and making his whole body shake. When the spasm finally passed, he looked up at Isolde. He held up the hand he'd used to cover his mouth, and she saw that there was a smear of bright blood across the palm.

His fever bright eyes were streaming, but he managed to give her another fleeting ghost of a smile as he rasped, in barely a whisper, "Silent as the grave."

"MY NAME," SAID THE MAIDEN, "IS Niamh of the Golden Hair. I am the daughter of the King of the Land of Youth, and that which has brought me here is the love of Oisin."

Then she turned to Oisin, and said, in a voice like clear water, like sweet honey wine, "Wilt thou go with me, Oisin, to my father's land? An earthly paradise is the land, delightful beyond all dreams. Fairer than aught thine eyes have ever seen. There all the year the fruit is on the tree, and all the year the bloom is on the flower."

Isolde paused in telling the story to look at Fidach. He'd lapsed into unconsciousness near dawn, and now, at the gray twilight of another day, he lay without moving, eyes closed, flecks of blood still on his lips and chin from the fits of coughing that had wracked him through the night.

Beside her, Eurig cleared his throat and said, "Won't be long, now, will it."

It was more statement than question, but Isolde shook her head. "No. Not long."

She could try rousing Fidach, try pouring another dose of horehound down his ravaged throat, but that would only be cruelty when he'd at last drifted beyond pain into peace. Instead she slipped her hand into the dying man's. She could feel each separate, knobby bone of his fingers, fragile as a bundle of sticks in hers, and his skin felt hot and dry.

"There with wild honey drip the forest trees; The stores of wine and mead shall never fail. Nor pain nor sickness knows the dweller there, Death and decay come near him never more."

IT WAS NEAR MIDNIGHT.

Isolde had long since finished the tale of Oisin and Niamh of the golden hair, and told countless others, besides, her words falling like the bubbling murmur of the stream into the forest quiet that had drawn in with the deepening dark. Now she'd fallen silent, still sitting beside Fidach, her hand still in his. Cath and Eurig had built up the fire and sat, one on either side, with Cabal lying at Eurig's feet. And Cath, a short while before, had surprised her by drawing a crudely carved wooden flute from some inner fold of his tunic. Now he sat with his feet planted square apart, huge hands moving with surprising grace and speed as he played a soft, lilting tune that seemed to rise like the coils of wood smoke into the air and yet twine about them, close as the shadows of the night.

Through all the stories, all the songs Cath had played, Fidach had lain without moving, the blankets that covered his gaunt body scarcely even rising and falling as he breathed. Now, though, at this darkest hour, his eyelids flickered, then lifted. His leaf-brown gaze was bleared, but his eyes traveled from Eurig to Cath to the sky above, and then finally came to rest on Isolde.

He drew breath, coughed, and then the glimmer of a smile touched his thin mouth. "Funny," he said. He spoke between labored gasps, his voice a thready breath of sound so faint that Isolde barely caught the words. "All the ways I could have died in my time . . . and it turns out to be safe in bed . . . with a beautiful woman holding my hand."

Isolde looked at his gaunt face, at the swirling Pritani warrior's tattoos on his cheekbones, and thought of what he'd told her. *I had a sister, long ago.* That, she realized, was all she actually knew for certain of Fidach, a man who'd constructed his own persona, his own public face, and worn it like a mask, nearly till the end.

Through the haze of her own tears, she thought she felt a press of his fingers against hers, so slight she might have only imagined it. Then he coughed again, a harsh, rattling gasp of air. His eyes flickered closed. And Isolde knew that Fidach was gone.

Chapter 10

*T*HE WIND OUTSIDE WAS RISING, *the rain gusting against the sides of the tent, making them billow inward, the guy lines threatening to rip free of their pegs. The man before her wore a gold circlet about his brow and sat with a grave, careworn face, looking at the scroll she'd brought. Hope wasn't a thing she usually allowed herself, but gods, she hoped he'd agree to the bargain. That the whole bloody, filthy waste of yet another battle could be avoided this time.*

The man looked up. "You may tell Lord Marche—"

Isolde jerked awake to find that Cabal was beside her, whining and anxiously butting his head against her neck. She sat up, pushing the hair from her eyes, patting the big dog mechanically.

She'd carried and heated water from this stream to wash Fidach's body the night before, while Cath and Eurig dug a grave in the spot they'd chosen, a soft, mossy patch of ground beneath the shade of a spreading pine. She could hear the scrape of shovels even now; they must be nearly done.

And as Isolde had readied Fidach for his final resting place, she'd murmured the words to an old song she could remember her grandmother singing long ago, one that bid the lingering spirit farewell, giving it leave to depart. And then, when she'd wrapped Fidach's body in the clean traveling cloak that would be his shroud, she'd come here, to sit by the bubbling stream. Because even as her lips had shaped the ancient words of the parting song, she'd kept hearing the echo of what Fidach had told her of Caer Peris and Madoc's son.

She'd been tired, though, after the sleepless nights of caring for

Fidach. And so, instead of the vision she'd half hoped for, she'd fallen asleep. Dreamed. And woken with a now familiar tugging ache, as of a pain she could neither heal nor share.

Isolde looped an arm about Cabal's neck. The dream had been of Trystan. She remembered the details more clearly than those of any other before. Trystan meeting with a man—a king—hearing that king say, *You may tell Lord Marche*—

Isolde shivered and looked up at the roughly carved stone altar again. At the skull, cup of the Old Ones who had seen these waters as a portal to the Otherworld. She could see, still, with hideously chill clarity the vision she'd had of Trystan and Marche, locked in a sword fight that could only end in death. Could hear, in the rippling murmur of the stream, the voice of the nameless man who came to tell her that Trystan had been wounded—fatally so.

Or had the dream been an answer—or a warning—to her? *You may tell Lord Marche*—

Marche. She rarely thought of him now. Rarely had to stop herself from thinking of him, either, which mattered to her far more.

Now, though, the memory of Marche's face rose before her. A black-haired, broad-chested man. Maybe handsome, once, though age now had coarsened him, leaving his skin scored with broken veins, his dark eyes puffy and ravaged.

She'd not set eyes on him since he'd forced her into marriage, and then had her tried before the king's council for a witch and a devil's whore. Hadn't seen him since she'd glimpsed him in flashes of the Sight: a man who felt nothing now but rage and pain, and who used both to stuff down fear of what he'd done, what he'd become. A man who ate and drank and had all turn to ashes in his mouth, because what he wanted with a longing like a poisoned arrow twisting in his chest had been buried seven years ago under the ground at Camlann.

And Marche might be at Caer Peris. However shaky the allegiance, Marche and Octa were still allies.

Isolde closed her eyes. Risk her life, and she risked the baby's life, as well. A boy with his father's blue eyes, if the vision she'd glimpsed in the abbey chapel were true. And yet . . .

And yet she—maybe she alone—had a hope of saving Madoc's son, of stopping Madoc from treason.

Isolde hugged Cabal tightly, rested her cheek a moment against the rough prickle of his fur. Then she bent, scooping up water from the stream to quickly wash her face and hands.

She tried, as she rose and brushed crumbs of leaf mold from the skirt of her gown, to fix in her mind the memory of her grandmother's voice whispering *Courage*.

Cath and Eurig were eating bread and some small tart, sour berries Eurig had found, and Isolde let them serve her with a portion of the food and give her a cup of water from the stream. She dipped the bread into the water to soften it, took a few mouthfuls, and then said, "You told me that Trystan had a job to do, and that he'd asked you to keep me safe until it was done. Do you have any idea how long he meant that to be? Or what he's doing?"

She spoke steadily. Because if she kept seeing Trystan's face as he walked away from her, even if she felt as though whatever threads she'd tried to spin, binding her to Trystan, were now pulled tight to the point of breaking inside her, she had to hold fast to her own decision now.

Cath and Eurig exchanged a glance, and then Eurig shook his head. "Not for certain he didn't. Why?"

Isolde set her cup of water down and gave Cabal the last of the bread. "Because there's to be another meeting of the king's council in about a week's time. And I want to attend."

Eurig and Cath exchanged another long look, and this time it was Cath who said, "Why?"

Isolde drew in her breath, locking her hands tight together in her lap, knowing how much depended on her getting this right. Then she began, going briefly over what the two men already knew of Madoc's treason, then repeating what Fidach had told her the night before. And then, step by step, she laid out the plan that had formed as though of its own accord while she sat by Fidach's body and sang his spirit on its way.

Finally she stopped speaking and looked from one to the other of the two men. The stream behind them splashed and murmured, and from somewhere in the trees came the raucous, scolding call of a jay.

Eurig's round, jowly face was grimy in the gray morning light and creased in an anxious frown. Cath looked thoughtful. He scratched his jaw, then spoke. "All you say may be true enough. But

I'd have to be a good bit sicker of living than I am to let you walk straight into danger when Trystan had made me swear I'd see you came to no harm."

He glanced at Eurig, who grimaced and gave a short nod of confirmation. So Trystan could walk away from her, leaving her to fear for him with every breath she took, so long as he'd Cath and Eurig here to ensure that he didn't have to fear for her.

Isolde said, meeting Cath's bright blue gaze, "You told me that you have both a daughter and a son." She turned to Eurig. "And I know you had a son, as well." She saw pain cross Eurig's face at the mention of the boy he'd not seen in years—but made herself go on. "We've just buried Fidach. You know what Octa of Kent did to him. Madoc's son, Rhun, is only five years old. Five years old and a captive—just as Fidach was—of Octa." She stopped, then said, her voice very quiet, "Can you look at me and say that if it were your son"—she turned to Eurig—"or yours, Cath, you wouldn't want someone to at least try to get him free?"

For a moment, the forest clearing was quiet again, the air blurred by the shadows of dawn, the silence lengthening all about them. Then Cath blew out a breath. "Christ's avenging chickens."

"You don't agree?"

"Oh, I agree all right." Cath's mouth twisted. "All too well. So does Eurig, there." He jerked his head at the other man. "We're just sitting here and wondering which of us is going to draw the short straw and get to be the one who explains it to Trystan."

Isolde drew what felt like her first real breath since she'd risen from her place by the stream. "Then you'll help me get to the king's council meeting? Unless Madoc has changed it, there'll be a gathering at the next turning of the moon."

Cath watched her a moment. "What would you do if I said we wouldn't?"

"I'd say that you'd have to tie me hand and foot and set a constant guard if you meant to keep me here. Because I'd be grateful beyond words for your help. But even without it, I'd have to try this all the same."

Cath's eyes stayed steady on hers, but then he gave a short grunt of a laugh. "Well, then."

He glanced at Eurig, who seemed to understand the unspoken question in his look, for he nodded, passing a hand across his bald crown. "Aye." Eurig spoke with his usual slow, sober deliberation. "I'm with you. Can't see that there's any other choice to be made."

OCTA OF KENT EYED THE PILE of gold before him, leathery face impassive, eyes hard. "And you found this as part of the hidden storehouse guarded by Cerdic's men?" He barely waited for Trystan's short nod. Trystan could see the other man's gaze turning distant, thoughts following an inner track as he came to the inevitable conclusion. After a moment he said in a voice that grated with anger, "Bribes. Intended as payment to any man willing to turn traitor and allow Cerdic's men past our defense here."

This time Trystan had been poured a cup of dark—and undoubtedly expensive—imported wine by one of Octa's body slaves. He took a swallow and said, "As you say."

Octa's hall was unchanged in the weeks since last he'd sat at this table with the Kentish king. There were the same painted shields, war axes, and swords hung on the timbered walls, and the air was still thick with smoke from the central hearth. There were the same greasy-haired, leather-clad warriors sprawled in the straw that littered the floor of the lower half of the room, drinking ale and wagering on a fight between two war hounds and playing at dice.

And there was the same old woman seated on a pile of furs and tapestried pillows in the corner of the room nearest to where he and Octa sat. Still swathed in shawls and a dark head cloth, head bent as she spun a cloud of wool into a single even thread. Still a strangely dissonant note in what was clearly Octa of Kent and his warrior's domain.

Tonight there'd been no keen, penetrating look in Trystan's direction; since Trystan had sat down opposite Octa at the wooden table, the old woman hadn't spared them so much as a glance, but kept her gaze lowered, body hunched, as she bent over her work. But Trystan had long before this trained himself to an awareness of being watched and observed; by now it was instinct, a cold knife prick on his skin that he recognized without conscious need for thought. And, letting his gaze drift briefly to the old woman's corner, he knew by the tension in the woman's swathed shoulders, the tilt of her head, that she was listening attentively to the talk between himself and Octa all the same.

Octa shifted position, and Trystan pulled both his attention and his gaze back to the man opposite him. "So, my friend." Octa reached to take one of the gold pieces from the heap on the table, turning it between two fingers so that the clearly marked stamp of *GEVVISSÆ CYNING*—King Cerdic of Wessex—caught the light. "This relationship may indeed prove profitable to us both. You've done better than I expected you might."

Thanks would have been a mistake, so Trystan only took another swallow from his cup of wine.

Octa frowned at the gold piece a moment more, rubbed the edge with his thumb, then dropped it with a clink back on the larger pile. Trystan knew a search would be made in the coming days of the personal effects of all Octa's fighting men. And he sent a silent apology towards any poor devils who'd already accepted Cerdic's bribes. A futile hope that there would be none who had.

He'd already weighed the good he might do against just how much his conscience would stand. But he'd have needed a lot more of Octa's wine before he could sit here and think without any guilt of the men—albeit traitors—and the unpleasant deaths they were soon to suffer.

Still, he wasn't done here. He'd delivered the gold, had given Octa the report of burning Cerdic's hidden storehouse, which would serve as a warning to Cerdic that his plans of attack were known. That had gained him a measure of Octa's trust, insofar as Octa trusted anyone at all. Time to go on with the other half of his purpose in being here.

This, at any rate, he could contemplate without the faintest compunction.

Trystan pushed the half-empty cup of wine aside and said, careful to keep his tone casual, without too much interest or inflection, "I overheard the guards speaking while I was watching the place." He'd have been equally feeble-witted to let Octa know about Daka and Piye, so he'd been careful to imply that in finding Cerdic's store-house he'd acted alone. "They were saying that there'd been far more gold than this when Cerdic first had the place built and stocked with supplies. But that they'd already been hit. Raided by a band of Marche of Cornwall's men."

A ship sails on gentle seas.
At its prow a maiden stands,
Morgan of the fairies.
Forever young, forever fair,
Her raven locks caught on the wind,
She calls the magic from her heart.
It runs through her fingers,
Like sand, like time.

ISOLDE STOOD IN THE SHADOWS AT the back of the King's council hall, listening to Taliesin's song. His voice, the plucked notes of the harp, the words themselves, seemed to shimmer like moonlight on water.

Night had long since fallen, and the hall was filled with smoke and leaping shadows from the torches set on the walls. No one, since she'd slipped inside the door, had noticed her; dressed in the travel-stained gown she'd worn from the abbey, she might easily have passed for one of the serving women who moved around the room with pitchers of ale.

The narrow room was crowded, torchlight glinting off the gold of torques and armbands the council men and their warriors wore, their bright-colored cloaks and leather war gear and the polished hilts of knives and swords. At the moment, all eyes were fixed on the front of the room, where the bard played.

Green meadows and cool wind,
blood soaks the grass below.
They called him Arthur.
He looks up at the sky
He turns his head at the rising breeze.
Catching sight of the ancient ship,

His eyes fall closed.
She has come. At last
She has come.

Listening, Isolde could feel an almost throbbing power in the music that seemed to echo a voice deep in the ancient hill fort itself. It wasn't hard to imagine tonight that the Old Ones who had sacrificed themselves to secure the foundations of this place, succumbed to suffering the sacred triple death, had opened a small crack to the Otherworld, through which their voices could still be heard. Listening, Isolde wondered whether in dying they had foreseen the need for the protection they cast—not only in their time, but in this one, now.

The sea whitens; the dawn brings light.
All is peace at last
The King's wounds are healed.
Arthur sleeps
In Ynys Afallach, the realm of Avalon.

Taliesin's song ended, the plucked crystal pure notes of his harp and the clear notes of his voice blending, quivering in the air, and then melting into silence. For a moment, all was still in the hall, as still as the space between heartbeats, the space between breaths.

It made for an odd contrast. Taliesin, plump and sleek in his rich cream-colored tunic and jewel-colored cloak, his mouth still twisted with something like bitterness, black eyes sharp with a kind of sullen anger at the world. And yet his voice and his lily-white, graceful hands seemed to call up not only the echo of that ancient buried voice but a deep, wordless longing, as well.

Even Isolde had felt it. She couldn't honestly think the songs of Arthur's glorious reign any less a children's bedtime tale than the thought of Morgan magically healing the king of his wounds, granting him mist-filled eternal rest on the sacred Glass Isle.

But as she had listened to Taliesin, even she had felt a deep pull of sadness, an ache for the world, the past age that had come and now gone—or, if not the true past, at least the glimmering tapestry world of the song.

Isolde made herself draw a breath. Because now that Taliesin's song was ended, the moment she had been waiting for had nearly come.

For nearly a week now, Isolde had been sleeping under the stars with only her traveling cloak for cover, washing in brooks and streams, eating what plants and berries she could gather and what game Cabal, Cath, and Eurig between them could hunt. It felt strange, now, to return to the newly built council hall and the hill fort she'd visited only a month before. To realize that she still had a place here, among the rulers of Britain. A place, and a task to perform.

And if, standing here, she wished with a hollow ache under her breastbone that she might have caught even the briefest glimpse of Trystan's face in one of those brooks and streams in which she'd bathed, she knew that she absolutely couldn't afford to let herself think of that now.

She, Cath, and Eurig had arrived at the hill fort near sundown, just in time to watch the sun's fiery rays gilding the wooden ramparts and rings of earthworks as they made their way upwards towards the crown of the hill. The guards posted had been Cynlas of Rhos's men, standing at the heavy main gates beneath burning torches whipped into banners of flame by the night breeze. They'd been surprised at Isolde's sudden appearance—and with an escort of only two men. But they'd recognized her at once and had without hesitation let her enter the fort.

And so, leaving Cath and Eurig with Cabal, Isolde had slipped inside the council hall. In time to hear Cerdic, his sculptured face grim, addressing the company at large.

A cache of Cerdic's armies had been raided, the grain and gold stored there stolen and the cache house itself burned. Strangely, the men who had been posted on guard at the site had only been struck unconscious and trussed up so that the goods could be removed. They'd been able to tell their story: that the band who had attacked had worn the blue boar badge of Marche of Cornwall.

Before the company, Cerdic had called for his sword, opened a cut across the flat of his palm, and smeared the blood over his own shield with a vow to spill Lord Marche's blood even as he had spilled his own. He had already dispatched fifty of his own spear-men to march north with Meurig of Gwent and his men. Now he pledged to send at least a hundred more—and pledged, too, in blood, his renewed allegiance to Britain's cause.

The council meeting had gone on, though the news they dis-cussed had been nothing Isolde had not already heard. On the road coming here, they had seen ominous columns of thick black smoke on the horizon, marking another settlement raided and burned by Octa's warlords, who still controlled the lands around the borders of Kent, and twice Isolde and her companions had met with small par-ties of exhausted travelers, fleeing the wreckage to whatever safety could be found in the war-torn land.

Isolde had offered to treat their hurts, had salved burns and stitched cuts and treated frightened, hollow-eyed children and ba-bies' coughs with what medicines she'd brought with her from the abbey and what herbs could be gathered from the woods through which they passed. And as she'd worked, Eurig and Cath had talked with the men and learned what news was to be had. Despite the renewed raids in the east, the situation along the coast appeared un-changed, Britain's united armies and Octa's at a standoff, neither side gaining, neither side losing ground.

Now Taliesin had finished playing, and the men were stirring in their places along the benches, preparing to rise. Isolde drew in her breath, and, before the meeting could start to disburse, stepped swiftly out from her place in the shadows and into the center of the council hall.

Madoc saw her first. Isolde saw his eyes flare wide with shock, his whole body jerk back as though burned. She kept her gaze on him as she moved forward, through the rows of benches towards the front of the room. Her heart was beating hard and fast. But it was for this she'd come. If she couldn't succeed now, tonight, then she'd risked herself for nothing—and Britain was truly lost, as well.

"Lady Isolde." Madoc had himself under control; only someone watching closely would have seen the tightness at the corners of his eyes, the jerk of a muscle at the edge of his mouth. "I am thankful beyond measure to see you here tonight—and safe. I—we—under-stood you had been abducted from the abbey."

He could hardly have said anything less. But all the same, Isolde could almost believe there was a flare of genuine relief in his dark eyes.

She heard the ripple of surprise go round the room as the rest of the men caught sight of her, and she bowed her head. "Thank you, my lord Madoc. There was an attempt at abduction, as you say. But thanks to the loyalty of friends, I am safe. As you see." Then she drew in her breath, and before Madoc could reply, said what she'd planned, what she'd gone over again and again on the long journey here. "I fear, though, that I must bring you ill news. Concerning your son."

She saw shock tighten Madoc's expression once again, and this time she thought there was anger, as well, in his scarred face. But here, before the watching eyes of the entire assembled council, he could do nothing but say in a harsh voice, as she'd known he would, "My son?"

Isolde ordered herself to go carefully, not to let herself slip into haste or uncertainty or fear. *You have only one chance. No room for mistakes. You have to get this right.*

She took another step forward, keeping her gaze steady on Madoc's face. "I am sorry beyond words to be the bearer of such ill news, my lord. But your son has been abducted, as I nearly was, and is now hostage of Octa of Kent."

Another wave of shock swept the room, and Isolde heard several startled outcries and exclamations. She never looked away from Madoc, though, but instead went on, raising her voice just a little to be heard over the clamor, speaking as steadily as before. "But I can at least tell you where your son is being held. And I can—I think—offer you a means of ensuring his safe return."

THE FIRE IN THE GREAT CENTRAL hall had burned down to glowing embers, and the timbered walls of the council hall were melting into deepening shadows. The men were gone. Isolde sat alone with Madoc on one of the benches at the head of the hall.

Listening to the distant, mournful call of an owl outside, to the sounds of the camp all about them settling for the night, Isolde

remembered sitting with Madoc of Gwynedd this way once before, in the empty council hall at Tintagel, after all the rest of the
king's council were gone. That had been the night when, learning
of Marche's treason, the council had chosen him High King. Then
they'd sat in exhausted silence, like two survivors of a war.

Now the silence between them was different—though, strangely,
it was untouched by tension or strain. It felt to Isolde more like a
pause, a drawing of breath, before what they both knew was inevitably to come.

But when at last Madoc spoke, the words were scarcely those
Isolde had expected. "Your Hereric is as fine a hand with the horses
as you claimed. He's much valued among the stablemen. Though I'm
sure he'll be glad to see you again."

"I'll be glad to see him, as well."

Madoc looked at her searchingly. "You had no fear for him?"

"No." And it was true. She'd never doubted that Madoc would
keep the promise he'd made in the abbey chapel weeks ago. "You
gave me your word." Isolde heard Madoc let out his breath, saw
him briefly close his eyes. There was a moment's pause, and then
she said, voicing the unspoken truth that rested between them,
"We both know that the council's decision matters little. You could
easily send word to Octa, warn him that my offer of allegiance is
merely a ploy."

She had tonight outlined the plan that had come to her at Fidach's gravesite. And, almost to her surprise, the council had agreed
to what she'd proposed. She was to travel to Caer Peris, and, as Lady
of Camelerd, offer Octa an oath of fealty in exchange for his protection. Octa might be wary—suspicious, even—but the prospect of
gaining control of Camelerd without even a fight would almost certainly be enough to gain her admittance inside Octa's walls.

Where she might be able to make contact with Madoc's son,
Rhun, and discover how he might safely be smuggled out of the fortress and away from Octa's hands.

Now Madoc was watching her curiously, a look Isolde couldn't
quite read behind his black eyes. "You have a great deal of courage,
Lady Isolde," he said. "Both to come here at all and to propose such
a mission for yourself."

"Perhaps. But as I've discovered these last weeks, there is danger everywhere just now. Even barricaded inside a Christian abbey's walls, with your men posted as guards, I was not safe. And my safety will be even less assured should Octa and Marche win the war."

Meeting Madoc's gaze, she thought that the look in his eyes might almost have been one of relief, or hope. She couldn't be certain. But it was enough to make her ask, directly and without further waiting, "Are you going to send word to Octa that my proposed oath of fealty is merely a ploy?"

Madoc was silent a space before answering, his eyes on the dying embers of the fire before them. Finally, he let out a breath and ran a hand down his face. "You must have believed I would not, else you'd not have come here tonight."

His tone implied a question. But instead of answering, Isolde asked one in return. "Do any of your men know of your agreement with Octa?"

Madoc bent his shoulders, bracing his forearms on his knees and flexing his hands, watching the play of muscles beneath the skin. "No. None."

"And have you . . ." Isolde paused. "Have you yet given Octa all the information you might have done? All he might use against us in a final push to end the war?"

Slowly, Madoc shook his head once more. "I have not. Though Octa of Kent believes I have done." Slowly, his head lifted, and Isolde saw that there was a slight, humorless smile playing about the corners of his mouth. "You are saying, Lady Isolde, that in my own heart I have not been fully committed to betraying Britain's cause."

"I'm saying that you are not so far committed now that you cannot yet turn back. I told you that once before, and it is still true tonight." Isolde leaned forward a little, clasping her hands tight in her lap. "You have done no irretrievable harm. Committed no crime which may not yet be turned into good."

She paused, willing Madoc to listen, willing whatever fates were governing this night—whatever protective spirits of the Old Ones who might linger here—to please, *please* let her find the words that would sway him as she'd not managed to before. She drew in her breath, then went on. "I remember speaking about you to Kian, when you came to Dinas Emrys months ago. Do you remember that day? It was just after Kian had been captured. Just after he'd lost his eye."

Madoc's gaze was fixed on the dying fire, the last faint glow of light and shadow playing across his face, but she saw him flinch, and without looking at her he gave a short, wordless nod.

Isolde went on, her voice wavering a bit as she remembered Kian sitting in her workroom, bruised and bloody, while she applied a compress to the raw wound. "Kian said that you were the kind of man who doesn't tolerate weakness—not in yourself, nor in your men. But he said . . . his words were that he doubted there was one among your army who wouldn't follow you into a wolves' den, waving a haunch of raw meat."

She stopped. She thought there might have been a sheen of moisture in Madoc's gaze. But he said nothing, and he kept his gaze turned away.

Isolde realized her hands were clasped so tightly together that her wrists and fingers ached. She said, "In Kian's eyes—in the eyes of all the men who've given you their fighting oaths—you are still that man. And, more than that, in their eyes you need never be anything *but* that man. The one they would follow without question into the thick of battle. The one they would willingly, proudly, give their lives to serve."

Finally, Madoc turned to face her. His face worked, and his chest rose and fell as though he struggled for air. "You are suggesting—"

"Go before the council," Isolde said. "Tell them of the offer Octa made you. And your agreement with him need never, so far as any but the two of us know, be anything but a clever ploy to get past Octa's defenses. Lure him into a false alliance so that he may be caught off guard and defeated once and for all."

Isolde touched Madoc's arm. "You may have felt when Octa took your son hostage that you had no choice but to agree to what he asked." Outside in the encampment, one of the war hounds howled, but Isolde held Madoc's gaze with her own, forcing him not to look away, silently willing him to believe what she said. "But you *do* have a choice now."

On the central hearth, a glowing log flared briefly red, then collapsed into gray ash. The silence pooled and spread out. Then: "No," Madoc said quietly. "I do not."

And then, before Isolde could speak, before the lurch she felt could turn to sickening disappointment, Madoc's mouth lifted in another smile. An easier smile, this time. He drew a breath, then let it out. "Go to Caer Peris, Lady Isolde. As the council agreed tonight. And I thank you." His voice was quiet and a little husky in the big, still room.

His eyes met hers. Silence fell between them, and seemed to stretch out for an endlessly long moment, the quiet isolation of the empty hall seeming to draw in all around. Madoc's hand lifted, as though he were about to reach for her, and he said, his voice nearly a whisper, now, "I wish . . ."

The place of High King is a lonely one, Madoc had told her once. And she'd never thought, really, that his proposal of marriage had come from more than the knowledge that she, too, knew what that kind of loneliness was. But now, just for an instant, the look in Madoc's gaze was so raw that Isolde felt her breath catch.

He stopped before saying what it was he wished. His hand fell, his mouth tightened, and he looked away.

Isolde couldn't stop herself from reaching out, touching his arm again. "I am truly sorry," she said quietly. "But I thank you, as well."

She felt Madoc's muscles tighten under her touch. But he turned to give her another brief smile. "Go to Caer Peris," he said again. And then his expression shifted, hardened and set into something like his old one, that of a man of action, a leader in battle and war. He smiled grimly, balled his fingers, struck his fist against the palm of his hand. "And between us—between all Britain's united forces— may we succeed in nailing Octa of Kent's hide to the wall."

BOOK III

Chapter 11

THE AIR AT CAER PERIS smelt of salt and ocean and far distant
lands. Isolde leaned against the waist-high stone wall of the
ramparts, looking out across the wave-capped waters that spread
out before her, watching a gull wheel and circle on the wind that
whipped at her skirts and hair.

She'd lived at Tintagel, built on a jutting edge of Cornwall,
where the land, the very walls of the castle seemed poised to tumble
into the sea. The ocean was no stranger to her. But it felt different
here, somehow. Tintagel's walls had echoed like a bard's song with
tales of the past—of Uther the Pendragon and his Queen Ygraine,
and a night when Arthur, savior of Britain, had been made by the
magic of Myrddin.

But here, at Caer Peris, she could feel no echo, even, of the
Roman legionaries who had built this fortress on the shore—built
it for defense against the very Saxon tribes who held it now. Instead,
the thick stone walls seemed to look outwards, and the salt-scented
wind that whipped at her hair and skirts seemed to sing of the far-
off countries that lay beyond vast expanse of the sea.

Or maybe she only imagined it did, because she wished, at this
moment, to be anywhere but here.

The fortress was built in the curve of a natural harbor whose
white chalk cliffs rose starkly from the shingled coastline. From
where Isolde stood, looking out towards the open sea, she could see
the long, dark shape of the channel island of Ynys Gywth, called

Wihte Ealond, by Cerdic and his forces, who held it now. On the landward side, the fortress was surrounded by brackish marsh stretching away in a flat plain that eventually gave way to farming and grazing land for goats and sheep and wild ponies.

Here and there clumps of gorse bloomed, spiky yellow flames against the gray brown boggy heath. But few animals save the wild ponies now remained, not after the recent siege that had been waged here. Even now, two months later, the ravens and other carrion birds still circled the fields where the battle had been fought, and at night Isolde's skin pricked coldly with the sounds of the wolves that came to dig in the shallow graves.

Overhead, a gull screamed and wheeled on the gusting breeze, and Isolde followed its circles with her eyes. To the north, the land rose to a crest of turfed and pastured hill, beyond which stretched thick forest, the same forest in which Madoc and his armies were now encamped.

Isolde had asked Madoc, the last time she'd spoken to him, whether the already shaky alliance between Britain's forces and Cerdic's had been weakened by the destruction of Cerdic's secret storehouse, the loss of his gold, and the discovery—though no one on the council had outright said as much—that Cerdic had been planning to move independently against Octa of Kent.

Madoc's face had been tense, his eyes dark with strain. That he was already regretting having agreed to Isolde's journey to Caer Peris had been plain. But at the question, his face had lightened into a brief, tired smile.

"If anything, this has strengthened the alliance. Cerdic is now determined to focus his energies on cooperating and uniting fully with our plans of battle. And on defeating Marche—which, as you may imagine, pleases Meurig of Gwent. Few things bring men together like hatred of a common foe."

Madoc had paused, then, eyes on Isolde, before finally bursting out, "I wish to God I could send a greater force of men to guard you."

Isolde wished it, as well, but she forced a small smile. "Eurig and Cath will go with me. And you've granted me Kian. There's no one else I'd sooner trust, no one I'd want with me more than those three."

Save for Trystan. But she wasn't letting herself think of Trystan, then or now.

Especially now, when for all the protection Kian, Cath, and Eurig could offer her, they might as well have been sleeping with Arthur in the mists of the Glass Isle.

She did, at least, still have Cabal. She had left the big dog asleep on a rug spread before the hearth of the room in the fortress's guest hall, where she'd spent the night.

They had arrived at the wide, heavily guarded landgate of the fortress the previous evening, just as the rays of the setting sun were bathing the walls of Caer Peris in crimson and setting the spread of ocean behind it afire. And they'd been admitted as soon as Isolde had identified herself, led past the storehouses and smith's shops and soldiers' barracks to the stone-built inner fortification—and from there to Octa of Kent's hall.

Again and again on the road coming here, she'd wondered what she would do if Octa recognized her as the woman responsible for the very nearly crushing defeat he'd suffered at Cerdic's hands. And not once had she been able to think of a single plan that stood even a remote chance of saving her or her companions' lives if that fear were to come true.

But Octa had received her without a glimmer of recognition in his chilly gaze. And Isolde had been glad of the preparation that meeting had offered. Glad that Octa of Kent's hard face and steely, almost empty eyes—his long braided hair and necklace of human finger bones and beard dipped in black pitch—didn't take her completely by surprise.

The Saxon king had offered her a chair beside his own and a cup of thick, sweet dark wine. And he had accepted her story that for the safety of herself and her lands, she wished to ally Camelerd with what she had come to believe must prove the winning side of the war. Indeed, he'd believed her so readily, had questioned her so little and paid such perfunctory attention to the answers she gave, that Isolde, remembering, felt slithering unease brush along her spine.

She'd been prepared for a lengthy interrogation—for having to tread carefully, to keep all her wits about her to parry questions and persuade Octa that she came in good faith. To have her story accepted almost before she'd finished it's telling had felt off, somehow, indefinably wrong.

But Octa had offered her the hospitality of the fortress for as long as she wished to stay. Only as the audience was drawing to a close had he looked at her directly and smiled, displaying teeth worn to little more than brown stumps.

"I offer your bodyguards the same hospitality, of course. They will be housed with my warriors in the men's hall. And you will be guarded by two of my own men, to honor our new alliance. I insist."

She'd agreed, because plainly she'd had no choice but to give her consent.

And so far, she had been safe. She had been awarded a place near—although thankfully not beside—Octa's at the evening meal the night before in the great hall. And she'd been allotted a room of her own, furnished with carved wooden bed and table and thick silvery furs on the floor. And a maidservant—a blue eyed, stolidly built woman perhaps ten years older than herself and as silent and impassive as her guards—to fetch and carry for her and help her dress.

And now, after a night of fitful sleep on the carved wooden bed, she stood on the fortress ramparts, watching the morning sun sparkle on the waves below. Trying, still, to block out all uneasiness or fear—and to ignore the presence of the two armed and helmeted bodyguards Octa had assigned her, who had taken up their duties the night before.

She didn't even know their names. She had asked, but Octa must have given orders not to speak with her, because both men had only stared fixedly straight ahead at the question and ignored it as completely as though they'd not heard. Grim-faced and steely-eyed, they had followed a few paces behind every step she'd taken this morning, from the moment she'd left her room. Though once atop the ramparts they'd started a sparring match with their heavy wooden-shafted spears.

Isolde had been paying little mind to their grunts and shouts and the crash of the wooden spear shafts coming together, but now, glancing towards them, she caught a few words, spoken in the Saxon tongue.

"Block me, you arse-licking son of a whore!" That was the older of the two guards, a gray-haired man of forty-odd. His helmet was of leather, tufted with wolf's fur, and beneath it his face was grim and remorseless, his features hard-bitten and scarred by a lifetime's battles as well as by the deep pitted marks of some child-hood pox.

The other guard was a much younger man—scarcely more than a boy, really—with flaxen hair, a tall, lanky form, and a pale-eyed, narrow face that would be bony one day, but as yet hadn't quite lost the softness of youth. He was panting now, his cheeks streaked with sweat as he struggled to dodge, block, and parry the older man's lightning-swift thrusts.

The gray-haired man brought his spear up, and, holding it cross-wise as a wooden staff, delivered a smashing blow that sent the younger guard crashing to the ground. "I said block me!" he growled. "Wodin's tree, you might as well use the knife at your belt to cut off your scabby cock and give it to the lady, there. She'd make a better warrior than you."

As he spoke, he shot a glance over his shoulder at Isolde. His eyes were a flat, almost colorless blue, and something in their gaze, half dislike, half thinly veiled contempt, made Isolde say before she could stop herself, "The lady doubts it. But she does understand some of the Saxon tongue."

If she'd been remotely in a mood for humor, it would have been funny to watch the gray-haired guard's face go from contemptu-ous to slack-jawed, to see the faint stain of color rise up his thickly muscled neck. He stared at her a moment. Then, without a word, he turned, hauled the younger man to his feet, and resumed the spar-ring match where they'd left off.

Isolde turned back to lean against the outer wall and look out across the wave-capped water, silently cursing herself. She'd spent nearly the whole of her life nursing wounded soldiers. It wasn't as though she'd never heard rough language before. So why—she clenched her hands—why, in the name of the maiden, mother, and crone, did she have to let herself lose her temper now of all times?

A gust of wind whipped a strand of hair across her face and she thrust it viciously back. In gaining entrance and Octa's—however precarious—acceptance, she had still accomplished not even half of her purpose here. She had still to find a doubtless frightened five-year-old boy and discover a way to get him free from here.

And more than that, she had to learn enough of the fort's defenses that she could help Madoc and the rest of the council formulate a plan for breaching the defenses of Caer Peris and defeating Octa once and for all. Which was impossible task enough without senselessly antagonizing her guards. Or ensuring that she'd overhear nothing useful by giving away her familiarity with the Saxon tongue.

Lackwit!

Isolde walked a short distance further along the outer wall, shading her eyes against the sun. And then felt sudden, tingling cold crawl the length of her spine as the guards, Madoc's son, even her own position here were instantly pushed to the back of her mind.

She stood on the eastern side of the fort, just above the water gate that formed one of the two main entrances to the outer Roman built walls. The other entrance was the wide, heavily fortified landgate on Caer Peris's western front. It was a powerful stronghold for any man's army. The man who controlled Caer Peris held not only the fortress itself, but the natural harbor below her, as well.

And from where she stood, Isolde could see the ships that filled the harbor. Several small trading vessels, that would bring food and fresh supplies to the army within, allowing Octa to withstand a siege nearly indefinitely. But that wasn't what had caught her eye. Beside the trading vessels, bobbing slightly in the waves, rode a fleet of a dozen and more sleek, dragon-prowed ships. Warships. And not Octa's own fleet, either, because Isolde could see several more vessels that had been drawn aground on the narrow shingled beach, all flying Octa's totem of a white horse's head on a blood-red background.

These warships must be newly come; she could see, too, an encampment laid out at the tops of the stark chalk cliffs, the army tents looking small and harmless as children's toys from this distance, the men milling about the camp like a swarm of ants.

Isolde blinked the dazzle of sunlight from her eyes, made herself ignore the stab of fear at the base of her spine, and counted the number of ships and then the number of tents once, and then again. Then she stood staring unblinkingly down, eyes dazzled by the sun and stinging salt wind and the glittering waves. If she was right, Madoc and the rest of Britain's forces had to contend not only with Octa's own army, the warriors that had a month and more ago captured this fortress from Cerdic's men. Now, if they were to defeat Octa, they had to face a force of at least five hundred more.

A sound behind Isolde made her turn to see her guards pausing in their match of spears and, both breathing hard now, moving aside from the stair to allow two people to pass. One was a bent, white-haired old woman whom Isolde had seen at the evening meal in the hall the night before, swathed in shawls and seated on a pile of fur-covered cushions just behind Octa's own chair. And the other . . .

The other was a dark-haired boy, looking very small and slight, standing bent-headed and unresponsive at the old woman's side. The older of the two guards spoke briefly to the woman, and the boy went rigid, hands tightening to fists, then turned so that his face was hidden from Isolde. But she'd already seen his eyes. Very dark eyes—a rarity, here, in this Saxon stronghold. And very nearly the mirror of Madoc's own.

The old woman moved across the ramparts with a bent, slightly limping gate, and the boy, after a moment's hesitation, followed, his gate shuffling and slow, his head bent and his gaze trained on the ground. When she reached the outer wall, not far from where Isolde herself stood, the old woman turned and touched the boy lightly on the shoulder. He stiffened again at the touch, shoulders hunching, and didn't look at her, instead moving away to begin a slow progress along the walkway's curving edge. He never looked up, that Isolde could see, never even glanced at the glimmering expanse of sunlit water that stretched out around them on three sides. His gaze re-mained firmly fixed on the ground, and he paused only to kick idly at the stones of the outer wall.

The old woman watched him a moment, then seemed to sigh and moved to approach the segment of wall where Isolde stood. She made Isolde a small bow of greeting, though she didn't speak, only turned away, looking out as Isolde had done on the wave-capped expanse of blue gray-sea stretched out below.

Her face was hook-nosed, fierce, and strongly molded, despite wrinkles upon wrinkles of loosened, paper-dry skin, and Isolde thought there was a resemblance to someone she knew or had recently seen that for the moment she couldn't quite identify. Her brows were bushy white, and below them her pale blue eyes looked out on the world through a film of age.

Isolde was wondering whether she ought offer some greeting when abruptly the old woman turned to her, fixing the rheumy blue gaze on her face.

"For forty years now," she said, "I have watched our men fight and forge alliances and bleed and battle to carve out kingdoms here. We came because of a starving time in Jutland. A time when the rains came without ceasing and the crops rotted in the fields. The old and the children sickened and died, and the horses were butchered for meat, and women smothered their newborn babes because one more mouth could not be fed and they could not bear to watch the babes slowly starve. So the longboats were launched. And we came here."

How old would she have been then? Isolde wondered. Thirty? Thirty-five? Studying her face now, Isolde thought she could catch just a glimpse of the woman she must have been then: blond-haired and straight-backed, her blue eyes still keen and clear and her face as yet unlined but no less fierce.

As though she'd heard the thought, the old woman's eyes met hers. "I had lost a husband to the fighting and three children to the hunger. I felt I had nothing more to be lost. And since then I have watched our people wedded to the land through blood and sweat and toil. Though I don't"—her voice turned slightly wry, and she gave Isolde a quick glance from under her brows—"expect you to agree."

Isolde didn't answer at once. She looked down towards the dragon-prowed warships and the army encampment below. Then she said, slowly, "I don't know." The words were in keeping with the role she played here. And yet she found they were also not—entirely—untrue. "For generations on generations, Britons have fought other Britons for the land and wealth this country provides. Does that mean our men alone have the right to kill and maim one another over kingdoms?"

The old woman tipped her head back and laughed at that, a surprisingly deep, throaty chuckle that seemed somehow too large for her wizened frame. "Very true." Then she stopped, the smile fading to be replaced once more by the look of almost eerie calm. "Though it would also be true to argue that after a lifetime of warfare, my brother has now become so drunk on blood that he has run mad with it." Her tone was calm, almost unconcerned, and she added, fingers still steadily guiding the spindle and thread, "Still, even a king cannot live forever. And Octa has sons who are not—not yet—the man their father has become."

Isolde had been asking herself whether she might risk a question about the newly arrived warships, but at that she caught herself up sharply, realization striking her. "Your brother," she repeated. "Then . . ."

The old woman glanced up at her and nodded, a small, strange little half smile playing about the edges of her thin mouth. "Your pardon. I ought to have presented myself formally before now. I am sister to Octa. Daughter of Hengist, son of Uictgils, son of Uitta, son of Uecta, and so on back"—another wry smile touched her mouth—"to the great god Woden himself, if my brother is to be believed." She straightened and made Isolde a small, oddly graceful bow. "My name is Godgyth."

Isolde returned the bow. "And I'm—"

Again Godgyth stopped her before she could finish. "Yes, I know." The milky blue gaze moved over Isolde from head to foot, taking in, Isolde was sure, every detail of her appearance, hair, and clothes.

Since she'd arrived at Madoc's hill fort with little more than her cloak and the three travel-stained sets of shifts and gowns with which she'd left the abbey, there had been a hurried and united effort amongst the women's hall to outfit her with clothes more credibly those of a princess seeking alliance with a foreign lord. Her hair was caught back in a net of silver thread, and she wore silver drops in her ears and a heavy bracelet about each wrist. Her gown was of pale green with bands of flowered embroidery at the sleeves and hem—a gift from the young wife of one of Huel of Rhegged's chieftans. Its folds smelled, just faintly, of the aniseed and southernwood with which it had been packed to keep mice and insects away, but its high waist hid the slight curve of the child that had by now begun to show.

Godgyth's eyes, though, seemed to linger on Isolde's middle before traveling back to her face, and she said again, "I know who you are. And," she added, "why you have come here."

Perhaps strangely, Isolde hadn't, until now, been afraid. Not even on learning that Godgyth was sister to Octa. Now, though, she felt uneasiness trickle in like icy water through a crack. She was only partially relieved when, without waiting for a reply, Godgyth turned away, squinting a little as she, too, looked down at the sleek painted vessels bobbing in the waves far below.

"And I know, too, that the starving times are not ended. Every year will bring more longboats to these shores. More men, hungry for land and a new place to call home. Britons may fight, but our people will not be driven back. We have farmed and fought here, paid for our lands in blood and toil and will hold them, make no mistake of that."

Isolde thought of Cerdic of Wessex, saying much the same on a night weeks ago after the meeting in the council hall. She said, after a moment, "And so where will it end, do you think?"

Godgyth shook her head, eyes still on her spinning. "As to that, I cannot say. I cannot tell endings. Though don't tell my brother I have said so." A small, slightly grim twist of amusement lifted the corners of her mouth and narrowed her eyes. "He keeps me on at his court because he believes I can read the web of *Wyrd*—fate, in your tongue. Because he believes in my power of . . . we call it *spae*. You would say prophecy, I think. The power to see into the future and alter its course. Octa believes I can do this. Believes that my weavings"—she lifted the spindle and thread—"can trap the power of the three Norns—fates—who sit at the foot of the great world tree and spin out the thread of our lives."

Godgyth paused, eyes on the shimmering line of horizon where blue water met blue sky. Then she said, still in the same calm, slightly lilting tone, "My brother Octa is a hard man—and a cruel one. I have known him from an infant in the cradle, from a boy gifted by my father with his first *saex* and spear—and it is true. Blood will tell. And we come, I think, from a cruel line, Octa and I. A line of warriors who take without fear and without counting cost."

She paused, gaze distant. Then: "But my brother is also . . . I do not know the word in your tongue. In ours we would say *ofertæle*. Readily gulled into believing in a power beyond the mortal, beyond the ordinary world. Most fighting men are. The result, perhaps, of living with death constantly hovering at their backs. They seek always some some safeguard. Something that will guarantee them their lives." She made a small, derisive gesture. "It makes them easy prey to anyone with a quick wit and ready tongue and a handful of worthless charms to sell."

Isolde thought of all the little tokens she found on wounded soldiers: twists of knotted thread and scraps of embroidery stitched by sweethearts and wives, and said, "Not only the men."

But Godgyth had gone on without hearing, mouth twisting up at the edges. "And my brother, like many men of his kind believes in magic. And I should thank the gods he does, else I would be nothing but a helpless old woman left to drool in the sun. Or cast out to starve. So, yes." Her lips stretched in another mirthless smile. "Thank Woden and Freya and all the other gods of our homeland across the sea, Octa of the Bloody Knife believes that words have the power to harm or to heal—that the wind may be captured in a knotted length of thread . . . so."

Godgyth broke off a length of the thread she had already spun and deftly twisted it into a series of knots, then handed the result to Isolde. "Here—take it. For you."

She leaned forward as she spoke, and Isolde caught a gust of some strongly potent spirits on her breath. Which explained the slight slurring of her words, the faintly unfocused look of her rheumy eyes.

"Thank you." Isolde took the knotted thread between her fingers, then looked up, brows lifted in slight puzzlement. "For taming the wind?"

"No." Godgyth didn't look up. "*That one*"—she laid very slight emphasis on the words—"is to be used in childbirth. Untie the knots when the first labor pains come on—the babe will enter the world without trouble, then, and without threat to the mother's life."

Isolde's heart skipped, the trickle of uneasiness flowing faster, now, and her hands stilled on the twist of thread as she forced herself not to react. *Octa believes I can read the web of Wyrd*, Godgyth had said. She'd not actually claimed she did indeed hold the power of Otherwordly sight. But it wasn't as though Isolde could tell herself that such a thing weren't possible.

She said with an effort to speak calmly, "You speak the British language very well."

"Ah, well." Godgyth made a small, dismissive gesture with one hand, another small, tight smile curving her mouth. "I've had many Briton slaves to serve me over the years."

She paused a moment, head bent over her spinning, then said, in a different tone, "I have heard tales of your grandmother, Lady Isolde. Morgan, sister of Arthur. She was a powerful seeress, so they say."

Godgyth did glance up then, rheumy eyes suddenly masked, opaque as milky stones.

Isolde ordered herself to hold Godgyth's gaze. The old woman might be half gone in drink, but there was a purpose to this, all the same. Isolde could feel an almost palpable force running beneath Godgyth's words.

An order of Octa's? Telling his sister to try to trap a questionable ally into an admission that her purpose here was not what it seemed?

It might be. Even Godgyth's slighting words in regard to her brother might have been a trap, a ploy to lull Isolde into false confidence. And yet there had been a strange note about the older woman's voice when she'd asked her question about Morgan that made Isolde's skin prickle with something like warning.

Without waiting for an answer, Godgyth turned to stare out across the fortress walls, eyes distant, the slurring of her words more pronounced now. "The Lady Morgan believed, I suppose, in the gods of this land." With one age-twisted hand she gestured towards the ridge of rolling green hills, pasture, and forest beyond the fortress walls.

Cadfaelhod, mistress of stars. Isolde could almost imagine she heard her grandmother's voice in the wind gusting over those same hills. *Blodeuwedd, lily maid. Morrigan, goddess of battle and magic.* All gone—or at least sleeping—in the Old One's hollow hills and crystal isles.

The set of Godgyth's shoulders was almost angry. But then she turned back to Isolde.

"There will be a *symbel* in two days' time." Her wizened face was serene once more, and she set the amber-weighted drop spindle to spinning again. "A banquet to honor an expected guest of my brother. Like the Lady Morgan, I, too, cast auguries." Her jaw hardened. "So if you wish to see me prophesy, you should attend. I will wear my black lambskin cloak and sit on the high seat, and drink a porridge made from the hearts of all the living creatures which may be found within these walls. And chant the wisdom chants and cast the future of what and where Octa's next battle is to be."

Isolde fingered the knots Godgyth had tied—knots to be loosened at the birthing of a child. "And do your prophecies come true?" she asked.

Godgyth raised her head, and for the briefest instant Isolde thought there was a trace of unexpected sympathy in the clouded blue eyes. "I cannot give you endings. But I told you that before."

Isolde heard in the words an echo of her grandmother's voice from weeks before, and her skin prickled as she turned Godgyth's knotted length of thread over in her fingers. A picture swirled together in her mind's eye: Trystan, returning to the glade where she and the other men had been camped and finding them gone. Sifting through the cold ashes of what had been their campfire. Finding all that now remained the heaped earth and small cairn of stones over Fidach's grave.

Isolde dug her nails hard into her palms. She had herself survived seven years as High Queen by pretending power she didn't have. She knew how it was done—all the tricks of watching faces, noting starts and sudden intakes of breath, by watching eyes. If Godgyth couldn't actually read the future, she would surely be able to read her face if she were careless enough to give anything away.

Though she thought, too, despite the slurred voice, despite the reek of alcohol on her breath, that something more than only Godgyth's words reminded her, just faintly, of Morgan.

Godgyth watched her, head a little on one side, then asked, "And what are you thinking now?"

"I was thinking that you remind me of my grandmother, just a bit."

"Ah." Godgyth seemed to consider her a moment, then she asked, sharply, "You loved her, I think?"

Isolde's eyes suddenly stung, but she said, steadily, "Very much."

Godgyth's eyes seemed to search Isolde's a moment more, and then a surprisingly sweet smile broke out on her fierce, sculptured old face. "Then I thank you," she said, with another of those jerky and yet oddly graceful bows.

She might have said more, but a step behind them made Isolde turn to see that the dark-haired boy had finished his slow circuit of the ramparts and returned to where they stood. He took no notice of either Godgyth or Isolde, only came to a halt and stood stiffly a little distance away head bowed, eyes fixed on the ground.

Godgyth watched him a moment in silence, and Isolde thought, just briefly, that a flash of some indefinable emotion crossed her features, swift as the clouds that raced across the blue sky above. But whether it was anger or sympathy—or even satisfaction—she couldn't have told. Still watching the child, she said, voice calm as before, "He's been like that since he came. He never speaks. He's not said a word since my brother brought him here."

Seen up close, the child's small face was even more a mirror of Madoc's—as it had been before the scarring burns—than Isolde had first thought. His expression was pinched by a look of fierce, almost adult tension, as though he were trying with every part of his will to be brave, not to give way to tears or show how frightened he was. And he had, too, Isolde saw with a twist of anger, a fading bruise over one eye.

Isolde glanced up at Godgyth, but the old woman had half turned away, eyes once more on her spinning. No way to know whether this was permission, or a trap, or merely indifference. But the chance was too precious to let slip by.

Isolde bent, crouching down so that she was on a level with the boy. "Are you Rhun?"

She'd spoken softly, but still the boy's small hands clenched, his whole body seeming to still, like a hare at sight of a hunting dog. He didn't look up, but stood with his head bowed, staring down at the ground.

Isolde waited a moment, then said, "I'm glad to meet you at last. I know your father, you know." She kept her voice quiet, trying to put as much reassurance and understanding into the words as she could, to say that she knew his world had been ripped apart and turned on its head—and in his place she would have hated any and all adults, too, when it was their arbitrary dictates that had brought him here.

And maybe it worked, at least a bit, or maybe it was only the mention of Madoc that caught his attention. Slowly, slowly, Rhun's head lifted and he regarded her warily, thickly lashed black eyes dark with mistrust. Then a heavy step sounded behind her, and a pair of booted feet appeared in Isolde's field of view to the right. Looking up, she saw that it was the older of the two guards, the man with the grizzled hair and pockmarked face.

He said, shortly, "You come down now." He spoke the British tongue far less well than Godgyth, his voice harsh and grating—and even now he didn't look at Isolde directly but stood at attention and addressed the air directly above her head.

Isolde quenched a flare of anger, both for the interruption and for the fear his presence clearly caused the boy, who had instantly ducked his head, shoulders tensing once more. And who had, the Goddess knew, plainly known fear enough these last months.

But she could hardly argue—not without drawing suspicion—so she rose to her feet, smoothed her wind-tossed shawl, and said, dividing her words between Godgyth and the child, "Good-bye, then. I hope we'll meet again soon."

Godgyth regarded her a moment. Her tongue flicked across her lips again, and then she said, "I hope we may, as well." She paused, then asked, abruptly, "You're a healer, are you not? As your grandmother was?"

Isolde nodded, startled by the suddenness of the question. "That's right."

"Good." Godgyth stopped again, and when she went on her eyes were once more eerily masked, opaque in the bright sunlight. "I think it likely you may . . . find an outlet for your skills here before too long."

"LADY?"

It was the older guard speaking to her again, and Isolde looked up, surprised. They were crossing Caer Peris's sprawling inner courtyard, walking past the men's barracks, the grain storehouses, and the smoke-filled smith's forge on the way back to the innermost garrison that housed Isolde's own room. The two bodyguards were walking beside her, one on either side, and again it was the older, gray-haired man who spoke.

His pockmarked face was as grim and implacable as ever, and Isolde braced herself, wondering if she was to be rebuked for having spoken to Rhun.

"Yes?"

The guardsman frowned, then said, in a gruff, heavily accented voice, "The Lady Godgyth say—"

He broke off as the younger guardsman tripped over a clump of loose straw and staggered a pace or two before regaining his footing. "Thor's bollocks, can't you even watch where you're going, you whining cur? Or have you got cow dung for brains as well as—" The gray-haired man stopped again with a quick look at Isolde, as though belatedly recalling that she understood the Saxon tongue. He said nothing, though, only fixed his eyes straight ahead and continued in his heavily accented British.

"The Lady Godgyth say you are healer?"

Isolde tried to guess where this was leading, but couldn't. She nodded and said, "That's right."

They were passing the practice yard, where a group of warriors drilled with axes and short swords, and her guard waited until they'd left the noise and shouting behind before he said, keeping his gaze trained straight ahead, "You can make . . . love charm?"

His voice was still gratingly rough, and the question seemed so absolutely, fantastically unlikely that Isolde thought for a moment she must have misunderstood, or that the guardsman had gotten the British word wrong. She said, blankly, "A love charm?"

The gray-haired guard still didn't look at her, but nodded.

Or this could be a trick, some sort of elaborate revenge for her having embarrassed him during the sparring match on the ramparts? Just for a moment, looking at the Saxon man's remorseless, battle-scarred face and thinking of the way he'd just stopped her from speaking to Rhun, Isolde wished that she could bring herself to prescribe some truly vile potion and call it a love philter. She wouldn't even have to invent one. She'd heard of dozens from her various patients—all that their mothers or grandmothers or cousin's aunts swore by. Something to do with mouse droppings and ram's urine— and that would likely make him sick enough that he'd not be able to follow her anywhere, regardless of Octa's orders.

Her conscience, though, taking the form of her grandmother's voice, whispered that a healer's first and sacred duty was to never knowingly cause harm.

Which was, Isolde thought, purely unfair, because she wasn't at all sure whether Morgan, had she been the one here now, would have scrupled to take this chance to sicken her guard.

The Morgan in her mind's eyes gave her an unrepentant smile. *Perhaps not. But that doesn't mean I didn't raise you to be a better person than I ever was.*

Isolde drew breath. She had, at any rate, to answer the guardsman. Offer him something harmless—some mild herbal draft—and she might, possibly, win a small degree of his trust. And the gods knew she could do with an ally here.

Isolde looked up at the man beside her again. For all his foul mouth and stolid warrior's looks, she didn't think him a fool. Offer him a charm that failed—which it would, unless she was lucky to an impossible degree—and she'd draw his anger and lose far more than she might possibly gain.

"I'm sorry," she said. "I don't know any love charms."

The guard's head turned, and for a moment his gaze, flat and almost colorlessly blue, met hers. Impossible to tell whether he was angry or offended or simply unsurprised that she couldn't give him what he asked. Then he turned away again and gave another curt nod. Isolde thought the line of his mouth might have hardened, slightly, but he said only, in the same gruff voice, "I see."

"GOAT-BASTARD!" THE SAXON DROVE A FURIOUS fist into Trystan's stomach and spat the words, spittle spraying Trystan's face.

Trystan clenched his teeth. It wasn't as though he'd never done this before: shut down all emotion, all thought beyond the next move, beyond action and reaction. This time was harder, though. He had to force himself to hang limp, head drooping between the iron grip of two of Octa's warriors; force himself not to fight back, not to give way to the seething fury that pounded behind his eyeballs.

Gods, he missed being detached from the past, having the memories shut up in a box he never looked inside. Being a man without a name, without a country or home. All that had ended with the sight of Isolde's face, nearly a year ago. The first time he'd seen her in seven years. Since Camlann.

Though for all that, it was a memory of Isolde's face he fixed on now as the man—a red-faced older man with no neck and the foulest-smelling breath Trystan had ever encountered—punched him again.

It was dark, and a light rain was falling, turning the summer night raw and chill. No Neck and the other two warriors who made up this border patrol of Octa's were growing tired of Trystan's lack of response, anxious to return to their campfire and their ale. The blows were becoming more perfunctory, the curses they spat at him bored in tone.

Let them amuse themselves a short while longer and he could fake being struck unconscious by one of the blows, wait till their guard was relaxed, and then make his escape. Get back to Daka and Piye, who would have already raided the nearby encampment of Cerdic's men, traveling north towards the border of Gwent as agreed in the council meeting weeks before.

Their role was part of the plan. But he needed the reports of Marche's men in this area not to depend on his word alone. Which was why he was here, wearing the scavenged uniform of Marche's guard and playing the part of one of Marche's scouts, stupid enough to have fallen into the enemy's hands.

He'd already given Octa's men a sullen—and fabricated—account of a troop of Marche's warriors making their way south, raiding encampments and settlements that should, by Octa's lights, have been his alone.

Now—Trystan grunted as No Neck landed another punch—he just had to stay in control a short while longer. Refuse to fight back. Though he knew he could reach the knife hidden in his boot and wipe the oily smirk off No Neck's face. Do to him what he should have done to Marche . . .

Trystan swore at himself, caught himself before he could jerk free of his captors' hands.

It was early yet, and the blow just landed not all that hard, but Trystan groaned again and made himself go completely slack, hanging limp and heavy between the other two men. They dropped him, kicked him once or twice to be certain he really was unconscious. But they soon gave it up. He'd been right. They were bored with him.

"Not going to give us any more tonight. You might as well tie him up." No Neck grunted the order at one of the younger men, then stumped off towards the campfire they'd left at Trystan's appearance an hour before, and a moment later Trystan heard the slosh of a skin of ale.

The younger guard, whom No Neck had ordered to see him tied up, stooped and bound Trystan's wrists together with a leather thong. Bound them in front of his body, which was a bloody stupid mistake to make, but Trystan wasn't about to put him right.

He lay quiet, eyes closed, breathing heavily through his mouth. The bruises from the beating throbbed and were going to hurt like the devil tomorrow, but Trystan ignored the pain for now. Didn't even let himself think of Marche and the plans yet to be carried out. He concentrated instead on Isolde's face, on pushing the anger, the simmering potential for violence back into its box, shutting it off, detaching himself from it before it could take hold.

Ignoring the hatred that still, after seven years, felt like hot coals burning a way through his skin.

SHE STARED INTO HER OWN FACE, pity curling in the pit of her stomach as she opened her mouth and spoke in a voice that was at once alien and her own. "I'm sorry, Lady Isolde. He was wounded. Fatally so. He didn't—"

Isolde woke with a gasp, her heart pounding, the image of her own face, the dream's voice still so vivid in her mind's eye that for a moment they blotted out all awareness of the curtained bed and the guest hall chamber around her.

It must be about midnight, to judge by the slant of silvery moonlight that filtered through the room's single narrow window. Isolde sat up and tried to stop shaking, tried to slow the frantic hammer of blood in her ears, the ice cold memory of the dream spreading through her like ripples on a pond. The Sight didn't always show true. There was *may be* and *has been* and *will be*—and never a flicker of a hint of which of the three she'd seen.

Still, the knock at her door made her heart stumble then start again, slamming hard against her ribs. Isolde drew a slow breath. No one at Caer Peris knew of her connection to Trystan. This could not be—was *not*—the messenger the dream had presaged.

Her skin still felt clammy, though, as she pushed the tangled hair back from her eyes and slid out of bed, catching up her cloak and wrapping it about her over her thin lawn night robe on her way to the door. Cabal, too, had woken at the noise, and now rose from his bed by the hearth, the fur on his neck standing on end, teeth bared in a low growl.

"Good dog, Cabal." Isolde put a hand on his neck, and the rough prickle of his fur, the awareness of the power in the muscles beneath the big dog's brown and white coat, steadied her a bit. "Quiet, now."

When she opened the door she found the older, gray-haired guard standing outside, fist upraised to knock a second time. Isolde's heart lurched again, her mind flashing to what this midnight summons might—almost had to—mean. That Octa had learned somehow that her offer of alliance was a lie.

Making her voice as steady as she could, she said, "What is it?"

The guardsman carried a covered lantern in one hand, and in its guttering light his face looked implacable as ever. "I—" He stopped, gaze fixed over Isolde's shoulder. "Horse ill. In stables. You come?"

Isolde hesitated, trying to catch her breath. Then she asked, "Is there a name I can call you by?"

Just for an instant the guardsman's eyes met hers, then flashed away again, focusing again on a point behind her, inside the room. He was silent so long Isolde thought it must be another unspoken refusal to answer. But then he jerked out, "Ulf, lady."

Isolde studied his pockmarked face a long moment. Save for Cabal, she was alone here. If Octa had indeed summoned her, he and his guards could make her attend without any recourse to tricks or pretense.

And anything, or almost anything, was better than going back to bed and lying alone in the dark with the memory of the dream pressing against her eyes and its voice whispering in her ears.

One hand still resting lightly on Cabal's neck, she said, "All right then, Ulf. Give me a moment to get dressed, and then I'll come."

ISOLDE STRAIGHTENED FROM WHERE SHE'D BEEN bending over the horse that lay on its side amidst piles of clean, sweet-smelling straw. Ulf had given the stallion's name as Hræfn—Raven, in the Saxon language. And true to name, the animal was a pure, glossy black— and must, in health, have been a breathtakingly handsome animal, with a powerful neck and back, long legs, and a shapely head. Now, though, the horse's sides heaved in and out as he breathed, a thick yellow discharge oozing from his nose, and the night hush was broken every few moments by his harsh, dry coughs.

Isolde pushed a bucket filled with the broth she'd made from leeks and heartsease flowers under Hræfn's nose. The stallion's eyes were dull, but his ears twitched and after a moment or two he lowered his nose to the bucket and drank.

This was the third draft of the broth she'd given him, and each time he'd drunk the whole. Was that a good sign? She didn't know. The leeks and heartsease draft was what she would have given a man or woman who coughed this way. Whether it would work on a stallion she couldn't be sure.

Isolde sat back, pushing the hair out of her eyes and trying as she had several times already tonight to call up all she did know of horses and their care. As a small girl, she'd visited Trystan often when he'd worked as assistant to the crabbed and elderly horse trainer in her father's stables; had brought apples and carrots to feed to the animals gentle enough to take food from her hands.

And her grandmother had sometimes been called out to doctor war mounts, as well. Isolde could remember as a child going with her to the stables to fetch and carry and serve as an extra pair of hands. Horses were, Morgan had said, usually a good deal more deserving of a healer's attention than any man, and made for far better patients, as well.

Isolde turned from the black stallion, glancing at the small figure who sat huddled in a corner of the narrow horse stall. Ulf had sent to Godgyth for the leeks and heartsease, since the stallion would need more than Isolde had in the meager stores she carried in her box of medicines. And to her astonishment, both had been delivered by the boy Rhun, blinking dazedly, eyes still a little puffy as though he'd been roused from sound sleep.

Now, watching the boy as he sat in the corner, shoulders hunched, head bowed, Isolde felt a pricking cold across her skin as Godgyth's words on the ramparts came back to her. *I think it likely you may find an outlet for your skills here before too long.*

But even if Godgyth hadn't foreseen Hræfn's sickness and Ulf's request, she had, at least, sent Rhun here. Had given Isolde the chance for . . . what?

If she was supposed to be winning the boy's trust, she'd so far failed. She'd tried speaking to Rhun several times, but he hadn't moved, hadn't even looked at her or at the horse. Though they were at least alone. Ulf was keeping watch outside the stables. To be sure they weren't seen or interrupted by any others of Octa's guard, Isolde supposed. Ulf had said nothing, but the nervous twitch of the Saxon man's hands was enough to make her nearly certain that Octa of Kent would have no pity to spare for a sick or dying stallion, or for a healer who tried to save it.

Isolde moved to the small brazier, intending to start heating another measure of the broth. She bent over the copper cook pot. And then she froze.

She'd been holding all thoughts of Trystan, all her tightly stretched fears for him, ruthlessly at bay, knowing that there was nothing she could possibly do for him, no way she could even know for certain where he was or what dangers he faced. But now, as though something waiting for her had broken free, a lighting flash of Trystan's face appeared on the surface of the water in the cauldron.

He wore his battle face, eyes hard, all emotion, all thoughts but those of combat shut out. He was backlit by what looked like firelight, the flickering shadows showing a darkening bruise on his cheekbone and a trail of dried blood over one eye. He had a knife clenched between his teeth and was sawing at a leather thong that bound his wrists together.

Isolde froze, feeling as though her heart were trying to force river mud through her veins, as though she were trying to breathe in something far thicker and more cloying than air. As she watched, the final fibers of leather broke, the thong fell away, and Trystan was instantly on his feet, every muscle tense and poised. This time, she could only see, not hear, so she didn't know what drew his attention. But his head lifted, eyes fixing on something beyond her narrow field of view, and Isolde saw a muscle jump in his jaw.

She had to clench her hands against the urge to reach towards the waters, to drag from them more than what she could see through their small window. And then three men stepped forward, towards Trystan, spears and battle-axes drawn. Saxons, all of them, by their blond hair and braided beards.

Still, she saw Trystan's expression as he faced them unflinchingly, saw the various options flick through his mind and the instant of realization that he'd no other choice but to stand and fight, armed with nothing but a knife against two axes and three spears. He said something—a taunt or insult, it must have been—because the biggest of the three Saxons, a red-faced older man, gave what looked like a bellow of rage and charged, blade swinging.

Isolde sat as though paralyzed while Trystan stood in the face of the Saxon man's charge. And then, at the last possible moment, just as the gleaming axe was about to descend, Trystan dove forward, rolled under the arcing blade, knocked the Saxon's legs from under him, and dealt him a blow to the jaw that made him sag to the ground, eyes rolling back in his head.

Instantly, Trystan was on his feet again, pausing only to catch up the Saxon's fallen axe before turning to face the remaining two. And then . . .

The vision shattered and broke, and Isolde was left staring into the water inside the cook pot. She sat still. Tried to breathe slowly, until her heart no longer raced and her whole body no longer flashed hot and cold. Still, it was like dragging herself out of a black swamp to bring her attention back to the stable and the sick horse at her side. The dazzle of lantern light hurt her eyes, and everything seemed unnaturally, painfully clear; each blade of straw, each hair of Hræfn's mane cut her vision like a crystal of ice.

Beside her, Hræfn coughed again, and Isolde made herself rise, kindle a fire in the brazier with hands that still felt cold and stiff, dropped more of the dried purple heartsease flowers into the pot atop the glowing coals.

Isolde made herself draw a breath. She could see Rhun's small, hunched figure out of the corner of her vision. Looking as frightened as she felt.

Isolde rubbed the big stallion's ears in slow circles, as she could dimly remember Trystan doing years ago when a frightened or yet untrained horse needed to be soothed. Rhun had pulled his knees up, folding himself more tightly even at her sideways glance. She forced herself not to look at him again. "I'm going to tell you a story." She whispered the words to Hræfn, but she was aware of every line of Rhun's pinched shoulders, the hard, tight line of his small mouth.

She had to believe there was a purpose in being here. Something beyond seeing Trystan—

Isolde snapped off the thought. Trystan was alive. His face might be bruised, he might be moving as though his ribs ached, but he hadn't been killed. It wasn't possible that she would have felt nothing if he'd actually died. So stop thinking anything else. Stop thinking about him lying in the dirt, staring with dead, lifeless blue eyes up at the night sky.

"I'm going to tell you a story," she said again, keeping her eyes on the black horse. "About a stallion. And a boy I knew, years ago."

The horse breathed out in a gusty sigh, and Isolde shifted, watching the play of shadow the lantern cast on the opposite wall.

"The stallion's name was Cadfael—Battle Prince—and he was a dappled gray instead of black. But you're still a bit like him, I think." She lightly rubbed Hræfn's neck and felt the muscles ripple under the skin. "Cadfael was wounded in battle, a deep sword cut on his left hind leg. Everyone thought he'd have to be put down."

Isolde paused. The lantern guttered, making the play of light and shadow shiver and dance. "But Trystan—that's the boy I was speaking of—thought it wasn't so much the injury that troubled the horse—that was healed—but just plain fear that it would hurt again. So he started to work with Cadfael. The pain had turned him, so that he'd try to bite anyone who came near. But Trystan kept coming to see him, day after day, just talking to him. And then, when Cadfael had started to trust him a bit, Trystan started to walk him, just slowly, around the stable yard."

A bubbling hiss from the cook pot made her look up to see that the heartsease and leek broth had come to a boil. Isolde rose swiftly and lifted the pot from the heat, using a fold of her cloak to protect her hand. She set it on the floor to cool, then turned back to Hræfn.

She wasn't sure what made her break her resolution and look over at Rhun. Some slight movement, maybe, a rustle in the straw from the corner where he sat. But when she glanced over at him, she found the boy sitting up, the pinched, strained look gone from his face, his black eyes still a little wary, but interested, curious as he watched her.

I feel as though I'm exactly where I'm supposed to be, doing what I'm meant to be doing. Gods, she would love, right now, to be able to believe that true.

Instantly, before she could frighten him by her notice, Isolde turned away, crossed back to the sick horse, and sat down again in the straw by his head. She could feel Rhun's gaze still on her, but she forced herself not to look in his direction again.

"And bit by bit, Cadfael got well again." Isolde stopped, fingers momentarily stilling on Hræfn's glossy mane as she remembered. "Trystan let me ride him, just at first—just to get him used to wearing a saddle and bridle again."

She paused. In the sweet hay-scented silence of the stable, Hræfn shifted and coughed again. "Of course, Cadfael's getting well meant that he could be ridden into battle again. I was heartbroken." Isolde turned her free hand over, looking down at the thin pink handfasting scar across her palm. "Trystan carved me a little wooden model of Cadfael, though."

Isolde stopped and looked up, risking another glance in Rhun's direction. He was still watching her, and as Isolde looked up his eyes met hers. Isolde held her breath. But the child didn't look away. Only sat very still, staring at her with serious, thickly lashed dark eyes.

And then a step sounded in the doorway of the stall. Isolde turned to see that Ulf had returned. And out of the corner of her gaze, she saw that Rhun had instantly flinched back, tucking his head to his chest, huddling into his corner once more. Isolde felt a stab of anger. But Ulf had checked in the doorway and was looking past her, apparently frozen in place by what he saw.

Isolde turned. At sight of his master, Hræfn had lifted his head from the straw. He was still too weak to rise, but he gave a faint shake of his mane, a soft whicker, and a twitch of his tail.

Ulf's throat worked as he swallowed once, then again, and Isolde thought she saw just a very brief shimmer of moisture in his eyes, even if all he said was, "Looks better." Then he cleared his throat. "Daylight soon. You and the boy must go."

TOO DAMNED CLOSE.

Safe in the cover of a thick grove of oak trees, Trystan wiped the blade of his knife on a clump of springy grass growing amidst the roots and returned it to his belt. Not his escape. The three Saxon men had been far enough gone in drink that they'd barely been able to keep their feet under them, much less wage an effective fight. No, what had been too damned close was how near he'd come to killing the three of them instead of only knocking them unconscious as he had.

Not that, of all the lives on his conscience, these would have been the ones to keep him awake at night. But it would have made for a hell of a wasted effort if he'd gone to the trouble of getting himself captured, taking their beating so that he could sow false information about Marche in their minds, and then killed them all before they could tell anyone what they'd learned.

Trystan dragged himself to his feet, swearing under his breath as every muscle in his body screamed in protest. Not that even that helped with silencing the remembered voice in his head. *Cur. Bastard brat. Midden scum.*

A hell of a long way he'd come since then. Maybe it was true what they said about fate being in the blood.

Something tugged at the edge of his awareness, and bruises not withstanding, Trystan reflexively dropped flat-bellied to the ground even before his conscious mind fully registered the acrid tang of smoke from somewhere up ahead.

He was approaching the crest of a rise in the land. Still keeping flat to the ground, he crawled on his elbows to the top and looked down into the forest clearing below. A war band's camp. A couple of goat-hide tents for whoever the leaders were. Bedrolls on the ground for the rest, at this early hour still occupied by grunting and snoring men.

The sky in the east was lightening, though, with the dawn, and that, combined with the light of a guard fire, enabled Trystan to see the shadows of the sentries stationed at intervals around the camp's perimeter. And to see the badge on the bands about their arms. The blue boar of Cornwall. Marche of Cornwall's men.

Trystan lay absolutely still, breathing in the dew-wet bracken. Then slowly, soundlessly, he began to work his way backwards down the embankment until, once more screened by the cover of thick trees, he could safely stand. A camp of Marche's men. Here. They were even, roughly speaking, where he'd told the three members of Octa's patrol they would be.

Trystan felt a grim, soundless laugh break against his rib cage. His eyes strayed towards the crest of the slope he'd climbed, details of trees and scrub appearing, now, in the growing light of dawn. What the seven hells were they doing here? Raiding in Octa's territory, as he'd also claimed to Octa's guard?

Well, it was possible, he supposed. He'd chosen the lie because it was one he'd judged Octa would readily believe; because he knew that Octa and Marche trusted one another to honor their alliance about as much as they would have trusted a wolf among a flock of sheep. It wasn't out of the question that Marche, uneasy in his agreement with Octa, was doing exactly what he, Trystan, had claimed.

Trystan's gaze lingered on the helmeted sentry whose outline he could just see near the top of the hill, a short distance away from the spot where he himself had lain. Was Marche himself likely to be there? Asleep in one of the tents in the middle of the camp?

His hand twitched towards his knife, as, just for an instant, he thought of all the times through the years that he'd forced seething anger back, back far enough that he could detach himself from it and step away. All the times he'd pictured Isolde's face in order to fight down the demon potential for violence inside him. If he turned into his father, he wouldn't deserve the trust he always saw in her eyes. And he was going to be worthy of her someday, when they were both grown.

Worthy of her. Right.

Trystan let out a slow breath, forced his fingers to relax their grip on the knife. If he was willing to risk his life for Isolde, he couldn't get himself killed with the mission only half done. He turned away, slipping silently back the way he'd come through the trees. At any rate, he'd have something to tell Octa of Kent when he got back to Octa's fort.

Chapter 12

"THIS IS THE MAN."

Isolde looked up to find Octa's gaze, watchful and cold as a snake's, fixed on her. The Saxon king wore a tunic with ill-cured wolf's fur at the neck and cuffs. His greasy, white-streaked hair was loose on his shoulders, the ends of his mustache and beard still matted together with what looked like black pine pitch. He gestured to the man who lay sprawled amidst the filthy piles of straw on the floor. "Can anything be done for him?"

Isolde looked down at the unconscious man, seeing, even in this dim light, the cuts and puffy, darkening bruises on his face, bad enough to nearly obscure his features, the angry, black-crusted lashes on his back, the marks heavy-booted feet had left about his ribs. His hands were tightly bound behind his back at an angle that must have been excruciating, or would have been, had he been aware enough to feel anything at all.

The small stone-built room stank of rotting straw and human waste and, stronger than all, a thick, acrid smell of despair and fear. Isolde had to summon every scrap of will not to react to the faint challenge she could see in Octa's coldly pale eyes.

That was the purpose, the entire purpose, in his summoning her here. She knew it, and she still had to call up a memory of all those who depended, just now, on her staying alive—on not drawing Octa's wrath while she was entirely under his power.

Rhun . . . Madoc . . . Kian . . . Eurig . . . Cath . . . the tiny spark of life that would be quenched if she were careless enough to lose her own. All of them flashed through her mind. But it was the memory of Trystan she held to—Trystan, as she'd Seen him in the scrying waters the night before, bruised and bloodied and wearing his battle face, all feeling, all emotion plainly shut down.

The remembrance steadied her, somehow, made it easier to push her own churning mix of anger and fear far, far back, until she could move to kneel beside the unconscious man as though he were just another wounded soldier, like any of the countless others who had come into her care.

Which in a way he was. A wounded, unconscious, bleeding man, with hurts to assess and tend, like any of the rest. Save that he lay not in her infirmary or even in a tented battlefield medicine station, but in a fetid, damp, stiflingly hot prison cell.

She had been dressing in her room that morning when Ulf brought word that Octa was summoning her. She was to attend him at once, and bring whatever medicines and herbs she had with her. Isolde thought there might have been a trace of reluctance in the guardsman's voice as he repeated Octa's order. But that might have been only her own imagining. Certainly if he recalled, in speaking to her, anything of the night they'd spent laboring to save the life of his horse, he'd betrayed no sign of it either by word or look.

Nor did it show now, as Isolde knelt on the prison cell floor and took stock of the unconscious man's hurts, a prisoner whom Octa and his guardsmen had interrogated—Octa's word—until he could tell them nothing more.

Isolde glanced from the prisoner's battered features to Ulf, who stood on guard by the door, pale, flat eyes fixed straight ahead. She wondered whether he had been one of those whose fists and feet had struck the blows.

She could feel Octa's serpent-cold gaze on her still, and forcing herself not to look up, Isolde moved to run her hands lightly over the unconscious prisoner's chest, checking for broken ribs—and felt anger threaten to break free again, because, gods, there were four or five at least, besides the countless other bruises and bleeding cuts she'd already found.

She was gritting her teeth, the blood pounding behind her eyes with the effort of keeping her hands steady, of stopping herself from turning and striking Octa of Kent across his battle-hardened face.

At least, when she closed her eyes and reached out to the unconscious man in her mind, she could catch nothing from him. No thoughts, no fragments of memory, not even fear or awareness of pain. Still, after she'd finished taking stock of his hurts, Isolde laid her hand on the man's chest and concentrated every part of her will on a kind of wordless message of reassurance or comfort, a hope that he might know before he died that someone had touched him who wished him peace instead of harm.

There was little else she could do for him. His breathing was heavy and slow, and when she'd pulled back the blackened lid of one eye, his pupil had stayed unresponsive and fixed. She doubted he'd ever wake again. And if he did—

Isolde felt sickness churn through her all over again. Because there was no way she could say, absolutely, that the injured man wouldn't wake to further nightmare and torture, further pain. She couldn't even give the prisoner a draft to be sure he never did wake.

This was a test. Another test of good faith.

"I'm sorry, lord." She looked up at Octa and was faintly surprised to hear that she had, indeed, succeeded in making her voice sound steady and calm. "But he's beyond my help."

For an endlessly long moment, Octa's eyes met hers. And then: "I see." Octa took a step towards her and said, voice rising, brows drawn, "I see that you are either a liar or as worthless to me as a healer as a whore is to a gelded slave."

He wants you angry. Isolde held herself still, fighting the urge to flinch back or press herself up against the moisture-slick wall. *He wants you afraid.*

Godgyth had called Octa drunk on bloodshed, had said that after a lifetime of war he had run mad. And with the jagged feel of the unconscious prisoner's broken ribs still tingling in her fingertips, Isolde could all too easily believe that true.

She'd seen a beggar once, afflicted with a sickness that killed from the outside in—a disease that deadened once healthy flesh of hands and feet, face and nose, leaving it lumpy, white, and chill as a dead man's. Maybe it was in some measure the same with all warriors who rode out to battle year after year. The pain, the blood, the constant fighting and threat of death blunted and deadened all feeling until the men felt nothing at all save exaltation at the kill.

But it was true, too, that even standing here with him in this tiny prison cell, Octa seemed somehow unreal, more like the character in all the vile stories of his atrocities than like a flesh-and-blood man. Trying to guess at the thoughts that went on behind his chill blue stare was like running against a blank stone wall.

Octa had, Isolde thought, built up an image of himself as a man to be looked on with terror. Octa the king, Octa of the Bloody Knife. His confidence, his self-importance were as bloated as one of the in- flated pig's bladders children batted amongst themselves at autumn slaughter time.

Which meant that she couldn't give in to fear, or, she knew of a certainty, he would crush her as thoughtlessly as he would crush a fly. But neither could she risk saying or doing anything at all that Octa would view as a challenge to his authority, a knife-prick puncture to that swollen image of himself.

Isolde ignored the racing of her pulse, the clammy sweat that prickled her skin. She lowered her gaze to say, "I'm sorry you think so, lord."

Octa didn't answer at once. Eyes like twin stagnant lakes met Isolde's. Then, abruptly, he nodded a dismissal. "That will be all."

Isolde bowed her head in acknowledgment, bending to pick up the scrip of medicines she'd brought from her room. Only then did she say, "This prisoner—is he one of Cynric's men?"

Octa had turned for the door, but at that he instantly whipped round, his ice pale eyes contracting and sharpening as they once again focused on hers. Something hard stirred behind his gaze, and Isolde again had the impression of hostility—hatred, even—kept under tight control.

Which was in itself frightening. She couldn't imagine Octa of Kent ever troubling to reign in anger. And she could think of no harmless reason why he should do so now. When at last he spoke, though, he said only, his voice almost a growl, "Why should you think that?"

Isolde made herself keep breathing, willed herself to hold tight to the memory of Trystan's face. If Trystan could face a fight against three men at once, she could face Octa of Kent now.

"No reason. Only that I understood you to have captured Cynric himself and all his men when you took Caer Peris from him."

For what seemed another eternal heartbeat of time, Octa's eyes held hers. Then he gave a harsh bark of a laugh. "If this were one of Cynric's warriors, his flayed skin would even now be hanging above the door of my feasting hall."

He turned to the cell door again, this time jerking it open to let in a wash of comparatively cooler, cleaner air. And then, before more than a flicker of shaky relief could flash through Isolde, Octa turned back and smiled, a smile so far removed from any real feeling that it was in itself frightening.

"There will be a *symbel* tonight—a feast in the great hall to honor a new ally of mine. It is my wish that you should likewise attend."

OCTA'S HALL WAS MORE CROWDED THAN Isolde had ever seen. Many of the assembled warriors were Octa's, but several groups of tall, fair-haired men with mustaches braided to long points were surely from the encampment she'd glimpsed outside. They were dressed differently from the rest, in iron helmets with gleaming bronze cheek guards and bronze boars mounted on the crests, while the price of their gleaming mail shirts of linked metal chains would have kept an ordinary foot soldier in food and clothing for two years and more.

Octa's white horse-head totem stood at the head of the hall—a real horse head for tonight, tanned and preserved and set with a pair of polished stones for eyes, the whole mounted on a scarlet-draped warrior spear. And the newcomers had bowed to the totem, and again to Octa, and kissed the gem-crusted ring he wore on his left hand. But more than one, Isolde saw, carried a shield with a painted raven's crest—an emblem used by no Saxon king that she knew of—and they kept to themselves, mingling little among Octa's men.

The air was thick with smoke, heavy with the mingled scents of mead, sweat, unwashed bodies, and roasted meat. Isolde hadn't been troubled by sickness in the last two or three weeks, but sitting in her place at the king's table and watching the mail-coated warriors lifting horns of ale, she felt queasy, her head pounding with the heat and the noise.

Ulf and the other guard, the younger man whose name she still didn't know, were standing behind her, one on either side. And Godgyth was standing at the head of the room, a dazzling figure despite her hunched shoulders and yellowed skin, dressed in a saffron-dyed tunic and skirt with gold and glass chains about her neck and heavy gold rings hanging from her ears.

Godgyth was alone tonight; Isolde had looked for Rhun as soon as she came in, but the boy was nowhere to be seen among the attendants in the hall. As she had told Isolde on the ramparts, Godgyth had her own role to play in tonight's rituals. She had entered some time after the rest were assembled, paused a moment in the doorway to draw all eyes to her, and then hobbled slowly to the front of the hall to stand before the company and cast a charm of protection across the hall for the night to keep out all malign spirits that might be circling, intent on doing harm.

Her voice, wavering and age-cracked as it was, had silenced the already half-drunken laughter and shouts of the men. Now, in the expectant hush that had fallen, she moved forward with surprising grace, towards the fire that burned beneath the smoke hole in the center of the roof, raised her hands, and threw in a double fistful of herbs. A cloud of thick, sweet-smelling smoke rose, billowed, and dissolved in the already hazy air. And then Godgyth raised her hands again and a pair of leather-clad warriors dragged a great black bull into the center of the room.

The beast was bellowing with terror, eyes rolling in its massive head, and Isolde turned her head away as Godgyth drew a wide, gleaming blade from the folds of her robe. She couldn't block out the noise, though, or the cloying, rusty hot smell.

When she looked back, a scarlet pool stained the floor rushes in the center of the hall and Godgyth's gnarled hands were wet to the wrists. The bull had been carved up, its flesh placed in gleaming copper cauldrons hung over the central flames, its blood collected in a chased copper bowl.

Godgyth dipped a crudely made broom of bundled twigs into the bowl, then whirled, skirts and shawls and sparse white hair flying outwards as she splattered a crimson rain of blood in all directions. Then she stopped to raise her arms again, high above her head. Watching, Isolde felt a shiver curl through her at the remote, exalted look in the old woman's milky eyes.

"For Woden." Godgyth half sang the words. "Who traded his own eye for a drink from the Well of Urd, that he might gain the knowledge of true Sight. May Woden's vision be our guide this night. May Woden cast his spear over the heads of King Octa's army that this blood bring victory to our warriors in the battles to come."

Silence, thick and heavy as the scent of herbs and smoke and blood, held the hall. And then a great roar of approval went up from the men, a huge welling of sound that seemed as palpable a force as the silence had been. Godgyth bowed and stepped back, and Octa himself moved forward into her place.

"HERE. FOR YOU." GODGYTH SET A cup into Isolde's hand. The old woman's nails were still rimmed scarlet with the bull's blood. "The first cup poured from the *eula bora*—the ale bearer's—horn. Soon, as soon as the king's speech is done, I will serve all the others who have come to the *symbel*."

Now that the public performance was done, the slight slurring of Godgyth's speech was more pronounced, the smell of her breath and the owlish blink of her rheumy eyes making it plain she'd already drunk several cups herself. She nodded, making the gold earrings sway and spark in the torchlight. "That is the purpose of the night, you know. Apart from allowing Octa's guest of honor to swear his fealty, I pour the mead into the cups and drinking horns of all those who attend. Just as the Well of Urd from which Woden drank waters the World Tree where the Norns carve our fates into the bark. And all at the *symbel* may step into the flow of *wryd*. Gain the power to shape our future. Weave our own fate."

Godgyth spoke in a low undertone, but even still her voice held the eerie, almost prophetic lilt as it had done on the ramparts days before. And yet at the same time Isolde had the impression that the words were oddly mechanical in a way that not only drunkenness could explain, the air of prophecy merely an indifferently performed act. Godgyth was watching her with a curiously intent, almost hungry look on her withered face, head and shoulders slanted a little forward—as though she were waiting for something, Isolde thought.

Out of politeness, she was about to raise the cup to her mouth. She didn't know what made her turn to look up to her left where Ulf stood. Maybe the guardsman had shifted in place, or made some sound that carried over the noise of the hall. But as she was lifting the cup, she happened to glance up and met Ulf's gaze.

The guard's face was as immobile as before, the set of his mouth as unrelenting. But as his eyes met Isolde's, he looked from her to the cup of mead in her hands. And then, though his expression didn't alter by even a twitch of muscle, he shook his head.

Isolde held very still. Studying Ulf's face, she was half ready to believe she'd imagined that quick warning. Except that she knew she hadn't.

With an effort, she recollected herself and turned back to Godgyth, making some automatic reply that even she scarcely heard. She shouldn't feel shaken. Whatever had prompted Ulf's gesture of warning—for warning it had definitely been—it told her nothing but what she'd already known. That if she couldn't entirely trust her guard, neither was Godgyth anyone she could trust.

Isolde thought there might have been the smallest, the very smallest, flash of disappointment across Godgyth's hook-nosed face as she set the mead cup down untasted. But that truly might have been only her own imagining, her own readiness, at this moment, to read sinister motives even if none was there.

Octa, standing at the head of the room, had been addressing the assembly in a deep, gratingly powerful voice. Much of what he said simply washed past Isolde, but she thought he had made a series of declarations of his own past deeds, battles won, enemies slain—and swore further victories before the gods.

Now he finished with a sweeping gesture towards the rows of assembled warriors and what were plainly words of long-standing ritual. "*Site nu to symle and onsæl meoto. Sigehreð secgum, swain sefa hwette.*"

Another expectant hush fell across the room. Isolde thought that this time the swiftly masked expression that passed across Godgyth's face was one of reluctance. But she turned from Isolde and rose a little stiffly to her feet, bearing her golden pitcher and limping forward to pour mead into the drinking horn Octa held for her.

And then she lifted the chased bowl of the sacrificed bull's blood again and dipped a gold ring into the sticky scarlet pool inside. "May Woden hear the vows spoken tonight. May he gather all who fall in battle to feast at the tables in his warrior's hall. May he crush any who would dare to break their vows beneath his mighty heel."

She began to move around the company at large, pouring mead for the rest of the assembled warriors. As she poured, each man lifted his drinking horn, laid his hand over the blood-smeared gold ring, and swore an oath, and Godgyth spoke a few words to each man in reply. Sometimes approval, sometimes half-teasing flattery, sometimes a fierce challenge of whatever boast he had made: a vow to kill ten Britons with a single stroke of the sword. To capture a hundred Briton women for the army's pleasure. A promise to bring Octa the head of Cerdic of Wessex himself.

Isolde would have liked to discount it, disbelieve it all. She would have been glad if listening to boast after boast of how Octa's warriors planned to slaughter Britain's people and carve up her kingdoms like so much fresh game had not sent cold like icy rain trickling across her skin. But there was something fearsome, dignified, and imposing about the words that rolled off each man's tongue.

And there was something strangely—bizarrely—beautiful about the ceremony, as well. Even Godgyth, hunch-shouldered and slow as she moved around the room, seemed somehow transformed by the fierce, alien magic of the night. Watching, Isolde thought that it wouldn't have been hard to believe that Godgyth might at any moment throw off the old-woman's disguise, peel away the wrinkled face and frail, stooped form, and emerge as one of the very goddesses she'd invoked earlier, young and beautiful and bathed in Otherworldly light.

A blunt-featured man with a braided mustache and thick gold bands about his muscular arms had moved to a stool set at the front of the hall, directly before Octa's raised chair, and now sat with a carved wooden harp propped on his knees, reciting the verses of what sounded like a tale or poem. His voice was deep, unmelodic, and gruff, and instead of playing a melody, his fingers plucked the harp strings in rhythmic emphasis of the words he spoke.

And yet there was something in voice and playing combined that made Isolde think of Taliesin's songs. Some power twined up from the words and strummed notes and made her feel for a moment as though this gathering had slipped free the bounds of time, entered a realm in which the past breathed, where *has been* and *will be* became one and the same.

Godgyth continued to move around the room. The boasts and vows continued, the playing went on. Isolde looked up to find Ulf still standing beside her. She hesitated a moment, then gestured towards the harper and asked, "What is it that he recites?"

At first Isolde thought the guardsman wasn't going to respond. But then he said, in an undertone, "Old story. Tale of a great hero who killed the monster plaguing a king's hall."

Isolde drew in her breath, looking up into Ulf's face. "And what was it that Godgyth put in my cup?"

She hadn't expected an answer. But to her surprise, Ulf said, for once directly meeting her gaze, "Nothing good." Then he stopped, the corners of his mouth pinching shut. "Quiet, now. Honor guest of King Octa—"

But the rest of what he said was lost on Isolde. The whole room seemed to tilt crazily, and Ulf's voice, together with all the rest of the noise of the hall, was blotted out by a dull roar as she stared at the man who had risen from his place among the assembly and was walking towards the front of the hall. A young man, broad-shouldered and tall, with gold-brown hair laced back at the nape of his neck. His face handsome, lean and a little angular, with startlingly blue eyes set under slanted brows.

Trystan. Here in Octa's Hall. Honor Guest at Octa of Kent's *symbol.*

He wore plain gray breeches, boots, and a leather jerkin, and had a fading bruise over one cheekbone. He moved a little stiffly, as though he were trying not to limp. Which, Isolde thought above the pounding in her ears, proved the truth of what she'd glimpsed in the stables two nights before. Not that she'd ever doubted the vision true.

He came forward. And then his head turned, and she knew the moment he saw her, because his face went utterly, carefully blank, and he checked a moment in his progress towards Octa's raised chair. Then he turned back to Octa and crossed the remaining distance to stand before the Saxon king.

Isolde could read tension in the line of his shoulders, but he didn't look at her again, only dropped smoothly to one knee before Octa and spoke a few words. Octa made some sort of reply, then gestured for Trystan to rise, and gave him a heavy gold ring.

Isolde felt as though she'd been forcibly detached from her own body. The formal ritual went on and on, Godgyth appearing to offer Trystan a cup of mead, Trystan raising it to his lips and drinking, then making his own vows before Octa and the gods.

Godgyth poured more mead in his cup each time he spoke, each time seemed to challenge his words, judging—at least Isolde assumed that was what she was doing—the worth of his oath. Each time raising the crude bundle of green twigs and splattering him with droplets from the bowl of bull's blood.

All three spoke rapidly and in the Saxon tongue. Still, Isolde would probably have understood at least some of what was said if she'd made any effort to attend. As it was, the words rang in her ears as meaningless noise while she sat, heart racing, her eyes—the only part of her that still felt under her control—locked on Trystan's bruised face and grim, slightly shadowed eyes.

Though, after the first wave of shock had run like cold, tingling fire from her head to the tips of her fingers, she hardly even felt surprised. Of course Octa's new ally, his guest of honor tonight, would be Trystan. Why wouldn't it be?

Why wouldn't Trystan—Isolde gritted her teeth so hard it made her head ache—why wouldn't he have maneuvered himself into the most dangerous mission, the most dangerous position he could possibly have found?

The speeches seemed to last an eternity, an endless, nightmare eternity of questions and answers, smoke, and the splatters of sticky scarlet from Godgyth's twig wands, and long before the finish, Isolde's every muscle was screaming with tight impatience for them to be done. Finally Godgyth filled Trystan's cup one last time, this time moving to fill Octa's, too. Both men drank. Godgyth brought something wrapped in gold cloth from the shadows behind Octa's chair—an ancient brown human thigh bone, Isolde saw, likewise smeared with the freshly sacrificed bull's blood.

Trystan placed his hand on the bone and spoke a final formula of words, some kind of ritual oath, Isolde thought, with the part of her mind still capable of conscious thought.

Octa replied, standing to address the company at large, arms outspread, his silvery blond hair spilling over the shoulders of his wolf-skin cloak, the smoky torchlight flickering over his face. Isolde thought he gave the assembly an account of the missions Trystan had carried out for him—information gathered, gold and stores of grain won—though she registered only a word or two here and there.

Another great roar of approval went up from the crowd of assembled men, several warriors pounding the floor or beating on their shields with the butts of spears or swords. And then it was over. Octa raised his hand and scattered gold rings into the crowd then shouted an order towards the doorway, summoning a straggling line of dirty, sullen-looking slave girls.

He lifted his voice and promised them all more gold, more women, and certain entrance into the great Warrior's Hall of endless battles and roasted boar and ceaselessly flowing mead from the teat of the magical goat Heidrún if they fought with valor, slaked themselves on the blood of their foes, and fell on the point of an enemy sword.

Trystan had drawn back towards the edge of the room, the harsh light from a torch just above him casting shadows across his face and patching his body with light and dark.

The harper stepped forward again, and this time was joined by several more, a thin, one-legged man with a carved wooden flute, a lyre player, a man carrying a drum. They started to play, and the solemn order of the hall broke and dissolved, some of the men pulling serving maids and slave girls into a whirling dance, others pushing towards wooden tables set out across the rear of the hall on which Isolde now saw a feast laid.

What none of the assembled warriors did was to approach Octa himself. The Saxon king drew back, regarding the company with a hard, watchful gaze. Octa was a king to be feared. But scarcely loved.

Many others from the assembled crowd of warriors approached Trystan, though, to clasp wrists with him or pound him on the back, so that for a few moments Isolde lost sight of him in the crowd as she sat, still frozen, even her thoughts only just beginning to thaw.

And then suddenly he was there, standing before her, near enough that she could have reached out and touched the bruise on his cheekbone.

ISOLDE WAS HERE.

He'd just gone through hell and back to keep her safe from Octa of Kent. And here she was. Sitting in a place of honor in Octa's great hall.

Trystan drew in his breath and managed to suppress the dozen or so curses that had been running through his head since he'd first caught sight of her. None of them was remotely adequate in any case.

She was staring at him, plainly as shocked to see him here as he was to see her. And he didn't dare speak to her. Not openly. Not here.

But she spoke first, in a voice pitched to anyone standing near enough to overhear, "More mead? Of course. Here, take mine." Swiftly, she took a cup from the table, rose from her place and stepped forward, putting a cup into his hands. Then she lowered her voice. "Don't drink it, though. I think Godgyth—Octa's sister—put something in it. Some kind of potion. I don't know what."

Trystan looked blankly at the cup in his hands and tried to force coherent thought to emerge through the muck that had evidently taken the place of his mind. "What—"

Isolde didn't let him finish, though, but took a step towards him. "Holy Goddess Mother, Trys, what are you doing here?" She was near enough that he could see the tiny flecks of gold the fire brought out in her gray eyes, the pulse of blood under the pale skin of her throat. "What were you thinking of? What if—" She stopped herself, plainly trying to keep her voice from rising. "What if someone had recognized you? What if Marche had been here?"

Trystan managed to keep silent. But Isolde must have read at least a partial answer in his face, because her eyes widened slightly, and then flooded with sudden tears. "You didn't care, did you?" Her voice was barely a whisper, now. "You didn't care whether Marche was here and could tell Octa who you really are. You'd have just—what? Drawn your sword, right in front of Octa, before Marche could speak, and cut Marche's throat? Even if it meant you were killed yourself before you'd so much as drawn your next breath?"

Her voice was tight, her eyes still swimming. Trystan felt something inside him snap as every emotion, every memory he'd suppressed over the last days tore free and the sour, churning anger rose up in a wave. "And what about you?" he heard himself say. "When you told me Marche wasn't entirely a monster, I didn't expect to find you here, sharing bread and mead with his chief allies. Arguing against my taking his worthless life."

Isolde's eyes widened, and Trystan silently cursed himself. She was looking at him as though he'd struck her. Which he might as well have done, at that.

As though he needed another goddamn reminder of why he didn't allow that sleeping demon in his chest to break free.

Behind them, the drumbeat and the piper played a wild, shrill tune. Isolde was still staring at him, tears still standing in her eyes. Then she blinked, took a breath, and wiped her cheeks with the heels of her hands. "I don't care two straws about Marche." Her voice was fierce. "I care about *you*. And even if you survive whatever it is you're doing now, even if you live through taking your own father's life, I don't think you need one more scar on your spirit. One more nightmare to make you lie awake at night."

Her cheeks were flushed, and her mouth trembled slightly.

Gods, and he'd thought being apart from her had been torture. It didn't even begin to compare to standing here with her right in front of him and *not* being able to tell her the truth about where he'd been and why he was here now, pretending allegiance to a man he trusted less than a feral dog.

And then one of Octa's guard's stepped towards them. Who, Trystan's automatic defenses now informed him, had been standing to one side and watching them for some time.

Now the guard looked from Trystan to Isolde, one hand moving to the hilt of the knife in his belt. "This man bothering you, lady?"

At least his reflexes were still working, even if he'd temporarily lost his mind. Trystan stepped instantly backwards, making his own expression a careful blank, and turned to the guard, ready to say—what?

Before he could frame any kind of response, though, Isolde, too, had stepped back and turned to the gray-haired man. She drew a steadying breath, then said, her voice almost her usual one, "No. He's done nothing. It's just . . . the hall is growing hot, and the smoke is making my head ache. I think I'd like to go back to my room."

ISOLDE SCARCELY NOTICED THE CROWDS OF laughing, shouting, half-drunken warriors she and Ulf had to push through to reach the door of the hall. Barely even noticed the treacherous roll underfoot of the gnawed beef bones that littered the floor. Even after they stepped from the hall into the comparatively silent night air, it was a moment before she realized that Ulf was speaking.

"I . . . am sorry to ask more of you," he was saying stiffly. "After Hræfn." The guard kept his gaze trained straight ahead, staring at the dark outlines of the army garrison ahead.

After the smoke and bright color and raucous noise of the hall, the comparative silence outside was almost shocking, the night darkness pressing like a palpable force against Isolde's eyes. A breeze whipped the torches set about the ramparts into bright tattered banners of flame, and the air carried the faint tang of smoke, as well as the smells of mud and horses from the stables and the practice yards. But these were overlaid, washed clean by the the cool, salt scent of the sea, and the first breath Isolde drew felt almost like a draft of water on her parched throat.

She drew another steadying breath and looked up at the guard beside her, telling herself to be careful. Though at least whatever Ulf was saying didn't sound as though it were anything to do with Trystan.

"I'm sorry," she said. "What did you say?"

They were passing beneath a pair of torches set into brackets on an outer wall, and she thought she saw a slight flush creep up into the guard's pockmarked face. He didn't answer at once, then seemed to force himself to speak. "I said, I know you saved Hræfn. That I am . . . in your debt for that. But I would ask . . ." Again he paused, then added in the same gruff tone, "I would ask another favor. If you would."

It was embarrassment, Isolde realized abruptly, that was roughening his voice, making him avoid her gaze. She asked, after a moment's pause, "What is the favor?"

The flush on Ulf's skin deepened, and he seemed to struggle with himself for the space of another few paces before saying, "You remember . . . what I asked you before. What you said you couldn't do. The . . . love charm."

Isolde's head was still pounding, every word she and Trystan had exchanged echoing in her ears with each fresh throb, and she felt all at once exhausted—completely, utterly tired of trying to maneuver her way among all the potential dangers and pitfalls and hidden motivations of this place.

Which was just too bad. She was here, regardless of what Trystan had done, regardless of what dangers he was in now. She said, carefully, "I remember."

Ulf sucked in a breath, let it out in a gusty rush, and then said, "I am thinking about Ymma. I know you say you have no magic. But I wanted to ask you if you could . . . speak to her. For me. Since she is serving maid to you now."

In the days she'd been at Caer Peris, the serving woman Ymma had, apart from telling Isolde her name, spoken only three phrases to Isolde in stiff, heavily accented British. *Yes, lady, No, lady,* and *Good night, lady.* Isolde couldn't recall her saying anything else, and any attempts she'd made to speak with the other woman had been met with blank stares. Indeed, it had taken her a moment even to associate the name Ymma with the stolid, fair-haired maidservant who fetched her water for washing and helped her dress and undress morning and night.

Now she glanced sideways at Ulf's shadowed face, trying to decide what, if anything, lay behind this request. But if his awkward embarrassment was only some sort of pretense or ploy, he was doing an amazingly fine job. And try as she might, Isolde couldn't see what Ulf—or Octa—could possibly gain by asking her to play match-maker between her assigned bodyguard and her serving maid.

Someone among the revelers in the great hall had started a drinking song; the sound of many slurred voices floated out to them across the night. Isolde walked a few paces in silence, then said, "Why me? Surely there must be someone else who knows her better."

But Ulf was shaking his head. "Don't know many here. None well."

Isolde looked up at him, startled. "But you're one of Octa's own army, aren't you?"

To her surprise, Ulf shook his head again. "I am oath-sworn to Eormenric. Octa's son. Eormenric is . . . not here. Octa gave him a mission." Ulf shrugged. "I was chosen to stay behind to guard the fortress here."

And then, before Isolde could frame another question to ask him, though, Ulf went on, kicking at a loose tuft of straw that lay in their path. "There is a battle coming. Soon. Between your people and mine. Maybe I will live through it. Maybe not. But I—" He stopped. "I would like to be married, before I die."

Just for a moment, a flash of something vulnerable appeared on his face. Isolde felt an unexpectedly sharp pang. When battle came, she had to hope that Britain's forces would triumph and that Octa's—and so Ulf's—would lose, and not only hope it, but do her best to ensure that Ulf and all the other warriors here met with as crushing a defeat as could be dealt.

They were nearing the door to the stairwell that would lead to her room, and Isolde paused beneath another pair of torches set on the wall and looked up at her guard. "And Ymma would be your choice of a wife?" she asked.

Ulf rubbed his nose and shrugged again. "Good as any."

"Good as . . ." Isolde caught herself. She shouldn't judge. Maybe Ymma and Ulf would grow into love. Maybe they would marry and find the kind of happiness the harpers sang of. Her thoughts flashed instantly to Trystan, standing before the hall and swearing the ritual oaths on Octa's blood-smeared human bone.

Someone might as well.

They reached the door where Isolde paused, her hand on the stone frame, and turned back to face Ulf. Music and laughter spilled out from the great hall, though they were far enough away now that she could also hear the ever-present throbbing voice of the sea. "That man," Isolde said, "the prisoner Octa asked me to treat earlier today."

Ulf didn't pretend not to understand what she was asking. "He lives. But still unconscious, lady."

"And if he does wake?"

Isolde thought something flashed across Ulf's pale gaze, as he said, "He wakes, I think it likely he will not live long." He paused, then went on, seeming to choose his words with care. "If he wakes, and I am on duty . . ." Ulf scratched his chin and stared out into the night, then said, deliberately, "Prisoners try to escape sometimes. If this man wakes while I on guard, I think he will try . . . attack me, maybe." He turned, meeting Isolde's eyes. "I would have no choice but to kill him—quickly and cleanly. You understand?"

Isolde searched his face, trying to weigh the truth of his words. Slowly, she nodded. "Yes. I do." She stopped. "And I think you should just speak to Ymma yourself. She's one of the serving maids on duty in the feasting hall tonight. Go back and see her now. She . . . she'll listen to you, I'm sure. But if not, yes, I'll speak to her."

HOURS LATER, ISOLDE LAY ON THE bed in her allotted room and stared unseeingly into a shadowed darkness lit only by the pale blue moonbeams that filtered through a single narrow window set high on the wall. The *symbel* was still going on in the great hall; she could hear the shouts and music and laughter, fainter here, but still clear in the summer night. She realized, listening, that she'd left before hearing Godgyth's prophecies, and she wondered just for a moment what victories the older woman had promised Octa and his warriors tonight.

Then she turned over and stared up at the plastered ceiling above her head. She'd long since given up on the prospect of sleep. She kept seeing Trystan's face, hearing his voice, tight with control, in that brief, bitter exchange. And she kept hearing Mother Berthildis's words. *You think you can save him—from himself, if need be?*

She'd thought of them often in the last weeks, but tonight they lodged tight in her chest like never before. She couldn't save Trystan. No one could save a man who didn't want to be saved. She couldn't break him free from whatever long shadow of the past had trapped him now, even if by some miracle she could force him into actually talking to her. Telling her why he was here, pretending allegiance to Octa of Kent, swearing oaths he already planned to break.

Because it was a pretense. If she was sure of anything, it was that.

She could see Trystan stepping back from her as Ulf interrupted them, the guarded, controlled look falling instantly over his face. This was the mission she'd guessed at, read in his eyes at their parting weeks ago; the mission he didn't expect to survive.

Isolde closed her eyes. She thought of the night she'd married Trystan, when, as she'd told Mother Berthildis, she'd felt as though she followed a course as fixed as the path of the stars across the night sky.

But then, she'd hardly be the first to look into her own heart and call the desires there a god or goddess.

And then she felt it.

From four years before, she remembered the first stirrings of an unborn child as a tiny flutter. The lightest, smallest beating of hidden bird's wings, gone almost before you were sure there'd been any movement at all. This was different. A definite tug, a thump, like the beat of a second pulse, like a fish rippling the surface of a pond. As though the child inside her had wanted there to be no question at all about making his presence known.

Isolde's own pulse skittered to a stop and then started again. She spread her palm over the spot where she'd felt the movement. And felt another ripple of movement, stronger this time. She pressed her eyes closed.

For a moment she felt nothing, saw nothing but the darkness of her closed lids. And then, before more than the first chill trickle of disappointment could seep through her, a flash of an image filled her mind—though it didn't at first seem an answer to what she'd asked.

What she saw was a confused jumble of fragments, the same fragments of vision she remembered dreaming twice before. Mud and blood, torn flesh, clashing shields and swords and endlessly screaming men.

And then suddenly, without any conscious thought at all, she was up off the bed, searching the darkness for her clothes—pulling on skirt and tunic, boots, her dark traveling cloak. Her fingers were icy cold but completely steady, moving almost of their own accord to fasten laces, tug the garments swiftly over her head. When she opened the door to her room, she saw that her guards were absent, Ulf and the fair-haired younger man nowhere to be seen.

She spared a thought to wonder whether this meant that Ulf had, indeed, gone back to the great hall to make his suit to Ymma, and whether he'd succeeded or failed. But, oddly, she felt no surprise that she'd been left alone and unwatched for the night.

She felt as if something were calling her in a voice like the silent keening of an abandoned field of battle, like the constant murmur of the sea. She paused only a moment in the doorway, closing her eyes, thinking, *Where? Where do I find him? Where do I go?*

Chapter 13

*T*HE CLASH OF SHIELDS AND *swords was relentless, the screams like the souls of the damned in hell. Trystan raised his own blade to block the swing of a charging horseman and deflected the blow, even as he saw the man on his right go down under another mounted man's charge.*

It was Bradach; he lay gasping on the mud-churned ground, a bubbling hole in his chest fringed by the broken ends of ribs and tatters of muscle and sinew. No chance he'd live more than an hour, if as long. They had about another half moment before the pair of riders turned and were on them again. Trystan raised his sword and ended Bradach's gasps with a single quick stroke, blocking out even momentary pity or regret. Blocking, too, the knowledge that but for him, Bradach and the others who'd already fallen wouldn't have died at all.

Trystan wrenched his mind back. Back to staying alive another moment, keeping as many of his men as possible from getting themselves killed. Luc, the damned thirteen-year-old fool, was standing there gaping like a cod as Arthur's warriors charged, spear and shield lowered in a positive invitation to be run through on one of their swords. Trystan hauled him roughly back, thrust the boy behind him, and brought his sword up in a thrust that cut through the belly of the nearest rider's horse. The beast went down, thrashing, screaming in pain, though the rider jumped clear. Trystan yanked his blade free—

—and then the nightmare miraculously broke and he was back on the patch of ground he'd stretched out on for the night, under a gnarled apple tree in the fort's kitchen garden, because it was the one place in Caer Peris where he'd been reasonably sure of being left alone. Except, no, he was still dreaming. Because Isolde was there, walking lightly towards him across the grass, stopping just before him as she had in a hundred other waking and sleeping dreams. The moonlight filtering through the branches above lighted her gray eyes, touched her delicate features to something almost unwordly, pure and lily pale.

"You're so beautiful."

She smiled a little at that. "Is that meant for an apology?"

The memory of all he'd said to her tonight thudded home— worse, in a way, that the lingering reek of mud and blood and the pounding suffocation of the nightmare he'd been lost in a moment before. "I am sorry."

"It's all right." She dropped to the ground beside him, tucking her feet under her. "I hate it even more when you won't let yourself lose your temper or shout back at me. You don't let yourself get angry often enough."

Not often enough. "You have no idea. I . . ."

He knew he wouldn't be able to touch her, but he reached a hand towards her all the same. And then jerked back as—score another one for the god with the malignant sense of humor—his fingers met smooth, warm skin. "Jesus God, you're here!"

Trystan sat up fast enough to make his already swimming senses lurch and spin.

Isolde's brows drew together in a puzzled frown. "I'm here?"

Trystan shook his head. "I thought I was . . . that you were . . ."

Isolde was looking at him as though he'd lost his mind—which probably wasn't far off. He ran a hand across his face. "Isa, you can't be here. You can't be seen here like this, with me. It's—"

But she stopped him before he could finish. "It's all right. Everyone is still at the *symbel*. Even the guards Octa assigned me. It's safe—there's no one to see."

His heart was still hammering with remnants of the dream. If he loved her, he had to stay away, keep his distance. And yet he knew absolutely that he was never going to fight the temptation of having Isolde actually here, actually beside him, as well as block out the avalanche of memories the dream had called down.

Trystan ran his hands down his face again. "It's not just that. I'm not . . ." He had no idea what he was going to say. "I can't—"

She stopped him again, reaching out, touching his cheek lightly with one hand, her gaze softening as she looked at him. "I know," she said. "That's why I'm here."

Trystan froze, ordering himself to breath in. Breath out.

He should get up, see she got safely back to her room, and then come back here.

And he couldn't do it. The best he could do was clear his throat and say, hoarsely, "I've had about five times too much of Octa's mead for this to be a good idea."

Isolde smiled one-sidedly at him again. But then the smile faded and she said, looking up to meet his gaze, "What were you dreaming about? You cried out something, just as I came up, but I couldn't tell what."

Thank the gods for small mercies, at any rate.

But Isolde didn't seem to expect a reply. Instead she moved her hand to smooth the hair back from his face, her fingers cool and soft against his skin. "You need to be with someone tonight, Trys." Her voice was almost a whisper. "Please, please, let it be me."

He was going to regret this. But, as though watching himself from a distance, Trystan saw himself lean back against the tree and reach to pull Isolde with him, so that his arm was around her and she was half sitting, half lying against him, her head on his shoulder.

She shifted a little, turning her head to ask, suddenly, "Do you ever pray?"

The surprise of her question was a distraction, at any rate. Trystan said, automatically, "No." And then, at her questioning look, he sighed and leaned back against the rough tree trunk. "I gave up on praying when I was . . . when I was in the mines."

Even at the mention of the word, the stench of burning metal from the smelting fires seemed to catch at the back of his throat. "I used to pray every minute, every hour, that I'd find a way to escape. But then after a while I—" Trystan caught himself.

Although it wasn't as if she didn't know about the years he'd spent a slave, a prisoner in a tin mining camp, breathing air practically solid with dust, trapped in the swelteringly hot dark without water or food for days at a time. Staying alive moment by moment, breath by breath.

And knowing all the while that it was his own god-cursed fault he was prisoner there. That this was justice, even. Assuming that there was any such thing in the mess men had made of the world.

Isolde took his left hand in hers, ran her fingers lightly along the disfiguring scars, keepsakes from some of the prison camp guards. "And yet you did get free," she said.

Trystan gave a brief laugh. "So the gods work on some kind of delayed fulfillment system? Maybe."

Isolde was silent a long moment. And then she said, "Trys? What do you really think about the war?"

This, at least, he'd been expecting. "Between Britons and Saxons, do you mean?" Trystan tipped his head back, looking up at the network of branches above, trying to ignore the fact that she was still holding his hand, that her head still rested against his shoulder. "Why? Because I'm here in Octa's camp?"

But Isolde gave a quick, impatient shake of her head. "Don't be stupid. As if you meant a single word of all those oaths you swore to Octa tonight. No, I meant . . . I grew up hearing stories of Arthur slaying the Saxon hordes. Stories that made the Saxon armies sound barely one step removed from hordes of demons. Not that I believed in them completely, not that I don't know of all the horrible, ugly deeds British warriors have committed on their raids of Saxon settlements, Saxon lands." She paused again and shifted a little, turning her head to look up at the night sky. "But some of those tales—of Octa, at least—are true. I know that, as well. And yet tonight was . . . it was beautiful, in a way. The stories and the singing and the oaths the warriors swore. And Octa—whatever he is himself, he's surrounded by men who are . . . just men. Warriors, but still men like any others. I just . . ." Her voice trailed off.

The all-too familiar nightmare was still clinging like battle mud, and when Trystan opened his mouth, he heard himself say, "War's always a stupid, bloody waste. And I long ago gave up on thinking one side deserved more than the other to win. But if I—"

Why not come right out and tell her he'd bargained with Octa of Kent to protect her? See just how willing she was to stand back and keep safe then.

But Isolde pulled back a little to look up at him, gray eyes luminous, unearthly beautiful in the moonlight. "But if you saw a chance of stopping it, stopping the war, how could you not take that chance?" She gave him a small smile at the expression on his face. "That's what you were going to say, isn't it?"

Trystan cleared his throat. "Isa, I—"

She shook her head, though, stopping whatever it was he'd been about to say. He wasn't even sure. "Don't bother. I know you, Trys."

Her eyes were still on his. And for a long moment, Trystan could only sit, staring at her. Then she settled back against him, and he felt his hand come up seemingly of its own accord to trail lightly along her jaw, slide through her dark hair. Her breath was a soft, tickling warmth against his throat. And then she said, "Trys? If you could be anywhere at all right now, where would it be?"

Here with you.

At least he managed not to say it aloud. Trystan watched a tattered patch of cloud drift across the face of the moon and said, after a moment, "On a boat—sailing somewhere."

Isolde shifted a little. "Where to?"

He shrugged. "Anywhere. It doesn't matter. Just sailing." He stopped. "On a boat you're . . . free. There's the sky and the wind and the sea. Nothing else exists, or at least you can pretend it doesn't."

He felt her nod against his shoulder, and then she slipped a hand into his and said, softly, "I'm sorry your boat was burned."

Trystan shrugged again. "Not your fault."

"I'm still sorry."

There was another moment's quiet. God, he was tired. Trystan's eyes felt gritty, and he let them slide briefly closed. Maybe he could do the same now. Pretend that nothing else existed but this moment, here, with her lying close beside him. Lose himself in the touch of her fingers, the feel of her at his side, the soft, sweet scent of her hair.

And then she drew back a little again, touching his cheek as she asked, very softly, "What were you dreaming about, Trys?" Her eyes searched his face. "Please tell me. Maybe the nightmare would go away if you told me about it."

Trystan kept silent. After a long moment, Isolde said, still looking up at him, "Who do you talk to, Trys? You don't talk to Kian or

Cath or Eurig or even Fidach—I know. I asked them. So who do you go to when there's something you can't bear alone?"

His mind flashed to all the nights she'd come and sat beside him amidst the filthy, hellish stink of the mines. Not just the dreams, but all the times he'd imagined her there himself, sitting in the dark beside him, holding his hand, telling some story or tale. Or listening while he talked with that *You can say anything, tell me anything*, look in her eyes.

"You." The word was out before he could check himself.

Isolde's eyes widened as though with surprise. "Me?" She shook her head. "You don't, though. Not really. You'll tell me what happened, but as though it all happened to someone else and not you at all. Years ago, with your father, or . . . you'll say you were a prisoner in a mining camp. But you never say how you felt. Whether you were angry or afraid or—"

Trystan didn't think he'd reacted visibly. But Isolde broke off, her look softening. "I'm sorry, Trys." Her voice, too, was soft. "You know, I could stay here—be with you for the rest of the night."

Another avalanche of memory hit, this time of all the nights at the abbey with Isolde sharing his bed, laughing with him in the dark. Lying awake and listening to her soft breathing, because even if he'd dared let himself fall asleep more often than he had done, he'd not have wanted to miss a single moment of being with her, holding her that way.

Trystan stood up so quickly he almost knocked Isolde over.

Well done. Maybe he could make her cry again while he was at it.

He pushed a hand through his hair, trying desperately not to think about what she'd just offered. "Isa, I—" His voice sounded raspy. "I can't let you. You deserve better than that. Better than—"

"Than you?" Isolde finished for him. She looked up at him, moonlight playing across her upturned face. "You've said that before. But better how? Better than the best man I've ever known? Better than the man who's risked his life twice in the last two turnings of the moon to save mine?"

"Don't you understand?" His voice was roughened by trying to keep some sort of a rein on the emotion churning inside him, the clash of wanting to reach for her and knowing he couldn't. "I did swear I'd keep you safe. But that means keeping you safe from myself above all else."

She frowned a little, remaining. "What do you mean?"

And for the second time that night, Trystan felt something inside him snap, felt the anger slip free. "Goddamn it, Isa. Kian lost an eye. Hereric lost an arm. Are you seeing any kind of pattern about what happens to those close to me?"

His chest tightened painfully as he saw her flinch at his tone. He'd have thought there was a limit to just how much of a swine he could feel in a single night.

Apparently not.

Trystan drew in a breath, forcing his voice, the anger back under his control. "If anything happened to you because of me . . . Please, Isa, don't ask me to live with that."

Isolde got to her feet. "Then don't ask me to live with it, either!" Her eyes flashed in her pale face. But then she stepped towards him, laying a hand on his arm, turning his wrist so that she could fit her right hand against his, palm to palm. "I gave you a marriage vow, Trys." She spoke more quietly, now. "That means if you need me, I'm here." She stopped, her gaze on his. "I know you've been on your own most of your life." She raised her free hand to lightly touch his brow. "All the hardest times, you've been alone. But right now, tonight, you don't have to be."

Trystan didn't speak. He just stood, the lean, hard-muscled lines of his shoulders, the planes of his face shadowed by the moonlight filtering through the trees. Looking at her. Their palms still fitted together, handfasting scar to handfasting scar. Even in the moonlight Isolde could see the scattered droplets of dried blood on the neck and shoulders of his shirt from Godgyth's rituals.

Isolde would have given anything right then to know what he was thinking. She couldn't guess, though. His face was one she remembered from years ago, shutting out all emotion, revealing nothing of what he thought or felt. She couldn't even tell whether he was about to turn on his heel and walk away from her without looking back. So she drew in her breath and said, "What were you dreaming about, Trys? Once before back at the abbey you said your mother's name when you were dreaming. Was the nightmare tonight about her?"

Trystan swore softly, but he didn't resist as she tugged him down so that they were once more sitting on the patch of grass under the apple tree. "Isa, you make me . . ."

"What, Trys?" Isolde leaned forward, her free hand sliding up his shoulder to the back of his neck. "Please tell me. What happened to your mother? I know she died just before Camlann, but—"

"After." It was spoken on a rough exhalation of breath, as though he hadn't meant to speak at all, as though the single word had forced itself out into the night stillness of its own will.

Isolde looked up, startled. "What?"

"She died after Camlann." Trystan's voice still sounded harsh, and he dropped his head into his hands. "Did I say I'd had too much to drink? If you really want to help, maybe you could go inside and get about another barrelful of Octa's mead, because if you're going to make me talk about this I'm going to need it all."

Isolde thought his first words had been spoken almost involuntarily, but now he went on before she could answer, as though some inner dam had broken and the words had to flow until their source ran dry. "You want to know what happened to my mother? I killed her. She didn't just die. She died by my hand."

Isolde's breath stopped. The soft summer air was sweet with the scents of fresh earth and herbs and growing things. Please, she thought, let him keep talking. Please, let her not do anything to break this cobweb-fragile moment of intimacy.

Aloud she said nothing, only tightened her hand on Trystan's—though she doubted he even felt it. He wasn't looking at her, but instead stared off into the night-darkened garden, a muscle jumping in the side of his jaw. "It was just after Camlann. My mother was there. In the army encampment. My . . . Marche had ordered her to come. He'd promised that—" Trystan broke off again. "Never mind. It was just as much a lie as every goddamn thing else he ever said."

He was still staring out into the garden, though she knew he wasn't seeing the shadowy shapes of growing herbs and trees. Then his shoulders moved convulsively as though throwing off a memory before it could take hold. "You know what happened at the battle. At the last possible moment Marche turned his coat and betrayed your father so that he—" Trystan broke off with a short, bitter laugh. "So that we were on the winning side. Even if Arthur was dead. I'd not honestly expected I'd live through the battle. Especially since—" The line of his mouth tightened. "But at the end of it, there I was, alive. I came back from—"

Trystan checked himself again. "I came back to my father's war tent. Covered in mud and blood and tired enough to be practically seeing double. And my mother was there. Lying on the ground." His voice was still flat and tonelessly hard, but Isolde felt the sudden tension in the hand she held, sensed the stiffening of his frame. "She was . . . Marche had . . . God, he must have broken nearly every bone in her body."

Isolde felt his fingers clench, then deliberately loosen. "She was still alive. Barely. Enough to know who I was. Her one eye was swollen completely shut and her lip was split and bleeding. But she saw me and managed to say"—Trystan broke off, but he went on with the same still-muscled control—"to say, 'Finish it . . . please. Just kill me. Let me die now.'"

He fell silent, and Isolde sat utterly motionless, feeling Trystan's every word twist in her like an arrow. She didn't dare interrupt him to speak, though—only sat, holding her breath while she counted four interminable beats of her own pulse, then five, before at last Trystan went on, voice roughening just slightly. "It wasn't as if I'd never seen men wounded, beaten bloody in battle. I could see well enough she was . . ." His mouth clamped shut, muscles jumping in his jaw, and he gave another shake of his head as though trying to dislodge the memory. "At most she'd have lived another day or two, and in godawful pain. So I—" He stopped and exhaled hard, thumb pressed against the bridge of his nose. When he looked up he was back in control, his voice flat. "So I did what she wanted. It was . . . quick, at least. She didn't suffer any more."

Isolde couldn't bear it any longer. "Trys—" She started to reach for him, but he stopped her.

"Don't."

The sharpness of the word made her check the movement before she could touch him. The muscle was jumping in his jaw again, and she knew he didn't want her sympathy. Didn't even want love just now. And she knew with aching certainty that she couldn't make this any harder for him, or say anything that might make him stop speaking.

Finally Trystan said, "I couldn't be . . . She'd died for me long before that. Maybe for herself, as well. I think that was the first time in years I'd heard her say more than yes or no. But—"

He stopped, Isolde could see a brief reflection of how he must have looked on that day, seven years before. And then, abruptly, he turned back to her with another of those mirthless laughs. "So. Now you know the truth. Not only couldn't I protect her, I was the one to take her life. Still want to spend the night out here with me?"

His voice, too, was harsh, as though he'd stepped backwards behind some internal wall, closing himself off both from her and from all he'd just told her. Isolde remembered saying to her grandmother, years before, *He almost never smiles.* And Morgan saying, with a gentleness that was surprising, *It's because he has no one in his life to love him.*

His flatly spoken question hung now between them, and Isolde wondered what she could possibly find to say.

Her heart was twisted too tightly for her to speak, though, even if she'd been able to find the right words. So, for answer, she leaned forward and kissed him, touching her lips to his.

Trystan froze, then jerked backwards, catching hold of her hand when she reached for his face. "Isa, I . . ." At least the still-muscled, frighteningly expressionless look had cracked; he sounded as though he were working to steady his breathing. "This can't possibly be what you want. Not really. I—"

Isolde didn't let him finish. "Trys, when I told you that Marche had forced me into marrying him, did it change what you felt for me?"

Trystan pushed a hand through his hair. "God, no, of course not, but—"

"But it's easier to believe I'm here because you carved me a wooden horse when I was ten than because I might actually love you the same way? Because I do love you that way. Whether you like it or not."

Isolde stopped for breath and then said, more softly, "I don't *still* want to spend tonight with you. I don't want to *anyway*, or *even though*. I just want to. I—" She stopped. "I wish I could take it away. The choice you had to make. The memories you've had to carry all these years. But it's for you I wish it—it doesn't change anything about what I want or feel."

Trystan said nothing, only looked at her, eyes shadowed in the moonlight. But his grip on her fingers had relaxed, and she freed her hand and gently reached to touch his face, the stubble of the day's beard on his jaw rough against her fingertips. "Please, Trys. Let me stay with you. Just for tonight. It doesn't have to be more than that. You don't have to promise anything about what happens tomorrow."

It wasn't a lie—not exactly. She did want just one more night with him, if that were all he could give her, would take it gladly. A part of her, too, was silently praying to the herb-scented currents of air all around them to please, please, let him say yes.

The remembered vision of three nights ago seemed to press against her like the surrounding darkness itself, clutching at her like birds' claws. *I'm sorry, Lady Isolde. He was wounded. Fatally so.*

And something in this moonlit garden seemed to whisper to her that if only she could keep him in her arms for a night, she might— just might—be able to hold back that future. Change *will be* into *might have been.*

She drew in a breath and then said, searching his face, her voice almost a whisper, "Do you want me to stay?"

Trystan pressed his eyes briefly shut. "You know I do. But you can't—"

Isolde stopped him before he could go on. "Trys, I've spent weeks and *weeks* fearing for you with every breath I took. Not knowing where you were, not knowing for certain whether you were even still alive or whether I would ever see you again." In spite of her best efforts, the vision's echo made her voice shake and her eyes flood with tears. She blinked and drew another breath and then whispered, voice still unsteady, "How could I not want one more night of being your wife—whatever happens in the morning? How could I possibly not want one more night in your arms?"

The garden was hushed, the sweet scent of herbs and dewy grass alive all about them. A cricket chirped nearby. For a moment, time itself seemed to hang suspended as she looked up into Trystan's face. He had gone absolutely, utterly still. Isolde wasn't even sure he was breathing. She saw, though, or at least desperately hoped she did, the mingled pain and longing at the back of his gaze, and she saw his fingers stir, as though he were trying to stop himself reaching for her.

She leaned forward and kissed him again, lightly brushing her mouth across his. Still he didn't move, but this time she could feel him shaking with the effort he was making not to respond.

And then she felt him tense and stiffen as he looked past her at something beyond. He said, voice intense but lowered to a barely audible murmur, "I need you to hit me—strike me across the face—say something angry. As though you'd come here alone and I accosted you. Make it convincing." And then, before Isolde could voice disbelief or confusion, he went on, the next words sending an instant slither of cold across her skin, "Someone just came into the garden. Someone watching us."

She didn't argue, didn't even hesitate. Trystan found himself thanking the gods for her nerve even as she lifted a hand and struck him with the flat of her palm.

"How dare you? Do you know who I am?" Her pretense at anger was equally convincing. Although maybe that was because she didn't have to pretend all that hard.

The shadow by the garden gate—too dark to tell who it was, too dark to say even whether it was male or female—hadn't moved. Trystan shook his head to clear it. "No idea, but pretty girls who wander alone at night shouldn't object to a kiss or two." He slurred his words so that he sounded far gone in drink. *Further gone, don't you mean?*, a voice in the back of his head commented sourly. "Come over here, love, and you can introduce yourself."

Isolde gave him one last look from wide, brimming eyes, her lips silently shaping words. *Don't forget. Please.*

And then she turned on her heel and was away, walking swiftly across the grass towards the garden gate, shoulders and back stiff with a credible show of outrage. The shadow by the garden wall moved and then vanished through the gate at her approach, and Trystan swore silently under his breath. All to the good, he supposed, but it meant, too that any chance of finding out who the watcher had been was almost certainly lost for good.

He waited a count of ten and then followed after Isolde, moving quickly and silently and keeping to the darkest shadows so that he, too, would be all but invisible should whoever it had been return and try their hand at another round of spying. But he passed through the garden gate—and as he'd thought, the fortress compound was utterly deserted, the flagged pavements and stone walls lit in patches by the flaring torches, the only sounds the continued shouts and drunken laughter from the feasting hall.

Trystan stood and watched Isolde cross to the inner garrison, watched her step through the door that would lead to the room she'd been assigned. He stood a long moment, eyes on that doorway and the deeper shadow into which she'd vanished. Then he let out his breath, turned, and made his way silently back through the garden to the apple tree, dropping onto the patch of grass where what felt like six lifetime's ago he'd made a bed for the night.

As if he was going to sleep, with the memory of every word he and Isolde had spoken beating in his head like a war drum. He hadn't even had the wits to ask her what she was doing here, at Caer Peris, in the heart of Octa's camp.

Not that he couldn't guess. Whether she was here because she'd known, somehow, that he would be coming, or whether this was some mission of the king's council. It didn't matter. She'd have walked straight into any den of wolves, without flinching, without hesitation, if that was what had to be done.

From somewhere in the fortress a dog barked and then yelped as though in pain; someone must have started a fight between two of the war hounds. Trystan closed his eyes. The entire evening was still replaying in his mind. From the moment he'd set eyes on her in the feasting hall to the memory of all he'd told her out here.

Trystan threw up an arm across his eyes and thought that he ought to feel something. Renewed guilt. The old hatred eating its way through his skin. And yet . . .

What he felt most was a wave of disgusted anger at himself,

because the mere fact that she hadn't left, hadn't run away screaming, was making stupid, irrational hope well up in his chest.

A vision swam up out of the surrounding darkness: Isolde, slender and graceful and so beautiful it actually hurt as she knelt before him in the moonlight, leaning forward to touch her lips to his.

Trystan swore and rolled onto his back, staring up at the ragged patches of sky visible through the network of leaves and branches above. Maybe if he tried thinking about that watching shadow, tried asking himself just how much whoever it was might have seen . . .

Though he supposed he owed whoever it had been a debt of gratitude. He ought to be relieved.

Relief. Right. That was the feeling uppermost in his mind right now. Not unanswered desire jangling along his every nerve. Relief.

Let me stay with you. Just for tonight. It doesn't have to be more than that.

Trystan closed his eyes, feeling the recollection of Isolde's words pump through his blood.

No chance on God's green earth would he have been strong enough to refuse that offer on his own.

"CAN'T SAY I LIKE IT," CATH said.

Isolde made herself breathe. She was standing with Cath, Kian, and Eurig outside the men's practice yard. Within sight of the garden where she'd sat with Trystan the night before. They were alone; after last night's revels, which had ended only with the sunrise, the fortress was all but deserted at this hour of the morning, though a pair of warriors too drunk to find their beds lay sprawled and snoring on the cobbles outside the men's hall.

And she ought to have been glad to see the three men again for this, the first time they'd spoken freely since their arrival at Caer Peris. She ought to have been, and was, thankful beyond words that none of them had come to harm.

Trystan, though, was gone. Departed before dawn this morning on some further mission for Octa of Kent, before Isolde could even see him, much less speak to him again. She'd not even have known he was gone at all save that Ulf had told her when she'd come out of her room an hour earlier and asked after Octa's guest of honor, careful not to speak his name.

Ulf had been red-eyed and blinking after last night's *symbel,* though still at his duties as usual. He'd seemed to notice nothing odd about her question. But he'd told her that Trystan was gone. All Octa's private guard knew of it, it seemed. Trystan had left at first light on another mission for his newly sworn lord.

And now Isolde had to persuade Cath, Kian, and Eurig, to leave her as well and go after him. She tried to force back the raging impatience, the icy shaking under her breastbone. "I will be safe. And I've spoken to Octa already. He's accepted my offer of the services of you three as my honor guard. All you need do is follow—and find—Trystan."

Octa, unlike the rest of his guard, had been clear-eyed and steady-handed this morning. Whatever Octa of Kent's weaknesses or vices might be, excess of drink was not one. He'd listened in cold silence as Isolde made her careful offer of her own honor guard to aide his new ally. But he'd agreed, which was all she could spare attention for or care about now.

Isolde looked from Cath to Eurig, whose homely face was as worried and reluctant as Cath's, and then turned to Kian, who was watching her in silence, rubbing the scar on his cheek with the back of his thumb.

"I don't like it, either," he said, answering the question she'd not asked. The harsh early-morning light made his face look even grimmer. "Don't like your being here in the first place. Like the idea of leaving you alone here a sight less."

"I won't be alone. I'll have Cabal with me." The big dog sat close at her side, and Isolde put a hand on his brindled neck. She could see Kian opening his mouth, about to argue, but she stopped him before he could begin. "Kian, you know Trystan. All three of you do." She included Cath and Eurig in her glance. "Have you ever known him to keep himself from danger? Have you ever known him not to—"

Despite herself her voice cracked slightly. She couldn't even have said why she was so afraid, where the cold, black dread that now hung over her had come from, or why she was so absolutely, utterly sure that she had to persuade Kian and the others to follow wherever Trystan had gone.

And yet that made it worse, in a way—that there was no solid reason for her fear. The terror that had gripped her from the moment she'd heard Ulf's announcement that Trystan was gone felt like a child's nightmare monster, looming unknown and shapeless in the dark.

She dug her nails into her palms again. "Have you ever known Trystan not to walk straight into the most horrifying risks imaginable if that's the only way to get a mission done? Any of you?"

She saw unwilling acknowledgment flash in Kian's remaining eye. "And you think Trystan's in danger now?" Kian said.

Isolde nodded, the beginnings of queasy relief making her words come in a tumbled rush. "I'm sure of it. I don't know where he is or what he's doing, but I know that unless you go after him, there's every likelihood he'll get himself killed. Please"—she looked from Kian to Cath to Eurig and back again—"please say you'll do it."

Kian was silent. Then, slowly, his head moved in a nod, and Isolde had to stiffen to keep from sinking to the ground, muscles suddenly limp. Before she could speak, though, Kian rubbed his scar again and said, "And what if Marche of Cornwall should happen to join Octa while you're alone here? Could happen, you know. They're allies, the two of them. Have you thought of that?"

Marche's face—dark, heavy-featured, and brutal, with ravaged eyes—rose before her at Kian's words. Once the thought of facing Marche again, for the first time since he'd forced her into a marriage of one nights would have filled her with loathing and fear intense enough to make her ill. Now, though, the thought scarcely touched her, except as a stomach-clenching reason why Kian might, after all, refuse to leave her here alone.

"I had thought of it." Isolde spoke steadily as before. "But I promise you, even if it happens, I'll come to no harm."

Involuntarily her hand went to the girdle of her gown. Strange, she thought, that the very unborn baby who could be her undoing among the men of the king's council should be almost her sole safeguard now.

"I promise you, I'll be safe." Her gaze met Kian's. "You told me once that Trystan was a good friend to you. That he'd saved your life more times than you could ever repay. Please promise me you'll do your best to see him safe, as well."

Kian's harsh-featured expression didn't alter, the grim set of his mouth didn't soften or even change. But his remaining eye was bright as he tipped his head in a nod and said, gruffly, "That's not a hard promise to make."

Chapter 14

"MARCHE OF CORNWALL IS HERE?" Isolde's whole body felt like one tingling mass of shock and her voice sounded tinny and far away. Beside her, Cabal whined, and she automatically put a hand on his neck to quiet him.

Ulf nodded. "He and a war party rode in tonight. Octa welcomed them in hall, said—" The guard stopped and shot Isolde a quick glance in which an odd blend of reluctance, embarrassment, and, she thought, something almost like sympathy showed in his blue eyes. "Octa said Lady Isolde of Camelerd and Marche of Cornwall had been wedded once before. Now that both his allies are both here, be wedded again."

Isolde stared. But there seemed, at least, to be a limit to the number of shocks that could be absorbed in a single evening, because she scarcely even felt surprised. No, what she felt, most of all, was anger. The Sight, ever a mocking joke, had given her a shadowy, ominous sense of danger to Trystan, and not even a warning hint of what she faced now. But the anger that hissed through her blood was at herself, for not having foreseen this, Sight or no.

In the brief eternity since Ulf had spoken, she had relived in memory every interview she'd had with Octa of Kent since arriving at Caer Peris. And she had had time to castigate herself for not putting together the fragments that now came together in her mind as a chilling whole.

Of course Octa of Kent would have welcomed her here. Of course he'd have bided his time, suppressed any hostility he felt for the woman whose lands had still not fallen to the combined forces of himself and Marche. He'd known that all he had to do was wait, summon Marche here, and declare Marche her husband and lord, and so, king of Camelerd.

Camelerd's armies might hold out against a direct attack. They might even have fought with bitter armed resistance had Isolde's ostensible capitulation to Octa a few days before been real. But if they were given news that their lady was actually wedded to Marche . . .

Isolde gripped the sides of her chair. She was sitting by the cold hearth in the room she'd been assigned; after a day spent trying to imagine every step Kian, Cath, and Eurig might have taken in their search for Trystan, she'd been unable to face the thought of the evening meal in the great hall.

Which was, as it turned out, lucky, in a way. At least she hadn't had to face this news before the watching eyes of Octa's court.

She tightened her hands until the chair's wooden frame bit into her palms. The pain was oddly steadying, a single bright central spark in the fog of disbelieving panic that had formed in her mind.

She waited until she could be absolutely sure that her voice wouldn't shake, then looked up at Ulf, and said, "Very well. You may tell Lord Marche that I will see him now, here."

"LORD MARCHE OF CORNWALL, LADY."

Isolde's heart jerked against her side. She was alone. She'd shut Cabal into the tiny privy room that opened off her own. If she'd have been thankful beyond words for his solid bulk at her side, she didn't trust him not to attack if he felt her threatened. And she didn't doubt for a moment that Marche would draw a knife or sword and run Cabal through if Cabal sprang.

So she drew a breath and held herself very still. She'd had what seemed an impossibly short while to steady herself between Ulf's departure and his return. But she'd imagined many times in the months since she'd last seen Marche what she would feel on seeing him again—not only since that brief marriage, but since she'd been able to summon him in the scrying waters, slide into his mind, and hear his thoughts as her own.

Fear, hatred, anger—she'd imagined them all. That and the

stomach-turning possibility that he'd been aware of her as she'd been of him; that he'd felt her silent presence inside his head.

But what struck her most at sight of the man who followed Ulf into the room was, more than anything, shock at how much he'd changed in the last half year and more. When she'd seen Marche last almost a year ago, his dark, blunt-featured face had been brutal, yes, heavy and weathered by a lifetime spent on campaign, but he had still borne the lingering remnants of having been a handsome man in youth.

Now Marche of Cornwall looked ghastly. Bloated and ill, with a pasty, twitching face and bloodshot eyes, his once thick black hair now sparse and gray. His nose and cheeks bore a telltale network of the red, broken veins caused by heavy drink; in fact, his gaze looked glassy and his steps were slightly unsteady even as he came forward into the room.

Unwillingly, but instantly, Isolde reached towards him in her mind. The prospect turned her stomach, but she had to know, now, at once, whether she could still step inside Marche's mind. She fixed her eyes on his puffy, drink-glazed ones and felt . . .

Nothing. Not even a flicker in the space inside where she heard or felt the Sight, not a tug or even a whisper in her mind. That door was closed, and instinctively she knew it had closed once and for all.

The knowledge let her draw her first full breath, let her incline her head in a brief but steady nod of greeting as he stepped into the room.

She had felt, too, occasional flashes of unwilling pity for Marche of Cornwall, that he had, as Cath had once put it, to live inside his own skin. But what filled her now, on top of the shock, was incredulous amazement that the wreck of a man before her had ever been for her a figure of nightmare terrors and fear.

Marche of Cornwall was afraid himself. She'd glimpsed it in the scrying waters months before; had felt the raging fury he used to push down all fear, not only of the man he'd become but of the trap in which he presently found himself. The iron-barred cage he'd built around him in first swearing allegiance with Octa of Kent.

But she'd not have needed the Sight or the recollection of those visions to know that the man before her was filled with the mad, panicked fury of a wolf caught in a hunter's snare, willing to gnaw through his own flesh and bone to get free.

Marche was a king, and a king's son. He'd been born to rule Cornwall, had through a lifetime of battles—through even the wreck of Camlann—kept his borders fast and held his throne. And now he stood teetering on the brink of losing it all. Of seeing Cornwall—the fishing villages, the settlements, the rich tin mines—become nothing but fertile ground for Octa and his warriors to plow, an added source to line Octa's coffers with gold.

Marche came weavingly forward, and Isolde barely had to make an effort to hold herself still in the face of his advance; hardly had to work to shut out the memories stirred by the reek of ale and sour vomit on his breath.

"Lady Isolde." His voice, though, was as she remembered, deep and with the rasp of steel on steel. A chill crawled the length of Isolde's spine—one she had to work harder, this time, to ignore. "I understand you are now once more my wedded wife."

His drink-glazed dark eyes strayed to the curtained bed in the corner, and just for a moment memories of another night nearly a year before swamped Isolde, making bile rise in her throat. Lying in bed and waiting for Marche. Thrusting a cedar- and mandrake-smeared rag deep inside her. And risking her life to do it, because if Marche had known she had taken measures to keep from conceiving his child, he would have had her killed in an instant.

From behind the closed door of the privy room, Cabal whined, and Isolde snapped the memories off at the root, forced back the wave of fear that was beginning to spread like grease over her skin.

If she'd not married Marche, she'd be dead—buried and turning to dust in a cold unmarked grave. And she'd always known, from the moment he'd left her to salve her bruises and wash herself over and over again, that she would have to face Marche again to fully reclaim what he'd taken from her that night.

Isolde met Marche's eyes. Puffy. Exhausted and glazed with the effects of wine and ale. Even if the channel through which she'd entered his mind was closed now, she could see in the depths of their gaze a reflection of the man whose thoughts she'd seen. A man who—she saw it with the suddenness of a whip crack—raged and savaged and killed because his soul was like a serpent, eternally gnawing on his own tail. Marche of Cornwall might hate, might take joy in destruction, but he hated himself most of all.

She thought of Mother Berthildis, telling her months before that the visions of Marche were sent to her that she might forgive him for all he'd done. Mother Berthildis, who now lay with half her body deadened and called it with utter certainty the wisdom of God.

Isolde hadn't known then whether the abbess's words were true or no. And right now, facing Marche himself, couldn't find it in her to care. She found a spark of anger, let it kindle into a hard, bright blaze.

She raised her head. "So King Octa decrees, Lord Marche. But you should know before this goes further that as we speak I am carrying another man's child. Take one step nearer—try to force yourself into my bed—and that child is your son and heir."

She saw rage flare behind the haze of drink in Marche's eyes. He raised his hand as though to strike her across the face. The blow never landed, though. Ulf, unnoticed, had come up behind Marche and in a blur of motion reached out and caught hold of the other man's upraised arm.

For a long moment, they stood like that, seemingly frozen in place. Marche drunkenly unsteady in Ulf's grasp, blinking at Isolde through furious eyes; Ulf as impassive as always, but still keeping tight hold on Marche's forearm.

In the silence that followed, Isolde heard Cabal's whines turn into near-frantic barks, heard him throw himself hard against the closed door. And then, in a single jerky movement, Marche turned, wrenched himself free from Ulf's hold, and was gone in a swirl of the green traveling cloak he wore. For the briefest instant, Ulf's eyes met Isolde's. Then Ulf turned and, without a word, followed Marche from the room. It was only when the door had shut behind both of them that Isolde realized she was shaking from head to foot.

She stared at the closed door a long moment. Still shivering, she got up, and crossed to open the privy room door. Cabal bounded out, nearly knocking her to the ground, and she knelt to put her arms around him. Just for a moment, she let herself bury her face in his fur, forget everything but the rasp of his tongue on her wrist as she willed her frantically beating heart to slow.

No time, though. She didn't have time to realize or even think about all that had just occurred. However deep Marche's hatred ran, he wouldn't willingly give her the chance of claiming another man's child for his. Whatever else Marche was, he was proud. And that pride had kept her safe for tonight.

But Marche was also under Octa's thumb. Coldly, deadly afraid of the ally whose greater power now had him effectively caught in a trap: obey the Saxon king's will or die. Owain of Powys had allied with Octa and died. Marche would surely know by now that he was no more indispensable than Owain had been.

And Isolde didn't for a moment imagine that Octa would have the slightest compunction about seeing her wedded and bedded by Marche, regardless of whether she carried Trystan's child.

Isolde closed her eyes, wishing that Morgan would choose now to appear before her. Or that she could feel again that tiny, pond-ripple stirring of the baby in her womb.

Or that Trystan were here.

She pushed that thought ruthlessly, almost angrily aside. So long as she was making up happy endings, she might as well wish that Trystan was not only here, but telling her he loved her and would never leave her again.

THE KNOCK AT HER DOOR MADE Isolde freeze, her heart slamming against her ribs again at the inevitable thought that Marche must have returned. When she'd made herself rise, though, and cross to the door, furiously ordering her hands not to shake as she lifted the latch, she found it was Godgyth who stood in the passage outside, her dress windblown and her white hair covered by an incredibly ancient and dirty shawl.

After all that had already occurred, Isolde couldn't even be surprised. She stared at the old woman blankly and as Godgyth almost pushed her way into the room. Godgyth shut the door behind her. Then she said, "You want to get free of Caer Peris. I'm here to help you."

Maybe it was a good thing to be beyond registering shock. Isolde blinked at Godgyth, drew in her breath, signaled Cabal to lie down by the hearth. Then she said, "Why should you wish to do that?"

Godgyth limped towards the room's single wooden table, picked up a pot of salve from Isolde's medicine box, and then put it down again to say, abruptly, "I saw you in the garden last night. You and your young man. My brother's so-called ally."

Or maybe she was still capable of shock after all. Isolde had to swallow twice before she could make her voice steady enough to answer. "That was you?"

"It was." Godgyth's voice was quiet, almost gentle, and she moved to lay a hand on Isolde's arm. "And I may be old. But I'm not so old that I cannot still recognize true love when I see it."

Her fingers were smooth, unpleasantly cool and slippery against Isolde's skin, her eyes masked and as eerily opaque as before.

Isolde drew back from her touch. "I'd keep to playing the seeress if I were you. It's far more convincing."

She half expected anger, but instead the old woman threw back her head and laughed her surprisingly rich, throaty chuckle. "I'm very sure it is. Though that doesn't stop what I said from being—at least in part—true. No, wait, hear me out." This as Isolde started to speak. "You're quite right. For all your youth and your pretty face and your looking, to be blunt, as though a strong wind would blow you away, you're not a fool. I was wrong to speak to you as though you were."

She paused, running one clawlike finger lightly around the table's edge, then shot Isolde a sharp sidelong glance. "What if I told you that I've no doubt my brother King Octa would kill you as easily as breathing if your death suited him. But with you wedded to Lord Marche, it may suit him better for now to keep you alive. And I've no wish to be replaced in my position of wise woman and prophetess should that occur."

Godgyth's eyes shifted focus, and something remote and not a little sad washed across her wizened face. "The gods of this land don't speak to me. Perhaps the gods of Britain are more powerful than I would have believed. Or perhaps it is only that I am too old." She glanced sidelong at Isolde once again. "Whatever the reason, any powers I have are but a dim reflection of what they once were. I catch flashes of vision merely. Dark shapes, as though seen through a fog at night, with the occasional bright flash, no more." A dry smile tightened the edges of her mouth and she made Isolde one of her oddly graceful half bows. "But that does not mean that I cannot yet recognize power in someone else."

That, Isolde thought, was almost funny, when she hadn't known about Marche or had the wit to piece together Octa's plan. When her mind was still utterly blank as to what her next move should be—whether, for that matter, she should even think of trusting the old woman standing before her now.

She didn't argue, though. Godgyth went on, speaking in the old, slightly lilting, singsong tone. "I knew, at least, that your alliance with my brother was pretense, that you had come here for the boy. Madoc of Gwynedd's son. I even thought, if I am honest, of appearing to aid you in a plan to get the boy free from here. And then informing Octa before you could get far away and so increasing my worth in Octa's sight." She shot another wry glance at Isolde. "I may have little real power, you see. But I have learned to make good use of what I do possess. To bend circumstances as far as possible to my aid."

Isolde had caught her breath by now. She said, "I do see. And is there any reason why I should believe you're not carrying out exactly that scheme now?"

The old woman's mouth stretched again, the smile this time almost like a grin that bared nearly toothless gums. "None. I could be lying. You could step out of this room straight into a contingent of Octa's guard. But—" With sudden, surprising swiftness, she limped to the room's single window and drew back the shutters, throwing them wide. "An assurance of good faith. Should you believe in such things."

The air that rushed into the room was damp, smelling of salt and the sea. And curling with tendrils of fog, ghostly white in the candlelight. Isolde crossed to look out. A thick sea mist had rolled in, covering all. She could barely see the glow of torches from the ramparts. And nothing at all of the fortress spread out below. It might have been engineered to cover an escape.

Slowly, she turned back to Godgyth, who nodded and, as though in confirmation, gave a small flick of her fingers and offered Isolde a knotted piece of string. "Yes. This one is for summoning a fog. No wind will rise to clear the mist until these knots are undone." And then, before Isolde could answer, before she could even decide how she meant to respond, Godgyth leaned forward and put a clawlike hand over hers. "I was a mother, once. That I do still remember well. And I would think that for the sake of the child you carry, you would be willing to take the risk of believing me now."

Her skin felt as cool and as slippery-smooth as before. But her voice had changed, not softening, quite, but taking on a quality Isolde had never heard from her before.

Isolde drew in a slow breath, then made up her mind. "All right." She nodded. "I do believe you. Tell me what you would have me do."

ISOLDE SAT AT THE OPEN WINDOW, staring out at the thick fog that still blanketed the night. Godgyth had been proven right so far, at least. The air was without wind or any hint the mist would soon clear. The hours since Godgyth had gone had passed with agonizing slowness, broken only by the occasional disembodied voice from one of the guards on the ramparts outside, the words eerily muffled by the fog.

Now, though, it must be nearly time. Isolde rose and picked up the bundle of belongings she'd already packed: her medicine box, some bread and cheese left from her supper tray, a change of clothes, all wrapped together in her traveling cloak. She clicked her fingers together and instantly Cabal, who had been asleep on the hearth, was alert and at her side. She went to the door and eased it open, gritting her teeth as the hinges gave a creak that sounded like a scream in the still night. And then she froze at the sight of Ulf, standing outside.

The guardsman turned at the sound of the door's opening, and Isolde willed herself not to stare at him in horror.

Goddess, why hadn't she thought of this? If she'd considered it at all, she'd assumed Godgyth must have planned for all the details of her escape tonight, including getting free of the guard Octa had set.

But the old woman had, in fact, said nothing at all about having to evade Ulf or the younger man, who at least wasn't here now.

And at least Ulf appeared to have noticed nothing amiss yet. He looked more embarrassed than anything else. "I am . . . glad to speak with you, lady. Thank you for telling me to speak with Ymma last night." The guard paused and then a slow, utterly unaccustomed smile spread over his hard-bitten face. "She says she will have me."

Isolde's mind was racing, but she instantly summoned up an answering smile. "I'm very glad." She found it was true, too, whatever else she now felt.

Ulf gave a small, gruff nod of acknowledgment, then said, still with the edge of embarrassment in his tone, "I wanted to see . . . to ask if you are all right. From before. When Lord Marche—"

He stopped abruptly, looking at her more closely, seeming for the first time to take in her outdoor clothes and sturdy boots and the bundle of possessions she carried under one arm. Though it could at best have been only been a matter of time before he did notice them—he'd have had to be blind not to. Isolde's fingers clenched on Cabal's collar, dread tightening inside her once more as she met Ulf's pale, steady blue gaze.

Then the guardsman said, "There was something else, lady. I . . . am not sleeping well these last nights. Do you have something . . . some potion, maybe . . . help me sleep more soundly tonight?"

For a moment, Isolde could only stare at him. "I do have something," she said at last. She touched the bundled shape of her medicine box. "Poppy syrup. I have it here. But—"

Ulf stopped her. "You give to me. And I will . . ." He paused, the continued steadiness of his gaze weighing the words. "I will go and share a horn of ale with the guard at the northern gate. You understand?"

Isolde's throat felt all at once impossibly tight. "I understand. But I want you to promise me that you'll not face punishment for this. Octa doesn't strike me as likely to forgive a guard who fails in his duties."

Ulf shook his head. "Not my duty tonight."

Isolde stared at him for the second time. "What?"

"Not my duty." Another of those slow smiles spread across Ulf's face, broader this time, than before. "Before I go to northern gate, I will find Lord Marche's men and tell them Marche orders them—" He stopped, searching for the word. "Orders them to replace me as guard outside your door. Marche will be pissing himself in drink by now if he's carried on the way he began tonight." A flicker of contempt curled his lip. "Not likely to remember different. In morning, when you are gone"—Ulf raised his burly shoulders in a shrug—"must have been on Marche's men's watch. And besides," he added, "I will not be here much longer. Eormenric is—"

Abruptly, he checked himself. Isolde nearly asked him a question, nearly tried to frame a way that would validate the half-guess she'd made as to where Eormenric, Octa's son, must be. But she, too, stopped herself before she could try. She and Ulf stood on opposite sides of a generations-old war, for all he was aiding her now. Unfair to ask of him anything more.

She said, simply, "Thank you."

Ulf gestured, waving the thanks away, then shot her another swift glance. "One more thing, lady. I . . . I visited the stables today. Hræfn is recovered. I'd say ready to ride. If"—his pale gaze met Isolde's—"if the rider is someone small. Not too heavy a load."

For a moment, Isolde could only stare. Then she made herself find her voice. "I can't let you—"

Ulf interrupted, voice again implacably flat, harsh as before. "You let nothing. I do nothing. Only tell you Hræfn well enough to be ridden. No more." He paused, blinking, and Isolde thought there might have been another of those brief glimmers of moisture in his eyes. Or maybe only a trick of the passage's flickering torchlight. The guard scowled and added, gruffly, "Horse a piss-poor scabby beast, anyway. No loss if—" He stopped, throat bobbing as he swallowed. "If the great farting bag of guts somehow . . . stolen in the night."

"WOULD YOU CARE TO LIVE PAST this morning?" Cath's tone was pleasant, amiable, even, but the youth in Kian's grasp still paled. He cast a wild-eyed, terrified look about the tree-lined clearing, as though hoping some of his fellows would miraculously appear—or at least for an equally miraculous means of escape. Finding neither, he swallowed convulsively, the movement making the knife point Cath held at his throat bob.

Trystan suppressed a twitch of guilt. This job came under the category of frightening children; the guardsman they'd captured was barely more than a wet-behind-the-ears boy, for all he wore Octa's badge on his scrawny arm. And at that, Trystan hadn't trusted himself to keep hold on his temper. Not after his last encounter with Octa's guards. Not with images of every hell-cursed danger that could by now have befallen Isolde swarming like angry wasps behind his eyes. Which was why Cath was the one doing the questioning now and not him.

That, and the fact that even if the boy was a half-wit, he'd recognize in Trystan Octa's purported ally and informant. From the moment the youth had been spotted, Trystan had kept out of sight, and now stood in the shadow of a spreading oak, screened by shade and branches—and by the sun at his back—from the boy's view.

And Cath, to do him justice, made for a good terror-inducing figure. Taller than the boy by double a man's handspan, his black beard knotted with leaves and bits of twig and his black hair standing on end, he looked like something out of the wilder tales.

"Good, I'll take that for a yes, then." Cath's beard parted in a ferocious grin. "You'd like to live past today. And since that's the case, I'll suggest you get started on telling us what you know about what's happened to the Lady Isolde."

The Saxon youth's throat bobbed again. "I don't know anything. Only that she was gone from the fortress this morning. Her and one of the war mounts from the stables, a black. And Lord Octa raged up and down the hall and swore we'd better find her if we wanted to keep our hides."

"Did he, now?" Cath's thumb idly caressed the hilt of the knife, pressing it just slightly more firmly against the boy's throat. The youth flinched, and Cath said, "Well, much as I'd hate to keep Octa from the fun of skinning you alive, I'd say you've got more immediate troubles to fret yourself over than Octa, my lad, if you're lying to us now."

"I don't lie." The Saxon boy's voice was thready and high-pitched. "I swear it. The Lady Isolde was gone from her room this morning, and a black stallion gone from the stables. That's all I know." He finished with a string of oaths and a prayer to the gods in his own tongue.

Cath, still holding the knife, flashed a questioning glance at Trystan, which Trystan, from his place of concealment, answered with an nod.

"Right, then." Cath sheathed the knife with a flourish, but then leaned forward, baring his teeth again as he peered into the boy's face. The youth, who had sagged visibly, flinched again. "Get out of my sight. Pray I never lay eyes on you again."

Kian, standing behind, released his grip on the boy's arms. The Saxon stared a moment, gulped, and then stared a moment more, as though unable to take in the import of Cath's words. Then, face still white with terror, he turned and fled, the crashing of branches marking his blundering way through the trees.

Cath stood looking after him, then, when the sounds of the Saxon's panicked flight had started to fade, cast another look of inquiry at Trystan. Trystan gave another nod, and Cath moved off silently in the direction the youth had taken.

Trystan waited a count of fifty, then stepped out from the tree's shade. Kian raised a questioning brow. "Think he was lying?"

Maybe one of these days Trystan would be able to stop wincing inwardly every time his gaze fell on the patch over Kian's right eye. It wasn't likely to be today, though. Trystan forced himself not to look away. God knew that was the least he owed the other man.

He shrugged. "I think he was too terrified to lie about his own name. But better to be sure." Which was why Cath had followed him, on the off chance that the youth knew more than he'd said.

Kian grunted agreement, rubbing the scar on his face with the back of his thumb. "Think he'll report back to Octa about seeing us?"

"Tell Octa he was fool enough to get himself captured and nearly dirtied his breeches with fear when you questioned him?" Trystan shook his head. "I doubt it. But even if he does, what does he have to tell? That the lady Isolde's honor guard was searching for her. No surprise there. Nothing lost, unless you were hoping to get back into Caer Peris as a guest again."

"Ha." Kian gave a short bark of laughter. "Not likely. I've had enough goat-piss vinegar Saxon wine and the slop they call food to last a lifetime." He paused, and Trystan could see the next words hovering on his tongue.

He cut Kian off. "Don't say it. You did everything you could." The stinging hornets still buzzed inside his head, but he forced a measure of lightness into the words. He owed Kian that, as well. "I've been trying to keep Isolde from trouble practically since the time she could walk. I don't think it can be done."

Kian had been scowling at the ground in a way Trystan knew tokened suppressed worry or guilt, but some of the grimness in his face lifted at that. He grunted again. "Same might be said of some others I could name." He paused, scanning the surrounding forest. "We'll find her. If she's on horseback it shouldn't be too hard to pick up a trail."

Trystan nodded. What went unsaid was the likelihood that Octa's men would pick up her trail and find her first. He exhaled, pushing exhaustion and fear both far, far back. Christ knew he didn't have time for either, now.

"Did she say anything that might give you an idea of the direction she was taking?"

Kian shook his head. "Nothing. Would have sworn she'd no thought of leaving Caer Peris at all, else I'd not have left her there." His jaw hardened slightly as he spoke the final words.

"I know."

Kian nodded acknowledgment, then said, "You want to wait for Cath to get back?"

Wait. Trystan's skin was already itching and crawling with the urge to be out, searching, away from here, but he said, "Give it another hour. If he's not back by then, we'll separate—start looking for the horse's track." Already they'd split into two parties, Eurig, Piye, and Daka heading east, Trystan, Cath and Kian to the west.

Kian nodded, and then said, eyes still on the surrounding trees, "And after one of us finds her? What then?"

Trystan looked at him, brows drawn. "What then? You're oathsworn to Madoc, aren't you?"

"Oh, aye." Kian scratched his chin again. "But orders were to serve Lady Isolde. And now she's ordered me to stay close to you. And . . ." He paused, his single eye swiveling to meet Trystan's head on. "Seems to me like you might have need of someone to guard your back about now. If all she said about what you're mixed up in is true."

God's wounds. Trystan made an effort to control his tone. He looked at the leather patch over Kian's right eye. "I'd say you've already done more than your share."

"What, this?" Kian raised a hand and touched the eye patch. "And they say it's the Christians who live to make martyrs of themselves. Last I checked I was a grown man, make my own choices. Should be able to defend myself. Next you'll be wanting to tell me you're to blame for this, too, I suppose?" He gestured to the scar that ran along the side of his face from temple to jaw. Mark of the wound he'd gotten at Camlann. Trystan fought off the memories that slapped him across the face.

"Look, you're oath-sworn to a king who deserves your loyalty a hell of a lot more than I do, can you just leave it at that?" The words came out more harshly than he'd meant, and he drew in his breath. "You've guarded my back more times than I can count, and there's no one I'd sooner have there. But this isn't your fight. It's not worth losing your life over."

"And it's worth losing yours?" Kian's brows drew together and he gave Trystan a long, keen look. He scratched his chin, then said, abruptly, "She's frightened for you. That's why she sent us out after you."

Trystan managed to keep silent. After a moment, Kian let out a half-exasperated, half-angry breath. "Fine, then. You want to owe me something for this?" He touched the patch again. "Find Lady Isolde. Find her and stay by her and don't make her fear for you anymore. She deserves better." He stopped, scowling at Trystan, one eye narrowed. "God knows I owe you my life a dozen times over. But if you do anything to hurt her, God help me, I'm going to have to beat you black and blue."

Trystan tightened his jaw. "Don't worry. If I do anything more to hurt her, I'll have to stand still and let you."

Chapter 15

DO YOU WANT SOMETHING TO eat?" Isolde held out a roll of bread, from the parcel Godgyth had packed, to the small figure hunched at her side. Rhun had to be hungry. They'd traveled nearly the whole of the raw, misty night, walking when it was too dark for them to ride, and so far he'd eaten nothing at all. But he only hunched his shoulders, curling more tightly in on himself, eyes fixed on the ground. Nor had he so far spoken a single word, from the time they'd left Caer Peris until now.

Isolde hesitated, then quietly replaced the bread in Hræfn's saddlebag. She was lucky that Rhun had come with her at all and luckier still that they'd made it this far—away from the fortress and the flat expanse of the shore's open plain and into the thickly forested hills to the north.

After she'd parted from Ulf, the whole of their escape had gone with almost frightening ease, from leading Hræfn from the dark and deserted stables to meeting Godgyth and Rhun as planned, in a sheltered spot behind the garrison and near the fortress's outer wall. Godgyth hadn't spoken, had asked no questions, but instead led the way unhesitatingly to the north gate, where she eyed without surprise the figures of Ulf and the other guard, sprawled on the ground, deep in their drugged sleep, a flaccid wineskin lying empty on the ground nearby.

"Yes. I thought so." Gogdyth had nodded as though in confirmation. Her breath had been once more thick with the reek of wine, but she'd given Isolde a sidelong glance and another gleam of her nearly toothless smile. "I told you I had the occasional bright flash of real vision in the dark."

The fog had lasted throughout the night. Rain had even fallen in a penetrating mist that chilled and soaked them to the skin. But by necessity their path had to skirt the edges of the army encampment that perched atop the cliffs, and they'd managed it without being seen. The watch fires had been smoking sullenly, the guards whose figures could be glimpsed against the flames hunched in their cloaks against the pervading wet.

Now, leaning against the trunk of the tree she had chosen as a place for brief rest, Isolde pushed tendrils of damp hair off the back of her neck and took a swallow of lukewarm water from the skin that Godgyth had likewise packed. The sun had risen only an hour or two ago, but already the day was sticky and warm, the mist beginning to burn off. Godgyth had promised only no wind to drive the fog away; she'd said nothing about heat or sun.

Isolde shivered despite the heat as Godgyth's further parting words returned. "I can undertake only to see you and the boy safely outside these walls. My brother will doubtless send scouting parties in pursuit when he discovers you gone. If one such party should find you . . ."

She'd not needed to finish. Isolde replaced the cap on the waterskin and tried to summon the energy to make her aching and exhausted muscles rise and move on.

Before she could pull herself to her feet, though, a sudden high whine filled the air and, as though the recollection of Godgyth's warning had summoned it, an arrow struck the trunk of the tree with a meaty thud and hung, quivering, just above her head.

Isolde reacted instinctively, almost before she thought she was up, catching hold of Rhun's hand, dragging the boy with her further up the slope, her pulse hammering painfully hard in her ears as she struggled to take in the truth of what was happening. Cabal bounded alongside, crashing through the underbrush, and from behind she heard a high-pitched whinny from Hræfn. The horse had been browsing in a patch of grass a few paces away from where they'd sat, and Isolde glanced back, heart contracting at the thought that he might have been struck by an arrow.

Another bolt whined overhead, this one striking a tree trunk off to their right, and Isolde jerked round, dragging on Rhun's hand, hauling the boy on. Nothing she could do for Hræfn. No time even to hesitate. *Run—get away—you have to run.* The words were a frantic drumbeat in time to the thump of her heart as she pulled Rhun upwards in a stumbling rush.

An archer—gods, how close behind them must he be? She couldn't make herself remember anything of an arrow's range. But he must be close, surely. Her back and shoulders felt horribly naked and exposed, her every muscle aching with the need to look back and see. But she made herself go on, moving with what seemed agonizingly slowness, stinging branches whipping at her face, catching at her clothes and hair, Rhun's increasingly leaden weight dragging on her arm.

The boy was flagging; he couldn't go on much farther, and there was no chance the two of them could outrun a grown man. A thick screen of holly bushes grew just ahead at the foot of a steeper slope, and Isolde dragged Rhun behind them, collapsing beside him onto the ground. For what felt like an endlessly long moment, it seemed impossible that the dark, sharply pricking leaves before them wouldn't part, that a figure with a bow and arrow wouldn't loom over them at any moment. But nothing happened. All about them, the forest was utterly, eerily still, the only sounds the soft rustle of branches and their ragged gasps as they fought for breath.

Isolde made herself look round, made herself breathe more quietly. The spot she'd chosen almost blindly was a better one than she could have hoped, sheltered from behind by a boulder that had tumbled to lie at the base of the slope, and holly branches hid them from view. A good place to hide.

Too good. Any searcher that came upon this place would surely look here.

Isolde pressed her hands hard against her eyes, shivering as cold perspiration dried on her skin. She glanced at Rhun. The boy was huddled beside her, ashen cheeks streaked with rivulets of sweat, dark eyes dilated wide with terror. And if she was going to keep him—and herself—alive, she had to think.

Cabal butted his head against her shoulder and she rubbed his neck, steadied a little by the rough prickle of the big dog's fur against her palm.

It had been stupid of the faceless archer to fire at them from a distance. Stupid to drive them into flight when he could instead have crept up on them unawares.

She drew in slow breaths, remembering something an old, seasoned warrior had told her once, when he'd come under her care for a broken hand. *You need to keep a vision of the future if you're going to survive a fight,* he'd said. *You picture yourself alive after the battle is over and don't for any reason let that picture go.*

Isolde closed her eyes and conjured up a picture of Trystan. Trystan reaching to take a tiny, swaddled infant from her arms. The baby's face was red, his hair still damp from birth, but he blinked and looked up at Trystan with his father's blue eyes. Isolde watched Trystan touch a miniature clenched fist with one finger, watched him cup the small, fuzzy head in one hand.

She held tight to the picture for a long moment. Then she opened her eyes and let out a breath. *Now think how you're going to survive.*

The forest was eerily quiet, and she inched forward as silently as she could until she could look through a chink in the stiffly curling leaves. No sign of their pursuer. No sign at all of life other than theirs. Although—gods—she was going to have to risk coming out of concealment to try to obscure their trail. Their panicked flight, a track through the damp leaves that pointed the way to their hiding place as clearly as a painted sign.

A track. Isolde stopped, looking again at the path of churned leaves on the forest floor. A clearly marked trail.

Swiftly, she turned back to the boy at her side. "Rhun?" She tried to make her voice sound quiet, reassuring and calm. "Rhun, I need you to wait here for me. Wait here and keep absolutely quiet and still until I tell you it's safe to leave. Can you do that?"

Rhun didn't respond—she wasn't even sure he heard. He was hugging his arms tightly about himself, staring intently at the ground, occasional tremors wracking his small, rigid frame. Mingled fear and the frantic need for haste drummed through her. But Rhun was five years old and utterly terrified. He barely knew her and had no real reason to trust her. Frighten him any further and she might panic him into fleeing the moment he was left on his own.

Isolde dropped to her knees close beside him, though she was careful not to actually touch him in any way. "Rhun, I know you're frightened. I am, too. But you have to trust me when I say that the only way we'll be safe is if you stay here. Stay here until I come back for you. And then we'll go to find your father. All right?"

For a long moment, Rhun stayed absolutely still, thin shoulders hunched, eyes still fixed on the ground. Then, without looking at her, his dark head moved in a tiny jerky nod. Only the smallest movement—Isolde could almost have thought she'd imagined it. But there was no time for more.

Isolde rose, the back of her neck still prickling with the feeling of exposure, and stepped from their place of concealment. The hem of her gown caught on a branch, and she yanked it free, quickly scuffing through the leaves, obscuring the trail they'd made moments before. Then she made a new trail, one leading further up the slope, dragging her feet to be sure the marks were plain.

She kept tight hold on Cabal's collar and walked until she was out of sight of the place she'd left Rhun—and came to a place where another tumbled boulder leaned against the hill face and made a spot behind which someone feeling pursuit might hide. Still dragging her feet to mark the path she'd taken, she moved quickly into the small space of concealment and reached for a thin, low-hanging branch on one of the trees nearby.

The branch was springy and green and her hands were shaking, so it took her several agonizing moments before she could wrench the slender bottom portion of the bough free. But finally it gave, and she held in her hands a makeshift broom. Isolde paused a moment, trying to slow the frantic hammering of blood in her ears. She couldn't have much time left. She mustn't panic now.

Clicking her fingers to summon Cabal, she stepped out from behind the rock and moved to a place almost directly opposite, behind the thick burled trunk of an ancient oak tree, brushing away the footmarks they made as she went. When finally she stopped, she pressed herself tightly against the trees rough bark and looked back the way she'd come. A clearly marked track of churned leaves and twigs led up the slope to the rock, as though someone fleeing pursuit had run this way and then gone to ground.

Good enough? Good enough to deceive anyone experienced in tracking?

Another seemingly endless length of time passed while she stood, pressed close against the tree, and then Cabal stiffened, the hair on his neck rising, teeth bared in a silent growl. Isolde froze, flashing first hot then icy cold as a moment later she heard what Cabal's more sensitive ears had already picked up. From somewhere close by, the soft snap of twigs and crunch of leaves beneath booted feet.

He stepped into the clearing a moment later, a big, burly man dressed in a leather jerkin and breeches, with tatters of greasy blond hair hanging past his shoulders. Isolde had only a glimpse of his face as he passed heart-stoppingly close to where she stood: a heavy-boned, slightly stupid face, with a network of broken veins like a spider's web covering his cheeks and nose.

Isolde's heart was beating hard enough to make her feel sick, and for a moment fear seemed to press in on her, compressing the air around her into something too thick and solid to draw into her lungs. But the man had slung his bow and arrow over one shoulder and moved towards the shelter of rocks straight ahead with a wicked-looking hunting knife already drawn, the corner of his mouth visible to Isolde curved in a small smile.

Another moment and he'd realize the space behind the boulder was empty, would turn around and start hunting anew. Isolde forced her stiff lips apart and gave Cabal a low-voiced command.

The big dog bounded forward in a blur of motion, leapt, and brought the Saxon crashing to the ground. Isolde heard the man's bellow of surprise and fury turn to a scream of pain. Every muscle in her body was screaming at her to run, to turn away or at least hide her eyes. But she stood unable to move, watching the brief, vicious struggle amidst the damp earth and leaves.

It didn't take long. Cabal was so gentle with her, always, that she sometimes forgot he was trained as a war hound. When the Saxon at last lay still, his lifeless body sprawled on the ground, Cabal's jaws and muzzle were smeared with scarlet and the man's throat was a torn, mangled mass of ripped muscle and blood.

Cabal stood a moment, paws planted on the Saxon's chest, growling over his kill. Then he shook himself all over, like a dog coming out of water, and came padding back to Isolde.

Waves of nausea were churning inside her, and she wanted overwhelmingly to flinch away. But she didn't. Instead she gulped air and rested a shaking hand on the big dog's back.

A voice spoke in the back of her head. A knife. There were undoubtedly more searchers out combing the woods all around her. She was unarmed. And this man had carried a knife.

It took her several long moments before she could force herself to approach and kneel by the body. The Saxon man had landed heavily on the knife as he fell, driving the blade deeply into his shoulder, and she lost the struggle not to be sick as she pulled it free then stumbled back, gagging.

She'd seen death before, many, many times. But never a death for which she, herself, was responsible.

If he'd found them, the nameless Saxon archer would have killed her and Rhun both. She'd seen his face as he moved towards the spot where he'd thought them hidden, and she didn't for a moment doubt that it had been a question of their lives or his. That knowledge wasn't helping, though, to dissolve the guilt that had lodged in her heart the moment she'd given Cabal the order to attack.

But she had the knife: a long, bone-handled *seax* with a broad blade. And, for right now, she and Rhun were safe.

SHE BARELY REMEMBERED MAKING HER WAY back to the spot where she'd left Rhun, though she let out a quick breath of relief at sight of him, still huddled up where she'd left him behind the screen of leaves. He glanced up at the sound of her approach, then jerked back, eyes wide in his pale, pinched-looking face, and Isolde had a sudden flash of how she must look, her hands and gown smeared with the dead Saxon's blood.

Rhun, after that first, terrified look, hunched over, trembling, hiding his face. And when Isolde spoke his name in a voice as soft and reassuring as she could make it, he only shrank farther away, burrowing into the leaves on the slope behind him. Isolde's heart ached for him, for the terror his five-year-old body was trying to contain. But her first, purely selfish, thought was that, maiden, mother, and crone, she couldn't—absolutely couldn't—face this now.

Isolde summoned every last scrap of control, every reserve of strength she could muster. "Rhun? It's all right. I'm not going to hurt you, and I promise you I won't let anyone else hurt you, either. But we need to leave here now."

If they could wait for night to fall, there was a chance they could elude pursuit under cover of darkness. In fleeing Caer Peris, she'd chosen a route roughly towards the area she knew Madoc and his men occupied. If they could only get safely through the long hours of daylight today, there was a chance, at least, she could find her way to the king's encampment by night.

Rhun didn't respond by so much as a glance or even a twitch of muscle, and Isolde felt an almost overwhelming urge to sink down onto the ground beside him, close her eyes, and simply wait for someone to appear who would take this whole situation off her hands. But where there had been one man sent in pursuit of them, there would undoubtedly be more.

She drew a breath, trying desperately to think of words that might persuade Rhun to get up and go on. But then Cabal padded forward, butted Rhun's shoulder, thrust his nose under the crook of the boy's elbow. Rhun looked up.

Cabal's muzzle was still bloodied, and Isolde wouldn't have blamed Rhun if he'd been more terrified still by the sight. Instead, though, he stared at the big dog, dark eyes for the first time losing their glassy, unseeingly look of fear. And then slowly . . . slowly, his hand came up and he reached to stroke Cabal's ears, and Cabal responded with a swipe at the boy's face with his tongue.

It was as though that touch had broken some internal dam. Rhun's face crumpled, and he started to cry, great, frightened, tearing sobs that shook his small frame. And Isolde knelt beside Rhun, gathering him tight against her, holding him close. He stiffened at the first touch. But then she felt his arms come around her neck and he clung to her, his face pressed against her shoulder, hot tears soaking through the fabric of her gown.

"Shh, it's all right." Isolde held him and rocked him, keeping up a murmur of soft, soothing words—for herself as much as for Rhun—comforting, reassuring, making promises she really had no right to make. "It's all right, Rhun. I promise. We just have to be brave a little longer and then everything is going to be all right."

TRYSTAN SPOTTED THE HORSE AS HE rounded a curve of the hill. Its bridle had gotten caught in a thicket of briars, and the poor beast must have been struggling to free itself for some time, because its mane was rough and filled with brambles, its neck scored by angry scratches where the thorns had dug in. The stallion was exhausted now, head hanging low, though it reared as he approached and snorted in renewed terror, eyes rolling, nostrils flaring wide.

Trystan moved slowly forward, keeping his body turned un-threateningly sideways, speaking in a low, calming tone. "All right. Easy there, boy. Got yourself into a mess there, haven't you? Just hold still. Steady, now, and we'll soon have you free."

Keeping up a steady flow of words, he worked to untangle the bridle from the thorns until at last the great animal stood shivering, ears twitching, black coat streaked with a lather of sweat—but free of the briars.

And he'd been right. This was the horse Isolde had taken from Caer Peris. A glance in the saddlebags, hanging by a single broken strap, showed some clothes, a parcel of food, and something he rec-ognized at once as Isolde's medicine box.

Trystan pushed away the unpleasant, crawling sensation that gripped him, the thought that Isolde would never willingly have left this behind, even if for some reason she'd had to abandon the horse. He rubbed the stallion's neck, and the horse snorted again and blew in his ear. "All right, old man. That's better, isn't it? Now let's see whether you can help me find her."

ISOLDE CAME AWAKE WITH A JOLT, cold fear hissing outwards to her very fingertips. She and Rhun had been lucky to find this place: a small, dry, natural cave set into the hillside they'd been climbing, the entrance visible from without only as a crevice in the rock. She'd dragged a few branches across the opening to conceal it further before they'd crept inside, hours before. Rhun had been exhausted, steps dragging, eyes still swollen with crying. But he'd clung tightly to her hand, and, curled up beside her on the floor of the cave, he'd fallen asleep almost at once.

Isolde hadn't meant to sleep, but she must have, to be jolted awake this way. And she knew, instantly and with cold certainty, what had wakened her. The sound of a footfall just outside.

She looked down at Rhun, still soundly asleep and looking horribly, terrifyingly vulnerable, small face relaxed, one fist curled tightly under his grubby cheek. Cabal, too, had heard the sound. The dog was on his feet, staring at the cave's entrance, fur bristling, and Isolde put a hand around his muzzle in silent warning to be still.

The footsteps drew nearer, and she held absolutely still, with all her strength willing whoever it was to pass by without noticing the entrance to the cave. Then she realized, with a fresh burst of panic, that the footsteps outside had checked and come to a halt. The branches across the mouth of the cave rustled, stirred.

Isolde's heart was tripping so hard it was almost impossible to breathe, but she clenched her hand tightly around the hilt of the knife she'd taken from the dead Saxon and made herself get soundlessly to her feet.

And then she swayed, the cave walls spinning around her at sight of the man who appeared in the rock doorway.

Isolde's vision darkened and she would have fallen if Trystan hadn't been so quick to catch her. "Holy God, Isa. Are you hurt? What happened?"

He was holding her tightly, one hand running over her, checking for injury, and remembering the bloodstains on her gown, now stiffened and dried, Isolde managed to say, "I'm all right. I'm fine."

Trystan was still gripping her almost painfully tightly. "Aren't you the one who told me fine is when you're not bleeding?"

"I'm not. It's . . . It's not my blood."

Her senses were still reeling, still trying to decide whether Trystan could actually be here or whether this was only some terror-induced fantasy, and her voice wavered on the final words, throat constricting at the thought of having to live the whole nightmare over by telling Trystan what had happened.

Trystan went still, but to her overwhelming relief, he didn't ask what she meant; didn't ask her anything at all. He only looked down at her a long moment and then nodded and said, "I found your bags, and the horse. He's outside. But here are your things if you want to change." He held out the leather pack she now saw he'd carried slung over one arm. "I'll go outside and scout around a bit—I won't be long."

Isolde knew he'd left on purpose, so that he'd not have to be in the cave with her while she undressed. Still, she felt a little steadier when she'd stripped off the bloodstained gown, washed her face, arms, and hands in some of the water from the waterskin, and dressed in the clean tunic and skirt she'd packed at Caer Peris what now felt like a lifetime ago.

She drank some of the water, and then looked down at Rhun. But the boy was still sleeping soundly, and she decided to let him get as much rest as he could. Time enough to see if she could get him to eat and drink something when he woke. She gave Cabal some of the water, though, pouring it into her cupped hand so he could lap it with his tongue, and was breaking off a slab of bread for him when the branches at the mouth of the cave parted again and Trystan returned.

"All's quiet. But I tethered the horse a bit farther away so he doesn't point the way straight here." Trystan spoke quietly, eyes on the sleeping child curled up on the floor near the back of the cave, and Isolde answered the question before he could ask.

"He's Madoc's son. Rhun."

Trystan nodded. He seemed to hesitate, then dropped to the ground across from her, stretching his booted feet out and scratching Cabal behind the ears when the dog came to thrust his nose under Trystan's palm.

Isolde rubbed her gritty eyes. She kept half expecting to wake and find herself abruptly back in her bed at Caer Peris. Expecting at any moment that Marche—

She stopped herself.

"That's why I went to Caer Peris. To get Rhun free." The words came in a tumbled rush. "And to learn anything I could of Octa of Kent's defenses. Not that I succeeded in discovering much but that his son Eormenric isn't at Caer Peris, but encamped somewhere not

far distant. By his father's orders, so one of Eormenric's men said."
She stopped, trying to keep from shivering as she glanced back to-
wards the boy's sleeping form. "Rhun and I did get away, though.
Octa was keeping him hostage. To force Madoc's compliance."

"I know. Kian told me."

"Kian?" Isolde's head came up with a start. "You saw him? And
the others? They're all right?"

"Last I saw them they all were." Trystan seemed about to say
something more, but then stopped himself. The cool quiet of the cave
pooled around them a moment, and then Trystan looked up at her
and said, in a different tone, "Do you want to tell me what happened?"

"I—" Isolde shut her eyes, biting her lip hard. Trystan had lived
through this the gods only knew how many times. He'd killed men
before. Had in the past been forced to kill to protect her. If she
blamed herself now for the choice she'd made, she blamed him and
all the other fighting men she'd known.

She knew it, but it still took all her efforts to force out an account of what happened, the words coming in short bursts from a
throat that felt impossibly tight.

Trystan listened without interrupting and then said, eyes steady
on hers, "It wasn't your fault. You couldn't have done anything else."

"I know." Despite her struggle, Isolde felt her eyes flood with
tears and she bit her lip again. "It's just that I'm a healer. I'm supposed to help people when they're hurt. And this man . . . I killed
him." She had to stop. Her whole body felt icy cold, and she had to
clench her jaw to keep her teeth from chattering.

"No you didn't."

She looked across at Trystan. "Maybe Cabal did the actual killing, but—"

Trystan's hand moved as though he were about to reach for her,
and remembering their last meeting in the orchard, Isolde wondered
whether he was actually going to let himself touch her. He checked
the movement, though, hand dropping back to his side, and her brief
flicker of hope died.

Trystan shook his head and said, "I don't mean that. The Saxon
gave up the right to his life when he tried to kill you and the boy.
You didn't kill him—he killed himself."

Isolde drew a shaky breath and scrubbed at her eyes. "Is that how you get through it?"

Trystan's shoulders moved. "Sometimes."

Isolde's fingers rubbed at a worn patch on the hem of her skirt. "And does it ever get any easier?"

Trystan tilted his head back, leaning against the rock wall. His face was shadowed by the dim light of the cave, hard to read, but Isolde thought his voice, when he spoke, sounded tired. "No. But then I'm not sure it ever should be easy."

Isolde swallowed and nodded. "I—"

Before she could finish, though, there was a gasp and a sudden frightened cry from the rear of the cave, and she realized that Rhun had woken and caught sight of Trystan.

"Rhun, it's all right." Swiftly, she rose and went to kneel at the boy's side. "It's all right. He's a friend. His name's Trystan."

She wondered, even as she moved to put an arm around the boy, whether the fragile bond of trust established earlier had broken, whether Rhun would now flinch away from her touch. But after the first quick stiffening of his thin shoulders, he relaxed against her, dark eyes shifting from the dazed look of interrupted sleep to wariness.

"The Trystan you told the story about? With the horse?"

They were, Isolde realized, the first words she'd ever heard him speak; he had a small, gravelly, and strangely unchildlike voice that contrasted oddly with his small frame. But not wanting to frighten him any more by making too much of his finally broken silence, Isolde said, only, "That's right."

She saw Trystan give her a quick glance as he, too, rose and came to the back of the cave. Rhun had tensed again at his approach, though, turning his face into Isolde's shoulder, and she said, "You don't have to be frightened. It's all—"

"He's not frightened." Trystan spoke quietly, crouching before the boy so that his face was on a level with Rhun's. "Just has too much sense to trust a stranger. Isn't that right?"

He addressed the last question to the boy, his pose absolutely relaxed and calm, voice filled with the same complete assurance he would have used to quiet a panicked horse years before. Rhun's head slowly turned, his wary dark gaze fixing on Trystan's face. Cabal had followed Trystan, and now whined softly and licked Trystan's hand. Trystan rumpled the big dog's ears. "Cabal likes me, though, so I can't be all that bad. What do you say?"

He held out a hand to Rhun. The child looked at him a long moment, and then very slowly put out his own small, dirt-smeared hand, taking the one Trystan had offered. Rhun nodded as their palms clasped, with the almost adult gravity Isolde remembered from before. And then he leaned back against Isolde, putting a grubby thumb into his mouth.

"AND IN THE NAME OF EUROLWYN daughter of Gwdolwyn the Dwarf, Teleri daughter of Peul, Indeg daughter of Garwy the Tall, Morfudd daughter of Urien Rheged, fair Gwenlliant the magnanimous maiden, Creiddylad daughter of Lludd Silver-hand (the maiden of most majesty that was ever in the Island of Britain and its three adjacent islands. And for her Gwythyr son of Greidawl and Gwyn son of Nudd fight forever each May-calends till the day of doom), Ellylw daughter of Neol Hang-cock (and she lived three generations), Esyllt Whiteneck and Esyllt Slenderneck—in the name of all these did Culhwch son of Cilydd invoke his boon."

Isolde stopped speaking, but the boy beside her didn't open his eyes or even stir. She waited a moment, then covered him with a blanket and came to sit across from Trystan. She looked exhausted, gray eyes smudged with weariness, her face pale in the green-tinged afternoon light that filtered through the branches at the mouth of the cave.

"Culhwch and Olwen did the trick, then?" Trystan kept his voice low.

She nodded, pushing a strand of black hair back from her face. "I picked the story with the dullest beginning I could think of. Listening to Culhwch invoke everyone he can think of to claim his right to marry Olwen would put anyone to sleep."

Trystan's whole body was still thrumming with the total, icy terror that had filled him at first sight of her, bloodstained and ashen-faced and about to crumple to the ground. Even the memory of the twenty endlessly long heartbeats it had taken for him to see she wasn't actually hurt was enough to set his pulse pounding all over again.

"You should rest, as well."

She shook her head. "I don't think I could sleep. Not after—" She stopped herself, but Trystan saw her rubbing at the smears of rusty red that still stained her fingernails, saw the tremor that shook her.

This time he reached for her before he could check himself, wiping the trace of moisture on her cheek away with his thumb, chest tightening with a wave of possessiveness he knew he had no right to feel. "I'm sorry."

She looked up at him. "Why should you be sorry?"

"I'm sorry I didn't find you in time to save you from this."

"So then you could be the one feeling this way?" She was silent a moment, then said, "You could put your arms around me now."

"I . . . don't think that's such a good idea."

"Not a good idea." She nodded, a small, humorless smile twisting her mouth. "I thought you'd probably say that."

The look in her eyes made something in his chest twist and tighten all over again. "Isa, I can't—" What could he possibly say? "I don't want to make you unhappy."

"You don't want to make me unhappy." Isolde choked on something between a ragged laugh and a sob. "That's funny, Trys. That's really, really funny."

Then she stopped, her expression changing at whatever she saw in his face. "I'm sorry. Maybe you should just . . . leave me alone for a little while. Rhun and I didn't sleep at all last night; we were trying to get as far from Caer Peris as we could. And then there was the Saxon man"—her voice wavered—"and that besides having Marche arrive at Octa's fort, and having Octa declare us married again and . . ."

The burst of fiery red fury that shot across Trystan's field of vision was almost enough to blot out his sight. He—just—managed to say, "Octa did what?"

Isolde said, quickly, "It's all right. He—Marche—never touched me. I told you, I'm fine. But still, I had to see him and speak to him, and I'm so tired I—" She stopped, rubbing a hand across her cheek and swallowing again. "I've got about half a moment left before I start crying, and once that happens I'm not going to be able to stop. So please, please don't list all the reasons we can't be together now. If you can't help, just . . . just leave me alone for a little while."

She spoke the last words in an unsteady rush, dropping her head onto her raised knees. Trystan didn't let himself think. "You were right," he said. "You do scare me."

Well, he'd surprised her, at any rate. Her expression, as she raised her head, couldn't have looked more shocked if Cabal had got up and started reciting a bard's epic battle poem.

His heart was pounding, but he forced himself to go on. "You said once that I don't let myself talk about . . . about anything that matters. That I don't let myself get angry often enough. But I'm not—"

He stopped. But Isolde was still staring at him, waiting for him to go on. So he said, "I . . . My father used to get angry. You know what it was like. What he did. My mother died because my father was so goddamned good at letting himself get angry. And I . . . God, I hated him for it. For all of it. But he—"

Trystan stopped again, chest clenching, the words sticking like rocks in his throat. But he kept going.

"His own father was the same. Not that he talked about it. But I knew, just from things I heard. Things he sometimes let slip. His own father was a roaring drunk who beat the hell out of him every chance he got. And, Christ, I could understand in a way why Marche turned out the way he did. After he'd been at me, after I'd seen what he'd done to . . . to my mother, I'd be angry enough to slaughter the whole world." He rubbed a hand across the back of his neck. "I knew I couldn't let myself get angry that way, though. Because then I was letting myself turn into the same monster he could be. But it doesn't matter. The anger's still there, like something trying to claw its way out through my skin. And after everything I've . . . everything I've seen and done these last seven years, there's a part of me that's . . . I can see myself turning into him . . . turning into someone like Marche. I can see myself hurting you, and Holy Mother, Isa, I would rather die any death you could name than live to see that actually happen."

Isolde looked up at him. Then she said, "Madoc said weeks ago that I'm a healer, that I want there to be a cure for everything. But that some things can't—shouldn't—be healed."

Madoc again. A memory of the way Madoc had looked at her at the council meeting flashed across Trystan's vision. If he'd any honor at all, he should tell her now that she should marry Madoc. That even with all the mistakes he'd made, Madoc was undoubtedly the better man.

And yet he wasn't saying it, was he? He was just sitting here, the blood pounding blackly behind his eyes even at the thought of her wedded to anyone else.

Isolde leaned forward, brushing his cheek lightly with the back of her hand. Trystan suppressed a shudder that threatened to shatter the last remaining threads of his control.

"I don't believe that, though. Scars may last forever, but you can make the hurt go. And you are not your father, Trys." Her voice was soft, like cool, sweet water. "You could never, ever turn into the man he is. Don't you know that?"

Her face was upturned, her tear-bright gaze on his. But it was the complete, perfect trust and belief he could read in her eyes that was making the fool hope well up in his chest, sending rivers of fire jolting through his veins.

He absolutely couldn't let himself reach for her, pull her to him. Lower his head and cover her sweet mouth with—

Trystan tore his gaze away and said the first thing that came into his head. "Why didn't you believe I was actually working for Octa?"

At least it broke the moment. Isolde, thank the gods, sat back a little and just looked at him a moment, her face serious, gray eyes very grave. "Why don't I think you're working for Octa? Well, I could say that it's because I know you too well to think such a thing even for a moment. And it would be true. I do know you, Trys. Better than to believe you'd ever swear allegiance to a man like Octa of Kent. But that's not the real reason. The real reason is—"

Her voice wavered momentarily and her slender throat contracted as she swallowed before going on. "The real reason is that I didn't know what might happen back at Caer Peris. Whether I'd live to see you again, or whether I'd be caught trying to get Rhun away and Octa would have me killed. It could still happen. I don't even know what will happen an hour from now, what will happen when we have to leave this cave. If I do die, I don't want it to be while I'm thinking ill of you. And if you—" She stopped, blinking as tears filled her eyes, and reached out to lightly touch his face again. "And if you go out and get yourself killed the way you seem determined to do, I want you to know absolutely that I never, even for a moment, stopped loving you or trusting you."

Trystan reached for her. He reached for her, pulled her to him, hands sliding up her jaw to tangle in her hair. Kissed her, because it was that or have everything he'd been trying not to let himself feel, everything he'd been trying desperately not to tell her, break free of all the inner restraints he'd set and come pouring out in a crashing wave. Because kissing her kept him from thinking, and he couldn't stand to think just now. Because if he was kissing her he only felt the softness of her lips, the melting sweetness of her body pressed against his, her cool, smooth fingers on his skin.

Bare hours ago, he'd been living with the stomach-clenching fear that even if he found her it would be too late—that she'd been wounded, even dead. But instead she was here and warm and alive and—God—in his arms. He kissed her hungrily, desperately, and she kissed him back just as fiercely, clinging to him, winding her arms about his neck to pull him closer still. He kissed her eyes and her lips and the beating pulse in her throat, sweet liquid fire pounding through him in a coursing—

A branch snapped somewhere outside. Trystan froze, breathing hard. Another branch snapped as though beneath someone's booted foot, and he made himself pull back, put his hands on Isolde's shoulders, and put her gently—and silently—away from him. She caught hold of his hand, though, before he could rise. Her black hair was tumbled all about her face, and she was breathing as quickly as he was, but above her rose-flushed cheeks her eyes were frightened.

Please don't go out there. He could read the words in her look as clearly as though she'd spoken aloud. With an effort that was like pushing a boulder weight off his chest, Trystan forced his mind to jolt into rational thought, to flip quickly through the possibilities, the way this could play out.

He'd dragged more branches and spread an armful of clinging vines across the mouth of the cave when he'd come back from tethering the horse; no one should be able to see it unless they were looking. And if there was a chance whoever was out there might pass by, this was a fight he didn't need to have. One that might draw the attention of anyone else in the area, as well, if it made enough noise.

He settled for drawing the knife at his belt. He was still holding on to Isolde, though, and somehow before he'd realized it he'd drawn her close again, his free arm around her even as he fixed his eyes on the mouth of the cave and waited for anything to stir, any sign that the entrance had been seen. He heard leaves crunch outside, and felt Isolde shiver as she leaned against him, her head tucked under his chin to rest on his shoulder.

A pause, and the footsteps sounded again. Only one pair. One man. Trystan adjusted his grip on the knife but stayed motionless, making his breathing even and slow. The moments dragged by. More footsteps, slowly tracing a path up the slope, with pauses during which Trystan could picture the searcher outside stopping to scan the surrounding trees and ground. It seemed to go on a long time. But at last the heavy footfalls, the snap of leaves and twigs faded from earshot, leaving the cave emptily still.

Isolde was still pressed close against him, her heart a steady beat against his side, the softness of her hair brushing his neck. Trystan waited until he could be sure this wasn't some trap, that the searcher hadn't merely drawn off to watch the cave until they emerged. Then he shifted, looking down, about to tell Isolde that it was safe to move. And saw that she'd fallen asleep, her fingers loosely twined in his, her head still resting against his chest.

Trystan sat looking down at her. Holy mother, what had he done? He could hear Kian's voice, ordering him to find Isolde—find her and not make her unhappy or hurt her again. And yet he'd just . . .

He might as well have turned into a monster just like Marche. He hadn't thought of her, of all she'd just been through. Hadn't even considered the boy asleep just feet away at the rear of the cave. That she'd kissed him back was no excuse. If she'd asked him to stop, would he have been able to?

Trystan free hand clenched and he looked down at Isolde again. She looked about twelve years old, lashes spread out on her cheeks, her hair slipping out of its confining braid. He shook his head. Gods. She should have been afraid—or at the very least tensely waiting to see whether they were discovered by the searcher outside. But instead she'd fallen asleep in his arms, trusting that he'd protect her.

Trystan tipped his head back against the cave wall and shut his eyes, thinking of Luc and Bradach and all the others who'd died choking on mud and blood because of him.

Not Isolde, though. He could protect her and get her safely to Madoc's camp. Not allow her name be added to the list he carried in his mind of lives he should have saved.

The memory of how Madoc had looked at her slid across the others in his mind's eye, making him clench his jaw. But he'd rather see her wedded to Madoc—would sooner face having to picture her waking up every morning in Madoc's bed—then risk hurting her again.

He'd get her to Madoc's encampment. And then—

Trystan stopped, watching the shadows lengthen across the opposite wall. He'd not been letting himself think ahead to the future. He'd seen this as a series of steps. Carry out the mission he'd set himself. See Isolde safe from all threat by either Octa or Marche. Then go back to his old life, the old way of living moment by moment, day by day. The life in which Isolde could have no part.

Now, though, he was abruptly back in the council meeting he'd attended weeks before. Listening to the talk of Cynric, Cerdic's prisoner son. And thinking of that night now, a way opened before him, one that would see Isolde protected and might even bring a halt to the war. But one that he himself almost certainly wouldn't survive.

Trystan looked down at Isolde's sleeping face again, traced the line of her brow, the delicate curve of her cheek. He'd always known he hadn't much to give her but his life.

Then he lowered her gently onto the blanket already spread on the cave floor. He covered her with his cloak and moved to sit near the mouth of the cave. The movement roused Cabal, who padded over, whining softly, and thrust a wet nose under Trystan's palm. Trystan scratched the dog's neck, his eyes still on Isolde. Cabal whined again, and Trystan tousled his ears, drawing a happy thump of Cabal's tail. Trystan let out a breath, tipping his head back against the wall, one hand still resting on Cabal's head as the dog settled beside him with a sigh. "Look after her, will you, boy?" he said. "Keep her safe for me after I'm gone."

ISOLDE WOKE TO EARLY-MORNING SUNLIGHT SLANTING through the entrance of the cave. She blinked at the rough stone walls, momentarily disoriented as she tried to remember where she was and how she'd come here, then felt a jolt of fear as memory returned with the simultaneous realization that both Trystan and Rhun were gone.

She sat up quickly, and realized she could hear voices from outside the cave. Trystan's; a softer one she now recognized as Rhun's. The voices were too low for her to make out the words, but they sounded easy, relaxed. So she got up more slowly than she would have otherwise, washed her face and hands in some of the water from the waterskin, and combed her fingers through the tangles in her hair.

Her muscles ached after the strain of the last day, and she was ravenously hungry, which seemed wrong, after all that had happened. But she seemed hungry all the time, these last days, and she found some of the dry bread and hard, crumbly cheese in the traveling pack before going outside.

Trystan and Rhun were sitting with their backs to her, side by side on a low, flat rock near the entrance to the cave. A little distance away, Cabal lay sprawled asleep in a patch of early sun, paws twitching in some mysterious dog's dream.

"Grip it this way," Trystan was saying, and Isolde, chewing the last of the bread, saw that he had taken the knife from his belt and was showing Rhun the proper grip on the wooden hilt. "Fingers here, thumb around there, right? Good, now you try."

Rhun glanced up at him nervously but bit his lip and took the knife, his movements hesitant and a little clumsy as he tried to arrange his fingers in a duplicate of the grip Trystan had showed him. Before he could manage it, he fumbled, the knife slipping from his grasp. He tried to catch it, then winced, putting his finger into his mouth.

"Did you cut yourself? Let me see." Trystan held out a hand, and

Rhun, after another moment's hesitation, took the finger from his mouth. His small face looked unwilling, but he held it for Trystan to see, cringing a little—more because he expected a reprimand, Isolde thought, than because he was much hurt.

"Not so bad." Trystan used his thumb to wipe a bead of blood away from the tip of Rhun's finger. "You'll live, I'd say."

Rhun said something, a muttered apology maybe, because Trystan clapped the boy's shoulder and said, easily, "That's all right. You bleed in practice so that you don't in battle. Just try again. You'll get it this time."

Isolde stood still, feeling as though time had briefly rippled, showing her a scene from ten years before: Trystan, twelve years old to her ten, teaching her to throw a knife in the same way. Though in secret, because combat skills weren't considered, save perhaps by Morgan, to be proper occupation for the daughter of a king.

Rhun relaxed again, and, brow furrowing in concentration, took up the knife and arranged his fingers around the hilt. This time Trystan helped him, guiding the boy's hand until he held the knife in a passable battle grip, blade at the ready. "That's it. You—" Trystan stopped as he glanced up and saw Isolde.

He wore an undyed linen shirt open at the collar, the sleeves rolled up over his forearms. A shaft of sun lit the lean planes of his face, gilding the stubble of beard on his jaw. He looked her up and down in exaggerated wonderment. "So that's what you look like with your eyes open. Rhun and I were starting to wonder whether you'd sleep all day."

He looked tired, Isolde thought, despite the smile he gave her. His eyelids were slightly reddened, and she wondered whether he himself had slept at all. She knew she'd fallen asleep against his shoulder when the searcher, whoever he was, had been outside. And she had a vague memory of his shifting her gently onto the ground and covering her with a cloak sometime during the night or maybe early dawn. But she'd slept too soundly to recall anything more.

"Is everything . . . ?"

Trystan nodded. "All's quiet. No sign of anyone around. We were just having some practice at knife throwing." He tipped his head towards the boy at his side. "You should ask Isolde to teach you, Rhun. She didn't used to be too bad. For a girl."

He threw her another grin, and Isolde thought that it wasn't only weariness; Trystan seemed different somehow this morning. Easier, or more at peace. Which should have been cause for happiness, or at least relief, she thought, as she remembered all that they'd said to each other last night. Instead, though, she felt cold fear snaking about her heart as she watched him and thought that he looked not so much as though he'd finally made peace with his past as like a man who'd burned his bridges behind him, set his course, and wouldn't look back.

She made herself smile in return, though, and said, "Was that a challenge? Because if it was, I'll bet you any odds you'd like that I can hit the target of your choice."

"Do you, now?" Trystan eyed her, then cocked an eyebrow at Rhun. "I don't think we can let her make a claim like that without proof to back it up, do you, Rhun?"

Rhun truly was starting to relax. A shy smile—the first Isolde had ever seen from him—spread across his small face as he shook his head.

"Name your target, then." Isolde held out a hand for the knife, fitting her fingers round the hilt when Rhun put it into her palm. Trystan looked round, eyes narrowed, then gestured to a tree maybe ten paces away. "See the knot on that tree trunk over there?"

Isolde's brows lifted. "You could at least make it a challenge." She drew her arm back, hearing an echo of Trystan's long-ago voice in her head. *Wrist straight, shoulder level, follow through with your arm.* She let the knife fly; it sailed through the air, struck the knot in the tree with a dull thunk, and hung, stuck fast by the blade.

Eyes wide, Rhun raced across to pull the knife free and returned it to her. "Can you do it again?"

"Probably." Isolde smiled, then glanced up at Trystan. "Unless you want to pick another target? One that takes some effort this time?"

Trystan shrugged. "Just starting easy. Though that wasn't bad, I'll grant you."

Isolde raised an eyebrow again. "Do you want to add the 'for a girl' part?"

"Not when you're the one holding the knife, at any rate."

Isolde laughed, the sound echoed by a small, chuckly one from Rhun. And then she felt it again: a purposeful, rippling little thump like the tug of memory as the baby inside her kicked and stretched tiny limbs.

Trystan was still watching her, and said, "Something wrong?"

Isolde shook her head. She wanted with a twist in her heart that was almost physical pain to tell him, to say that she was imagining one day seeing him like this with his own son. Watching the baby she'd just felt stirring look up at Trystan with the same look of mingled respect and complete adoration Rhun was giving him now.

But she could still hear what he'd said the night before. *I can see myself turning into him . . . turning into someone like Marche.* If she scared him already, what would he feel knowing he'd be a father himself by Samhain?

And she was unwilling to let go of this moment, besides, to do anything that would shatter the peace of this all too brief time together, when she could almost pretend that nothing else existed but the here and now of the summer breeze rustling the trees, the call of birdsong, the quick flash of Trystan's smile.

The sun was climbing higher in the sky, though, the morning light turning from pale rose to deeper gold. And from somewhere in the trees nearby came the throaty trill of a dove, like a mournful reminder that soon they'd have to pack up and be gone.

So she said, only, "Just pick your target. Though I think if you're going to do all this talking you ought to have to try for it as well."

"IT'S A PATROL OF MADOC'S MEN." Trystan dropped from the lowest limb of the fir tree he'd climbed to the ground beside Isolde and rubbed a smear of sap from his hands. "Heading this way. They'll cross paths with us if we keep straight on."

"Madoc's men." Isolde stared at him. She'd been prepared for danger, for the news that the party Cabal had scented over the next rise in the land was one of Octa's war bands. She'd been ready for fear, for the news that they would have to draw back, find somewhere safe to hide until any searchers passed by. But Madoc's men! She'd not been ready for them at all.

It was early afternoon. They'd left the cave and their makeshift campsite after eating the remains of the food Isolde had brought from Caer Peris, had found Hræfn still tethered where Trystan had left him, safe and unharmed. Trystan had known the direction of Madoc's camp, though Isolde hadn't asked how, and they'd been traveling for several hours, Isolde and Trystan walking, Rhun astride Hræfn's broad back.

Isolde had known this moment was coming, the moment when she and Rhun would have to go on alone, leaving Trystan behind. But she'd been putting off thinking of it from moment to moment. And now that it had suddenly arrived, she felt as though something inside her were falling, spinning away into darkness, as though the black uncertainty of the future gaped like a chasm on the leaf-strewn ground at their feet.

Rhun had drawn a few paces ahead, still perched on Hræfn's back. Isolde glanced at him, then slowly turned back to Trystan, swallowing, blinking hard. "I never even asked how you found us yesterday. Or how you knew to be searching for us at all. Everyone at Caer Peris said you'd gone."

Trystan had been squinting ahead through the trees in the direction he'd just scouted from above, but he turned at that. "How I knew you'd escaped Octa's fort?" He just looked at her a moment. Then he said, "Do you think I'd have left you on your own there for one moment longer than I had to? I'd never have left at all, except that I knew I had to make Octa believe I was still following orders from him. But I circled round and came back almost at once. Met with Kian and the others, and—"

He stopped, shaking his head. Isolde felt a lump rise in her throat again. "Why are you doing this? Pretending to be Octa's man?"

Trystan didn't answer at once, just looked at her. At last he said, "You said you trusted me. How can I deserve that trust if I don't do whatever I'm able to end this fighting? If I knew there were lives I could save and just walked away?"

The sun at his back threw his face into shadow, leached the color from his hair and clothes, blurred and shaded the hard-muscled planes of his body so that he looked suddenly remote as his gaze had been, like the figure in a tale, or the death fetch Isolde had once imagined she saw.

Her heart lurched hard, her stomach twisting as memories of the old visions flickered across her mind's eye. Trystan and Marche battling savagely with swords. Someone coming to tell her that Trystan had died of fatal wounds. Her vision darkened and she might have fallen if Trystan hadn't put out a hand to catch her.

"Isa?" His voice seemed to come from a long way off. "What is it? What's wrong?"

Isolde felt too sick, too dizzy for a moment to speak. "I . . . nothing. It's nothing."

Trystan's hands shifted so that he held her shoulders, his touch warm even through the fabric of her gown. "You looked at me and saw something. What was it? Tell me."

Isolde looked up at him, losing herself for a moment in the blue of his eyes. If this really were the last time she spoke with him, the last chance she had . . .

Her throat felt dry, her lips stiff, but she said in a whisper, "I saw you and Marche. In combat. Fighting with swords."

Something passed like a swift shadow across Trystan's face, then hardened. He nodded. "That's all?"

Death. Isolde clenched her teeth shut before she could say the word. Before she could grant the vision added reality by speaking of it aloud. "That's all."

Trystan's hands were still on her shoulders, and she drew a step nearer, still looking up into his grimly set face. She saw some of the control flicker in his face just briefly as his eyes met hers—saw, just for an instant, a reflection of the night before cross his blue gaze. His lips on hers, her arms about his neck, his hands tangled in her hair.

Trystan's hand moved, as though he were about to reach for her. But then he clenched his fingers, arm dropping back to his side. Stepped back and away.

Isolde blinked. Tightened her own hands. "You're never going to let yourself touch me again, are you?"

"Isa—" He stopped. She waited, but he didn't go on. And all at once, Isolde felt searing fear stab her again like the blade of a sword.

She caught hold of Trystan's hand. "Promise me this won't be the last time I see you."

"I can't—"

"I don't care." Isolde spoke almost angrily, tightening her grip on his, holding his gaze so that he couldn't look away. "I don't care what you think you can or can't do. Promise me that you'll find me—that I'll see you again—or I swear to you I'm not going another step forward from here." And then she drew a pace nearer to Trystan, still holding fast to his hand, and said, more softly, "Please, Trys. I'm not asking where you'll go from here or that you'll give up whatever it is you feel you need to do. Just that you'll try your utmost to see me once more. I'm not asking you to promise me any more than that."

For a long moment, Trystan's eyes met hers. And then he bowed his head. "All right. I promise you. You'll see me again."

BOOK IV

Chapter 16

ASK 'KING CERDIC WHY WE should squander the lives of our men in trying to thave his worthless son and his goat-thwiving war band? If Octa thlaughters the lot of them and hangs their entrails about hith hall, that'll only mean fewer Thaxons for us to kill."

Isolde turned slowly from Dywel of Logres's flushed, choleric face to Cerdic, seated, as before, beside Madoc at the head of the hall. "Do you honestly want me to translate that? I think it would sound about the same in your tongue as in mine."

Cerdic had been sitting in cool, level silence that was in a way more forceful than open anger would have been. He glanced up at Isolde, one of those small sparks of amusement at the back of his blue gaze, even if the grim line of his mouth neither relaxed nor changed. Isolde, meeting the look, had to order herself not to think of Trystan. Not to remember him swinging himself easily up onto Hræfn's broad back—she'd insisted he keep the stallion with him— and disappearing amidst the trees. Not to remember that two weeks had passed since then. Two weeks without a word.

Beside Cerdic, Madoc thumped the table before him with the flat of his hand and rapped out, "Enough! God's teeth, if you cannot control yourself better than a seaman in a whorehouse, Lord Dywel, you may leave. Now."

The two weeks since Isolde and Rhun had arrived in Madoc's encampment had been tense ones, when nearly every day brought word of a fresh skirmish with a raiding band of Octa's men, every

morning saw the greasy, ominous black column of smoke in the sky
that marked another settlement raided, another farm burned.

Still more ominous was the unavoidable truth that from what
the scouts reported of Octa's strength, the raids might have been far
worse. The infringements of Octa's troops were like lightning-quick
feints with a sword: mere testings and probings for weaknesses and
gaps in defense.

Madoc had withdrawn with his troops to the safety of the ancient hill fortress; the council met tonight in the same firelit hall
they'd met in weeks before. The fortress, though, had expanded to
shelter the refugees who streamed in from all sides, seeking protection from Octa's raids. Britons, who had lived in quiet subservience
on the Saxon lands for a generation and more. Saxon families, as
well—of Cerdic's churlish thanes and warlords, who now warily,
often grudgingly, approached Cerdic's Briton allies for aid.

And, looking from Madoc to Dywel, whose face darkened even
as he finally subsided onto his bench, Isolde thought that it was a
mark of just how perilous their position was that the Saxon refugees
had come here at all.

The weather for the last week and more had been close and
humid and oppressively hot. A filmy haze blurred the sun, dank
moisture coated the grass and leaves, and yet the skies remained
parched, barren of even a hint of cloud that might promise the relief of rain. The hill fort was crowded with families who huddled in
makeshift shelters of whatever they'd been able to find: blankets or
hides or cobbled-together boards. And from dawn to dusk the air
rang with the clash from the smith's forge, the shouts of men, the
babies' continual, fretful cries, and the bawling of those who tried to
earn a few copper coins or the occasional bronze ring from selling
grain or food.

Supplies were running low, and in this weather food was quick
to spoil; Isolde had treated countless numbers—men, women, and
children alike—who had eaten tainted meat or pottage made from
moldy grain. And already tonight at least three of those present at
this meeting of the council had had to lunge hurriedly for the door.

Even the most even-keeled among the men were short of temper, ready at the slightest imagined offense to bristle into shouts or

even blows. Already a group of Cerdic's warriors had come to blows with several of Meurig of Gwent's war band, bloodshed averted only by the furious intervention of the two kings. And even before Dywel of Logres's outburst, Isolde's skin had felt tight and prickling with the atmosphere of tension and strained nerves that thickened the air in the long, timbered room.

Madoc at least looked almost himself again, black eyes clear, if furious, broad shoulders straight. Only his slightly rasping voice and the deliberateness of his movements gave away how exhausted he truly was.

Isolde knew that he'd been in the saddle almost continuously these last three weeks, with barely a pause for rest or even food as he led the counterattacks that met Octa's forays into the surrounding lands. The rescue of Rhun had banished any hope of Octa's believing that the agreement between himself and Madoc still stood, nor would he be accepting information from Madoc that might bring about his defeat. Octa would now no sooner believe a report from Madoc than he would welcome Isolde back into his camp.

But, *I thank you, Lady Isolde*, Madoc had said, his voice turning husky, *with all that I am.*

Isolde had seen Madoc only a handful of times since then—once when she'd stitched a deep, ugly sword cut in the pad of his thumb. And a few more nights when he'd come to the women's hall where Rhun slept these days by Isolde's side, or sometimes with Cabal, if Isolde were busy among the sick refugees and wounded men.

Rhun often spent his days, too, with Cabal, and with Hereric, working with the war mounts stabled within the fort. Isolde still saw Rhun flinch instinctively away from any grown men, even his own father's warriors. Still saw him hunch his shoulders, if less and less often now, and look round him as though scarcely daring to believe the hill fort real, to let himself think he'd escaped Octa's guard. But with Hereric he was never afraid. Hereric was so gentle, and had so much of a boy's direct simplicity himself, that from the first Rhun's face had started to lose its strained, frightened look whenever the big man was near. The last time Isolde had visited them in the stables, she'd found Rhun frowning in fierce concentration while he practiced some of Hereric's finger signs.

Rhun was usually asleep when his father was able to break away from the duties of kingship long enough to come. But Isolde had seen Madoc sitting by Rhun's pallet in silence, for that short while allowing the grim line of his mouth to relax, his eyes to soften as he reached to touch his sleeping son's springy black curls so lightly that Rhun never even stirred.

Though certainly not even a flicker of that softness showed in Madoc's gaze now as he turned from Dywel and faced the roomful of men.

"You have heard, all of you, the Lady Isolde's account of what she learned while inside Octa of Kent's stronghold. Octa is receiving added support, warriors from across the sea. Swelling his ranks by at least five hundred men." Madoc cast a brief, inquiring glance at Isolde and she nodded confirmation. "And we all know, as well, that Octa will attack with all he has soon. In the next weeks, certainly. Perhaps even in the next days. I need hardly point out"—Madoc's jaw tightened—"that should we meet Octa's forces in battle as we stand now, we could as easily lose as win. Should we gain back the warriors Octa holds prisoner—Cerdic's son and his men—we stand a better chance of victory instead of crushing defeat. It is only that, a chance. But such a chance is better than none. Therefore"—Madoc's eye fell on Dywel—"we must free Cerdic's warriors from Octa's hands."

But it was Meurig of Gwent, not Dywel, who spoke into the brief silence that followed. Meurig, with his sallow face and narrow, pinched mouth, who stroked the feathers of the speckled falcon perched on his wrist and said, "I'm not sure I see, Lord Madoc, why we need face Octa of Kent in battle at all."

ISOLDE SAT IN THE EMPTY COUNCIL hall. It was over. The meeting ended, the kings and nobles and private guards of the council all withdrawn, the room deserted save for herself and a rustling in the thatched roof above that was probably rats. They swarmed over the hill fort these days.

She rubbed her eyes, the aching muscles in her back. She wasn't sure why she had remained, save that even thought of her cramped pallet among the multitude of others laid on the floor of the women's hall was enough to set her teeth on edge just now. And the empty council chamber was likely the only place in the crowded hill fort where she might be alone.

Even as the thought formed, though, footsteps sounded behind her, and she turned to see Madoc standing in the hide-covered entranceway. He stood a moment, then slowly came across to her and lowered himself wearily onto the bench at her side.

The tallow lamps that illumined the room were burning low, shadowing his scarred face and picking out with renewed clarity the lines of weariness carved about his mouth and eyes.

"So," he said. His voice, too, sounded raspy with fatigue. "What's done is done." He glanced at her. "You ought to be asleep, Lady Isolde. I suspect there is little you can do, now. Save perhaps"—his mouth twisted—"to make the infirmary ready for a veritable flood of wounded and broken men."

Madoc's gaze moved to a dusty black circle, drawn on the earthen floor with ash from the central hearth. A cluster of spears bristled at the circle's center, shafts upright, points buried deeply in the dirt. And two spears stood outside the circle's outer edge: one bearing the colors of Meurig of Gwent, the other those of Cynlas of Rhos.

The shouting, the raging, the endless argument and snarling debate had come down in the end to the casting of a vote. All save two of the king's council had proven loyal, had cast their spears into the circle along with Madoc's, thrown first of all. All save two. Meurig and Cynlas had elected to withdraw their troops immediately and return to guard their own lands.

"Marche's troops have withdrawn from my borders. The threat to Gwent is gone." Isolde could still hear the echo of Meurig's thin, self-righteous voice in the empty room. "Why should I now risk the lives of my men in defense of a land not my own?"

"And you think Octa will not march straight for the borders of Gwent should he win a victory over us here? You think he will not trample all over your lands? Burn your settlements and drag your women and children off for slaves as he has done here?" Madoc's face had been tight with contempt, though he'd kept his tone even.

Some of the disgust in the look Madoc gave him must have flicked Meurig on the raw; Isolde saw him hunch his shoulders and flinch as though at the bite of a stinging fly. But he only fed the bird on his arm a scrap of meat from some inner pocket of his heavily embroidered tunic and shook his head, chin jutting out. "I doubt Octa would have the resources for such a campaign so soon after this one. And in any case, all the more reason to make sure that the borders of my kingdom are as secure as I can make them."

Cynlas of Rhos had been less belligerent, his withdrawal of support quiet and half ashamed. But he'd said, "I have lost enough already. I can lose no more."

Now, seeing the muscles tighten in Madoc's jaw, Isolde knew he, too, was recalling Cynlas's words.

She said, "You did all you could. They were neither of them to be swayed."

"No." Madoc passed a hand through his black hair. "Cynlas and Meurig will march out with their armies at first light tomorrow. Not that Meurig's defection surprises me, the self-serving little son of a flaming—" He checked himself. "Swine. I always knew Meurig had about as much loyalty to the rest of us as that bloody damned bird of his. If that much. But Cynlas . . ."

Madoc's shoulders jerked, as though at the addition of another burden to an already heavy load, and his eyes remained fixed on the circle drawn on the ground. Isolde could almost see the thought pass through Madoc's mind that he had only himself to blame for Cynlas's withdrawal now—he, who was responsible for the most recent of Cynlas's defeats. And the recognition that he might have turned back from alliance with Octa, and yet doomed Britain to defeat after all.

Then he shook his head, visibly setting all such thoughts aside. Madoc was a warrior, first and last. He would know when it was only a waste of precious energy to spare time for useless guilt or regret.

"At any rate, they're gone. And we're to face Octa's forces with our numbers down by the three hundred spears of their armies combined."

"As you say."

A short silence fell, punctuated only by the squeaks and scrabblings of the rats above. Isolde brushed a smear of ash from the skirt of her green woollen gown and thought of the last time she'd entered this hall. When she'd persuaded Madoc and the others to let her go to Caer Peris in search of Rhun. When Taliesin had played a song of Arthur and Morgan and filled the room with a deep, wordless longing for days gone by.

Almost as though he'd picked up the thought, Madoc said, "Maybe I should have asked Taliesin to play tonight. Even a tissue of lies about Arthur's sunlit reign as High King couldn't have made the outcome any worse."

"Are they lies, do you think?"

Madoc only snorted. And then he said, in a different tone, "Rhun was awake tonight when I saw him."

Something in his voice made Isolde look up. "Was he?"

"He was. He was telling me"—Madoc gave her a sidelong look—"about a man who appeared, seemingly from nowhere, when you and he escaped from Caer Peris. A man who protected you, guided you back to where you met with my party of men."

Isolde kept her eyes fixed on the opposite wall, tracing the smutty black smear left by a lamp's flame. "Was he?" she said again.

"He said"—Madoc shot her another look from the corner of his eyes—"that this man had also taught him to throw a knife." He paused. "Quite a tale for the boy to have invented."

Madoc stopped again, seeming to wait. Then, when Isolde said nothing, he sighed. "Very well, Lady Isolde. But let me ask you: You had a messenger, one from your own lands, so you said, who guided you to Cerdic nearly four months ago. Would that same messenger have been a part of the battle at Camlann?"

Whatever Isolde had been expecting, it wasn't this. She said, slowly, "It is . . . possible. Why do you ask?"

Madoc's shoulders moved. "I suppose it matters little, on the brink of a battle like the one we face now. And yet . . ." His eyes turned unfocused at the recollection. "And yet I had time, after your departure, to recall your man's face, to think where it was I'd seen him before. It was at Camlann. The night before the fighting began."

Isolde went still. She couldn't let Madoc know about Trystan or that she carried Trystan's child. There was Marche at Caer Peris, within a day's ride from here. If Marche should learn Trystan, too, was nearby, he wouldn't rest until he'd seen him captured and killed. Not that she believed Madoc would give Trystan away. But it was simple fact that the more learned of a secret, the less likely it was that the secret would stay hidden for long.

Still, she couldn't stop herself asking, above the quickening of her heart, "You're sure that it was the same man?"

Madoc shrugged. "As sure as I can be, after nearly eight years. He was younger then. So were we all." He stopped, leaning back a little on the bench, gaze still distant as though he stared frowningly back across the years. "My father was king of Gwynedd then. Cadwallon. He was loyal to Arthur, for all he'd rebelled against the council's choice of Arthur as High King. But they'd been reconciled many years. He—and I—had fought many battles at Arthur's side, even before Camlann."

Madoc stopped again. "But I was speaking of the night before the battle. A filthy pig of a night. Rain coming down in torrents. Wind blowing a gale. No fire would stay lighted. Nothing to be had but sour ale and cold, half-spoiled food. Tents kept caving in. Not that they'd been much help in any case, with the water pouring in through all the chinks and the ground a river of mud." Madoc broke off to look up at Isolde. "What did you say?"

Isolde shook her head. Madoc's words had stirred something, some vague memory that brushed at the edges of her mind but was gone before she could grasp what it was. "Nothing. Go on. Please."

Madoc gave her a quick, intent glance, opened his mouth as though to speak, but then closed it again and instead went on. "I had guard duty at the High King—at Arthur's own camp. His was the one tent we had managed to keep from blowing over in the wind. And that was where I saw him, this man of yours. Coming out of Arthur's tent sometime around the middle watch that night."

Isolde looked up in surprise. "Out of Arthur's tent?"

Madoc nodded. "God alone knows how he'd gotten in, because we none of us guards had seen him come. Must have had the night vision of a bloody wildcat to have found his way, without being caught. But we guards were standing there, freezing our ba—our tails off in the pouring rain. And all at once the flaps to the king's tent opened, and there was this man, scarcely more than a lad, really. Didn't look to be more than sixteen, though he was no weakling or wet-behind-the-ears new conscript. You could see that. He had that edge men get in battle. He'd seen combat before, right enough. We all practically jumped out of our skins at the sight of him."

Madoc gave a short bark of a laugh. "And then we all scrambled to draw our swords." He glanced at Isolde, smile fading, eyes darkening with the memory. "All of us certain that the High King had been killed in his bed by one of Modred's spies. Satan's bollocks, I'd been in battles myself, but I'd never been more sick with fear in my life. Then Arthur himself stepped out from the tent. Dressed in his war gear, looking like he'd not slept in days. But alive. He came across to us and gave the order that we were to allow the lad to pass and not follow. That he had the High King's guarantee of safe passage."

Madoc stopped, eyes on the far wall. Then he slapped irritably at one of the stinging insects that were now as plentiful as the rats in the hill fort, and as though the gesture had broken a spell, looked up at Isolde. "So we let the lad pass by."

"And you're sure—" Isolde checked herself. She'd already asked Madoc whether he was sure the sixteen-year-old boy he'd glimpsed that night was the same man who'd undertaken to escort her to Cerdic's lands nearly five months ago. Trystan.

Madoc, though, answered as though she'd finished the question. "I only saw him for a moment. But the lantern light from the tent fell full on his face. I got a clear look. And I remembered him. The way you do remember a sight or a detail you've seen when you're almost pissing-yourself scared." He paused. "At any rate, you'll know the rest. Camlann was fought. Arthur was killed in any case. Not on my watch, though that was small comfort, at the time. And my father was killed, as well. Not on the battlefield. He died two days later of the wounds he got there. That . . . that was when I took the throne."

Madoc stopped. The glow of lamplight threw the scars on his face into relief, and showed up the beat of the pulse in his temple. Watching him, Isolde wondered whether he was thinking of the path that had led him from that night eight years ago to this night, now, where he stood once more on the brink of battle. But now in Arthur's place as High King.

She asked, suddenly, "You knew Arthur, then, what was he like?"

Once more, Madoc's gaze seemed to return from a long way away to focus on her. "That's right. You'd likely never have met Arthur, would you? Given who your—"

Madoc stopped abruptly with a conscious, half-embarrassed look at Isolde.

"Given who my father was?" Isolde thought of the father she'd barely known, who had died with Arthur on the field of Camlann and left her, at thirteen, to be reviled as the traitor's daughter from that time on. She said, "It's all right. It doesn't trouble me to speak of it, not anymore. No, I never met Arthur. I never even laid eyes on him that I can recall."

Madoc flexed the muscles of one hand, rubbing idly at the scabbed-over wound Isolde had stitched in his thumb. He nodded. "I see. Well, Arthur was . . . he was . . ." His voice trailed off and he sat quiet a moment. From outside, Isolde could hear the baying of a war hound and the fretful wail of a child from the women's hall. "I've known better men than Arthur," Madoc said at last. "I've known kinder ones. Cleverer ones. Even ones more skilled with spear and sword. But Arthur . . . was a king worth dying for."

And perhaps that was all—or enough—of what mattered. Enough to merit the bards' songs and hero tales, after all.

Isolde saw the shadow cross Madoc's dark gaze as he spoke the final words. She said, "I'm sure your men would say the same of you, Lord Madoc. Though I think they would say that you were a king worth living for, as well."

Madoc's eyes were still shadowed, but he forced a brief smile. "Let us hope they have the chance to do so." And then he rose to his feet. "I'll bid you good night now, Lady Isolde. I hope you rest well."

The suddenness of his leave-taking took Isolde by surprise. She blinked. "I . . . you don't want to know—" She stopped herself, met Madoc's eyes, and said, quietly, "Thank you, Lord Madoc. For not asking me anything more."

Madoc smiled again, a slightly easier smile this time. "I trusted you with the life of my son, Lady Isolde. I will trust now that if I needed to know the identity of the man Rhun spoke of, you would tell me. And besides"—the smile faded, leaving his face bleak, hard bitten with weariness once more—"as I said, I think it likely that questions of the past scarcely matter now."

WHEN MADOC HAD GONE, ISOLDE SAT in the silence of the council hall, hugging her knees and listening to the sounds of the hill fort, settled for the night under the close, oppressively still summer air. No trace of a breeze, not a hint of a thunderstorm that might break the spell of heat. She kept replaying Madoc's story again and again in her mind. Trystan, glimpsed at Arthur's tent on the eve of Camlann.

And what did that mean? She brushed at the sticky-feeling back of her neck. Nothing. It meant nothing at all, except maybe that Trystan would now have one more question to refuse to answer, one more story to refuse to tell—if he kept his word and sought her out one more time. If he lived so long.

Isolde sat for a long moment with her eyes closed. She'd tried every day since their parting to see Trystan in the scrying waters, even just a glimpse of his face that would let her know he was at least still alive. Always she'd seen nothing. Not Trystan. Not Marche. Even Morgan had seemed shadowy and indistinct when Isolde had given up on the waters and tried to summon up the remembered image of her grandmother's face.

So now she didn't even try to find a vessel for water; there was nothing here she could have used for scrying in any case, save maybe the battered drinking horn that had been dropped sometime during the meeting and had rolled under a bench a few paces away. She only sat, letting the heat and the night noises wrap around her until they blended and merged into something almost like silence. Focused all her thoughts on Trystan, on reaching towards him as she had before along a gossamer-thin thread of awareness stretched outwards into the night.

She sat quiet and very still until she felt a faint tingle, a slight warmth as though she'd stretched out a hand to a faintly burning point of light.

Maybe she felt it. Maybe she was only pretending she'd felt anything at all.

She rested her forehead on her raised knees as the recollection of Madoc's story rushed in. Trystan. Goddess, what would she say to him if he were actually here?

Is it true? Were you in Arthur's camp—Arthur's war tent—that night before Camlann?

And what would Trystan say? *If you trust me, don't ask me to answer.* Something like that, probably. Some answer that set her at a distance, kept him firmly behind his own walls, allowed her to share no part of his burdens at all.

Isolde clenched her hands before they could twitch with the urge to smash something. Perfect. She'd tried so hard all these long weeks not to be angry with Trystan. To let him keep a distance. To tell herself that the scars of the past weren't to be healed in a day or even a year.

And now she sat here, blazingly angry at him because of the way an imaginary Trystan she'd conjured up in her own mind answered her.

Isolde made herself breathe slowly. She thought of the tale of the maid who had held fast to her true love's hand while he was changed from serpent to beast to burning brand, and a line from the story floated up from memory. *They'll turn me in your arms, lady, into an esk and adder, But hold me fast, and fear me not, I am your babe's father.*

She felt the baby in her womb flip, stretching small legs and arms. A story. She should think of a story to tell the baby. Another one of Trystan, so that he—somehow since that brief vision in the chapel, she'd never doubted that the baby was a boy—might know who his father had been and still was.

She was all at once bone weary, though. Bone weary and shivering as the fear she'd been trying to hold off rushed in. And try as she might, no words seemed to come.

Finally, she closed her eyes, trying, without much success, to shut out the sound from outside: the barking dogs, the warriors shouting to one another across the practice yards. The harpers' songs spoke of the woad-painted blue warriors of the Old Ones asleep in caverns beneath such places as these, like Arthur himself, waiting to ride again in the hour of Britain's need.

She kept her eyes closed. At first there was nothing but the sound of her own breathing, the beat of her heart. Then—

It felt like a tug. Like a swift tightening of some unseen knot about her heart. Strong as whatever wordless summons had called her to the Caer Peris garden in the first place to hear the story Trystan would tell. Vigorous and forceful as the now frequent kicks and somersaults of the unborn child.

She felt as though her consciousness had dissolved, shattered, sending tiny fragments into the room, the night all around. She could feel the sharp fragments of straw in the roof, as though she herself were scrabbling through them along with the creatures whose squeaks and rustles seemed now unnaturally clear. She could taste on her tongue the smoke from the lamps, the musty, earthy smell of the rushes on the floor—and beyond that the thousand and one smells of the war camp. Straw and sweat and roasting meat, spilled ale and the sweet, milky breath of the crying baby in the women's hall.

And yet she felt, too, as though she were sinking into a deep, fast current that pulled her along, carrying her far out and away from here.

A small, distant part of her mind wondered if this were what the druids of the Old Ones had felt in the tales that spoke of souls being sent from their bodies to soar like birds. A part of her stood back in incredulous doubt, and at the same time begged anything that might be listening, *Let this not be just a dream. Let me not be just pretending this.*

But then—then he was there. Lying on the ground, arms folded, head pillowed on his bunched-up cloak, sword ready to hand even as he slept. His eyes were closed, but his head moved slightly, and his brow was furrowed as though in some dream.

Isolde's heart was beating so hard it felt too big for her chest, and each breath she took burned. It was a strange, half-frightening sensation: part of her aware of her body sitting alone in the empty council hall, aware of the pulse of her blood, the glow of lamplight dazzling her eyes.

And yet she saw just as clearly Trystan, sleeping on a patch of grassy turf beneath the shelter of an oak tree. Could feel a cool breeze on her cheeks as real as the earthen floor beneath her feet, hear the soft trill of a night bird somewhere in the tree under which Trystan lay.

For just a moment, the twin visions, twin sensations balanced. Equal weights to some inner scale. Two parts of a whole. Then the sights, the smells of the council chamber faded, entirely blotted out by the sight of Trystan, asleep before her on the ground, so near she could touch him if she put out her hand.

And, oddly, she didn't question what she had to do. Her pulse still racing, Isolde curled herself on the grass beside him, looking down at his sleeping face. His jaw was unshaved, and asleep this way, his face looked at once stern and somehow younger, not so far distant from the boy she'd grown up with years ago. Isolde stretched out a hand, touched his cheek—and felt nothing, saw her fingers pass through his skin as though through empty air.

Not so real, after all. And for a moment, her whole body felt pierced by the longing that this half of the sudden twin awareness could be the truer one, or that she could shed the part of her that remained in the empty council hall as a snake sheds its skin.

Trystan's head was still turning restlessly, though, still lost in the dream. Once before she'd reached him this way, through the layers of unconsciousness and the pain of a sword wound. And once before, too, she'd thought that a childishly simple feat compared to reaching him now, trying to heal a long-buried pain he didn't want to share. And she'd been right. Whatever power had carried her here seemed determined to bring her no further.

Again and again as she sat beside him, she tried reaching out towards Trystan in her mind, tried sending out the threads of awareness as she would have done with one of the wounded soldiers in her care. And again and again it was like running up against a solid stone wall. Until, with a slither of panic, she felt the delicate balance tipping, felt herself sliding back towards the self she'd left behind in the council hall.

Listen.

Isolde held very still. Maybe this was the land of the Mist Dwellers, the crack between the worlds, in which she now walked, and the voices of the small gods, those of the rocks and trees and streams that echoed in her ears. Gods of the Old Ones, now banished, or at least sleeping, like Arthur and his men. Gods of the old stories that Morgan had always said belonged to a world like this one.

She couldn't touch Trystan, but she watched the slow rise and fall of his chest, traced again and again the lean, strong lines of his face, a face she knew as well as she knew her own. She tried to empty herself of all thought, to let go all her own hopes and worries, let go the chill fear that made her want to batter at Trystan's mind like a child terrified by a locked door.

And then she felt it: a rush of cold, a flash across her vision of mud and blood and the agonized screams of horses and men, so sudden that her heart jerked hard against her ribs and she felt herself spiraling into darkness, the edges of Trystan's sleeping form starting to blur and fade.

She'd been tired and frightened when she began this, after a day of treating the sick and wounded, after the strain of the council meeting—after nearly two weeks of lying awake on her bed in the women's hall, listening to the soft sighs and rustles of the sleepers around her and waiting for word of Trystan that never came. And she could feel the renewed weight of her own weariness and fear, now, a dull ache dragging her back towards the council hall again.

With all her strength, Isolde ordered herself not to give way to either fatigue or panic, not to clutch desperately at the fading image of Trystan's face, the scent of the oak leaves and the glimmer of emerging stars in the sky above. She waited until the balance tipped back, until the sight of Trystan's sleeping form no longer shivered and threatened to darken into nothing.

She laid a hand on Trystan's brow, and this time she felt, or at least thought she felt, just the slightest touch of warmth on her palm. She drew breath, fixed her gaze on Trystan's face. *Tell me the story. Please.*

She heard it right away this time: clashing shields and swords, charging horsemen, screams like the damned souls in hell. And this time, even as she sat beside Trystan on the grassy ground, she could feel him, lost in the center of the nightmare, fighting for his life and the lives of the men around him. All the time blocking out a guilt bitter as gall, the knowledge that these deaths—this river of blood—lay on his hands.

And then she felt her awareness twine with his. Thin, fragile threads at first, but growing stronger, as though she'd been dissolved in a vision of the scrying waters, her own consciousness wholly submerged.

HE COULD PICTURE ARTHUR, SITTING ON his camp stool in the king's war tent the night before, reading the scroll from Marche. Looking up, dark, angular face sober, eyes very grave and hard. "You may tell Lord Marche—"

Trystan wrenched his mind back to the present. Back to staying alive another moment, keeping as many of his men as possible from getting themselves killed. Luc, the damned thirteen-year-old fool, was standing there gaping like a cod as Arthur's warriors charged, spear and shield lowered in a positive invitation to be run through on one of their swords. Trystan hauled him roughly back, thrust the boy behind him, and brought his sword up in a thrust that cut through the belly of the nearest rider's horse. The beast went down, thrashing, screaming in pain, though the rider jumped clear.

Trystan yanked his blade free and looked up to see, through the mingled blood and sweat that trickled into his eyes, a second wave of riders attacking on the heels of the first. All wearing the emblem of the blue boar of Cornwall.

Not that that should have come as any bloody great surprise. He'd already guessed that Marche—

THE CONNECTION SNAPPED SO SUDDENLY THAT Isolde gasped and nearly lost the struggle against the dragging force of her own weariness once again. The sharing of Trystan's vision had drained her; she could feel more strongly than ever the ache of exhaustion that seemed to dull her thoughts like fog.

Not yet. Isolde made an effort to clear her mind. She couldn't lose this yet—couldn't leave Trystan trapped in the depths of the battle nightmare. She closed her eyes, her palm still resting against his brow, holding tight to whatever gossamer connection that insubstantial touch might provide.

Trys?

For a moment she heard nothing, felt nothing but solid blankness again, and her heart stumbled. But then: *Isa?*

Isolde felt her heart constrict, felt tears rush to her eyes. She knew it was pointless, but she couldn't stop herself from moving as though to smooth the hair back from his brow, even though her touch only slid through him again. *I'm here.*

The lines of Trystan's face hardened, then seemed to relax, as though whatever nightmare had trapped him had lost its hold. *Gods, I wish you really were. I wish this weren't a dream.*

Isolde's every thought had been too much taken up by the shock of being here, by the need to hold on and not let herself be dragged away to be conscious of anything else. At Trystan's words, though, she felt something echo inside her like the sudden pulse of a drum, felt familiarity kindle in her like flame. Somehow, in some way, she'd been here—here with Trystan—this way before.

I told you. She hardly needed to think about the words that rose to her mind. *I'm here because you needed me to come. I won't let go.*

You should. She heard the bleak, bitter finality in Trystan's voice. *Though I suppose I might as well cut out my heart as think I could stop dreaming about you, wanting you here.*

Isolde laid a hand on his forehead, stabbed again by the searing wish that this could be real. That she could lie down here beside him, wrap her arms around him and actually feel the warmth of his body against hers. That she might never have to go back to her tired body in the council hall at all.

But that wasn't why she was here. *Not much time.* It was the same featherlight whisper she'd heard before, and it echoed her own awareness that she'd be called back to herself soon, that whatever had carried her here wouldn't or couldn't allow her to linger long.

The vision of Marche's face that flashed instantly across her mind was wavering, oddly unfamiliar, seen this way through Trystan's eyes. Heavy, brutal features, black eyes and bulging veins.

You saw me fighting with him, didn't you? I wish you'd told me whether I win or lose. Whether he lives or dies.

Isolde felt her throat close off. *You still hate him, don't you? Your father?*

Christ, I don't know. I did hate him. I do. I'd drain his blood from my veins if I could. And yet—

What, Trys?

But as though the thought had broken Trystan's sleep, she saw his eyelids start to flicker, and with that, the vision started to fade again, the pull of her own weariness grew all at once overpowering, inexorable as the undertow of a wave. She could feel herself sliding, slipping away into darkness. Back towards the council hall. Back towards the full weight of the duties—and fears—that awaited her there.

And she knew it wasn't why she'd come, knew that she might well despise herself for weakness when she returned to herself and the vision broke. But her heart was suddenly pounding, and she couldn't stop herself from thinking, just as the sight of his face was blurring before her eyes, *Please, please come back to me. There's a battle coming. A final battle. And I'm afraid—*

I'M AFRAID.

The words rang in Trystan's ears, even as he snapped back to consciousness and lay a moment with his heart trying to batter a way through his rib cage, asking himself whether he was losing his mind.

His hand had closed automatically on the hilt of his sword, and with the same automatic habit he hauled himself into a sitting position, listened, and swept the clearing with his eyes for any sign of danger or threat.

Nothing.

Trystan tightened his muscles, forcing the shaking that gripped his muscles to stop. Before he'd got it completely under control, a step sounded beside him. At least it was Kian. They had an unspoken agreement of long standing not to ask about each other's nightmares.

Kian squatted down on the grass beside him, face craggy in the patchy moonlight filtering through the trees. He looked at Trystan in silence, remaining eye taking in, no doubt, the fine tremors still running through him. But he said only, "You all right?"

"Fine."

The image of Isolde's face was still hanging before him, the sound of her voice still echoing in his mind. He was used to dreaming of her, but this time he'd have sworn she was actually there.

"You didn't—" Trystan caught himself. What was he going to say? *You didn't happen to see Isolde, did you? Just happening to be here, wandering around these woods at night?* Right.

He said, instead, "What's happened? Is something wrong?"

Kian shook his head. "Cath's got back, is all. And Daka and Piye." He gestured towards the campfire, where three figures sat tearing into roasted hare and cups of ale. "Thought you'd want to hear what they have to say."

HE'D MANAGED AT ANY RATE TO stop shivering by the time he reached the circle of firelight. Piye and Daka greeted him, downed the last of their food, and then melted off into the darkness to stand guard along with Kian. Trystan took a seat beside Cath, shook his head at the food Cath offered. "No thanks. What news, did you learn anything?"

Cath shook his head and said, around a mouthful of meat, "Not for threats or money." He tore off another mouthful, grimacing. "You know things have come to a bad pass when even bribery doesn't work. We questioned every hired mercenary, every camp follower and hanger-on of Octa's we could find and got piss-all. Except . . ."

"Well?"

Cath scratched at his beard. "Except one old-timer, a fisherman who sells to Caer Peris. Asked a lot of questions. Who we were and where we'd come from and where'd we get the coin we were offering so free, like."

"And you told him . . ."

Cath snorted and reached for his cup of ale. "Asked him did I have the look of a newborn babe? Because I'd been a good few years out of the cradle, the last time I checked. Tried to follow us, though, after that. Clumsy as a cow in boots and made twice as much noise.

Would've had to be blind, deaf, and feeble-witted not to notice him crashing along behind."

Trystan looked up with quickening interest. "So what did you do?"

"Let him tag along for a bit before we lost him." Cath shrugged. "Thought it might be useful, like, for him to think he could find us again."

He cocked an eyebrow in faint question, and Trystan nodded. "Could be. You did right." He paused, frowning into the snapping fire, then said, "Keep trying. And keep a watch on to see if anything comes of this." The lingering remnants of the dream crawling across his skin made him add, "If you're sure—"

Cath had been reaching for another haunch of rabbit but at that he turned to look up. "Look, we've had all that. I'm staying till this is finished and I've seen you out of it with a whole skin." He indicated the direction the other three men had gone. "Me and the others, as well."

Trystan allowed himself a silent oath. Well, it couldn't be that hard to slip away when the time came. So long as none of them—Cath or the others—suspected. He shrugged, reaching to pour himself a cup of ale, and said easily, "I just don't want to be the one to face your wife if I bring you back to her less than whole."

Cath chuckled, the lines of his face relaxing. "Oh, aye. It'd take a braver man than I am to cross her when she's roused." He stretched his booted feet towards the fire, leaning back against a fallen log. "And she's breeding again—due midwinter time."

Trystan's head jerked up. "And you're out here risking your neck with me? Christ, Cath."

Cath's shoulders moved again. "She'd not have heard of anything else. Besides, reckon I can take care of myself. You're the one for crazy stunts to get yourself killed."

"I'm not the one with the wife and family waiting at home, either."

"No?" Cath's swift, sidelong glance made the memory of Isolde's face, Isolde's voice, rush in and center like a dull throb behind his eyes. Not that it would have taken all that much. He'd been trying to cram remembrance back into its box since the moment he'd woken. "I'd have said you had the wife part right enough."

Promise me this won't be the last time I see you, Isolde had said. And he'd given her his word. Not actually intending to keep it—because that was the least she had to forgive him for. But, *I'm afraid.* The echo of those words was still like a toothache that covered his entire body.

Trystan passed a hand across his eyes. He really was losing his mind if he thought the dream and all the others like it anything but a fantasy of his own imagination. And yet the pounding urge to get up and head for Madoc's encampment straight off wasn't fading even in the smallest degree.

Trystan swore under his breath, drawing another questioning glance from Cath. *Tell me the story.* Isolde had said that in the dream, too. Fantasy or no, maybe it had always been craven cowardice to think he didn't at least owe her that much.

Besides, she'd be at Madoc's camp with the rest of Britain's forces. Given how little progress they'd made so far, that could be valuable.

Trystan tipped the remaining ale out onto the ground and made to rise. "Keep a watch out," he said again. "I'm off in the morning, but I'll be back in a day. Two at most."

Cath glance was edged with suspicion. "Off? Where are you off to?"

"Nothing dangerous." Trystan clapped him on the shoulder. "To keep a promise, that's all."

Chapter 17

ISOLDE FINISHED GATHERING HER SUPPLIES and straightened, stretching the ache in her lower back that was more or less a constant now, tipping her face to catch the very slight stirring of a breeze, barely enough to lift the sweat-damp hair from her neck. Then she looked over the rows of wounded men, trying to decide whether there were any who needed her urgent care, or whether she could simply go on to the next pallet in line.

It was late afternoon, the harsh golden glow of the sun dazzling, so that at first her gaze passed over the man on the opposite side of the infirmary tent without a second thought. There were so many among the refugees of the hill fort who came to hawk their wares amongst the rows of wounded: makers of ale or bread or cheese, old women selling charms against pain and the ill spirits that turned wounds bad; army harlots came sometimes to try their luck during the darkest watches of the night.

Sometimes even Taliesin came, jarringly incongruous in his spotless cream-colored cloak amidst the dust and blood and flies, to play his harp and sing one of the old hero songs, one of the Pendragon or Macsen Wledig. Usually he came at twilight, as the sun sank below the horizon and the shadows thickened into purple summer dusk, and his music floated out over the briefly still and peaceful fort.

Isolde let them all come, always, from Taliesin to the army whores. Men who had little to do but lie still and think of their own pain needed whatever distractions could be found.

This man—the one standing across the tent from Isolde—was a juggler. A skilled one, if the cheers and whistles of the men grouped around him was anything to go by. He was sending colored woollen balls spinning into the air, adding first one, then another, until they arced high above his head in a curve that moved so swiftly it was all but a rainbow blur. Isolde glanced at him briefly, then started to turn to the man on her other side, an older warrior with a broken right arm. Then she froze, slowly turned back, and looked at the juggler again.

Isolde was barely conscious of having crossed the space between them, but she must have done, because she found herself there, on the edge of the group of watchers. Looking at Trystan.

He looked just the same as he had during her vision of him: jaw unshaven, a healing scratch crossing his cheekbone, gold-brown hair tied at his neck. Just for a moment, his eyes met Isolde's. And then, as she watched, he caught the spinning balls neatly, one after the other, caught them, and dropped them into an open leather pack that lay at his feet on the ground.

There was a raucous burst of applause, and a few of the men even tossed him copper coins, several more shouting, *Again! Again!* Trystan wiped his brow with the sleeve of his shirt, shook his head, and grinned at the requests for more.

"You'd have to pay me more than that to keep juggling on a day like today. Give me a cup of ale, though, and I'll tell you a tale."

There was some shuffling among his audience, some good-natured attempts at bargaining, but in the end someone produced a dirty horn cup, someone else a skin of ale, doubtless warm, thin, and horribly sour, but Trystan thanked the giver and took a swallow before setting the cup down on the ground.

Isolde had been standing paralyzed, the laughter and talk passing by her as a wave of meaningless sound. But someone must have asked Trystan what his story was to be about, because—just for an instant—his blue gaze met hers again, and he said, "It's about a man. Who fell in love with a lady far too good ever to be his."

An appreciative murmur went round the group. Stories of war and battle were the favorites, of course. But any tale was listened to greedily by wounded soldiers; Isolde knew that. And one of doomed love was a close second best. Trystan took another swallow of ale and then began.

It was a stirring story, and he told it well; he'd always had the cool nerve and the instinct for the dramatic of a showman. Through it all, Isolde stood looking on and feeling still detached, as though she watched herself and the scene all around her from a great height. Or as though she were walking into an icy cold lake, water lapping at her waist, her chest, her neck and mouth as she drew nearer and nearer the wavering reflection of her own face.

Because Trystan was telling the story of how three months before she'd gulled Octa of Kent into the fatal attack that had given Britain at least a fighting chance. He changed the names, the details and conflicts of the tale, made it one of a time long ago, when dragons and giants and the elf race of the fairy mounds still roamed Britain's shores. Isolde doubted anyone else here would recognize it. But she knew, almost from the first words he spoke, that the story was the same.

His account of how she, or rather the heroine of the tale, had gone disguised into the camp of the enemy king drew a disbelieving snort from one of the listeners, an older, greasy-haired man with a split lip and a black eye. Trystan broke off long enough to grin at him again.

"I know, friend. Hard to credit, isn't it? Don't blame the tale, though. Blame the man who had to go and fall in love with—"

Save for those brief glances, he'd not looked at Isolde. Now, though, he turned to her, his gaze for once unguarded, giving her one of those rare looks when his whole heart seemed reflected in his intensely blue eyes. "Had to fall in love with the bravest woman ever born."

"Maybe—" Isolde hadn't even known she was going to speak until the word left her mouth, until she saw the heads of the listening men swivel round to her at the interruption of the tale. She was struck by a sudden memory of being in Octa's camp: the dark, the smell of men's unwashed bodies. Facing Octa in the squalid, filthy tent that passed for the king's quarters, and all the while being sick, not with fear for her own life, but with the knowledge that even if she survived the night she could well return to the abbey and find Trystan dead of the already near-fatal sword wound.

Isolde fought against the tightness in her throat. Trystan hadn't died. He'd lived to swear an oath of handfasting with her, to make the child whose kicks even now fluttered inside her. And now he was standing before her, alive, keeping his word to see her at least once last time.

"Maybe . . . if you could ask her, she'd say that she wasn't brave at all. She was terrified the whole time. But she kept thinking of him. The man she . . . she loved. Kept remembering all the times he'd faced danger and not been afraid. And then it was as though he were there with her the whole time, holding her hand."

The last words came out as barely a whisper. Trystan didn't answer, but only stood, eyes on hers. Finally the man with the black eye said, "Well, go on then. What happened?"

Trystan dragged his gaze away. "He, this man I was speaking of, gave an oath of allegiance to the enemy king."

It was one of the other men who interrupted this time, a young man—not much more than a boy, really—with a broken leg and a straggling first effort at a mustache. "Gave an oath of allegiance? Why'd he want to go and do a thing like that, then?"

"Well, he'd learned something, you see." The steadiness of Trystan's voice didn't alter, though just for a heartbeat his eyes once again found Isolde's. "He'd learned that this enemy king had discovered the name of the woman who'd tricked him. Knew her name and was bent on revenge. So the man made the king a bargain—his oath for her life."

The wave of shock went through her like the beat of a war drum.

"What?" Isolde's lips shaped the word, but no sound emerged. Luckily. At least none of the men had looked at her to notice anything amiss. She felt her whole body flash hot and cold, had to moisten dry lips before she could trust her voice enough to speak. "Why . . . why didn't he tell her?"

A faint, rueful smile touched the corners of Trystan's mouth and edged into his eyes. "Because he knew she'd risk herself again if she learned he was putting himself in danger on her account. She's . . ." He tore his eyes from hers, turning with an effort back to the circle of listening men. "She was brave, you see, as I said." He smiled briefly again. "Too brave and too good for this man by half. So he gave his allegiance to the enemy king. Though he was never, truth be told, planning to give the king all that much in the way of aid. The oath was a means towards bringing about the king's downfall so that she—his love—would be safe once and for all."

"Why—" Isolde was past caring about the number of times she interrupted the tale, past caring what the rest of Trystan's audience thought. She could see all too plainly where the story was leading, and the knowledge made each beat of her heart stab like the blade of a knife. "Why couldn't they have gone away together? Somewhere beyond this king's reach?"

Trystan looked at her again, something indefinable passing across his face. Then he said, "He couldn't ask her to do that. He had . . . chosen a path a long time ago. A wrong path, one that narrowed by the day. She deserves better than to walk that same road. Better than him."

"Shouldn't that be for her to decide?"

Trystan looked at her a long, long moment. Then: "She'd said, once, that she . . . that she trusted him. He'd ask her to trust him when he tells her that there's a story there she doesn't want to know—doesn't want him ever to tell." He stopped, drew a breath, and began again, voice steady, now, again controlled. "At any rate, he found a way. A way to bring about the king's defeat. Save her life— maybe thousands of others, as well. But that way meant . . . meant almost certainly losing his own. And so he found a way back to her because he wanted . . . he wanted to see her one last time."

When Isolde's sight cleared, she found she hadn't moved. Amazingly, she was still standing on the edge of the group, surrounded by the dust and the straw pallets, the buzzing flies, and the smell of blood from dozens of wounded men. The man with the black eye had chimed in again and was saying impatiently, "Well, so he found her again. What did he say?"

"He said . . ." Trystan was looking at her again. Longing and loss and love in his eyes. Isolde's own heart turned over, even as renewed pain arrowed in. Goddess, if he was letting himself look at her like that, he truly didn't think he was ever going to see her again.

"He said that he'd nothing to give her, nothing but his own life. And that he counts it well lost if it keeps her alive. And he told her"—Trystan's eyes were steady on hers—"that she shouldn't tie herself to him. That she should move on, make a new life for herself. Be happy. That if there were another man, one who was worthy of her, who could give her the kind of life she deserved, she should wed that other man."

"Maybe—" Isolde had to squeeze her eyes shut against the tears that burned behind her lids. She thought of the baby growing inside her. If Trystan went from here to his own death, the child would never know his father. But there was a battle coming. And if Octa and Marche's forces won—if she were killed—not only her own life would be lost. *No one should have to make a choice like this.*

Finally, when she could manage to speak, she said, "Maybe she'd say that she is the wife of one husband and will never be anything else. And she'd say that . . ." Her voice faltered and she had to swallow again. "That there's nothing he could say—nothing he could tell her—that would make her stop loving him."

She was looking at Trystan, and just for an instant, she thought she saw something—hesitation, maybe—flicker across his face. But then it was gone. Trystan looked away, then back towards her, seeming to force himself to hold her gaze. "He'd tell her . . . he'd say that she can't imagine how much he wishes he could actually be that man. The one he sees reflected in her eyes."

And then he looked up, gaze fixing on something behind Isolde. Looking round, Isolde saw them, as well: Madoc and Rhun, threading a way towards them through the pallets of wounded men. She knew the moment Rhun recognized Trystan, too; his small face lighted, and she saw him tug on his father's hand and say something excitedly into Madoc's ear.

Isolde made a quick, jerky movement, blood freezing as she turned back to where Trystan still stood, the center of the group of listening men. No chance for him to slip away—no chance even that he could avoid being seen.

Trystan shook his head again, though, said, "It's all right," in a voice almost too quiet for her to catch the words. He turned to go, and Isolde said.

"Wait! What are you—"

"I'll tell you." Again his eyes met hers. "But wait for Madoc. It's something he and the rest of the council should hear, as well."

· · ·

"SO, LADY ISOLDE."

Isolde glanced up to see that Cerdic had come to lower himself onto the bench beside her own seat in the council hall—slowly, as though his bones ached. The talk and debate were ended; serving maids crossed this way and that with what supplies could be spared to pass for an evening meal: cooked carrots and some stringy roasted venison that the hunters had brought in, bread made with flour so coarsely ground that bits of gravel from the millstones had been baked in.

And at the front of the room, Taliesin was playing, the sound of his music and the underlying voices of the men covering anything Isolde and Cerdic of Wessex might say.

> *Men went to Camlann with the dawn.*
> *True is the tale, death o'ertook them at Camlann.*
> *Since the brave one, the wall of battle, was slain,*
> *Since the earth covered Arthur,*
> *Poetry is now gone from Britain.*

Once before Isolde had listened with Cerdic to Taliesin's song. It seemed strange, now, nearly two full turnings of the moon later, to sit here with the Saxon king and listen to the song of Camlann again.

That had been afternoon; now it was night, hot and sultry.

Cerdic alone seemed untouched by the heat. His ermine-trimmed tunic was spotless, and the warrior's rings on his forearms, the heavy collar of gold about his neck, the gold beads in his plaited hair and beard gleamed in the smoky torchlight. He studied Isolde, blue eyes keen in his leathery face, and then said, "Courage, Lady Isolde. If all the prating Christians that infest the land these days are right, I shall be consigned to the kingdom of the damned in the next life. I don't know that I object strongly; their heaven sounds a dull enough place by all accounts. But what I am particular about is the way I get there. I assure you, I have no intention of being sent into the afterlife by Octa of Kent or his men."

Isolde locked her hands, watching the knuckles whiten under

the skin, and said, "You believe this plan stands a chance of success, then?"

"Oh, a chance, certainly." Cerdic's voice was dispassionate, his gaze judicial as he gazed at the room around them: the guardsman with their bright gleaming weapons, the meat, the horns of ale, the colored cloaks and painted shields. Watching him, Isolde was reminded of a golden hawk, looking down from a great height to the ground below. "I suppose whether that chance will be enough depends"—his voice turned slightly dry—"on my grandson. And on what we left waiting here make of the chance his mission buys."

Isolde stared straight ahead, a picture forming in her mind. Trystan, standing before the hastily assembled council and giving them an account—as true an account as could be made without mention of Isolde herself—of his movements over the last months. His false allegiance to Octa. His work at driving a wedge into the already widening rift between Octa and Marche.

He'd spoken, too, in blunt terms of Octa's current defenses and disposition of troops, though the knowledge did little good. None among the council had even tried to claim the intelligence enough to ensure a victory for Britain, only that it underscored their overwhelming need for more spears, more men before the brewing conflict came to a head.

Madoc had listened in silence while Trystan spoke, and then said, with equal bluntness, "All you say may be true. But why should we trust you enough to take your word?"

And Cerdic had sent a rumble of shock and muttered oaths rippling around the room when he'd stood in his place and said, voice calm, "You may take his word. He is my grandson."

Fortunate, maybe, Isolde thought as she sat beside Cerdic now, that Cynlas of Rhos had been among those to decamp, since he alone on the council might have identified Trystan as outlaw as well as Cerdic's kin. Fortunate, too, that Madoc himself had only looked from Cerdic to Trystan in intent silence and said no more.

Now it was over, though. The meeting finished. Trystan gone— with the council's favor—on another mission of intelligence, to learn where Octa had imprisoned Cerdic's son and warriors, if they still lived, and to free them in time to come to Britain's aid. Just as he'd intended from the first in coming here, to Madoc's camp.

Trystan had spoken with Cerdic, if briefly—an exchange of greeting, a formal recognition on Cerdic's part of the bond of shared blood. But save for those few brief exchanges under the eyes of the wounded outside, she herself hadn't—Isolde tore at a ragged nail on her thumb and watched a tiny bead of blood spring up where she pulled too hard—she hadn't even had a chance to say good-bye.

She blinked hard. Blinked before another memory—one of watching herself learn that Trystan was dead—could gather before her eyes. "You mean to take to the field of battle yourself, then, Lord Cerdic?" she asked, and was surprised, even as she spoke, at the tug of anxiety she felt, even in the midst of fear for Trystan.

"Despite my advanced years, do you mean?" The edges of Cerdic's thin mouth lifted in a wintry smile and he raised one eyebrow; despite her efforts, the worry must have come through in Isolde's voice after all. "I told you once, Lady Isolde, that I had come to the twilight of my life. Better that I should fall in battle than one of the young bloods with a life still before him, some might say. And besides, when my grandson displays such courage, can I do less?"

His voice was light, almost unconcerned, and he gestured with one age-gnarled hand. "Sacrifices are made in war. Men die. They say the spinners at the foot of the World Tree choose a man's time to die. But I had rather choose my own."

No use, Isolde thought, in trying to argue. No use to say that a warrior's death was small compensation for the loss of years' and more life. Cerdic would never believe her. Perhaps no warrior would. And useless, too, she knew, to ask Cerdic to take care, to guard his own life, as useless as making that same plea to Trystan would have been.

Almost as though he'd read the thought, Cerdic went on, "Whatever happens, though, I am glad to have seen my daughter's son before I die. For all I have many other grandsons, many other sons."

Isolde wasn't sure what made her speak. Whether it was only the wish that someone besides herself here might know the truth before the coming battle began, or whether it was part of that slithering fear for Cerdic she'd felt a moment before. But her eyes met Cerdic's, and she said, steadily, "A great-grandchild, as well."

Cerdic's brows lifted in a look so like Trystan's that Isolde's heart clenched again. The hall all around them seemed all at once very still, despite the voice of the harp, the clank of knives and platters and the talk of the men. Cerdic said nothing, though, only sat still a long moment, blue gaze holding hers. Isolde thought the very smallest trace of a smile might have touched the edges of his mouth. Then it was gone, and he nodded. "You must excuse me, Lady Isolde. I go to make my troops ready for war."

"JUST GIVE ME THE CHANCE TO get back at those filthy, turd-sucking dogs." The old man's eyes were wild and he hawked and spat on the ground. "That's all I ask. Just let me—"

He made a grotesque, toadlike figure, back bent nearly double, limbs twisted and shoulders crookedly askew under clothes that were little more than rags. His face, beneath a mane of grizzled hair, was so scarred as to be almost inhuman, and spittle dribbled at the corners of his twisted mouth and onto his chin.

Since it was the third time he'd repeated the words, Trystan cut in. "And here is the price we are willing to pay." He held out the brooch one of the council kings had offered: a good piece, formed of twisted gold, with a garnet the size of a man's thumbnail in the center. The old man stared at it a moment, eyes bulging, mouth hanging open. Then he snapped his mouth closed again, the muscles in his throat bobbing, and gave a brief, jerky nod.

"Fair enough. You've got yourself a bargain." One clawlike hand came out greedily to make a snatch at the gold, but he only shrugged when Trystan's fingers closed round the brooch once more. "As you like. Come back here tomorrow. Same time. And I'll take you to where Octa's got Cerdic's son stashed away."

Trystan didn't bother asking why they couldn't go now. He nodded, watching as the old man turned and scuttled towards the trees, his bowed legs and limping, awkward gait giving him the look of a crab seeking the shelter of its hole in the sand.

When he'd reached the edge of the tree line, Cath turned to

Trystan, one eyebrow raised. "You believe that? About the Saxons keeping him prisoner for years and breaking all his bones?"

Trystan shrugged. "Could be true. He'd not be the first. Not that it matters," he added after a moment's pause.

Cath's head jerked in confirmation. "Oh, aye. He was lying right enough. If he really had information to sell, he'd have haggled a bit as to the price you offered." Cath's grin flashed white in his dark beard. "Revenge may be sweet, but it's still not like to fill your belly or keep you warm through the winter, is it?"

Trystan nodded. "No, that was a mistake. He should have tried to bargain. And he should have asked for at least part of the payment in advance." Eyes still on the trees where the old man had vanished, he flipped the brooch into the air with his thumb, then caught it again on his palm. "The only question is, did someone send him, or did he come on his own?'

"You mean was he sent by Octa, or is he just some poor starving devil who heard we were looking for word of Cerdic's son and thought he'd try his luck?" Cath rubbed his jaw. "You want me to follow him?"

Trystan fingered the brooch, wishing the tension that had been carrying him along these last days hadn't picked this moment to depart. Its lack was leaving room for him to realize that he was tired and hungry, and that his skin felt gritty from nights of sleeping on the bare ground. Making it harder to keep memory pushed aside.

Trystan glanced towards the black stallion Isolde had left with him, now browsing on a patch of grass nearby. "No. I'll go. You get back to the others."

Cath made no move to go, only stood looking at him intently. "Not planning on coming back, are you?" he said at last.

Right. Probably it had always been craven cowardice to think he could get out of this, as well.

Trystan looked up at Cath. "I'm going to tell you something. I want your oath on it that you'll do nothing but stand here and listen."

·   ·   ·

'ISOLDE LIT THE CANDLES WITH UNSTEADY hands. Three candles, for the three faces of the goddess: maiden, mother, and crone. Or for the three faces of the Christ-God. Or whatever slow, beating voices of the Old Ones slept beneath this hill. Tonight she was willing to call on anyone—anything—for aid.

She closed her eyes.

She was in Madoc's war tent, a small, stuffy dwelling that smelled strongly of goat hide and sweat. But the long-awaited rain had threatened all evening, dark storm clouds massing low in a leaden sky, and the wounded had been moved for greater shelter into the council hall. Now Madoc and all the men save those left to guard the ramparts were out, away from the hill fort on patrol, and Madoc's tent was very nearly the only space in the whole of the en-campment where she could be sure of not being interrupted in what she had to do.

Twice before now, she'd summoned a memory of Morgan and asked her grandmother for help. Once in the chapel, where she'd been granted that brief flash of the child's face. And once two months ago, when Trystan had been dying of a deep sword wound—and she'd known that to save him she was going to have to reach him in the black depth of unconsciousness in which he lay.

Now she concentrated every scrap of her attention on calling up a memory of her grandmother's face, the delicate, eldritch features lined, crumpled by age, but strikingly beautiful, even still. *Please let me reach him again.*

Nothing at first, and then—

The vision of her grandmother seemed fainter tonight than be-fore, wavering and far removed, as though Morgan truly did stand just beyond the veil of the Otherworld.

Still, the part real, part imagined Morgan smiled just a bit. *One would think you believed the tales—the ones that credit me with the power of healing even fatal wounds.*

Would you?

Heal Arthur? Morgan's smile didn't fade, but it altered, somehow. *Perhaps I would. Perhaps I have.*

What does that mean?

Morgan laughed at that. Then her look softened as it rarely had in life, and Isolde would have sworn she felt a featherlight touch on her hair. *I wish I could help you, child. I would give anything if I only could. But you don't need me.*

WHEN ISOLDE OPENED HER EYES, HER hands were still shaking so much that she nearly slopped the water over the edges of the copper cauldron she'd taken for a scrying bowl.

She'd left Cabal outside, lying on guard in front of the tent's flap. Now the tent was hushed and still, the voices from the servant's quarters and women's hall, the noise from the refugees' makeshift shelters distant and at least partly muffled by the tent walls. Still shivering, Isolde dripped the sweet almond oil she'd brought in a flask into the water before her, then drew out the brooch that fastened the shoulder of her gown and pricked her finger deeply enough that a bright bead of blood welled up on the surface of the skin.

Three drops of oil to sweeten the waters. Three drops of blood as payment to lift the veil.

She knelt by the copper cauldron, staring at the wavering reflection of the candle flames, the swirling mixture of blood and oil, until her vision blurred.

And slowly, gradually, an image of Trystan's face took shape on the waters. Asleep—as she'd seen him before, though this time he lay on a roughly made bed of branches and dry leaves, the whole covered with his traveling cloak. Slowly, tentatively, Isolde reached out to him in her mind, trying to will herself into feeling the tugging, imperative summons she'd felt before.

The waters went dark. Isolde had to bite her lip to keep back an angry sound of frustration, to stop tears from rising to her eyes. She made her breathing slow. The vision of Trystan took shape again, cloudy at first and then growing clear. This time Isolde didn't try to reach out, but only sat still, staring unblinkingly at the waters until—

It happened more suddenly even than before: the shocking splintering of consciousness that made her separately aware of each noise, each small pulsing source of life all around, from the throaty bark of the war dogs outside, to the stiffening pain in the nearest sentry's knees, to the moths blundering against the walls of the tent.

And then she was there. Beside Trystan. Madoc's tent entirely gone, the balance tipped until she saw nothing but the lean lines of Trystan's face, his thin, mobile mouth relaxed in sleep, the gold-brown hair that had slipped free to hang over his brow. An owl's call, low and eerie, sounded from the trees nearby, and Isolde glanced up to see a black stallion—Hræfn—tethered nearby and asleep, neck bowed, head hanging low.

She felt the same piercing ache, the same yearning that this could be real—doubly so tonight, with the memory of their last meeting still so vivid in her mind. But slowly, slowly, unwilling to try anything that might risk the balance tipping back, she sat down beside him, reached towards him, willing the threads of her consciousness to twine with his. She'd asked Trystan, weeks before, who he talked to when there was something he couldn't bear alone—and he'd answered, *You.* Now she was desperately hoping—praying, even—that that would be true.

She hesitated a moment, then reached to lightly touch Trystan's scarred left hand, marked by his time as a slave in a Saxon mine. Start with the clearest, the most outwardly apparent of his scars.

It was harder—far harder—than with one of the wounded men. Partly because she continually had to silence the beating voice of her own fear. Partly because it seemed to her that even this way, lost in sleep, Trystan fought to keep all pain, all feeling pushed far back where she could barely even sense it, much less share. At first she felt only the present ache of weary muscles, a jammed finger, a dully throbbing bruise on his side.

She twined her fingers with his scarred ones, with her free hand reached to touch the slave's brand on his neck—though both times her touch only slid through Trystan as through empty air. And then—

Slowly she felt herself slip through tangled, jagged layers of memory until she was choking on dust, crawling through darkness so absolute it was like a solid weight, pressing her down. *A slave— a dead man, or as good as. Outside all law. Nothing to stop the guards killing him, chopping up the pieces, and feeding his guts to their dogs if*

that's what they choose. The world narrowed down to nothing but draw-
ing another breath, putting one foot in front of the other, surviving one
moment, one heartbeat more. Which was good, in a way. It stopped him
remembering why he was here—why he deserved to be here.

Isolde's own heart had started to pound, and she forced it to
slow, forced herself not to jerk back or let the threads of connection
snap. She sat still, with that same insubstantial touch holding fast to
Trystan's hand, tracing in the lines of his face the boy she'd grown up
with years ago, the one she'd lost at Camlann when he'd fought and
wound up somehow a slave in a tin mine.

Show me. Isolde made a picture of that boy Trystan in her mind:
sitting grim-faced, rigid and silent while she forced him into letting her salve his bruises and scrapes and cracked ribs. Enduring his
father's beatings without a single show of anger, without once shed-
ding a tear.

Tell me, she thought without words. *Show me.*

She listened, the threads of her consciousness sliding across
his, until her own body throbbed with the fiery pain of bruises on
bruises, until her own heart was pounding with pent-up rage—rage
she could never give way to, never show. Because if she let herself get
angry, she'd be halfway to turning into her father, and that meant
that Marche would have won. She felt the familiar bitterness in
her mouth, because as always she could only share this pain—she
couldn't lessen it or take it away.

But, *Tell me.* And she started to see more: pictures that flashed
through her mind like swift lightning strikes. Trystan's mother, fair-
haired and empty-eyed, like someone who had died and left only a
cringing husk of a body behind. Neither grateful to Trystan for trying to protect her from Marche nor angry on his account. Just . . .
dead. Gone.

Then Marche himself, face purple, suffused with rage, veins
throbbing in his neck like worms. *Cur . . . bastard brat . . . midden*
scum . . .

I know. Tell me.

And then herself, as she'd been at eleven or twelve, a gray-eyed
girl with raven hair braided down her back. Small, skinny, and—

Completely fearless. Gods, at eight she'd caught some of the older boys taunting and beating a younger, weaker one. She'd threatened to turn all the older ones into slugs and newts. They believed her, too—they knew who her grandmother was. Why she'd settled on him for a friend he'd never known—it wasn't as if he was usually much in the way of good company for a girl.

Isolde saw the boy Trystan in a practice yard, felt his heart pumping, his skin itching with sweat as he drilled again and again with bow and arrow, battle-axe and sword. *He didn't deserve her now, but he was going to make something of himself and deserve her someday.*

Isolde felt hot tears burning her eyes, spilling over her cheeks, and the sensation was almost enough to drag her back, back to the self she'd left behind in Madoc's tent. She couldn't let go—not now. Not *now*.

She drew a slow breath, then made another picture in her mind—this time made up of all the fragments, all the jagged pieces she'd glimpsed in her dreams. A night of driving rain . . . an enemy camp . . . a meeting with a king. *Was that how it was? Please. Tell me the story. Show me.*

Isolde felt his hand jerk in hers, felt his heart start to pound, and—

. . . clash of shields and swords . . . Bradach gasping on the mud-churned ground . . . broken ends of ribs and tatters of muscle and sinew.

Shhh, it's all right, Trys. It's all right. Isolde's heart was thumping erratically, too, and she tried to quiet it as she spoke to Trystan. *You told me about your mother. You trusted me that far. Tell me this story, as well.*

Tell you . . . God, Isa, I can't. I—

Jumbled pictures flashed across Isolde's mind, the overwhelming consciousness of Trystan's thoughts sweeping over her once again. The empty socket of Kian's lost eye . . . Hereric groaning in agony, skin the color of wet clay . . . the bandaged stump of Hereric's arm . . . a pale, fair-haired woman's battered face and crumpled, lifeless form.

You don't know me—you only think you do. I'm a curse. A walking curse. I shouldn't even let myself want you in a dream. Come near me and you'll be dragged down as well.

Stop it! Don't believe that—don't even think it! Isolde thought fiercely. *Kian and Cath and Hereric—and how many other men be-sides—would lay down their lives for you. Because they know you'd do the same for them. And I—Trys, those few weeks I had with you were the happiest I've ever known. You have to know that I wouldn't trade them for anything—whatever happens now.*

Silence. Silence and the sigh of the night breeze, the rustle of tree branches all around.

Isolde slipped her hand into Trystan's, felt again, just faintly, the smallest touch of warmth on her palm. She had a glimpse—just the briefest flash and no more. But she'd gone too far. Or not far enough. No way of knowing for sure. But Trystan's eyes snapped open and he sat up, instantly alert in the way of men trained to combat, one hand going automatically to his sword.

"No!" Isolde didn't know whether she'd actually shouted the word aloud. Her throat ached as though she had, even as the image of Trystan started to flicker and fade. With every last shred of strength in her reserves, she willed herself not to let go, begged anything that might have brought her here to let her stay a moment—even just a single heartbeat—more.

Trys?

"Isa? Isolde?" Trystan rubbed at his eyes, glance round him, then made a disgusted sound and muttered, "Christ, now I'm hearing you awake as well as asleep. I really must be going out of my mind."

Isolde's throat closed. Gods, there was so much more she'd thought to say, in time. *Your mother wouldn't want you to give up on life the way she did . . . Take care, be careful . . .* Even, *You're going to have a son.*

And now there was no time. No time for anything but the brief-est, simplest flash from her mind to his. And maybe this was all she would ever have been able to do, even if she'd been able to linger here this way for a year.

Didn't I tell you that I loved you no matter what was in your past? I've never lied to you, Trys. I never would.

Chapter 18

TRYSTAN CROUCHED IN THE REEDS, his eyes on the tor that rose up like a sharp knuckle from the flat expanse of swamp and marsh-land all around. Maybe the Christian priests were right about con-fessions being good for the soul. He wasn't actually worrying much about the state of his soul just now. Or feeling any lighter for having for the first and only time told someone about Camlann.

Would Cath have told Kian and the others by now? Trystan hadn't asked him not to—hadn't given Cath the chance to say any-thing much at all.

But giving Cath the truth had, at any rate, gotten him to this place on his own, with none of the other men to add to the weight on his conscience by risking their lives to help him.

Because the old cripple really had had information to sell. Not that there'd been a lamb's chance in a wolf den that he'd have actu-ally sold it or honored the bargain they'd made. Or done anything but stand back and smile while Trystan got his throat cut for his trouble of asking. But Trystan had followed him back to his master, the man who must have heard of the questions Cath and the others had been asking. Heard and bribed the old cripple to approach the strangers asking questions about Cerdic's son. One of Octa's thanes, as it had turned out. And Trystan had heard enough of their meet-ing to put together what he needed to know.

So now here he was. On his own. Ankle deep in brackish water, breathing air that stank of rotting plants, and swatting at the sting-ing insects that buzzed all around.

He had to credit Eormenric, though. If you wanted to conceal a prison camp housing half an army, this was the spot for it. *Ynys Witrin.* The bloody Glass Isle itself. Set amidst land that flooded entirely in winter, leaving the tor an island in a sea of bog and thickly reeded sea marsh. Wooden causeways had been built out over the wetlands for the locals who made a living from the fish and wild fowl to cross the marshes in safety, but they'd been burned, and some weeks since to judge by the waterlogged ash now left—Trystan's first sign, if he'd needed any, that those now in possession of the central Tor had something to hide.

The Tor was a gateway, so the old stories went, to the Otherworld, and the home of Gwyn ap Nudd, the Lord of the Underworld. And the last hiding place of the wonder-working cauldron of Ceridwen and a hundred more magical creatures and relics besides. If any of the local fisher folk and crofters noticed that the ancient fort atop the tor had been taken over by strangers, none of them was likely to risk an Otherworldly curse by telling it abroad, much less by approaching the place to know what went on behind the wooden ramparts.

And certainly the small band of monks huddled in their miserable little hermitage on one of the grassy hills that surrounded the Tor weren't likely to talk. Trystan had enjoyed—to use the term in the loosest possible sense—their hospitality the night before, and found them terrified one and all of the foreigners who'd taken possession a month or two ago.

Trystan cast a glance over his shoulder at the clump of yew trees, growing on a small patch of drier ground, where he'd tethered the stallion he'd ridden here, through the journey that had lasted two days and part of a night. The horse had been dragging by the end, head drooping, but still plodding gamely on. A good mount. Lucky that Isolde . . .

A lot of good it did to acknowledge that even thinking of Isolde made him feel like he was drowning. That even breathing hurt just now.

Trystan's jaw clenched. He'd had the chance to speak with Madoc while he'd been in the king's encampment. Not for long, but long enough to make a judgment about Madoc's character. Long enough to know he might even have liked the man if he hadn't been busy hating him from skin to guts.

A movement on the slope caught Trystan's attention. The sun was high overhead, and he narrowed his eyes against the glare. Yes, there it was. The main gate of the fort atop the tor had swung open, and a swell of riders and men on foot were streaming out as though a devil were riding on their heels. Or a threat of plague sickness.

Trystan allowed himself a small, grim smile. Nothing like fouling the encampment's water supply with the carcasses of a few rotting birds. He'd done it under cover of darkness the night before, since Eormenric seemed to be trusting in the tor's reputation—and the surrounding marshland—to keep intruders out. The guards posted around the earthen ramparts had proved themselves for the most part to be of the just-enough-training-to-be-stupid variety. Stupid and overconfident, trusting in their expensive leather and mail armor, their axes and gleaming spears and shields. Eormenric, son of Octa, might be a decent fighter himself, but he hadn't exactly been granted the best and brightest of his father's fighting men for this job.

Though at that Trystan supposed he owed Eormenric thanks for keeping Cerdic's son and warriors alive at all. Not that he believed Eormenric for a moment to be more merciful than his father. Only more mercenary, with a better eye to the main chance. Cerdic's son and the thanes who served him were valuable hostages, worth nearly their weight in gold. That and, better still, a sizable inroad into Cerdic's lands.

While Trystan had been inside the fortress walls, he'd spoken with some of the prisoned men—sleeping upright and chained together in the open square at the center of the camp, while the warriors not on guard duty snored in their tents all around. Through them, he'd had the word spread not to drink the water today, not that the prisoners were offered it all that often in any case, and to feign the same symptoms their guards would start to show.

And now here they came, those still unaffected by the fouled water supply. Fleeing what they'd almost certainly take to be a plague of sickness, the kind that often struck army camps in this kind of unrelenting heat. Trystan doubted any of Eormenric's men left behind would be in much of a condition to fight. And even if they were, the prisoners would now outnumber their guards. By at least three to one, if he'd rightly judged the number of men now streaming down the face of the tor and striking out along the narrow causeway of dry ground that would carry them across the marsh.

Trystan drew a fold of his cloak over his head so that he'd not be seen amidst the reeds. He waited until the vibration of the horses' pounding hooves had died away. Then he straightened and prepared to move.

TRYSTAN USED HIS SWORD TO SLASH aside the opening flap of yet another war tent. Empty, as nearly all the others had been. He'd found Cynric, eldest son of Cerdic of Wessex, alive, if weakened from nearly two months of living on what miserable slops of food the prisoners here had been fed. Still, Cynric had rallied quickly to take command of his men and to ask the name of the man who'd engineered their escape.

Trystan moved on to the next tent. Telling Cynric who he was would be one more complication he couldn't afford just now.

He remembered the look Cerdic had given him during their brief, private exchange after the council meeting. Coolly appraising, like a horse breeder trying to evaluate the bloodline of unknown stock. Not that he blamed Cerdic. Blood tie or no, it was a wonder the old man hadn't struck him dead on the spot, considering whose son he was.

Now Cynric and the rest of his warriors were raiding the fort's storehouses for supplies, while Trystan and a handful of others checked the tents for any of Octa's and Eormenric's men left behind. So far he'd found only three, puking their guts up and rolling in agony on the ground. No threat, maybe. But no help, either, in providing information on what Octa might—

Another goatskin flap—that of a tent on the edge of the fortress's central yard—was swept aside and Trystan froze.

A man. Wearing leather breeches and a dirty shirt, open at the throat. Sitting on the tent's single camp stool. Sitting—not lying down, as he would have been if he'd been sick like the rest. Trystan's mind registered that much, at least, even as a voice in the back of his head commented that this was, had to be, some trick of his own eyes.

But—son of a flaming goat—no. The man was aged. Changed. Gray hair where there had once been black. A network of broken veins beneath the puffy skin. Deep lines scored about the corners of the mouth and eyes.

Changed. But unmistakably King Marche of Cornwall.

Time seemed to grind to a momentary halt while Trystan stared and saw the same quick flare of shock reflected in Marche's black eyes.

Marche didn't speak. Didn't even hesitate. He lifted the sword that had lain on the earthen floor by his side and charged, head-on.

The blade nicked him on the wrist, and Trystan swore at himself for slowness, even as he sprang aside, reflexively raising his own weapon to block Marche's blow, with a savage chop of his blade that sent vibrations shooting up and down Trystan's raised arm. What had he been thinking? That once Marche recognized him, they'd settle in for a nice long chat? Pull up a couple of chairs and reminisce about old times?

And he might have known—Trystan flung Marche's blade off his own and circled, sword ready and upraised—he might have known that once the alliance with Octa failed, Marche would come here, whining and sniffing around Eormenric. Octa was an old man, and if Marche had lost the friendship of the father, he might yet stand a chance with the son.

Marche's face now was suffused with blood and his black eyes were narrowed nearly to slits. He made a harsh sound that might have been a laugh and charged again, swinging his sword in another savage, hacking arc that Trystan blocked again. And again. And again.

He'd seen Marche in combat before, seen the calculated fury with which he fought. Marche was a matchless swordsman. Whatever else he was. And now he was fighting with the demon violence of a man possessed. Hacking, slashing, ducking, and lunging on the beaten earth of the fort's practice yard. Sweat dripped into Trystan's eyes, his muscles cramping as he blocked each attack, and he felt—

Nothing.

The realization was almost enough to make Trystan drop his weapon, even as he spun in place, sword shrieking as it scraped the length of Marche's blade. If he'd let himself feel anything at Isolde's telling him that she'd seen this coming, it had been merely grim satisfaction that this outcome, at least, this fight, were that much closer to being assured. Now, though . . . it wasn't so much the detachment he'd trained himself to cultivate automatically in battle. Locking away all distractions, any thoughts that might clog his mind.

He was facing Marche in single combat. Combat to the death. Because he could see Marche's face, the look in Marche's eyes. There was no chance Marche would let more than one of them walk away from this alive. And yet he had to keep reminding himself whom he fought. Had to fight the feeling of watching himself from across the room, giving himself dispassionate advice like some kind of god-damned master of arms training raw recruits.

Balance . . . watch his eyes . . . he's trying to get under your guard . . . duck . . . spin . . . Metal clashed and shrieked as their blades met and were wrenched apart. March was smashing at him, again and again, trying to break through his guard. *Block that . . . he can't keep this up . . . he's tiring now . . .*

Another jolt went through Trystan as the shock of that realization struck. Furious as his attacks might be, Marche was tiring, and badly. His chest heaved, the breath hissed between his teeth, and sweat and blood from a cut over his eye sheeted over his face.

Steady . . . let him overbalance himself, and you've got him.

And it was true. It shouldn't be this easy. But it was. Marche raised his sword two-handed over his head and made a final, desperate charge. Trystan stood in the face of the attack, and then stepped aside. Marche stumbled—staggered—was knocked sprawling by Trystan's blow to the back of his head. And a moment later was lying prone on the ground, the point of Trystan's sword resting against his bared throat.

Marche's eyes met his. And for a lifetime . . . and then another lifetime . . . neither of them moved. They'd been fighting on a patch of barren, sun-baked ground between the rows of tents and the fort's outer earthen ramparts. Screened from view of the rest of the fort. No one to see Marche die if he slit his throat here and now.

Trystan's hand tightened on the hilt of his sword, but still he didn't move. And then Marche spoke, in a hoarse, rasping echo of the voice Trystan remembered from years before—the voice that had been the background to God knew how many nightmares.

"Are you going to kill me?"

A lifetime . . . another lifetime . . . the dazzle of sun overhead . . . the network of carved lines about Marche's eyes . . . the blood pulsing in his throat. *Not quite a monster.* That was what Isolde had said. "Can you give me a reason I shouldn't?"

Marche made another of those harsh sounds that might almost have been a laugh. "None." His teeth were bared, his chest heaving as he fought for air, and the words came in short bursts. "Though I'll at least . . . do you the favor . . . of not asking for your forgiveness before I die."

Time had already stretched and slowed; now it ground to a halt as a moment turned into an eternity of knife-sharp fragments. Marche's eyes, sunken in pouches of pasty flesh. Marche's heavy, sweat-reeking body and sparsely gray hair. The smell of dust and decay from the marshes, and the perfect blue sky arching overhead.

The cut on Trystan's forearm stung. A fly buzzed in his ears. His fingers shifted, adjusting his grip on the hilt of his sword. A single crimson bright head of blood welled up on Marche's neck.

Another eternity dragged by, in which Trystan saw the trampled dead on a blood- and mud-slicked field of battle from eight years before. His mother's broken body and lifeless, staring eyes. Isolde's face. Isolde's face—clear as the perfect blue sky above.

He lowered his sword. Jerked his head towards the abandoned earthen ramparts. "Get out of my sight. You can end your own miserable life. I'm not going to do it for you."

"AND YOU TRIED TO FOLLOW HIM?"

Kian snorted in response to the question. "*Tried* being the word. You ever try to follow Trystan when he's bent on not being tracked? Might as well try to get footprints and spoor off of sea fog. I know— we all know—he was to try to get word of King Cerdic's son. But if God knows just which direction he might have gone in, He's not anxious to share the knowing with us down here." Kian paused, rubbing the scar on his cheek with the back of his thumb, then added, a little gruffly and with a glance at Isolde's face, "I'm sorry. Knew you'd be fearing for him."

He'd been drilling with the rest of Madoc's warriors all morning; his grizzled hair was still sweat-damp, the indentation from his helmet plain.

The memory of the half answer she'd glimpsed in her last vision of Trystan passed like a scream through Isolde's mind. She said, "It's not your fault. Trystan makes his own choices. If he went off on his own, he must have had good reason for it."

Kian grunted. "Well, Piye and Daka are still out looking for him, may find him yet. They're rare good trackers, the both of them." He paused, then added, "You need a hand here? Reckon they can spare me outside for an hour or two."

They were in the room that had once been the council hall and now served as infirmary. The night before, the expected rains had come at last, in a violent deluge of storm and thunder and wind that shrieked like the *bean sidhe* of the old tales. The storm had done nothing to clear the air or lessen the heat, but the wind and driving force of the rain soaked the fort's already dwindling supplies of flour and food, turned the ground underfoot to a slippery ooze of black mud, and tore patches from the hall's thatched roofs to that the floor rushes and bedding had nearly all been soaked through.

Kian had arrived at the hill fort that morning, just after the rain had ceased and a hazy, watery sun was climbing in the sky. Cath and Eurig had been with him as well, and all three men had been pressed into service almost at once—Kian in his old capacity of one of Madoc's captains, Cath as a metal smith to repair dented and damaged armor and swords, while Eurig was helping to repair the damage done to tents and the village of crude refugees shelters outside, cleaning and oiling rusted weapons, clearing drainage ditches—and drilling, like Kian, with the rest of the encamped warriors.

Isolde and any of the serving women who could be spared had spent the morning sweeping wet floor rushes out from around the rows of wounded men and dragging straw bedding to be dried in the sun outside. Now, though, there was little more to be done beyond her usual rounds of the wounded men—and though several were tossing in restless fever dreams, none of them yet needed her urgent care. And even then there would be little enough good that she could do, with supplies running as low as they were. As always near fields of battle, there were far many more men in pain than could be granted the oblivion of one of her few remaining doses of poppy; those would have to be kept in reserve for the very worst of the wounds still to come.

Isolde pushed a loosened lock of hair back into her braid and shook her head in answer to Kian.

"No, that's all right. If you've an hour or two to spare, you ought to find yourself a bed. You look as though you need rest more than I need help here."

Kian grunted. "Today's like to be about the last chance any of us gets for rest, at that."

Isolde looked up sharply, skin prickling coldly at the grimness of Kian's tone. Kian nodded in response to the unasked question in her look. "Oh, aye. Can see the bastard's cookfires on the hills all around us. Not to mention it took Cath and Eurig and the rest of us damn near two days to work our way past them all. Octa's armies, making camp."

"Why haven't they attacked already?"

Kian's shoulders jerked. "We've the high ground here. Octa'll be hoping he can gull us into attacking first. Which we won't—King Madoc not being exactly a fool. He knows Octa and his thanes will lose patience soon enough." He rubbed the scar on his cheek again and grimaced. "The waiting's the second to worst part of battle. The worst being what happens when the waiting stops."

"And you think that will be soon?"

Kian gave a short nod of agreement. "Oh, aye," he said again. "I give it a day or two, no more." He gave Isolde a searching look, then added, "Can't say you shouldn't worry. But King Madoc's got a plan. Octa'll send a raiding party in to make a beginning attack, try to gauge just what we've got to set against them. But we won't answer it. We'll sit inside here and not be drawn. Make 'em think we're running low on arrows and fighting men. That'll draw the rest of Octa's army in, most like, thinking we'll be easy pickings."

Isolde met Kian's dark gaze. "And won't we?"

Kian let out his breath. "Aye, well. There's that. Still . . ." He paused and then said, in the gruff tone from before, "I'll be fighting with King Madoc myself. That's my sworn oath. But Cath and Eurig and the others—they know they're to get you away from here, if"— Kian scowled—"well, if the worst happens. They'll find you before a single one of Octa's warriors so much as touches boot leather to the ground inside these walls. Get you clear of here if it's the last thing they do."

No point in arguing. No use in saying that she didn't want any of them dying—or risking their lives—for her. Isolde said, "I know. Thank you."

Kian's head jerked in acknowledgment. Then he said, in a different tone, "I remember you . . . looked, once and saw . . . well, saw Trystan. At least got a feel for where he was, and whether he was dead or alive. I was—" Kian stopped and scratched his chin, his gaze turned away from Isolde, towards the rows of wounded men. "I was just wondering whether you'd . . . ah, tried looking again."

In the silence that followed, Isolde could hear the raspy breathing and occasional groans of dozens of wounded men. The squawking of chickens from outside, as the birds that had escaped from their storm-damaged coop were rounded up and returned. The soft rustle of Cabal's paws on the rush-strewn floor as he padded towards her from across the room. He had been spending most of his days outside with Rhun; now he seemed to appear as though by instinct to butt his head against Isolde's side.

Isolde rubbed her hand over Cabal's neck. "No. Or rather, I did try. But I've seen nothing. I'm sorry." She had tried, again and again, since the night in Madoc's war tent, to see Trystan. But even when she closed her eyes, she'd felt nothing but the unborn baby, whose growing presence had already made her spend a day in letting out the seams of her gowns. And who must be only a few short weeks away from being guessed at—even by male eyes.

Isolde caught herself. "I'm sorry," she said again. "I—"

And then she stopped, the words dying on her lips. She'd been facing the doorway of the hall, and so saw instantly when two guardsmen, Madoc's men, dragged a third man inside. A thickly built man with a heavy paunch and sparsely graying hair, his square-jawed, reddened face partially obscured by the blood that had dripped from a cut over one eye.

He wasn't unconscious; he walked between the two guards, carrying his own weight. But his arms were bound behind him at the wrists, and he stepped with a slow, dragging gait, the stiff set of his shoulders that of a man who held himself upright through sheer brute force of will.

Isolde stood staring. She had seen that same rigid stiffness before, in men under her care who were gnawed by biting, unendurable inner pain.

Madoc's men propelled their captive roughly across the room. Hauled him to a stop before her and Kian.

"Caught him trying to climb over the ramparts." The older of the two guards, a tall man with a drooping black mustache, pushed his helmet back to wipe sweat from his brow. "Says he'll only talk to you, Lady Isolde. You know who he is?"

The beat of her heart seemed far too loud. Isolde looked at the man trapped between the guards, feeling as though she were—had to be—in the midst of some fantastic dream. As though it were almost an insult that the room around her, the wounded men, the smell of sweat and blood and damp straw of the infirmary remained utterly unchanged.

His clothing was muddied, his tunic crumpled, sweat-stained and torn, though the remnants of fine gold embroidery about the hem and sleeves could still be seen through the caked-on dirt and blood. His eyes, hollowly black in a face that she now saw was swollen with purpling bruises, met hers without the faintest glimmer of feeling, the faintest show of interest in their dark gaze. He might have been dead on a field of battle, lifeless eyes staring unseeingly up at the sky.

Isolde wrenched her own gaze away: felt herself nod as she turned to the older guard. "I know him, yes," she heard herself say. "He's King Marche of Cornwall."

MARCHE OF CORNWALL LICKED HIS BLOODIED lips and shifted on the stool he'd been given, wincing in a way that made Isolde wonder whether he'd cracked ribs as well as the more obvious hurts. His eyes met hers, and just for a moment, the empty, soulless stare of a dead man, or a wild beast, lifted and something like anger flickered at the back of their gaze.

"You must be enjoying this, Lady Isolde." His voice sounded harsh, either with thirst or long disuse.

Was she? It was strange, Isolde thought, how little his anger touched her. And she scarcely spared a thought for the answer to that question. "I'm very sure, Lord Marche, that were our positions reversed, you would feel nothing but pleasure."

The room was lit only by what sunlight filtered in through the holes in the thatch above, the air stuffy and close, and the damp heat and smell of mildew made the place seem even smaller than it was. Marche had been dragged from the infirmary to Madoc's tent as soon as she'd made her identification. Now they were in a small hut behind the stables that had been used to store grain. The place had been rapidly converted to a holding cell, guards set at the door, the bonds that tied Marche's wrists and feet staked deep into the ground. Marche's gaze turned smoldering, but he neither spoke nor moved. And beside Isolde, Madoc, too, sat without speaking, eyes intent on the prisoner's bruised face.

Madoc had protested against Isolde's coming, had said it was too much to ask that she comply with Marche's demand to speak only with her. As had Kian. But Isolde had brushed both their objections aside as swiftly as she did Marche's anger now. Again and again, she had asked a question of the scrying waters, the Sight. Here was a chance for an answer. She had little thought to spare for anything else.

She added, "But our places are not changed. You must have known that this"—she gestured to the closely confined space around them—"was inevitable. And that you would be taken prisoner, if not instantly killed. Yet you came here deliberately. Why?"

The smoldering anger in Marche's gaze gleamed for a moment once more, though his expression didn't change. "Because if my death is assured, I can at least take Octa of Kent with me into hell."

Madoc stirred at that and spoke for the first time. "We are to take it then that the allegiance between yourself and King Octa no longer holds?"

For answer, Marche hawked and spat on the ground.

Madoc's eyes moved over the older man, from his puffy and bruised face to his bloodshot eyes and once powerful body run now to bloat and fat. This would, Isolde realized, be the first time Madoc had faced Marche in nearly a year, the first time since the swordfight in which Madoc, drugged by Marche to ensure his defeat, had fallen into the fire and suffered the burns that now scarred his face.

Madoc's expression now was difficult to read. Distaste, Isolde thought, mingled with disbelief. "And your warriors?" he asked.

Marche's gaze swiveled to Madoc and he moistened his lips again, the muscles of his face twitching, though the anger had died out of his eyes, leaving them darkly empty and deadened as before. "Decided they preferred Octa's gold to any oaths of loyalty sworn to me."

Hardly surprising. Marche had demanded treason—to Britain—of all his warriors a year before, when the alliance with Octa had been made. Men who had turned traitor once would find it far easier to betray oaths of loyalty a second time. Especially oaths sworn to the aging, wine-sodden wreck of a man before her, with his pasty skin and lifeless eyes.

Something akin to the unwilling pity Isolde had felt before stirred inside her. Pity and revulsion, both, as though she were seeing something at once shameful and obscenely vulnerable. Something raw and maimed that should never have been seen.

"And now you come here," Madoc said. "Offering what? A betrayal of Octa in exchange for your life?"

Marche let out a bark of a laugh at that, a caustic, raucous sound in the stifling heat of the little room. "You think I hope to save my life after what I've done? That I imagine a single man here wouldn't spill my guts as soon as look at me, and dance a victory on the offal?" He shifted again against the leather thongs that bound him hand and foot and said, gaze unflinching, voice still gratingly harsh, "No. Octa's forces will attack tomorrow at dawn. I offer what I know of his battle plans in exchange for a quick death—no more."

For a long moment, Madoc's gaze rested on Marche's face. "Tomorrow?"

"At dawn."

Madoc opened his mouth, but Marche spoke over him. "I'll say no more until you agree it's a bargain. I tell you what I know—and I die quickly. No torture. No trial." He gestured towards Isolde. "And I'll speak to her. No one else."

Madoc's gaze narrowed. "Why?"

Marche didn't answer.

Isolde thought Madoc was about to argue—to threaten, even, or say that Marche was scarcely in a position to make conditions. She laid a hand on Madoc's arm. "No. It's all right. I'll speak to him." Her voice sounded strange, but unnaturally steady. She neither knew for certain nor cared what lay behind Marche's demand, only that this gave her her chance. "It's all right. If what he says is true, if Octa's troops are to attack our position here tomorrow at dawn, this is an opportunity we can't afford not to take." She met Madoc's gaze, willing him to agree, to be convinced. "Wait just outside the door. I promise I'll leave—or call out at once—if there's need."

WHEN MADOC HAD GONE OUT—UNWILLINGLY, BUT still gone— Marche started to speak, but Isolde cut him off. She'd pushed all fear or thought of the approaching battle aside, together with all awareness of what she felt for the man before her now. Only distantly grateful that she had gotten fully beyond his power to make her fear him.

"When I leave this room, Lord Marche, King Madoc will ask me for an opinion of all you have said. I can tell him you speak the truth, or I can tell him you lie. If you want me to say that you speak true, you will answer—truly—the question I ask you now." She stopped, steadying herself, then said, "What happened to Trystan at Camlann?"

Isolde thought she caught a faint tightening of the muscles around Marche's eyes, but his expression didn't alter. And he didn't speak, only sat, staring at her impassively from under lowered brows. When it was plain he didn't intend to answer, Isolde said, "Very well. Shall I tell you how it was?"

Outside the storage hut's hot airlessness, she heard Madoc exchanging a word with the guard, the clang of weaponry and the pounding of hammers as men and women went about the work of repairing the storm's damage. Isolde kept her gaze fixed on Marche's face, though, letting remembrance of the dream fragments and visions she'd caught swirl and gather in her mind's eye.

"It was raining," she said, "that night before the battle at Camlann. And you charged Trystan with the mission of getting through the enemy lines to King Arthur's tent."

Isolde kept speaking, laying out, piece by piece, all she'd both guessed and Seen of that night eight years before. The whole of the prison that Trystan had carried inside for all these years since: his journey to Arthur. The answer Arthur had given Marche. And the battle that had followed: Modred's army defeated, both Arthur and Modred slain.

For a long moment after she'd done, Marche sat and stared at her. Unblinking. Unmoving. Finally, he said, "You know the whole." And then, with no change of expression, no emotion, "I hated him from the moment his whey-faced, drooping-papped bitch of a mother first laid him in my arms." He gave a harsh, grating laugh. "And now I owe him my life."

Isolde didn't move. She knew she hadn't moved, because through the momentary blurring of her vision, she could see her own hands, still clenched on her lap. When the blood had come back to her heart, she said, "You've seen Trystan?"

Marche sat staring at her for the space of another endless pause. Isolde could almost read the internal struggle behind the flatness of his gaze. On the one hand, the festering desire to deny all knowledge of Trystan; to make her suffer as he now suffered, if for a different cause. On the other, the risk he would take that she would simply leave, tell Madoc he lied—and deny him his revenge on Octa of Kent.

Revenge won. He might hate her, but at this moment he hated Octa far more. Marche said, in the same flat tone, "We met. We fought. And he won. He had me at his mercy. He could have taken my head off with one blow. Instead he spared my life."

Isolde felt as though something inside her were falling. She said, "Trystan's nothing like you. He never has been. Or—" She remembered the visions she'd glimpsed of Marche. The brief flashes where she'd read the thoughts of a man for whom rage was the only protection against gnawing pain and fear. Her lips felt stiff, but she said, eyes on Marche's, "Or maybe he is. Maybe he's like the man you might have been. If you'd taken a different path."

"If I'd taken a different path." Marche gave another caustic laugh. "If it had been up to me, I would have had him drowned at birth. Would have killed him at Camlann—or any other time before or since—and felt less than if I'd wrung a kitten's neck. And yet somehow"—just for a moment, the immobility of Marche's face cracked again, muscles jumping, mouth working as before—"yet he's grown into the kind of man of whom a father, any father, might be proud."

Marche stopped and the look was gone, anger replacing whatever else had stirred at the back of his dark gaze. "No, Lady Isolde. I am not, nor ever could have been, anything like him." His jaw worked. And then he ground out, "You can perhaps see why I choose to meet my own death—on my own terms—over living indebted to him."

THE NIGHT WAS MOONLESS, THE DARKENED sky hazy with cloud. Trystan lay in the grass, watching the flickering glow of camp fires on the opposite side of the valley, blazing out through the humid air that had cooled only slightly when the sun had gone down. Octa's fires. Octa's camp, where doubtless Octa and his warriors were smearing themselves with the blood of sacrificed goats and getting themselves pissing drunk in readiness for the battle to come. He could hear the call of their war drums from here.

At first the noise was only a vague irritation, but then the steady thud started to beat on the blankness of his mind, rousing him to resume the mental roster of steps that had carried him here, the list of tasks that remained. The two days' journey from Ynys Witrin—with what supplies had been pillaged from the fortress—made, in company with Cynric and his warriors. Not all had been well enough to make the march; some stragglers were still coming in, others had been left behind. But most were in fit enough shape to travel and to fight.

He could hear their occasional grunts and rustles now, as they lay sprawled all around him on the ground, asleep.

The beating war drum went on.

Cynric and his warriors were free. They'd made it back here, to where Madoc and Octa's armies were now encamped. Madoc's scouts had been found and sent back to their king with a message. Isolde was . . .

Trystan threw an arm up across his eyes. Heard in the incessant god-cursed drumbeats and Saxon war songs an echo of Cath's parting words. *You're sure that's what you want?*

Now there were no tasks that remained. Nothing left to be done. Trystan shifted, stared at the winking fires on the opposite hill, willing them not to turn into a memory of Marche's face.

One night more.

TALIESIN WAS PLAYING. THE SAME SONG he'd played before, the one of Camlann. Isolde stood at the edge of the fort's central square, in which a great bonfire blazed, and listened to the music that seemed to wrap around her, a part, almost, of the hot summer night and the hazy, eerily glowing sky above.

> *Men went to Camlann with the dawn.*
> *Their bravery cut short their lives.*
> *They stained their spears, splashed with blood.*

Madoc had ordered the remaining goats and sheep slaughtered so that tonight there might be roasted meat for all; had ordered the last of the ale barrels opened, the last skins of wine poured. Now, all about her, the folk of the hill fort, refugees and warriors alike, were eating, sharing cups of ale, even dancing, swirling in and out of the patches of shadow cast by the bonfire's leaping flames. Some of the warriors beat in time to Taliesin's song on their shields. Children shrieked and darted between their elders' legs at a game of chase, or—Isolde almost managed to smile at the sight of Rhun among these—sparred amongst themselves with sticks or wooden swords.

Even a handful of the wounded, those who could hobble or walk, had come out from the infirmary hall to stand as Isolde did on the edges of the crowd.

"Not eating?" Beside her, Kian was tearing into a haunch of roasted mutton with the fierce concentration of a man who'd been drilling with warriors all day and had taken small time to rest, much less eat. The bonfire's glow flickered over his craggy face and gleamed in his dark eye.

Hereric, Eurig, and Cath were there as well, like Kian weary and sweat-stained after a day's labors—and, like Kian, busy with platters of meat and horns of ale.

Isolde shook her head in answer to Kian. "I'm all right."

Men went to Camlann with the dawn.
Quicker to a field of blood
Than to a wedding.

Camlann again. Isolde saw in her mind's eye the tiny hut in which Marche now sat prisoner, bound hand and foot and staked to the ground.

"You were my father's man—his strongest ally," she'd said to him that afternoon. "But the night before Camlann, you turned on him. Betrayed your oath of allegiance and turned to King Arthur's side."

Until then, Marche had listened in unblinking silence, but at that, the hard mask had briefly shattered. His jaw worked, his mouth twisting in a spasm that might have been fury or pain, and his eyes blazed. "Your father—"

Only two words, spat out like bitter poison. And yet in them Isolde caught a glimpse as real and vivid as any she'd glimpsed through the Sight. She saw a man whose spurned love had turned to bitter hate. Whose rejected devotion had festered, spread, and de-stroyed all he touched. Her father—Britain—and himself, most of all. And now he was like a walking corpse. Drinking cup after cup of ale without ever quenching the burning thirst or even finding the peace of oblivion he sought. Eating and tasting nothing but gray ash. Because he'd not seen that when he betrayed Modred, his lord, on the fields of Camlann—killed him as surely as though he'd loosed an arrow at his heart—he'd also killed himself.

Now she saw Kian and the other three men exchange a look, and then Kian said, "Trystan'll have succeeded by now. Bound to have done. If he set out to free Cynric of Wessex, he'll have done it."

Isolde stared at the fire, the rest of her talk with Marche coming back in a sickening rush. All the truth that had lain buried for eight years.

She nodded, though. She wouldn't grant Marche the victory of telling anyone else. And Kian and the other three knew as well as she did the ways in which Britain's luck might yet fail. If Cynric and his warriors had been killed by Octa after all. If they couldn't reach the hill fort in time to join their spears and swords with Madoc's in the next day's battle. And even if they could, even if they did—

They were going to plunge headlong into the great, gaping maw of battle in less than a single night's time. Madoc and Cerdic and all their forces. Cath and Kian and Eurig. Trystan.

She could see in every leaping spark cast by the fire the broken bodies of all the battle-wounded men she'd ever treated. Every man she'd saved, every man she'd failed to save. Torn muscles and shattered ribs and jagged holes ripped in—

Cath cleared his throat. "If we all—" he started to say, but Isolde stopped him before he could finish.

"No. Please." Her voice wavered and she had to wait a moment before she could trust herself to go on. "This isn't a night for *ifs.*" She paused again, pushing the bloody pictures in her mind far, far back. "Tell me what you're going to do when the battle's over. When you're free to go where you like, do as you choose."

She thought Cath gave her a long look, as though he were sorry for her, or as though there were something he could tell her, and was debating whether to say. But then his familiar smile gleamed white in the shadows. "Right you are. Though if you think I've the nerve to say I'm going to do anything but get home to my wife and young 'uns when this here is all over, you've a better opinion of my courage than I do. And no use saying Glenda wouldn't hear of it, either. A wife always does." But his smile had changed and softened even at the mention of his wife's name.

Isolde said, unsteadily, "You're not oath-sworn to Madoc. You could go now."

Longing crossed Cath's eyes. But he shook his head. "Lot of good that would do if Octa's men win tomorrow and come pouring over the countryside, destroying everything in sight." He shook his head again. "No. I'll fight. And then I'll go back to my wife, tell my daughter and little lad that their da' hadn't thought to ever raise a sword again. But that he fought for them in a great battle—for them and to keep Britain free."

Cath stopped. "And that's enough about me, I reckon." He turned to Eurig. "What about you? Got plans for when all this is done?"

Eurig's round, homely face flushed slightly at the question. He'd been quiet until now, as he always was in a group—so quiet it was easy to almost forget he was there. Isolde remembered him telling her months ago, though, in a rare burst when he'd spoken freely of himself, that he'd had a wife, once, and a son. And lost both. Now she stood, blinking against the sting of the wood smoke and tears that kept threatening, waiting to hear what he'd say.

"Not plans, exactly," he said at last. "But I had thought that if—" He glanced at Isolde and checked himself. "That when I'd done with fighting I'd become a priest."

"A priest? Wearing a black robe and a cross o' the Christ?" Cath snorted, beard splitting in another grin as he tapped Eurig's bald skull. "Well, you'll not have to shave your head, at any rate. Got that part of it already down."

Eurig directed a good-natured jab at Cath's middle, and Cath doubled over in mock agony. Then he sobered, giving Eurig a curious glance. "You really mean it, then? Didn't even know you were a Christian."

Eurig flushed again, ducking his head. "Aye, well. A man's got to believe in something. And—" He stopped, as though searching for words. "A wife, a family—all you said you've got to go back to . . ." He looked at Cath. "Well, it's something that once you've had it—and had it perfect—you . . . well, you don't want it again. At least I . . ."

He stopped and exhaled, a soft burst of air. "Well, anyway"—he raised his head and looked from Isolde to the other three—"I've thought, times, that it'd be good to live for peace, not war, for a change. Feed the hungry, comfort the sick instead of training day in and out to carve men up with a sword or spear." Eurig rubbed at the back of his neck. "So that's why I'd thought to become a priest."

"You would—" Isolde stopped. "You'll make a good one." She

blinked hard again, then turned to Kian. "And what about you? You told me, once, that if you could, you'd buy a piece of land. Enough to raise a few crops and build a settle home. Is that what you'd choose still?"

Kian shrugged. He'd taken one of his little carvings—a badger—out of his scrip and begun taking off minuscule flecks of wood to create the animal's bushy tail. "It's a nice thought. But then so's a lot things. Like serving your king and dying with your boots on." He paused, squinting at the small carving a moment, then raised his gaze to Isolde. He gave her a long, searching look, his single eye dark on hers. Then finally he said, "Tell you one thing, though. If—*when* I see Trystan again, I'm going to kick his arse from here to Gwynedd for going off on his own like this and leaving you waiting and all the rest of us behind."

Taliesin's song had ended. Slowly, the talking, the laughter and noise died away into an expectant silence. A lone warrior beat a last, wild tattoo on his shield with the butt of his sword. And as though the sound had been a summons, a figure—Madoc—stepped out of the crowd. He wore a white cloak and a gleaming war helmet that caught and held the light of the fire's blaze. His sword hung at his side, and the gold torque of kingship shone about his brow. He raised his arms.

"We heard tonight of Camlann." Madoc's voice rang out. A warrior's voice, rough and a little harsh, and yet somehow no less a part of the still air and the warmth of a moonless summer night than Taliesin's song. "When Arthur, hope of Britain, fell. But I say to you tonight that our hope is not ended." Madoc's voice rose. "An hour ago, I received word from one of my scouts. Trystan, grandson of Cerdic of Wessex, has succeeded in locating and rescuing Prince Cynric and the other captive men. They are now camped within sight of the hill fort. And they fight tomorrow at our side."

A stir went round the croud. Exclamations, murmurs of wonder or approval. Cerdic had been standing amidst his bodyguard near the bonfire, the light gleaming on the golden caps of his braided white hair, the gold at his neck, the heavy brooch that fastened his cloak. For a moment, Isolde saw his face go slack with relief, but it was only a moment, the space of an indrawn breath, no more. The next he had straightened his shoulders and was once again stern and statue-proud.

Madoc was still speaking, though Isolde scarcely heard through the gray dizziness that had struck at first mention of Trystan's name.

"So I say to you tonight"—Madoc's voice rang out across the fortress yard—"I say that Arthur's not yet gone. He lives! So long as there are those willing to raise their swords—as I ask you here tonight to raise yours now—for Britain!"

He ended on a shout, drawing his own sword and swinging it above his head in a gleaming arc, firelight dancing off the blade.

For Britain! For Britain!

The cry was taken up by a swell of other voices, as, all around the glowing circle of firelight, men raised their swords and spears. Isolde, looking towards the cramped, tiny storage hut on the opposite side of the fortress, wondered what Marche thought, hearing the words.

Old men and young, men with pocked skin, men whose faces bore the marks of battle scars, warriors with grizzled beards and broken teeth, spearmen with gleaming bronze bands about powerful arms. Taliesin, stood beside Madoc at the fire, gilt-edged harp still clasped in his plump hands, the smoldering, mocking bitterness of his eyes and mouth still a jarring contrast to the pure, crystal notes of his song.

Isolde glanced at the men grouped about her: Kian, grim and craggy-featured, with the leather patch covering one eye. Cath, black-bearded and towering over the men around him by a head and more. Eurig and Daka and Piye. Hereric, solid and broad, the empty left sleeve of his shirt pinned up, and Rhun—changed out of recognition, almost, from the silent, white-faced boy Isolde had seen first at Caer Peris—laughing and clinging to the big man's good hand.

Further from the fire, on the fringes of the crowd, were clustered the women and children of the fort. Camp followers and cooks, washerwomen and petty kings' wives. Boys looking yearningly towards the swords and shields of the warriors. Babies still nursing at the breast in their mother's arms, oblivious of noise, crowds, and all.

Isolde saw them with unnatural clarity, almost the same sparkling clarity of a flash of the Sight. And then the firelit faces, the sights around her began to blur together through the tears that gathered in her eyes. Taliesin started to play again, though she barely caught the words.

> For he who searches for enlightenment
> Shall find confusion
> He who seeks to slay another
> Shall slay himself
> He who travels to the deepest reaches of the underworld
> Shall find heaven
> He who has lost his soul and cannot save himself
> Shall save us all.

It was with a start of surprise that Isolde realized that Madoc had left his place before the crowd and come to stand beside her.

"Lord Madoc." Kian and the other men were absorbed in the music, and Isolde drew a little away from them, towards Madoc, into the comparative shadow at the edge of the crowd. "You spoke well tonight."

Madoc's helmet was gone, his dark head bare, and he gave her a smile that was part wry, part a little sad, and part something that Isolde could not quite name, his gaze straying back to where Taliesin still played.

"Perhaps even lies have their place, if they give hope where there would otherwise be none." Madoc rubbed his forehead as though it ached. "God knows we all of us need hope tonight." He was silent, then turned towards the storage hut, where two of his men still stood guard on Marche—building and men alike just vague, shadowed shapes in the darkness beyond the reach of the bonfire's light. "If what he told you is true—"

"It was." Isolde saw Marche's face, heard the harsh echo of his voice in her ears. *The attack from the south is a feint. The main body of Octa's forces*—Marche's mouth had twisted—*and mine, will be massed to the north, waiting to cut Britain's armies down from behind as soon as they ride out from the fort.*

"It was true," she said again. "I'm sure of it."

Madoc nodded, scarred face at once weary and implacable in the shifting orange light. "Then it will be for tomorrow at dawn." He stopped, seeming to hesitate. Then: "Trystan's message was that he would fight with Cerdic's men when the battle begins."

Isolde watched the flames leaping towards the clouded, moonless sky. The shooting sparks and embers and flakes of black ash that drifted on hot air out over the now laughing, feasting crowds.

All the men in her infirmary. Torn muscles and shattered ribs and jagged holes ripped in skulls . . .

The last of the roasted goats had been carried out; beneath the tang of wood smoke the air was rich with the scent of the freshly cooked meat. Isolde watched Rhun tearing into the portion Hereric had gotten him, firelight gleaming on his small greasy hands and rounded cheeks. She said, finally, "I would have expected nothing else."

She was still watching the children, though she could feel Madoc's gaze on her. He said, quietly, "I'm sorry, Lady Isolde. Whatever his past, he seems a brave man, a good man. And God knows that tonight both I and Britain owe him more than can be easily repaid." He stopped again, then said, in a different tone, "And I know that he . . . that you and he . . ." Madoc cleared his throat. "If Trystan—"

Isolde pressed her eyes tight shut. What could she do? She couldn't scream. She couldn't ride out from the hill fort and demand that the fighting stop. Pointless even to wish or hope that Marche might be made to suffer for all he had done.

Isolde turned to Madoc, whose eyes now held the same raw vulnerability they'd held once before.

She said, "You're a good man, too, Lord Madoc. But don't. Please," she said again. "It's not a night for *ifs*."

Chapter 19

B LACK FLAKES OF ASH FROM the night's bonfire blew in Isolde's face as she crossed the fort's central square towards the stables and storage huts. A wind had sprung up during the night—a cool, ominous wind, damp with the promise of another approaching storm—and the dawn sky was leaden, heavy with low-hanging clouds.

Nothing remained of the night's feast save ashes, empty barrels of mead, and a scattering of gnawed bones on the muddied ground. The womenfolk—servants and wives and refugees—crossed to and fro, clearing up, gathering rubbish into heaps. But the men were gone. Silently and in the hour before first light, Madoc and the other kings of the council had led every able-bodied man, warriors and common folk alike, through the fortress gate to mass behind the outermost earthen ramparts for the battle to come.

Isolde had been there, at Cerdic's request, to buckle on his sword, help him on with a gleaming war helmet of iron and bronze. He had no queen, he said, and so she must perform the duty of arming the king for war. She'd knelt before Cerdic on the ground, fastening the heavy, jeweled sword belt about his waist as the other noblewomen had done for their men. And Cerdic had raised her to her feet, kissed her formally on both cheeks. The kiss of kinsman to kinswoman, and Isolde thought he might have been recalling their last talk outside the council hall. Though he'd said, only, "I thank you, Lady Isolde. And vow to do you honor on the field of battle today."

And above the broad cheek pieces of the helmet, his blue eyes had been hard and glittering, already lost in the fighting to come—and so like Trystan's that Isolde's heart had squeezed painfully tight.

She'd moved among the rest of Cerdic's army, then, and among Madoc's men, too, granting the requests of any who asked that she touch swords, spears, breastplates—or the charms of protection sewn into boot tops or cloaks—for luck. It still brought a strange feeling that so many men should want her to, that so many warriors should think that a touch, a word or two from her should have the same protective power of one of their Christ's crosses or rowan twigs. But if it gave confidence to any, she was more than willing to oblige.

Many of the men had looked at her with wondering speculation, or sometimes even sympathy, in their eyes. After the last meeting of the council, it had been impossible to keep secret where Trystan had gone. Or who he was. And word of the juggler who'd come to tell a tale for the Lady Isolde—and then proved to be grandson of Cerdic of Wessex—had spread like sea mist about the hill fort.

Isolde had bidden Cath and Kian and Eurig good-bye. Dry-eyed, because she'd let herself cry in the darkest hours after the feasting, so that she could see them off to battle and manage to smile. Now they were gone. And the very air currents about the great hill fort seemed to hold the same ominous, expectant promise of the storm clouds above.

Beside Isolde, Hereric touched her arm, and, broad brow furrowed in concern, made a rapid series of signs. *Not worry . . . Trystan be safe . . . come back . . .*

Isolde had told him the full truth of the news Madoc had brought her: that Trystan had succeeded in freeing Cynric and the other warriors and would fight with them today. She hadn't planned to—Hereric surely had enough cause for fear in knowing that Kian and the other men would take their places in Madoc's shield wall today. But he'd asked her in finger signs the night before whether there was any word of Trystan—with such pure, unwavering trust in his blue eyes that it had seemed like the basest insult not to share with him what she knew. From Madoc, at least. Neither Hereric nor anyone else knew of her meeting with Marche the day before.

"You sent Trystan, your son, to make the trip across enemy

territory and into Arthur's camp," she had said. "He might have been killed a dozen different ways. But you wouldn't have cared for that. Only that he delivered the message you sent."

And Marche had said, with a curl of his lip, "The Witch of Camelerd sees all."

But at least she needn't have worried for Hereric's peace of mind. Since she'd told him that Trystan would fight with the rest, the big man had shown not the smallest flicker of uncertainty or fear. Nothing but absolute confidence that Britain's forces would triumph and that Trystan and all the others would come through the fighting unharmed.

She was the one who kept misreading Hereric's gestures this morning, lagging so far behind in the translation that she caught only every other sign, because her own attention felt stretched tight as a drawn bowstring. She was only partially aware of the ashes and remnants of feasting around them; the rest of her awareness reached outwards, beyond the fortress walls, to imagine every soldier's movement, every smallest step towards—

Isolde broke off her thoughts with a feeling as though she'd been asleep and jolted awake by a kick in the chest. She and Hereric had been crossing the fortress towards Marche's prison cell. She'd been dreading facing him again, this morning of all mornings. But since she'd watched the gray dawn break over the ramparts as Madoc and Cerdic the rest of their leather-garbed armies made their silent departure for war, she'd felt overwhelmingly that she must go. She had to look into his eyes one more time, at least, and assure herself that he had spoken the truth about Oca's battle plans. Assure herself once more that her advice to Madoc, that he take Marche's word, wasn't going to lead Britain's troops straight into a death trap in an hour's time.

Now, though, any thought or question of facing Marche was sickeningly, obscenely beside the point. The guards outside the storage hut were gone—as Isolde had expected, with every man needed in the shield wall being formed outside. But the door to the shed was unbolted and ajar, swinging on its hinges in the rising wind. It was barely an hour past dawn, the ominous clouds hiding any trace of the rising sun, but there was enough gray light to see the whole of the shed's cramped interior: completely empty, save for a woman's crumpled body lying on the beaten earth floor.

Marche was gone.

After the first instant's stunned disbelief, Isolde crossed the remaining distance at a run and dropped to kneel beside the woman who lay sprawled facedown on the ground. She was one of the younger serving maids. Bethan . . . Betrys . . .

Blodwen, that was it. Isolde's mind cast about for and then found the name, her own heart racing as she turned the lolling head and felt quickly for a pulse in the serving maid's neck.

Blodwen. A plump, fair-haired young woman of maybe Isolde's own age, with a round, rosy-cheeked face, a scattering of freckles across a turned-up nose, and a mouth that had a trick of dropping open over her small white teeth. She'd lent a hand in the infirmary once or twice, and been cheerful and friendly, always, with a wink and a teasing word for each of the wounded men.

Now Blodwen had an ugly, purple swelling over one eye, nearly the size of a baby's fist. Her pulse was strong, and there were no other injuries that Isolde could find, but her dress—Isolde saw with a sick lurch of her stomach as she turned Blodwen's body over—had been torn open down the front, baring her breasts.

Blodwen shifted and moaned, and Isolde quickly pulled the torn fabric up to cover her as Hereric came to stand in the open door. Hereric's broad face was shocked, eyes puckered with alarm.

He gestured to Blodwen. *Marche*—Isolde thought the literal signs Hereric used meant *bad man*, but the import was clear—*hurt her?*

Isolde told herself savagely that she was not going to be sick. Not when Madoc had to be warned of Marche's escape. Not when at any moment Blodwen might regain consciousness.

Even as Isolde thought it, Blodwen's stubby-lashed eyelids flickered and bleary hazel eyes stared uncomprehendingly and without a trace of recognition into hers. And then, remembrance must have rushed in, because Blodwen's lips opened and she began to scream, harsh, tearing cries that rent the dawn hush of the half emptied fort.

"Shhh, you're safe. He's gone now. You're safe." Isolde put a hand on Blodwen's arm. Hereric, too, had dropped to kneel on the ground, his broad face still creased with worry, and it was to Hereric that Blodwen turned first, staring at him with the same blankly uncomprehending gaze. Then her face crumpled and she started to cry.

Hereric reached for her, his big, callused hand stroking her hair as he might have a child's, or the mane of one of the horses in his care. Isolde would have expected Blodwen to be frightened at a huge, one-armed Saxon man touching her so soon after whatever Marche had done. But maybe Blodwen recognized instinctively in Hereric whatever Rhun always had, because she clung to him, face hidden against his shoulder. And Hereric showed no surprise, only stroked her hair, rubbed her arm in slow, comforting circles, as though she truly were a panicked war mount.

Slowly, Blodwen's sobs died away to hiccuping gulps, and she sat up, rubbing red, swollen eyes as she turned back to Isolde. "Lady— it's my fault. My fault he got away. I should have—"

"Hush." Isolde stopped her. "Don't say that. Don't even think it. It's not your fault." She willed her voice to stay quiet, gentle and calm. "Can you tell me what happened? Did Marche—"

She had to stop. But Blodwen understood and scrubbed a hand once more across her eyes. "No. Not for want of trying. But he didn't do anything but tear my dress." Her voice was still uneven with crying, but her jaw hardened as she pulled the ragged edges of fabric at her breast more tightly closed. "I kneed him in the bollocks as hard as I could, then he heard something outside and settled for clouting me with his fist instead." Gingerly, she reached to touch the swelling lump on her forehead, wincing as her fingers connected with the bruised flesh. "Last I remember is seeing him turn and make off through the door."

Isolde drew breath, a stone weight lifting from her chest. That had been the worst of the nightmare into which she felt she'd suddenly been plunged—having to live with the knowledge that another woman had suffered what she had the year before because she'd asked Madoc to keep Marche prisoner rather than kill him at once.

Blodwen was still speaking, more easily now, though a shiver shook her as her gaze turned distant, lost in what had happened before. "King Madoc had given the order that Marche was to be fed.

So I got some bread and cheese and ale to bring him, after all the men rode out." She gestured, and for the first time Isolde noticed a wooden tray on the floor near the far wall, bread trampled into the mud, ale pot overturned. "He was . . ." Blodwen swallowed. "He was supposed to be tied up. But as soon as I opened the door he was up and on me and—"

She stopped, and Hereric laid a comforting hand on her arm.

Isolde's eyes went to the corner of the room, where the stakes to which Marche's bonds had been tied lay uprooted from the earthen floor. The rains must have softened the ground enough for Marche to wrench them free. Although—

Beside the stakes, the leather thongs that had bound Marche's hands and feet lay where he must have flung them off, and even in this gray, early light Isolde could see the deep russet color stains that marked each one. Softened ground or no, Marche must have torn both his wrists and ankles bloody with the effort to get free.

For what?

The sickness came back in a rush. She'd gotten the truth about Trystan. About Camlann. But Marche had escaped. And that meant that he'd either lied in what he'd told her of Octa's battle plans or that he was now planning to betray Britain once again and to approach Octa with what information he could sell.

Isolde turned to Hereric. "We have to get word to Madoc. We have to warn him."

And then she heard it. From outside the fortress walls. A blast of a war horn, followed by the roar of hundreds of voices, screaming insults, orders, war cries.

The battle had begun.

Isolde didn't even realize she'd swayed where she knelt until Hereric released Blodwen and put a hand on her shoulder. *Isolde . . .* She had no idea what else he signed, but she forced the pounding darkness, the roaring in her ears back, biting her lip until she tasted blood, until finally her vision cleared.

Too late. Too late to warn Madoc or Cerdic or any of the men who fought with them today. Too late to send searchers after Marche, even if there'd been any fighting men for her to send. *Too late for Trystan.*

"Hereric." Her voice still worked, even if the effort of forming words seemed almost unendurably hard. "Hereric, take care of Blodwen. See she lies down and has something to eat and drink. And then bring me some water—a basin, a pan, anything will do. Just bring it here. Please."

ISOLDE KNELT BY THE COPPER BASIN Hereric had brought her, staring at the waters until her eyes felt scorched, until every muscle in her body shook and her skin was clammy with sweat. She'd pricked her finger on the brooch that fastened the shoulder of her gown, added drops of both blood and sweet oil, though she'd no idea what difference in power—if any—that made. Outside the fortress walls, she could hear the impossibly loud roar of battle: screaming horses and shouting men, clashing shields and swords, loud as the end of the world, an echo of the frantic clamor in her own mind.

Her heart was colder than it had ever felt in her life, and just now she'd have prayed to anything—the voice of the hill fort, her grandmother, the God of the Christ—that if there were a veil between the Otherworld of Morgan's stories and this, it would lift for her here, today.

The blast of a war horn sounded outside, the noise running up Isolde's spine. Impossible to know whether the sound signaled retreat or advance. Impossible to know whether the tide of battle was running for Britain's forces or for Octa of Kent's.

Isolde shut her burning eyes, trying to block out the fear that hissed and crackled through her like flame through dry leaves.

"It was raining," she whispered, "the night before Camlann." She'd sat in this tiny, ill-lit room and spoken the same words once before—to Marche, as an accusation, a confirmation of all she'd guessed of what lay between him and Trystan. Now she kept her eyes shut and talked to the baby, that tiny part of Trystan she held safe inside her, and hoped with desperate intensity that somehow Trystan, too, might hear.

"Hard, driving rain that put out the watch fires and turned the fields into an ooze of black mud. And Marche of Cornwall sent Trystan—his own son—to make the trip across enemy territory and into Arthur's camp. He might have been killed a dozen different ways. But Marche wouldn't have cared for that. Only that he delivered the message Marche had sent. A message to King Arthur."

Isolde stopped, seeing the scene as Marche had described it, and as she'd glimpsed it through Trystan's eyes. The king's war tent, sagging under the relentless hiss of the rain. The guards outside, shivering and hunched in their cloaks. Trystan standing before King Arthur, handing him a tightly rolled square of parchment.

"I don't know what Marche had told Trystan. Not for sure. But I think Marche promised that what Trystan carried was a message from my father to Arthur, suing for peace. That if he succeeded in getting through to King Arthur's camp there could be an end to war without more bloodshed. He might—" Isolde drew a breath, this time seeing again the look in Trystan's eyes that night in the orchard in Caer Peris, when he'd spoken of his mother's death on the very day of Camlann. "King Marche might even have told Trystan to carry out the mission for his mother's sake, promised that if Trystan obeyed orders that night, Marche would let her go free, back to her father, King Cerdic."

A tug. The tiniest tightening about Isolde's heart, like those first fluttering kicks of the baby. But it was enough to make her open her eyes and, heart racing, look into the scrying waters one last time. As something beneath the surface moved, flickered, stirred, and . . .

If the fury of the battle outside had been stomach-clenchingly loud before, the sound now grew, swelled, pounded through Isolde's body until it felt as though she were tossed and pummeled by rocks in a mountain stream, as though her very bones would shake apart with the roar.

The vision in the scrying waters shimmered, took on form until she could see the battle whose clamor she heard. A maelstrom of bodies and blades, rearing horses and savagely swung axes, spears and bossed leather shields—all churning and seething beneath the leaden sky and low-hanging, sullen clouds.

Isolde saw Octa, face twisted and almost unrecognizable in the furious glee of battle, fighting on horseback beneath the scarlet stallion banner, his sword flashing, his mouth open in an exultant scream. All about him, guarding his flanks and rear, the mail-clad warriors she'd first seen on the cliffs of Caer Peris screamed frenzied curses and fought with a savage joy in the slaughter all about them that would have chilled Isolde if she'd not been too numbed by fear already to feel any colder.

She saw Cerdic, iron and bronze helmet dulled and red with blood, but standing at the forefront of his bodyguard, raising his sword above his head with the strength of a far younger man as he screamed a war cry at Octa's men.

She saw Madoc, too, as though she'd been granted the sight of the Morrigan in the tales, the death-maid goddess who flew over a field of battle in raven form and chose the men who were to fall.

Madoc's shield was painted with the scarlet pendragon of Britain. His scarred face was half hidden by the cheek pieces of his war helmet, and he was shouting orders to the men who formed his shield wall, roaring at them to hold, to fight, though it was plain they were being driven back and back.

Already one wing of Britain's shield wall had broken, the fighting there collapsed into a boiling chaos of screaming wounded, trampled bodies, broken shields and hacking axes and swords. Isolde saw some warriors, all wearing the badge of Cynric of Wessex, standing to fight, others fleeing in panic as Octa's men charged forward, cutting men down in an orgy of killing and blood.

She saw—

Trystan.

In the midst of all that great, devouring tide.

His hair was wet with sweat, his knuckles bloodied, and there was a patch of sticky crimson on the leg of his breeches just below the knee. But he wore his battle face, lean features set, eyes flat and hard as brilliant blue stones as he worked to drag an injured man, one of Cynric's, back from the fighting, towards a slight ridge of higher ground. Then he instantly plunged back into the fighting for another man whose right leg hung in shreds of bloodied muscle and bone.

Isolde sat frozen, watching as Trystan dragged another man to comparative safety, then went back, blocking the blows of axes and swords, lunging and slashing with his own blade. A leather-armored man with a wolf's tail strung on his helmet and a wolf's pelt on his back came at Trystan, blade swinging, and Trystan, without breaking stride, drove his sword hard under the other man's shield. The enemy fell, spitting blood, but then a rider—it had to be one of Marche's former men—loomed up behind him, swinging an already red and dripping blade high as he prepared to strike.

Isolde screamed. She'd no plan, no coherent thoughts at all, only a savage, vehement refusal to allow the sole purpose of this vision the Sight had granted her to be the chance to sit here and watch Trystan die. She screamed a warning, the blood roaring so loudly in her ears that the noise of battle was momentarily dulled. And as the wavering picture in the scrying vessel shimmered and shifted, she saw Trystan . . .

TRYSTAN DUCKED. THE GODS KNEW WHAT made him do it. One moment he was planting a foot on the dead enemy's belly to yank his sword free. The next some heightened awareness, some sharp stab of warning had made him turn and, without any conscious thought at all, spin under the mounted warrior's hacking blade, raising his shield so that the blow that should have taken off his head landed on the metal boss instead. The impact still nearly sent him through the ground, but he kept his footing, lunging upwards with his own weapon and thrusting the tip under the man's guard and into the exposed underbelly of the horse.

The animal reared, screaming in pain, nearly throwing its rider to the ground, then plunged off to the right, into the writhing sea of fighting men.

Trystan raised his shield to meet another onslaught of howling Saxons. Since their line in the shield wall had broken, the battle had turned into welter of death and bloodied, screaming men. Like some devilish replaying of the battle at Camlann. Watching the men around him go down under whirling blades and pounding horses hooves.

Block . . . thrust . . . parry a spear-thrust with his shield. Because he might not mind the thought of dying today. Might even have volunteered to take his place here, amidst Cynric and the rest of the formerly captive men, who, after a month's starvation, had been inevitably the weakest link in Britain's defenses. But damned if he was going to die without a fight. Or without taking as many of the enemy with him as he could. Octa's warriors—and Marche's. The ones on horseback had to be Marche's; save for a select handful, Octa's men fought on foot. And he'd seen any number of the riders' shields with a blue boar that had been hastily obscured by mud or lime wash.

At least Marche hadn't wormed his way back into Octa's favor after Trystan had spared his life.

Trystan parried another blow, knocking his opponent's shield aside—then swore as, some distance up ahead of him, he saw Cynric himself stagger and go down. Cerdic's son had been proving the name he'd won for himself as the best of his father's fighting men. He was a huge, broadly built man of forty-odd, with a braided flaxen beard, a crooked nose, and a ropy scar that ran the length of one powerful arm.

He and Trystan had been dragging back the wounded stranded at the forefront of the fighting when the shield wall had broken. And now—Trystan swore again—now he was down himself, with an enemy's spear lodged in his upper back.

Trystan thrust with the iron boss of his shield, pushing his opponent aside, hacking a path through the shoving, grunting, sweating mass of men towards the spot where he'd seen Cynric fall. At some point a crack, louder even than the clash of shields and swords, sounded overhead, a flash of lightning rent the sky, and the heavens opened in a torrent of rain. But Trystan scarcely noticed, save that the slither of mud made it harder to keep his footing as he fought a way to Cynric's side.

He blocked, ducked, parried blows from axes and spears—and then he was there, hauling Cynric up and backwards, out of the path of another mounted and charging warrior.

Cynric was still alive. The broken-off shaft of the spear was still lodged in his back, just below the collarbone, but he was thrashing around, trying to stand and bellowing like an enraged bull as Trystan's rough handling jarred his wound. God, he was heavy, though. Trystan's boots fought for purchase as he staggered backwards under Cynric's weight, dragging the other man one-handed while with the other arm he raised his shield above their heads to cover them both.

A hail of spear and axe blows thudded on the leather, the rain came down in torrents, soaking them both to the skin, making every step a struggle as Trystan fought against the weight of the clinging mud. Behind them, the ground rose slightly, a position marginally easier to defend, though before they'd crossed even half the distance, one of Octa's warriors loomed up, close enough that Trystan could see the spots of rot on the man's teeth, smell the stench of his breath when he yelled and raised his spear. Trystan braced himself.

Then the man's chest split open in a crimson gush, a sword point emerging through the leather jerkin. He fell, and his killer, a man wearing Madoc of Gwynedd's badge, his leather armor and helmet black and glistening as a seal's pelt with the rain, was climbing over the body to Trystan's side, hefting Cynric so that the Saxon man's weight was divided between him and Trystan.

Madoc's warrior raised his own shield and turned to shout at Trystan, "Keep going, can't you? Going to stand there all day?"

Kian. Rain dripping across the leather patch over his right eye; teeth bared in the grin of a man who'd survived, against all odds, the thick of battle raging on all sides.

Trystan shouldered his part of Cynric's weight, took up the staggering, sliding retreat to higher ground, even as he shouted, above the clash of shields and the noise of the rain, "What in the seven hells do you think you're doing here?"

Kian panted for breath, but his pace didn't falter as they dragged Cynric back between them. "Might ask you the same thing."

Christ on the cross. This was like a replay of Camlann—fighting amidst the bloodied remnants of a broken shield wall, watching the men around him die.

Trystan could see Octa's warriors forming a line, locking their shields together for another charge. Unless a few avenging angels decided to swoop in and lend a hand, they had moments—maybe just heartbeats—left to them.

"You want to get yourself killed?" he shouted at Kian.

Kian's grin widened, single eye gleaming in the storm-gray light, even as he thrust with the boss of his spear, knocking a lone attacker down into the mud and then kicking him savagely in the groin. "I can think of worse ways—and worse days—to die."

Trystan opened his mouth to shout a reply. And then he saw the man. Barely a half dozen paces away.

Wearing stolen armor—had to be, since it was Saxon made.

Iron helmet, mail shirt, round shield.

Marche's face, under the iron helmet's rim.

Marche. Face still battered with the bruises Trystan had given him. His eyes met Trystan's, and he froze.

And then, cutting across the crack of thunder, shouts of warriors, the screams of wounded men, came a blast on a war horn. Trystan's head snapped round. And then he felt a harsh breath of a laugh tear his throat. Not quite God's avenging angels, but maybe close enough.

Cerdic of Wessex, astride a cloud-pale charger. Leading a force of half a hundred screaming men.

ISOLDE'S EVERY MUSCLE SHOOK, AND SHE was drenched with sweat, her heart beating so hard it felt as though it would shatter her ribs. She'd no idea whether she'd helped—no idea whether she'd made any difference at all.

But she'd watched Trystan fighting amidst the driving rain, fighting to drag yet another wounded man back away from the worst of the slaughter. And she'd seen Trystan look up at Octa's re-forming shield wall, at Marche's traitor warriors, and seen in his eyes the look of a man who recognized his own death before him.

By that same sweeping vision—as though she truly had been granted a ravenlike sight of the field of battle, she'd seen, too, Cerdic of Wessex, astride his pale war mount and surrounded by his royal guard, still fighting with the strength of a man half his years. With every fiber in her body, every drop of her blood, with a force Isolde hadn't known she had, she'd willed Cerdic to look up, to turn, to see Trystan and the rest of the stranded men's plight.

By rowan, by ash, by maiden, mother, and crone.

She'd willed it so hard that she'd seemed to stand momentarily in the thick of the battle, smelling the mud and blood and hissing rain.

And just for a moment, she'd thought—almost—that she caught and held Cerdic's gaze.

She'd seen a quicksilver flash, no more, of one last image. Two men, facing each other on a rain-drenched, bloodied field of battle. Trystan and Marche.

And then the waters had gone utterly dark.

Isolde clenched her hands, and to the frantic drumming of her own heart, reached out, willed the edges of her consciousness to blur and dissolve into the pounding rain, the roar of battle outside.

TRYSTAN'S HAND TIGHTENED ON THE RAIN-SLICK hilt of his sword. And Marche froze. He could see Marche's warriors bringing their horses into line behind them, ready to sweep in and cut down any man Octa's happened to leave behind.

Marche's former warriors, with their shields repainted to make them Octa's men.

They were about to be caught in all the bloody mess of a clash between two opposing charges: Cerdic and Octa's armies. Marche's eyes remained locked on his.

Cerdic's war horn sounded again. The rain soaked through the leather of Trystan's armor. Moments—heartbeats—more.

Marche wasn't wounded. Wherever he'd gotten that armor, whatever prank of the gods had brought him here, he'd not been hurt.

The leather sword grip was damply cold on Trystan's palm. Water pelted down the blade. Another chance.

SHE COULDN'T SEE TRYSTAN. ISOLDE KNELT by the scrying waters and knew that she'd never felt so much hate for either the capricious power that governed the Sight. The darting images across the water's surface were a confused jumble: an axe, a hand clenching a sword, a man's screaming mouth or bloodied arm, ribbons of scarlet mingling with the pools of water and mud on the ground. Sometimes a picture flashed as quick as leaping fish and was gone too soon for her to even guess what it had been.

Her throat felt raw, as though she'd been screaming instead of whispering the words she'd repeated again and again. But she could see nothing of Trystan, nothing of Marche.

Suddenly a man charged on horseback, sword raised above his head, war cloak streaming out behind him like a banner. Cerdic led his band of warriors straight at Octa's shield wall. Giving the broken shield wall behind him a chance to re-form. Isolde saw Cerdic's horsemen push through the crush of battle, stabbing down with swords and spears at the enemy crouched behind their wall of shields. Saw the advance of Octa's men waver as men were crippled and killed. Then—

Mother of all the gods. Cold struck Isolde, echoing the clap of thunder outside. A chance spear cast by an unknown, faceless warrior. Nothing more. But it struck Cerdic in the side, in what must have been a gap in his plated armor. Because—time seemed to slow and stretch into eternal moments—Isolde saw his whole body clench in a rictus, then sway and topple from the white stallion's back.

And now time seemed to accelerate, too quickly for Isolde's blurred vision to take in. Cerdic's horse bolted, nostrils flaring, hooves flashing as it leapt across the bodies of crippled and dying men. Octa's warriors were continuing their crushing advance, shields raised. And Cerdic's forces, thrown into confusion by the loss of their leader, had faltered, were being pushed back, towards Madoc's shield wall.

She could see Madoc, bleeding freely from a gash in his side, his face ashy. But he was standing, holding the pendragon shield high above his head to guard against the hail of spears that struck his men.

"Shields!" Isolde heard him shout. "Hold!"

Octa himself was riding at the head of his army, his mouth still stretched in the savage grin of a man who laughs while he kills. Behind him, his men were forming a wedge, a deadly arrow point of shields and swords and spears. And Madoc's line was going to be crushed.

Isolde could see it already written, even in the waters. Britain's forces had barely had time to refortify their own shield wall. And they were still outnumbered.

Camlann all over again. But this time, Britain would be truly wrecked and destroyed, all hope of recovery trampled into the muddied ground.

And then—

He seemed to ride out of nowhere, appearing suddenly from the gray and sheeting rain, mounted on what Isolde knew to be Cerdic's panicked horse. He wore an iron helmet and a coat of gleaming mail, and he rode at a pounding gallop towards the arrow-wedge of Octa's warriors. Behind him, Cerdic's own forces sprang automatically to re-form, as though they believed the rider their king, somehow restored and returned.

The armored warrior rode straight for the very tip of Octa's arrow-wedge and straight for Octa himself. Isolde saw the rider raise his sword and swing it in a whistling arc: she saw the blade slice through Octa's neck as through dry straw; saw Octa's head fall to the ground.

The rider, too, fell, dragged down by the furious axe blows and spear thrusts of Octa's bodyguard. He vanished amidst a sea of furious men, but not before Isolde saw, in the wavering reflection before her, a glimpse of his face.

Iron helmet, mail shirt, round shield. Marche's face, under the iron helmet's rim.

Chapter 20

THE RAIN HAD FINALLY STOPPED during the night. Isolde stood in the infirmary tent that had been hastily erected beside the field of battle and, grateful for even a momentary excuse not to move, watched the glow of dawn breaking, turning the hills in the east to pale gold and the sky to rose. Soon, maybe even tonight, there would be time for feasting, for toasts of mead and ale to celebrate Britain's victory and Octa's defeat. But for now, on the edge of this bloodied field, the wounds were too raw, the win too new, for joy. The faces around Isolde—those who worked, as she did, to tend the wounded and clear away the dead—looked as dazed and exhausted as she felt.

At the far end of the tent, Cerdic of Wessex lay under his ermine-trimmed war cloak, sculptured face as proud and dignified in death as ever in life. Isolde had wept for him. But not for long. *I had rather choose my own time to die*, Cerdic had said. And just at the last, after he'd been carried into the infirmary tent, still bleeding from the wound in his side, he'd looked up at Isolde and smiled.

"I knew . . . you'd help me," he had whispered on an unsteady breath that might almost have been a laugh.

Perhaps she had.

Isolde turned away from the sunrise, went to clean and stitch the wounds and set the bones of a dozen more injured men. She stopped as she came to the body of another man who lay, unnoticed and almost pushed aside, on the very edge of the tent.

The stolen Saxon armor had been stripped away, looted by the victorious warriors who had stormed over the field after Octa fell and Octa's line irretrievably scattered and broke. A spear point was lodged in his chest, and blood from a dozen wounds and more had soaked his clothing. But his face, save for bruises, was almost untouched.

Isolde stood still, looking down at the thinning gray hair, matted now with blood, the heavy jaw and closed eyes. Already the whispers were spreading like fire amongst the victorious warriors, the injured men, the refugees from the hill fort alike. Stories of King Arthur, returning from his sleep on the Glass Isle to lead a final, desperate charge and strike off Octa's head with one blow of his faerie-forged sword.

Well, why not? She might, Isolde thought, be the only one who knew the truth. And she had no reason to tell what she knew.

Isolde moved to cross Marche of Cornwall's hands at his breast and thought of Blodwen's story, of her bruises and torn dress. She'd told Trystan once that Marche wasn't quite monster enough not to be revolted by what he'd become. But his face now, looked peaceful, even despite the bruises, despite the streaks of mud and blood. More peaceful that she'd ever have believed it could look in life. As though he'd been man and monster, both, and in death the monster had finally gone.

Isolde lifted a fold of his tattered cloak to cover Marche's face, and was struck with a vision of her grandmother's face. The most vivid by far she'd ever seen, so clear Isolde could almost believe she would touch Morgan's solid flesh if she put out her hand.

Mother Berthildis was there, as well. And real or no, Isolde knew with a bone-deep certainty that if there were an Otherworld—a world of the old tales, where time was an endless curve, where Morgan would heal Arthur's wounds and Marche of Cornwall might be transformed into King Arthur returned—if there were such a place hidden beyond a whisper-thin veil, then Mother Berthildis now walked there. With Morgan.

And Marche?

Mother Berthildis's face was as yellow, as wrinkled and toadlike as ever it had been while the abbess was alive. But Isolde smiled just a bit as she let the fold of cloak fall across Marche's death-still face.

You were right about forgiveness. I don't know whether I had to forgive Marche. But I'm glad, now, that I have.

Something made Isolde turn. Madoc was watching her from across the tent with utterly drained, pain-dark eyes.

Isolde forgot Marche, forgot the battle, forgot everything as she watched Madoc slowly cross to stand at her side. As though her own voice were nothing but an echo from a long, long way off, she heard herself say, "Trystan?"

And then she might as well have stepped from her own body and into Madoc's. Her whole body was numb, hollow, emptied out. An empty shell. Nothing inside left to feel. The pity on Madoc's face was far more sharp, far more real than anything of her own.

"I'm sorry, Lady Isolde. He was wounded. Fatally so."

She didn't scream, didn't faint, didn't cry. She stood, still breathing, heart beating in the barren wasteland inside.

"How can I . . ." Mingled pain and exhaustion and pity darkened Madoc's gaze. "Can I do anything for you?"

Isolde shut her eyes. She wasn't empty. There was a life inside her that grew by the day and would soon be apparent even to male eyes.

She thought of a promise she'd made that small, beating life weeks before. Then she looked up at Madoc, a distant spasm twisting through her as she remembered saying almost these same words to Trystan, on a night at the abbey when she'd reached him even in the depth of unconsciousness and pulled him back to her from death to life.

She swallowed the raw ache in her throat. Met Madoc's eyes. "You can marry me," she said.

ISOLDE STOOD AT THE END OF the path that led to the Caer Peris harbor.

It was all over: the endless meetings of the king's council, the forging of treaties, re-forming of boundaries and alliances. Both Meurig of Gwent and Cynlas of Rhos had returned when word of Britain's victory spread. Meurig brazenly, Cynlas with a naked look of shame in his eyes.

Eormenric, son of Octa, was to rule Kent. Cynric, Cerdic's son, would take his father's place on the Wessex throne. No chance, even with the recent victory, of pushing the Saxons back to the eastern shore, back across the sea to the lands from which they'd come, as Arthur had once promised, years before. But the lands Britain yet held in the west were to remain secure. And when Isolde had asked Madoc whether he thought the treaty forged by the council would last, he had shrugged and said, "Eormenric and Cynric are not the men their fathers were. Which may be no bad thing; the peace made here stands a chance of holding, at least."

Madoc. That was all behind her, as well: the betrothal and hand-fasting ceremonies to Britain's High King, both great affairs with huge trenchers of food and caskets of ale, gifts exchanges and prayers from Madoc's priests. Madoc in ermine-trimmed tunic and cloak, a heavy bronze torque about his neck and the gold circlet of kingship about his brow. Herself in a saffron-dyed gown stiff with gold embroidery, hair caught back with gold and garnet fillet cast in a twining pattern of flowers and vines.

All as unlike the handfasting Isolde had sworn to Trystan as could be imagined; that had made it easier to get through.

And now she stood here, at the mouth of the Caer Peris harbor, the sinking sun setting the water afire and turning the heavy walls of the fortress behind her to red-gold. Isolde's heart was beating unsteadily, and she had to hold tight to a fold of her cloak to keep her hands from shaking.

Kian and Eurig had come with her as far as the track that led to the harbor itself. Both men had offered to stay by her the rest of the way, but she'd thanked them and shaken her head. This she had to do alone.

Isolde put her hand on the small swelling of the unborn baby beneath her gown. *Almost alone.*

Octa's warships were gone, the harbor filled now with trading vessels and the small sailboats of the fisher folk. Isolde stood still, scanning the vessels that lined the harbor, hollow sickness striking her like a blow as she failed to find what she sought. Then her heart stopped. There, at the far edge of the water's curve. A small sailing vessel, trim and newly built with painted sides and crisp white sails.

A man stood on the deck, coiling a length of rope about a heavy wooden spool. A broad-shouldered man with a hard-muscled warrior's build and a lean, sun-browned face, his hair tied at the nape of his neck with a leather thong.

Trystan.

He wore breeches and a plain white shirt open at the throat, the sleeves rolled to the elbow, damp patches of sweat soaking through the back. He looked tired, his jaw stubbled by a day and more's growth of beard, but he was uninjured, so far as Isolde could see. The only mark on him was a healing bruise along one cheekbone.

More than she'd ever wanted anything in her life, Isolde wanted to give way to the tears pressing behind her eyes, to throw her arms around Trystan and never let go. And she wanted to shake him and shout at him for trying to leave like this. She did neither, though, but walked slowly to the water's edge, her pulse stuttering.

Trystan looked up when Isolde reached the end of the wooden plank that led onboard. He said nothing, though, even when Isolde stepped onto the deck of the ship, somehow moving steadily though now her heart was pounding so hard in her ears it blotted out the sound of the waves.

Trystan said nothing, only stood watching in silence as Isolde leaned against the gunwale.

Finally she gestured around them at the ship. "From Cynric?" she asked.

Trystan gave a short nod, though he didn't speak.

"Not much of a parting gift, considering you saved both his life and his throne."

Trystan shrugged. "All I asked for."

Isolde looked at him. "He doesn't know who you are, does he?"

Trystan didn't answer. Then he shook his head. "Better that way." There was another pause, filled with the steady lapping of the waves and the shouts of fishermen. Then Trystan said, "Who told you?"

She'd never believed him dead. Not for more than a brief, horrible instant when first she'd caught sight of Madoc's face as he'd come into the infirmary tent to repeat what Cath had told him. The deepest part of her had been certain, always, that she would know if Trystan had been killed. Though it had made hearing what Madoc told her worse, in a way, knowing that Trystan had chosen, of his own will, to leave her, to let her think him gone.

Now Isolde forced herself not to react to his tone. "Cath first, then Kian. Don't blame Cath, though. I'd just saved his life. He wasn't in much of a state to refuse anything I asked."

For all her efforts, the furious part of her must, at that moment, have been outweighing the relief, because she felt a flare of angry satisfaction at the shock that crossed Trystan's blue gaze.

"Cath was wounded? Is he—"

"Do you care? I thought that was the point, that you wanted to go away and forget us all."

Cath had been carried into her infirmary, bleeding from a sword gash that had laid open his leg nearly to the bone. Isolde had cleaned and cauterized the wound, had sat with him for three nights running, spoon-feeding him drafts of yarrow and poppy-laced wine. And then, when Cath's life was secure and he lay gray-faced but clear-eyed on his pallet in the infirmary, she'd asked him for the truth she already knew.

The corners of Trystan's mouth tightened, and Isolde relented, adding, more quietly, "He's fine. He's already on his way back to his wife and family."

She blinked away fresh tears—though happy ones—at the memory of how Cath, already mounted on the horse Madoc had given him for the journey, had paused in the act of bidding her good-bye. "Do you think my wife . . ." Cath had cleared his throat and gestured to the right leg—healing well, though he'd likely go lame all his life. "What's she going to say when she sees me come back to her like this?"

And Isolde had said, for once absolutely certain that her answer would be true, "She's going to say she's so happy to have you home again."

Now Trystan nodded briefly and a silence, filled with the scream of the gulls overhead and the shouts of the other fishermen, fell between them. Trystan's eyes were fixed on the glittering stretch of water beyond the harbor and at last he said, "I've been wounded how many times—and the battle where I make up my mind to die I come through with barely a scratch."

Isolde looked up at him, and said, softly, "Why?"

Trystan's shoulders jerked in an impatient shrug, though he didn't answer at once. "I suppose I—" And then he dragged his gaze back to hers, momentarily, at least. "It sounds insane when I say it. But I . . . I could almost see you, there in the midst of the battle. I could hear your voice and—" He stopped, turning back to her again. "You've saved my life for me, more times than I can count. I suppose I thought I owed it to you not to throw it away. To go on and . . . make something of myself that you'd not be ashamed of."

Isolde couldn't speak. Her throat was too tight. There was an-other moment's silence and then Trystan said, "I heard you'd married Madoc."

Isolde finally found her voice. "That was what you wanted, wasn't it? The reason you came to the hill fort that day?"

Trystan drew in a breath. "Madoc is . . . he's a good man." He had been looking out towards the open sea, but now dragged his gaze back to meet Isolde's. "I'm glad for you, Isa. I'm—"

And then, as Isolde continued to hold his gaze with her own, he broke off with a sound that was half disgusted exhalation, half angry laugh. "I could rip his head off with my bare hands."

Isolde drew what felt like her first full breath in days, suddenly felt the warmth of the day's brilliant sunlight on her skin. "Good. Then I'll tell you that my marriage to Madoc is about as real as your death."

Trystan's head came up with a jerk, but before he could speak Isolde went on, "It was never meant to be anything more than a way to grant Madoc—and after him, his son—control of Camelerd. I could have—and did—grant him the lands in charter. But I wanted there to be no doubts, no argument after . . . after I was gone. It was—" She remembered the look in Madoc's dark eyes when they'd spoken the marriage vows that would bind them together, but only for a space of days, and only in name. "It was good of Madoc to agree."

Trystan's brows drew together. "What—"

Isolde said steadily, "Isolde, Lady of Camelerd, died this morn-ing of a fever she caught working among the wounded—or from a broken heart, if you believe the stories being whispered around. She never recovered from the death of Trystan, son of Marche."

Trystan looked away again, out across the water, and Isolde said, "And Madoc has already been approached by the king of the Pritani country, offering a marriage alliance with his daughter. I'm sure the Pritani king will be delighted to learn that the alliance is still possible after all."

"She'll have buckteeth and crossed eyes, no doubt," Madoc had said at their final parting. But he'd smiled a bit as he'd said it.

And Isolde had shaken her head. "No. She'll have hair the color of a summer sunrise and eyes as blue as the sea. Or even if she doesn't, she'll recognize a good man's worth and you'll grow into love. Give Rhun an entire clan of little brothers and sisters in a few years time."

Madoc had laughed at that. And then, the smile fading, he'd bowed formally over Isolde's hand and added, voice turning husky, "I wish you all joy, Lady Isolde."

Isolde had touched her lips to his scarred cheek and said, "I thank you—for everything. And I wish you the same."

Trystan, though, was now shaking his head, already starting to step back from her as though he didn't trust himself to stay within reach. Only in one of those stories or bard's songs could this be that easy.

"Isa, I can't let you . . ." He shook his head again. "Don't do this."

"Don't do what? Don't love you?" Isolde took a step forward. She wasn't sure it was the right thing to say, but she was too angry at this moment to care. If Trystan had his way, she'd never see him again after today. No, if he'd truly had his way, she wouldn't even be here, wouldn't be speaking to him now. "Why not? Because of Camlann?"

Trystan stopped.

He said, "What do you mean?"

And Isolde drew a breath and said, quietly, "I know what happened, Trys. I know what Marche asked of you."

Still Trystan didn't move. He only stood, looking at her, and then, after a long moment said, in the same expressionless voice, "How?"

"Marche told me."

Trystan exhaled hard. "Marche told you. Perfect." He rubbed his forehead, then looked up, eyes angry in his set face. "You know I couldn't even kill him? All he'd done, and I couldn't even bring myself to take his life."

Isolde looked up at him. Risked taking one small step towards him as she said, still speaking softly, "Why not?"

Again Trystan gave a quick, impatient shrug. "I—Christ, I don't know. I could have. I've thought of it often enough, of sending him straight to hell. And I had the chance, twice. Once I even had my sword right up against his neck. But I . . ." He stopped, rubbing his forehead again. "It seemed so pointless, somehow. Like killing a bee after it's stung you. The bee's already torn its own guts out giving you the wound."

Trystan still looked out toward the open sea, but Isolde knew he was seeing again a rain-drenched battlefield. "He ran from me. He saw me, in the midst of the battle—and he ran." Trystan stopped again, then lifted one shoulder. "I didn't go after him."

"If you had, he'd not have been able to lead the charge that won the battle, defeated Octa and stopped the war."

Trystan gave another harsh laugh, and said, almost as though he'd read her thought, "I didn't kill him, so he gets the chance to be a hero. There's a bard's song in that somewhere."

There already was, but Isolde didn't say it. Instead she said, risking another small step forward, "Marche gave you a message, didn't he, the night before Camlann. For Arthur. He said he'd kill your mother unless you saw it delivered. And he told you it would make peace between Arthur and my father, and bring a halt to the war before any more blood was spilled. But instead . . ." Between Madoc and Marche and the glimpses she'd caught from Trystan himself, she knew the whole truth now. "Instead it was a betrayal. An offer to turn against my father in that final battle. It was the message that cost my father the war."

For a long moment, Trystan neither moved nor spoke. Then he turned, again forcing himself to meet her gaze. He let out a breath. "It wasn't for myself that I didn't tell you. Or—maybe at first it was. You were . . . the only good thing that had ever happened to me. I didn't want to see the look in your eyes after you knew the truth. And then after—" Trystan stopped. "I thought I owed it to you not to tell you that the man you'd married had killed your father and was the cause of his defeat at Camlann."

"So you were going to let me believe you were dead instead?"

Isolde's hands clenched and despite herself her voice shook as she said, "Didn't it occur to you, even once, that maybe if I knew the truth I wouldn't care?"

She'd shocked him with that; Trystan started to speak but she cut him off. "I said there was nothing you could tell me that could make me stop loving you. How could you think I would lie about something like that? Cath and Kian know the truth, and did they blame you for it? Kian fought at Camlann on my father's side, and he doesn't blame you. As he'd tell you himself if you ever gave him the chance."

"Already said I'd kick his arse from here to Gwynedd," was what Kian had actually said at their parting on the path leading to the harbor. "But you can tell him from me I'll kick it all the way back again if he doesn't stop thinking himself God almighty to be deciding for us poor mortals who we do and don't hold to blame."

Trystan was shaking his head. "Do you know how many men died because of me?"

"And how many lives did you save these last weeks? In this last battle?"

"That makes up for it?" Trystan's voice was still harsh.

"Did Marche's leading the final charge and killing Octa atone for all the evil he'd done in his life—all the hurts and ugliness and suffering he'd caused?" Isolde shook her head. "I don't think it can be as simple as that. But"—she looked up into Trystan's face—"you have saved countless lives these last weeks. Britain would have lost the battle if not for you. And you've men—Kian and Cath and Hereric and all the others—who would willingly lay down their lives for you. Why can't you see yourself through their eyes?" Isolde's eyes stung, but she whispered, "Why can't you see yourself through mine?"

Trystan said nothing, only looked out towards the channel island, a long, dark smudge on the glimmering stretch of open sea. Isolde drew in her breath, "You were fifteen and put in an impossible situation. Maybe you chose wrong. Maybe there was no right choice you could have made at all. Maybe even if Marche hadn't betrayed him, my father would have been killed or lost the war, and all the men who'd been oath sworn to serve him would still have died. None of that—*none* of it—makes any difference to my loving you now."

Trystan ran his hands down his face, though, taking another step backwards when she tried to touch his arm. "Isa, I can't let you do this. You can't want to give up everything just for me. What kind of life is that for you? What can I offer you? If you think you owe it to me to stay with me just because—"

Isolde's control abruptly snapped. "If I thought I owed you anything, it was the chance to be a father to the baby that will be born five months from now."

Isolde had thought Trystan motionless before, but it was nothing to the absolute, utter immobility that came over him now. A gull screamed overhead, the ocean-scented wind whipped at Isolde's skirts and tore at her hair. But Trystan stood without moving, his face as completely blank with shock as Isolde had ever seen, for a long moment, just staring at her. Then, very slowly, he sat down on the spool of rope so that his eyes were nearly on a level with hers.

He didn't speak, though. Didn't move. The silence stretched out until at last Isolde said, on a shaky breath, "I hadn't . . . meant to tell you quite that way."

Trystan passed a hand dazedly across his eyes. "You didn't—" He shook his head as though trying to clear it. "I . . . all these weeks. All the times I—Holy mother of God, Isa, how could you not have told me before?"

"If I had told you, would you still have gone after Fidach? Would you have left me at the abbey on my own?"

Trystan pushed a hand through his hair again. "God, no, of course I wouldn't."

"But part of you would have felt you should . . . would have felt you still owed Fidach to get him free. I know you, Trys. I didn't want burden you then, force you into making that choice. Not when it was really my fault the choice was there to be made."

"Your fault?" Trystan's look was still dazed, but one brow lifted at that. "I think I—" He looked at her as though he were trying to decide whether she was real or only imagined, but said, "I think I remember being there, too. It hasn't been that long."

Isolde hiccuped an unsteady laugh, and felt a first, tiny bubble of hope expand inside her. "I meant that I could have *tried* not to conceive a child. There are ways, herbs I could have taken. But I didn't. I didn't even try, because I wanted a child—no, I wanted *your* child—so much I couldn't breathe."

Her voice wavered as she reached out, touching Trystan's cheek. His skin was warm, rough with the sea's salt-laden breeze and the stubble of beard on his jaw. "I wanted *you*, Trys, before you think I'm here only because of the baby. I want you for my husband and the father of this child. I want the boy I grew up with. The man Cath named his son for. I want the man who took the time to teach Rhun to throw a knife and who kept his promises to me even when it might have gotten him killed and—"

Isolde had to stop and wait for her voice to steady before she could go on. "I asked you before how you could think I lied when I said I loved you no matter what. But I didn't mean that. I know how. I do. I know what your life was—has been. But please, please believe me now." Her voice was barely audible above the wind and the lapping of the waves. "I'm not giving up everything for you, Trys. The three of us together—you and me and our baby—that's my everything. This, right here, now."

The rays of the setting sun gilded the stubble of beard on Trystan's jaw and shadowed the planes of his face. Then, quite suddenly, he bowed his shoulders, dropping his head into his hands. When he finally looked up, Isolde saw that his eyes were wet.

He let out a breath and dashed the moisture away with the back of his hand, still staring at her as though unable to entirely believe her real. Then, very slowly, his hand came up to touch her cheek, the back of his knuckles brushing her skin. "You really want—"

"I really do." Isolde caught hold of his hand and fitted her palm against his, handfasting scar to handfasting scar.

There was a moment, a heartbeat when Isolde held her breath, stopped hearing the gulls or the fishermen's cries, when even the salt-scented breeze all around them seemed to still. And then—

She didn't know who moved first, but all at once she was in his arms. He was warm and solid and strong against her, holding her as tightly as she held him. After a long, long time she pulled back enough that she could look up at Trystan's face.

"There was another reason I didn't tell you before. About the baby, I mean. I wanted to wait until—until it could be happy news. I hoped—" She stopped, searching Trystan's gaze. "Are you happy about it?"

"Happy." Trystan let out a breath. "Of course I am. Happy and . . . terrified." He exhaled another half laugh. "I don't think I've ever been more terrified in my entire life. A child. How am I going to be a father?"

"You—" Isolde started to say. And then she felt it, stronger than ever. She took Trystan's hand and placed it over the place where she'd just felt the child move with kicks more vigorous and purposeful by the day. His left hand; she could feel the disfigured fingers, the rough edges of the scars. Her eyes searched his again. "Do you feel it?"

But she could see already in his face that he had. "God, that's—" He stopped. Shook his head.

Isolde looked up into Trystan's eyes, blue as the morning sky.

Time. She knew it would take time. The scars of a lifetime weren't going to be wiped out in a moment, not even in a year. But he'd let her see the tears in his eyes and admitted to being afraid, and was looking at her now as though he'd have been happy to stay here forever, feeling his son move.

Those were miracles enough for today. And there would be time, now. Time to tell him of how, as she'd witnessed the charters that would make Madoc and then Rhun Camelerd's king, she'd been struck by another of those moments when she knew—*knew*—that veil between this world and the Other was as thin as mist. She'd seen not her grandmother, but a beautiful woman, a stranger to her, with golden hair and gray eyes, who nodded and seemed to give her a glad smile.

There would be time to tell Trystan how Marche had looked, lying beside the field of battle, peaceful at last. Time even to tell him how, in the midst of the fighting, she'd whispered, again and again, *If you were willing to die for me, please, please be willing to live for me instead.*

"You're my husband, Trys." Isolde's voice was an unsteady whisper. "So long as you'll have me. I have nothing to offer you—no wealth, no lands. Only myself."

She could feel the baby kicking against Trystan's hand. All the links in her chain joined full circle, her points of light so close as to be almost one. Trystan cupped her face, his thumb tracing the line of her cheek as he looked at her, wonder still in his eyes. "You're all I've ever wanted. Forever and always."

Afterword

THERE HAVE BEEN PAIN, AND fever, and burning thirst. But those are gone now. For a moment I think I must already have died. But I can still feel my chest rise and fall. Feel the quick, thready beat of my own heart: a bird fluttering weakly in its cage.

I turn my head on the pillow, and I can see the room around me. Stone walls lit by a single candle's flickering light. And Isolde, asleep on a pallet drawn up close beside my bed. Worn out by all her care for me. I will not wake her. She badly needs rest. And there is nothing she can do for me now.

I know what this sudden lifting of pain means. Night has fallen. The end draws very near.

But for now, a strange, floating lightness fills my limbs. I feel myself sit up, push back the blankets and rise. And as though drawn by a force I can feel but cannot see, I cross to the hearth, where stands an ancient scrying bowl. Made of bronze, and chased with a swirling pattern: dragons of eternity, forever swallowing their own tails.

A gift from the Goddess, maybe, this sudden lightness, this sudden lifting of pain. But as I kneel by the scrying bowl, look into the waters within, I beg another gift in exchange. I will bear the pain of dying—I will bear the fever's burning thirst—for as long as my heart still beats, as long as there is breath left in my chest.

But let me see her. Let me see Isolde. Not *may be*, or *has been*, but what *will be*, for her, when I am gone. This I beg of the Goddess, in all her forms. Maiden, mother, and crone. By all her names. Morrigan. Cerridwen. Arianrhod, Mistress of the Silver Wheel.

For a moment, I see nothing in the waters but my own face, a ruin, now, of running sores. And I think the Goddess has turned her back on me indeed. But then, like a silver fish darting beneath the waters, something stirs. And I see . . .

She sits on the deck of a sailing boat, her skirts tucked up, dangling her bare feet over the side. She looks scarcely older than she does now, asleep on her pallet on the floor beside where I kneel. Raven-haired. Skin with the pearl white glow of apple blossoms. Wide, thickly lashed gray eyes.

But she holds a babe cradled in her arms, and smiles down at the child, humming a soft, age-old tune.

A tiny girl, the babe is, with gray eyes and wispy black curls. She grins a toothless, delighted grin and waves dimpled fists in the air. A beauty, she'll be. Like her mother. A good thing, I think, that she has two older brothers to be her devoted protectors lifelong.

Two boys are romping and playing now in the surf a little distance from where the boat is moored. Sturdy, healthy, handsome lads, with gold-brown hair and their father's blue eyes, splashing and laughing and digging for crabs in the sand. Six and seven years old, maybe, old enough to help with sailing a boat on journeys like the one they're returning from now.

Their father is making the ship ready to go, securing the black stallion they've bought from the trader in Gaul to be the year's new breeding stock. A great, glossy animal, with a graceful neck and a proud head. He'll sire fine mounts that will more than repay the price he cost.

The blue-eyed man finishes rigging the sails, then comes to sit by his wife's side, tickles the babe she holds under the chin, and tells her they'll have to leave her behind at the next port if her mother fills the boat up with any more bits of new plants and seeds and healing herbs to try growing in their garden at home.

But there's still wonder in his gaze when he looks at her, his life's love, as though he can't quite believe she's really his. As though he never for a moment stops being grateful beyond measure, beyond all words, for the gift of every day he has with her at his side.

He drops down over the side of the boat to haul apart the boys, who have started pummeling each other like all young lads do. Rumples their hair and tells them to stop behaving like wild hellions until supper, at least, and maybe they'll be able to make a good start for home.

They'll be glad, all of them, to reach their journey's end. These summer voyages over the sea are sweet, but sweeter still is to return.

The treaty that was made seven years ago yet holds. And though there are still raids and war—as there will always be so long as men have hands to raise swords—in their small corner of the Gwynedd hills, peace reigns. So they return, now, to a holding and a home that are neither too big nor too small. Not a grand place, but with room enough for a garden, for the boys to romp and play and fish in the rivers and streams, and then curl up by the hearth at night with an old brown-and-white war hound. The dog is too old, now, to join in their games, but beloved greatly all the same.

Lords from all corners of the land journey to barter for the fine horses their father breeds and trains—even to the king of Gwynedd himself, who comes yearly and brings his eldest son, grown now to nearly a young man. An old warrior comes often, too, a grizzled old man who wears a leather patch over one eye. He sits by the fire in the winter evenings, carving wooden soldiers and horses for the boys and birds and squirrels for the girl. And sometimes he'll give in to the boys' pleading and hold them spellbound with a tale of battles fought and won.

A big, broad-chested Saxon man sits by the hearth, as well, and teaches the boys to talk in finger signs, when he can be coaxed to leave the stables and the horses he helps to tend and train. And a great, black-haired, bushy-bearded bear of a man and his red-haired wife tend the smithy in the nearest settlement and visit often with their tumbling brood of daughters and sons. The house even gives a night or two's shelter, though rarely, to a wandering priest and a pair of brothers, twins with skin as black as coal.

And sometimes—rarer, far rarer still—a wandering harper comes to their door, begging shelter for a night and a hot meal. He offers to play in exchange for the food. A tale of Arthur, maybe, king that was and shall be, who, having saved all Britain, sleeps again undisturbed on his Glass Isle.

Or sometimes instead it's a love song, a tale of tragic love, sad enough to make a grown warrior weep. Of how Isolde the fair and Trystan, son of Marche, drank a magic draught that made them fall desperately in love.

Who knows how such tales are born? To find their beginning is like unwinding the weft in a weaving on the loom. But once begun, they spread like the ripples on a pond, like dry leaves scattering before the blast of the storm.

So the harper tells the tale of how they died, Trystan and Isolde, from broken hearts. And how from their graves grew two trees with their branches entwined.

And the young raven-haired mother I See in the scrying bowl— the raven-haired girl who sleeps, now, at my side—feels for a moment as though she walks into a crystal-still lake, drawing nearer and nearer the strange, wavering reflection that looks back at her with her own eyes.

But then she looks down at the babe in her arms, sleeping with dark lashes spread like tiny fans on rounded cheeks, small mouth puckered in some milky sweet infant's dream. At the boys, drowsing by the hearth, worn out by a day's chores and play. And then she catches sight of her husband, watching her across the room with eyes the color of the clear morning sky.

And other memories swirl across that wavering reflection in her mind: Lying in bed and watching her husband's face the day his oldest son was born, the day he reached to hold the tightly swaddled little form, cup the tiny, fuzzy head for the first time. All the night, many of them, when he's gotten out of bed to take a turn at comforting a crying babe so that she could sleep on. The way their baby girl gurgles and laughs when he swings her high in the air. Seeing him splash in the river with the boys and teach them to fish with hooks and wooden poles.

A night, more than seven years ago, now, when she lay twined close with him on the narrow bed in the tiny cabin of a rocking ship and knew, absolutely, that this was where she'd been meant to be since the stars began to move across the heavens and the stones themselves began keeping time.

She looks from her man to the wandering bard and then back again. And she smiles.

Author's Note

As in the first two books of the *Twilight of Avalon* trilogy, *Sunrise of Avalon* is a blending of historical fact and Arthurian legend. I have adhered as closely as possible to what facts are known about sixth-century Britain. However, the Arthurian cycle of stories and the Trystan and Isolde legend as we know it today are both very much grounded in the later Middle Ages, when they were first written down. Respecting the legends occasionally meant allowing an anachronism to creep into my story, such as the Abbey of Saint Eucherius, which is modeled on a later form of the monastic model than would have been found in sixth-century Wessex. My Trystan and Isolde's Britain is one that never quite existed, halfway between truth and tale, as, indeed, is the world of Arthurian legend itself.

Those familiar with the Trystan and Isolde legend will know that I've taken liberties with the tragic ending common to most versions of the story. However, there is a fragmentary early Welsh version of the tale that does end happily, with Trystan and Isolde united in marriage. And since I was basing my story on the earliest versions of Arthurian legend, I was happy to allow my Trystan and Isolde an ending that weaves that Welsh version together with the ending that appears in most later versions of the tale.

Acknowledgments

I WOULD LIKE TO THANK: MY daughters, Isabella and Vivienne—and Vivienne especially, this time around, for being obliging enough to wait on being born until I had finished the first draft of this book. My husband, Nathan, webmaster, babysitter, editor and general miracle worker, and all the rest of my wonderful family. My amazing, incredible writing partner Sarah, who wrote all the poetry that appears in this book. Visit her at www.sarahwoodbury.com, you will be very glad you did! Huge thanks to Shanra Lyn, for fantastic beta-reading, proofreading, and generally lovely support. I've also been so, so lucky in the number of wonderful book bloggers who have featured and reviewed my books, and I'd like to thank all of you, too. Thanks as always to my peerless agent, Jacques de Spoelberch. And a special thank you to my editor, Danielle Friedman, for truly helping me to make these books what they wanted to be: Trystan, Isolde, and I will always be grateful to you.

Touchstone Reading Group Guide

Sunrise of Avalon

Introduction

In the final installment of Anna Elliot's *Twilight of Avalon* trilogy, *Sunrise of Avalon*, Trystan and Isolde's love and secret wedding vows endure the ultimate test. As Octa of Kent and his ally, the traitorous Lord Marche, amass their armies for a great war against Britain, Trystan and Isolde are forced to make choices that will decide not only their future—and the future of their unborn child—but the future of Britain as well.

The rulers of the smaller kingdoms of Britain hold an alliance against Octa and Lord Marche, but Britain's High King Madoc knows their alliance to be a tenuous one. When Madoc's son is abducted by Octa's forces, Isolde embarks on a dangerous journey to recover young Rhun by pretending to seek alliance with Octa. She is successful, thanks to her bravery and the assistance of friends and confidantes, and Rhun is returned to his father's side.

Trystan, ever secretive and haunted by his past, is repeatedly called away on missions that prevent him from staying by Isolde, and Isolde's reoccurring visions of Trystan's ultimate face off with Lord Marche, perhaps resulting in Trystan's death, cause her to constantly fear for his safety. Only after the final battle has been fought and Britain has been saved can Trystan and Isolde's love prevail.

For Discussion

1. "[Trystan] made himself shift even more fully into the mind of combat, narrowed his focus to only here and now . . . Keeping Isolde safe was—had always been—the first" (page 39). Discuss the characters' main priorities in the novel. What do they seek to achieve? Which characters succeed in their quests, and which fail?

2. Although Isolde does not consider herself a Christian, she finds herself comforted by and in good company with the nuns of the Abbey of Saint Eucherius. How would you describe Isolde's relationship with the nuns, and why do you think they get along so well? What values do they have in common?

3. Return to page 54 and reread Mother Bethildis's reflections on faith. How do her words bring together the themes of faith and fate in the novel? What do you think Mother Bethildis means by "unexpectedly perfect"? Which other characters in the novel would agree with her assessment, and which do you think would differ in opinion?

4. How did you feel about Isolde's decision not to reveal her pregnancy to Trystan? Do you think it was wrong of her to do so, or did she make a wise choice? What does Isolde's decision reveal about her character and values?

5. Isolde regards Fidach as a man who has "deliberately created an identity for himself" (page 56) in order to keep others from truly knowing and from hurting him. Do you think her analysis is correct? Which other characters have created a persona that they wear "like a cloak" in order to protect their true selves from harm?

6. As Isolde worries about her vision of Trystan's possible death, she wonders if the future can be changed. And she is certainly

not the only character to do so: What opinions regarding the inevitability of fate are expressed by the various characters in the novel? Which do you find to be most aligned with your own views on destiny?

7. How would you describe the evolution of Isolde and Madoc's relationship throughout the course of the novel? Were you surprised by their marriage at the end of the book, or by Madoc agreeing to Isolde's false death? Why or why not?

8. The kings of the council—united to defeat Octa and Marche—hold a fragile alliance. As Madoc observes: "They'd be happy to plunder each other's lands and slaughter each other's warriors and rob each other's wealth as they would Octa's or Marche's" (page 128). Did you have confidence that they would be able to overcome Octa and Marche? How was Madoc able to keep them united?

9. How does Isolde's responsibility as a healer influence the novel's action? Do you think the outcome of the novel would have been different if she did not have "the sight"?

10. Similarly, towards the end of chapter five, Madoc suggests to Isolde that "there is that in this world which cannot be healed" (page 131). Though she does not respond to his suggestion, what do you think her reaction may have been? Would she have agreed?

11. Despite all the pain Lord Marche has caused, Isolde determines that he may be "not entirely a monster" (page 166) or that he at least regrets the man he has become. Did your opinion of Marche change throughout the novel and/or trilogy? Why do you think Trystan was unable to kill him when he had the chance during the battle, and what did you think of Marche's final charge?

12. Though the trilogy is set in Arthurian times, many of the struggles the characters face are similar to those people may face today. Was there a particular character to whom you felt you could relate to? What about that character drew you to her/him?

A Conversation with Anna Elliott

Which came first: your desire to write, or your interest in Arthurian legend?

I fell in love with Arthurian legend in college, years before I ever thought of writing my own retelling of one of the legends. It was such a joy and a privilege to get to live in my own version of the Arthurian world while I was writing the books.

The genre of historical fiction seems to grow in popularity every day. What do you think accounts for readers' interest in the genre?

Speaking for myself, I love history, and I love imagining the past and how different it must have been to live in a time without so many of the modern contrivances we take for granted today. And yet I love reading the primary sources and realizing how much of human nature and the human experience has remained the same throughout the ages: love, hate, faith, despair, hope. The essentials of life are constant, no matter how much the world around us changes.

The Twilight of Avalon trilogy has been read and praised by readers who are familiar with Arthurian legend, as well as readers who are encountering it for the first time. Did you have a specific audience in mind while you were writing these books?

I really didn't have a specific audience in mind, no, though I did try to make the trilogy accessible to both readers familiar with the original Arthur and Trystan and Isolde legends and readers who haven't encountered them before.

What books would you recommend to readers who want to learn more about the legend of Trystan and Isolde?

I have a gorgeous copy of a fifteenth century manuscript of the legend called *Illuminated Manuscripts: Tristan and Isolde*. It has all the gorgeous illuminations and illustrations from the medieval manuscript and really calls up the world of the story.

What was your research process like for the Twilight of Avalon trilogy?

I read all the Arthurian primary sources. Geoffrey of Monmouth's *History of the Kings of Britain* was the version of the story I'd decided to use as the basis for my book, so of course I read and re-read that, as well as Nennius's *Historia Brittonum*, another early source of Arthur material. I read the early Welsh Arthurian tales like *Culhwch and Olwen* and *The Dream of Rhonabwy*, as well as the later medieval legends like *Le Morte d'Arthur*. And then I also read both the Anglo Saxon Chronicle and Gildas's *De Excidio et Conquestu Britanniae*, neither of which mention Arthur, but which give a picture of the political climate in sixth-century Britain. (That being the age in which scholars agree a historical Arthur might have existed, it was also the period in which I'd decided to set my story.) And of course I also read all the available versions of the original Trystan and Isolde story.

I read every book I could get my hands on about Dark Age Britain in general, and the possibility of a historical Arthur in particular. Since I'd decided to make Tintagel Castle in Cornwall the setting for *Twilight of Avalon,* I also studied the archaeological work that's been done at the site. It's a fascinating place. The Arthurian connection has been largely discounted by scholars as mere literary invention. But the latest archaeological work has suggested that there was at least some kind of a princely fortress there during the fifth and sixth centuries, which would have been contemporary with King Arthur's time (if he did in fact exist).

And then, too, I pretty much had an enormous pile of research books on my desk throughout the writing process that I would constantly refer to as I worked. I would often need to double check a date or a place name or other historical reference, or look at pictures of Cornwall to refresh my mental image of the landscape I was writing about. And all the herbal medicine that Isolde uses meant a lot of research during the writing process as well, looking through early herbals and medical tracts to find cures that would have been known and used in sixth-century Britain.

In a review of *Twilight of Avalon*, *Publishers Weekly* acknowledges that the Britain created for this tale is "both familiar and distinctly alien" to fans of other medieval romances. In which ways do you think your Britain falls in line with the "norm," and in which ways is it set apart?

The Twilight of Avalon trilogy does present a version of the Trystan and Isolde story that's quite different from the original medieval tales. But the legend as we know it today is really very much a product of the courtly medieval style of literature, very much grounded in and shaped by chivalry and knightly honor. Essentially, the tale as it has come down to us reflects a twelfth- or thirteenth-century world and sensibility—which doesn't work so well when you try to drop it into sixth-century Britain, the age in which a historical Arthur might have lived. That was one of the main reasons I wound up being fairly free in my adaptation of the legend: to make it belong better to the world of Dark Age Britain I was uncovering—and falling in love with—in my research.

I did, though, try to stay true to what I considered the essential plot elements of the original Arthurian and Trystan and Isolde tales. In terms of Arthurian legends, I wanted to be sure to address the relationship between Arthur and Morgan and the conception of Modred, their son, as well as Modred and Arthur's final battle at Camlann. And I had to include the character of Merlin (or Myrddin), who has always been a particular favorite of mine and who just refused to be left out of my story. And then in terms of the Trystan and Isolde legends, I felt it was of course important to maintain the triangle between Marche, Trystan, and Isolde that forms the fundamental conflict of the original story, as well as Isolde's skill as a healer and Trystan's skill at swordsmanship and disguise.

In a previous interview, you mention that your characters "speak" to you and can sometimes inform you of the direction to take your stories. Which character in the Twilight of Avalon trilogy did you "speak" with the most, or feel the most connected to?

I truly love all my characters—even the villains!—but I'd have to say that I felt most connected to Isolde throughout the writing of the trilogy. I was inside her head and she was inside mine for three whole years. And I think (hope!) that she's the heart of the trilogy.

Were there ways in which writing the final book of the trilogy differed from writing the first two installments? Which book was the most difficult to write? Which book was your favorite to write?

Well, I was pregnant with my youngest the whole time I was writing *Sunrise*, the final book of the trilogy—which in many ways was amazing, since it made me feel so much more connected to Isolde carrying Trystan's baby throughout the book; it was that much easier for me to access her emotions. And then in other ways, I wouldn't necessarily recommend all the volatile pregnancy emotions as the perfect complement to bidding good-bye to your cast of characters! Even though I love where I left Trystan and Isolde, good-byes are hard.

For whatever reason, *Dark Moon of Avalon* was by far the easiest of the three books to write. I think *Sunrise* was the hardest, not only because it was last, but because I wanted to make sure all the plot threads from the first two books were woven together at the end. Still, I think *Sunrise* is my favorite of the three. Though that's a little like asking me to pick a favorite child. I really loved writing them all.

Did you know all along how you wanted your telling of Isolde and Trystan's story to end? Or did the "right" ending reveal itself to you along the way?

I did know all along how I wanted Isolde and Trystan's story to end. Not only that, but I actually wrote the very last scene of the third book first, before I'd even started work on Book 1. It was such a wonderful moment to actually reach that summit point in their story when I finally came to the end of writing Book 3.

Now that the Twilight of Avalon trilogy is complete, can you offer a glimpse into your next project?

Nothing definite yet, but you can stay posted on my website: www.annaelliottbooks.com.

Enhance Your Book Club

1. The Arthurian legend in all of its many forms has been passed from generation to generation for centuries. How has it been interpreted in various art forms and media outlets (film, literature, music, etc.)? If the members of your discussion group would like to further immerse themselves in this genre, consider choosing another novel from the Twilight of Avalon series for your next reading selection.

2. Isolde is a gifted storyteller by all accounts, and she tells a number of folk tales throughout the novel. Using resources online or at your local library, see if you can find records of some of the tales Isolde recounts.

3. Work together to create a chart of the characters in the Twilight of Avalon trilogy and their relationship to one another—a family tree of sorts. If your group enjoys creating the chart of relations, you may consider putting together a timeline of events as well. You can use these creations as resources during your discussion.

4. If the trilogy's main characters were alive today, what songs do you think they'd have on their iPods? Challenge the members of your group to draft playlists for their favorite characters.

5. To find out more about author Anna Elliot and her books, check out her website and blog at www.annaelliottbooks.com.

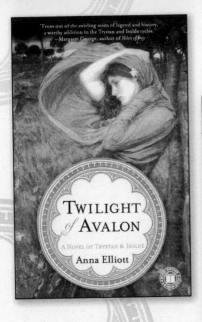
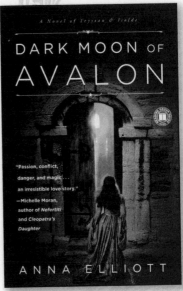